'Queensland is like a beautiful girl with lots of money. But stupid. For some reason she just loves to open her purse and bare her big pink arse to the world and say "Fuck me over, please" to all comers. And trust me, the fuckers come running.'

ANDREW MCGAHAN was born in Dalby, Queensland, but has lived and worked mostly in Brisbane. Since the publication of his first novel, the award-winning *Praise* in 1992, he has produced another novel, *1988*, a variety of stageplays including *Bait*, and most recently the award-winning screenplay for the feature film version of *Praise*. *Last Drinks* is his third novel.

ANDREW McGAHAN
LAST DRINKS

ALLEN & UNWIN

First published in 2000

Copyright © Andrew McGahan 2000

All rights reserved. No part of this book may be reproduced or transmitted in any form or by any means, electronic or mechanical, including photocopying, recording or by any information storage and retrieval system, without prior permission in writing from the publisher. *The Australian Copyright Act* 1968 (the Act) allows a maximum of one chapter or 10% of this book, whichever is the greater, to be photocopied by any educational institution for its educational purposes provided that the educational institution (or body that administers it) has given a remuneration notice to Copyright Agency Limited (CAL) under the Act.

Allen & Unwin
9 Atchison Street
St Leonards NSW 2065
Australia
Phone: (61 2) 8425 0100
Fax: (61 2) 9906 2218
Email: frontdesk@allen-unwin.com.au
Web: http://www.allenandunwin.com

National Library of Australia
Cataloguing-in-Publication entry:

McGahan, Andrew.
  Last Drinks.

  ISBN 1 86508 406 9.

  I. Title.

A823.3

Set in by 12/14 pt Bembo DOCUPRO, Sydney
Printed by Griffin Press, South Australia

10 9 8 7 6 5 4 3 2 1

Author's note

This is a work of fiction. While obviously inspired to some degree by the Fitzgerald inquiry and its era in Queensland, this is not, even for a moment, an historic or factual version of those times. In particular, no character in this book should be mistaken for any actual person, living or dead.

With special thanks to John Orr, who was more than generous with his time and knowledge. Thanks also to Shaune Gifford, Jo Jarrah and Carl Harrison-Ford for their advice and suggestions.

PROLOGUE

It was a cataclysm.

That was the only word for it. Like the fall of Rome, the fall of Troy. Like we'd flown too high and challenged the gods. It started out so small, just a whisper, but someone lost their nerve, someone let it slip, and suddenly it was the end.

People were scattering to the winds. Old friends wouldn't return my calls. And you know what I did on my last night as a government minister? I gathered up my papers and set them alight, right there in my office, let the fire blaze until the sprinklers came on and doused the whole mess. Later, the police arrived, warrants in hand, and found me there amongst the ashes.

'Take me in, boys,' I said.

And just watch while this whole fucking town goes up.

> Extract from untitled manuscript by Marvin McNulty (unpublished)

Unpublished?

Unfinished as well. And self-serving, but that was Marvin.

And what he called a cataclysm was more commonly known as the Inquiry, an investigation into official corruption in the state of Queensland, which ran from 1987 until the collapse of the government in 1989. All long ago. And in truth, no great cataclysm. To those outside of Queensland it was never much more than a diversion, another oddity from a place already long known to have gone mad. Outside of Australia, barely anyone heard of it at all. A government fell, yes, but it was a minor government, overseeing a bare three million souls. What was that in America, Asia, Africa? Governments fell all the time, much bigger ones. Great bodies of people were oppressed and displaced and suffered and died. What matter, then, the fate of a few dozen people like Marvin and his friends, or of a backwater state like sleepy, sunny Queensland?

No matter at all. Turns out Marvin was no friend of mine anyway.

And he won't ever finish his book now.

ONE

The phone then. Ringing and ringing.
I was asleep and it was cutting through warmth and dreams and tugging me awake. I raised my head, not knowing where I was, or when—back, just for a moment, to all the hungover mornings of times past. Then I shook my head and reached for the receiver. It was cold and black in my bedroom, and I was stone sober, not having taken a drink in years.
'What?' I said into the phone.
'George? It's Graham here. Sorry about the hour.'
I peered at the bedside table, looking for the time. The digital clock should have glowed there in the night, but there was nothing. I reached for the lamp.
'Why? What time is it?'
'Just going on five. Listen, you'd better get down here.'
I clicked the lamp switch, got nothing there either.
'Hey, Graham, you got lights?'
'No one's got lights. That's part of the problem.'
'What problem?'
'Um . . . look, we just need you here, quick, okay? At the station.'
Graham was the senior police sergeant of Highwood, and Highwood was a small mountain town on the border between Queensland and New South Wales. My refuge for the last ten years.
I sat up.
'You mean you need me professionally?'
'No . . . I'd say it was more of a personal matter.'
Professionally I was still working as a journalist. After a

fashion, at least, for while I had never reached any true heights in the field, there in Highwood I barely practised it at all. The *Highwood Herald* had a circulation of less than 3000, and apart from the semi-retired proprietor and editor, I was the only reporter on staff. It was a profound decline from the half million readers I had commanded in my day, but my day was gone, had ended in disgrace, and I was lucky anyone would employ me at all. I was more than lucky. Most of the others were in prison, or roaming the world in hiding. Me—I hadn't even driven from the state.

Personally though . . .

'What d'you mean, personally?' I said.

'Just get over here, George. We need you to identify somebody.'

And he was clicking the phone down.

I sat in the dark for a moment, blinking myself awake. Identify somebody? Did he mean identify some actual *body*? That didn't make any sense. It wasn't that people didn't die in Highwood, but I wasn't a local, not even after ten years of living there. I was nobody's relative and nobody's next of kin. Why would I be called? There wasn't a soul I knew in town that Graham didn't know just as well himself. If not better. So why call on me?

I got up, naked and shivering, and searched for clothes on the icy wooden floor. It was already well into spring by the calendar, but winter was lingering in the hills. I was acclimatised, perhaps, but still, I was well over forty years old and there was far less fat on me than there once had been. I flicked more light switches but nothing happened. I dressed by feel in the blackness. Then I padded from the bedroom through to the living room, in search of my shoes. In the fireplace a few embers still smouldered from the night before, the two armchairs drawn up before it. My shoes and yesterday's socks were warming there, and I slipped them on, went out into the night.

A clear mountain sky greeted me, the stars bright and chill. My breath puffed away into the air. In the east, above one of the high forested ridges that circled the town, there was only the barest hint of dawn. Below me spread the streets and houses of Highwood. My little wooden cottage, rented, lay high on a hill on the western fringe of town, and normally, even at this hour, there'd be a sprinkling of lights visible. Instead this morning there were only the dark folds of the valley, broken by a pale line of mist that followed the creek. There might not have been a town there at all. A power failure. Another one. The good folk of Highwood would be waking to heaters gone lifeless, and electric blankets as frigid as stone. They would not be happy.

Identify somebody?

Somebody was dead?

My car was no friend of the weather either, grinding noisily before starting. The heater jetted cold air as I wound down the dirt track that passed for my street, then on through the west side of town. There were no other cars, no streetlights burning. Dark houses huddled behind frosted windows. I drove across the bridge, mist curling up from the creek below, and on into the main street. At the southern end, close by Memorial Park, was the bureaucratic precinct. Council chambers, a district courthouse, a police station and a library. They were all sizeable stone buildings, raised in the thirties when Highwood was a booming timber town. The population had long since dwindled, and at an hour like this the whole area would normally be deserted. At best there might be a lone light outside the empty police station, illuminating a sign with a phone number that could be called in emergencies.

There was no light now, but the police station wasn't empty. Two police cars were parked outside and a dim glow that spoke of gas lamps suffused the windows. I pulled in and climbed the smooth stone steps, pushed open the swing doors. Three faces, shadowed by a gaslight that hissed and flared, turned to greet me. I knew them. Graham, and two of his constables, Tony and Maria—three-quarters of the district's complete police force, all of them in full uniform and wide awake, even though night shifts were unheard of in Highwood.

'Well?' I said.

They were grouped around the inquiries counter, surrounded in turn by their own looming shadows on the walls. On the counter itself, in the circle of light, was an array of items—socks and shoes, pants and a shirt. Someone's clothes. Graham came my way, and strangest of all, for we weren't friends by any means, he reached out to shake my hand, stiff and formal and somehow sympathetic.

'Thanks for coming, George.'

He turned back to the others. 'Tony, you two head back out to the substation. Get some coffee from somewhere for Tom, he'll be freezing. Set up the barriers and all the rest, then stay out of the way. George and I will be out in a while.'

They nodded, looking away from me and edging out the door. I waited until they were gone, the cold air swirling in with their passing.

'What's going on?' I asked.

Graham ushered me over to the counter. He was in his late forties, rounding out steadily, but in the yellow glow he looked older and thinner than usual—and a little unsure.

'I want you to look at this,' he said.

There was a wallet there amidst the clothes, its contents emptied out. There was no money, only a few crumpled papers. Graham rifled through them. I finally noticed he was wearing plastic gloves, and a chill not of the mountain air went through me. He held up something for me to see.

'Recognise it?'

I did. It was a press card. It stated that I, George Verney, was a fully accredited journalist in the employ of the Brisbane *Daily Times*—a fact which hadn't been true for a decade. The paper itself no longer existed. It had tumbled into ruin, like everything else.

'That's from years ago,' I said.

And even as I said it, as I thought about who would have one of my old cards after so much time, a surge of something like panic ran through me, unexpected and overwhelming. And then I remembered that the clothes on the desk belonged to a man, not a woman. Whoever it was, then, it wasn't her.

Graham was picking up another item, a driver's licence this time. It, too, was old, and long expired, but the face in the photograph wasn't old. It was young and clear and only slightly less terrible to see than if it had been her. Instead it was *him*.

'You know this man?' Graham asked, gently, seeing it all, perhaps, in my face.

I felt myself sinking into a chair.

The name on the licence said Charles Monohan. But no one had ever called him Charles. Not even when they'd arrested him.

'Charlie?' I asked. 'Charlie's dead?'

Graham nodded, his face sad as the gas lamp hissed like the wind of the afterlife.

'Very,' he said.

TWO

The heaters blew warm in Graham's police car as we drove north out of town. Over the eastern slopes the dawn was closer now, but down in the valley the light remained grey. Houses hunched in on themselves, cattle clustered forlornly in the paddocks, a dog scurried along the roadside, dodging our headlights. I felt detached from it all. Cold. I was on the way to witness the corpse of an old, old friend. If it was really him. And who could believe that? Charlie was the first. Before Marvin and Lindsay and Jeremy. Even before Maybellene. Not any friend. My oldest friend.

Graham was smoking as he drove. 'Any idea what he might have been doing up here?'

'No.'

'He didn't come to see you?'

'I haven't seen him in years. Not since I moved here.'

'Who else would he know in town?'

'I don't think there's anyone.'

'That card would suggest a connection.'

We drove in silence for a time.

'It's strange,' I said. 'I don't remember ever giving him one.'

There was no need. He knew where I lived, all my phone numbers. We saw each other every day. We were friends, we were business partners, I was best man at his wedding . . .

And the last time I'd tried to talk to him he was so bitter he'd refused to come to the phone. Later I'd heard that the damage to his mind was permanent, a light mental retardation, the doctors said. He would still be functional, but as for his intellectual abilities and some of his motor coordination, well . . . Maybellene said he became like a child. Frustrated with himself. Sulking. In the years since, I would picture him the way I'd known him first—his big red face and his giant hands, his narrow, intelligent eyes, smiling—and I'd try to imagine all of that gone. I'd try to imagine him as someone half vacant, someone brain-damaged and withdrawn. It was impossible, and I'd stop thinking about him. He was the one who had ended it anyway.

But then why, through it all, had he kept my card in his wallet?

No, the question was—why was he dead? And why here?

I stared out the window at the mountains, tall ridges climbing up on either side of the road, black with forest. Highwood was virtually surrounded by trees. High*grove* it had been called at first, late in the 1800s. They were striving for some sort of class, perhaps, but in truth it was only a logging camp. There wasn't anything like class for miles around. Highwood it became, and now the logging was gone. The useful wood had thinned out, national parks had been declared. Logging had been replaced by dairying, the sawmills superseded by a plant churning out milk, butter and cheese for a national chain. Lately, winegrowers had edged up from the lower hills. And last of all had come a few folk like myself, fleeing Brisbane to retire on cheap five or ten-acre blocks, and to live out their lives hobby farming, or painting, or potting, or growing marijuana. There was an art gallery in the main street now, and two new guest houses had opened in the last few years.

It was a hinterland town, on the verge of gentrification. The locals—the real locals—still prided themselves on being genuine country. I thought differently, sure enough, but being resident a mere ten years, who was I to anyone that mattered?

What would Charlie be doing up here? If it was him, if it was really him.

And I still couldn't believe it was.

We drove. Highwood fell behind, and we followed the road past dairy farms and plantations and the smaller subdivisions with their cement-brick huts, some with their chimneys already smoking. I caught a glimpse of a candle flickering in a window, and a woman's face over a sink. Her water would not be warm.

The police radio broke into life. 'Graham, it's Tony here.'

Graham picked it up. 'Yeah?'

'The two detectives from Brisbane have arrived. We've shown them everything.'

'I'm on my way.'

'They're not too happy that you moved the clothes.'

'The power workers moved them, not me. They weren't inside the substation anyway.'

'Just letting you know.'

Graham clicked the microphone back. 'It was a fuck-up,' he said to me. 'But when the boys from the power company got there, the first thing they found was the clothes, so naturally enough they went through them.'

He still seemed unnerved, pulling hard on his cigarette. I watched out the window. The houses and farms were thinning the further we got from town, and I wondered where it was we were headed.

'What's all this about a substation?' I said.

He glanced at me, hesitant. 'An electrical substation. The town's substation.'

I looked up. Powerlines ran alongside the road. I'd thought the blackout was just another line down, another transformer blown. It happened often enough up in the hills, and the repairs were never quick.

'This has something to do with the power failure?'

He nodded, but that was all.

'I don't understand,' I said.

'Wait. You'll have to look at it anyway. Let's just say for now he was electrocuted.'

I thought about that, and about the clothes back at the police station. A night as cold as the one we'd just had, and Charlie wasn't wearing his clothes? If it was him, of course, if it was *really* him.

'What was he doing at a substation?' I asked. 'Why was he there?'

Graham thought some more, then rolled down his window a little to toss out his cigarette butt. It was not a responsible thing to do in a forested area, but then no fire would ever start on a morning like this. Cold air sank around my feet as he wound the window up again.

'I don't think he went there by choice,' he said.

'What does that mean?'

'Leave it, George. We're almost there.'

And we drove into a black tunnel of trees.

I stared about, confused. Highwood lay high in the great ring of mountains that made up the Border Ranges, two hours south-west of Brisbane. There was only the one road that ran through the valley. It came winding up into the hills from the north, crossed the actual border just south of the town and then descended again into New South Wales. It was not much travelled, for the major interstate highways crossed the ranges further east or west. Up in the mountains there was no destination apart from Highwood itself, and here at the northern end of the valley the forest closed in tightly, crowding the driver for a mile or two. After that there was only the steep drop in the road, and then the long climb down, six or seven hundred metres, to the foothills. Where were we going?

Graham slowed the car. The forest was shadowed, as if dawn was still hours away, not minutes. Mist seeped from between the trees, rolling across the road. Finally Graham braked and turned off onto a narrow track that I'd never even noticed before, let alone driven down. It was damp and rutted, and the trees hung over it possessively, dripping moisture onto the windscreen. Graham flicked on the wipers. A fire glowed up ahead, at least I thought it was fire. After we'd run a hundred yards, however, I could see that it wasn't. It was the slow flash of police lights.

This was it, then. Something tightened in my stomach. I hadn't eaten since waking, couldn't have eaten. I felt hollow and cold and didn't want to leave the warmth of the car.

The track terminated in a clearing. Within the open space was a squat brick structure that had a door but no windows. Behind it was a fenced-off area which held a tangle of power lines and poles and things the name of which I didn't know. There were big signs on the building and the fences—warnings about trespassing and about dangerous voltages. And off to one side, a giant sentinel rising out of the trees, stood a naked steel tower that bore high-voltage powerlines away into the grey sky, off towards the mountain's rim and the descent.

Graham stopped the car and looked at me, his hand on the door handle.

'You ready?'

I was staring at all the vehicles and people crammed into the clearing. The other district police car was already there, its lights revolving steadily, plus one other car that was unmarked. There was an ambulance with its doors open, a dim light spilling out. There was a large truck with ladders and other gear on the back and the name of the power company written on the side. People were standing around in the gloom, some in uniform, some in hard hats. Someone was stretching police tape across a gate, although I couldn't see why—there would be no crowd here to keep away, no one would ever come here, surely, not to this little brick hut in the forest.

I gripped my own door handle, summoned the lie.

'I'm ready.'

THREE

It was cold again, outside the car, and faces everywhere were turned towards us. A man broke away from the group and came our way, buttoning his suit jacket against the morning.

'I'm Detective Kelly,' he said, shaking Graham's hand. Then he took mine. 'You're here to make the identification?'

'If I can,' I said.

Graham told the detective who I was, and the man studied me for a moment, as if somewhere the name meant something to him. 'He's already identified the licence photo,' Graham went on, 'but then, the person in there doesn't really look much like the photo. Not now.'

A shrieking erupted in the bush, and in a flurry of leaves a large white bird flapped from high in a tree, then soared off into the morning like a departing soul. We all paused and watched until it was gone. In the distance another chorus of bird calls rose, then fell away. Silence settled, apart from the mutter of voices, and the dripping of water.

'Strange place for something like this,' was all the detective said.

He was young, much younger than me, early thirties maybe, and that was disturbing. There was a time when I associated with police detectives, and back then they'd all seemed to be older, tougher, more capable men. This one wasn't like that. Maybe he thought he was tough and capable, maybe he really was, but to me his calm voice, his professional air, looked like an act, something learned in training. He was younger than me, that was all. He wasn't fat and he wasn't swilling free beer and grappling the women without bothering to pay. And I was older. Ten years older.

'You came up from Brisbane?' I asked. 'How long ago did this happen?'

He nodded towards the truck. 'The power boys say the substation blew about one a.m. The crew got up here about an hour later, from Boonah. They called the Highwood police and I'm told the sergeant here arrived about two-thirty. He put the call through to Brisbane and here we are. We don't know time of death yet, of course, but it's reasonable to assume it was connected to the power failure. A forensic team shouldn't be far behind us.'

One a.m. I'd been in bed only half an hour by then. And by Highwood standards I was almost nocturnal. The rest of the town would have been sleeping fast.

'George,' Graham said, 'we don't have to go in there right away.'

The three of us were walking towards the substation now. There was nothing to see apart from the vehicles and the men. But the door to the small brick building was open, and no one was looking that way. Whatever it was, it was in there.

We reached a group of three power workers. They were talking with another man in a suit, and we paused by them. 'So it was a lucky thing,' one of the workers was saying, and he stopped, looking at me.

'This is Detective Lewis,' Kelly said, and I shook another firm young hand. He was heavier, though, almost baby-faced, and seemed determined to be cheerful.

'I was just asking these guys,' he said to his colleague, 'how they got up here so quickly.'

The power workers glanced unhappily between the two detectives.

'We had a problem down at base that extended the afternoon shift through till after midnight,' the first one said, 'so we were still at the depot when the alarm went off.'

'Otherwise we might've had to wait till normal working hours, right?' Lewis said. 'I know you guys don't do a regular night duty outside of Brisbane any more.'

They shuffled their feet. 'It's not our fault. There's no money for overtime.'

Kelly wasn't interested. He was looking at the brick building. 'What exactly does this place do?'

The man shrugged. 'It's a substation. You got power coming out of the big generating stations, okay? They can send it out in any sort of voltage they want, but the lower the voltage the more resistance you get in the wires, so over hundreds of kilometres you'd lose a lot of power, just in heat. So instead they send it out high voltage, very high. The problem is, your average household or business can't use power at that voltage. So when the main line gets near a town, say, you put in a substation. It's basically a series of transformers, which scales the power from high voltage down to low. Then you can send it out to the consumer, and resistance isn't a problem because now the consumer is close by. The voltage is usually still a bit too high, though, so you have smaller substations and transformers street by street, which gets it down to 240 volts, or whatever you need.'

'But this is a big substation, right?' Kelly asked.

'Right. This is for the whole Highwood area.'

'So what sort of power have we got coming in?'

'240 000 volts.'

And silence fell again as everyone pondered the figure.

'Do you think he was hit with all of that?' Graham asked.

The worker thought, then shook his head. 'It's unlikely. But someone's been mucking around with the switchboard in there. The wires are all over the place. It could've been anything.'

And it seemed no one else had anything to say. I stared at the brick building. A substation. If I thought about it, I'd seen them everywhere, hundreds of them in cities and towns and along country roads, square and bland and forgettable. And yet they were like sewage pipes. Modern life revolved around them. A secret network, and this one most secret of all, hidden away on the mountains' edge.

The power worker tipped his hard hat upwards, and then back down. 'Um . . . you gonna get him out of there soon? Only with morning coming, we should get the supply back on.'

'Not until a team has been over it,' Kelly replied, official. 'And besides . . .'

He was looking at me. Graham took his meaning and laid a hand on my arm, and then it was just the two of us walking towards the brick building. Behind us the others remained, silent. The two ambulance men, over at their vehicle, dragged on cigarettes and looked away. They'd already been inside, of course. Everyone had, except me.

'What you'll see in there,' Graham said, his voice low, 'is pretty awful. But all you have to do is look at his face and tell us if you recognise him. Then we get straight out, okay?'

A sense of unreality was flowing over me, my feet didn't seem to be hitting the ground. The metal door to the substation hung open, and a soft glow came from inside. Another gas lamp. Even here, at the very source of power, there was still no electricity. Up close the building loomed larger, thick and windowless, like a blockhouse, surrounded by mist and darkness and cold. There was only the one narrow doorway, and the light flowing out seemed almost red. I could see nothing of what was inside. And then we were at the door, and going through.

I looked at the floor. I was ready for a body, and bodies were supposed to be on floors. But there was nothing on the floor, only naked concrete. The room was about fifteen feet square, the walls lined with equipment and panels. There was a desk and an old, tattered chair. And there was a smell, high and strong. For a sickening moment I thought—and maybe I'd almost been expecting it—but it wasn't that, it wasn't the smell of burning. Instead it was something familiar. Painfully, sweetly familiar. Something from a life lived years ago. It was that special mixture that all drinkers know, but only the old and hardened come to live with, to ignore, and finally to need. It was the ripe scent of alcohol and urine, inextricably fused, the one always leading to the other. Usually you smelt it in bars, or in back alleyways, or in boarding house rooms. Not on frozen mornings in concrete bunkers. Not unless they were prison cells. And then, to the right, I saw it.

'Is that him?' Graham asked.

I stared. And stared.

'Well?'

My mouth worked, got words out. 'I can't really tell.'

Graham cleared his throat. He took me closer, to within a yard of where the man stood, so that I could see the face more clearly, turned, as it was, away from the door. So I could see the right-hand side of the face . . .

'Well?'

And whatever doubts I'd had, now I knew. Charlie was marked, like Cain, and would always be instantly knowable. Even when he was like this.

'It's him,' I said.

Graham nodded. 'That, um, major injury to his face. It's not like the other wounds. It looks old and healed up, but it wasn't on his licence photo, so we were wondering . . .'

'It's old. He got it years ago. That's how I know for sure.'

'All right, that's all we need, George, we can go.'

But I couldn't go. I hadn't even made sense yet of what I was seeing. It was Charlie, sure enough, but it wasn't Charlie at all, not this thin scarecrow of a person, strung up against the wall. Not this old, old man. He was my age, Charlie, not even fifty, but this man . . .

He was naked and had his back to us, his chest to the wall. Only it wasn't a wall. It was a bank of power equipment, a switchboard. Metal doors had been opened and inside was a confusion of switches and coils and cables. His chest was pressed up hard against it all, his feet tied with wire to the panels, and his hands as well, above his head, so that he was spreadeagled against the switchboard, and even though he was dead, he couldn't fall. He looked like a convict ready for the whipping—no, like a convict already whipped, for his back was livid with small red marks. But they weren't from any whip. Lying at his feet were several cords which snaked back into the panels. The ends of the cords were stripped down to naked wires. Electrical wires.

And it was Charlie. His face, turned to his left, looked blank and stupid, with none of the life or thought that had worked within it once. I didn't know if that was death, or if that was how he'd looked ever since . . . light retardation, they'd said. Some loss of motor coordination. And his body looked ravaged by more than just electricity. So old, so thin.

Graham had a gentle hold of my arm. 'C'mon,' he was saying, pulling.

'But . . . but why this?' I said. 'Why would anyone do this?'

I was babbling. I wasn't looking at Charlie any more, I was staring all around the room, searching for someone else, for whoever did this, as if they might still be there, ready to explain themselves. And it was all crazy, what I was seeing now. Details stood out. There were beer cans everywhere. Empty, lying on their sides, a few dribbles of froth at their mouths. And there were bottles. Vodka bottles, two of them. Empty as well. A few puddles of alcohol, or urine maybe, on the floor. It was as if there'd been a party in there. And the smell, now that I knew its source, was fresh and strong as if someone had just gone out for another round. It was the sort of thing kids might have left behind, teenagers hiding out from their parents, drinking furtively. Just kids. Except for what was tied up against the wall.

'Why now?' I heard myself saying. 'Why would anyone do this now?'

But Graham wasn't listening. He was dragging me away and we were outside again and everything seemed brighter. The sky was a weak pink and the police lights had faded so that they appeared like toys. No one would look at me, and everywhere birds were screeching in the trees, thousands of them, greeting the day.

FOUR

Light always came late to Highwood, deep in its valley. Even so, by the time we all got back to the police station the sun had lifted high above the treetops and burnt away the mists in the gullies, the main street was flushed golden, and the townsfolk were up, driving and walking, going about their business. People chatted on the footpath. The power failure, that's what everyone would be talking about. At least until the real news spread. And it would spread. Faster than the power would be restored. The electricians had been kept waiting, and waiting. The forensic team and the photographer had spent over two hours with Charlie in that small, cold room before cutting him down.

And finally, too, Detectives Kelly and Lewis were catching on.

'Charles Monohan,' they were muttering, going through his clothes and staring at his licence. 'Charles Monohan.' We were all in Graham's office. I'd been dreading this, all through the long business out at the substation, while the light grew in the sky and the memory of what I'd seen took hold inside me. The detectives had been preoccupied, but Graham already knew, and the other two would remember, sooner or later.

'Charles Monohan,' said Kelly, turning my way. 'Why do I know that name?'

I didn't want to answer. For friendship's sake, possibly. But if it was an act of friendship, then it was ludicrously too little, and far too late.

'I don't know if you'd remember,' I said. 'How long have you been in the police force?'

'The police *service*,' he corrected, and I recalled that they'd changed the name, after all the troubles, in an attempt to salvage their public image. It hadn't worked. 'I've been in thirteen years.'

'Then it would have been not so long after you started. Charlie was arrested in 1988. For tax evasion.'

I had their attention, but they still weren't getting it. Graham only waited, as if it would all be better coming from me.

'And corruption,' I sighed. 'After the Inquiry.'

It was enough. In police circles, as well as in the political and media worlds, there were only two time-scales that defined Queensland. Before the Inquiry. And after it.

'Ah . . .' said Kelly, and turned to his colleague. '*That* Charles Monohan.'

Everything changed, as I'd known it would. Charlie as an innocent victim, strung up and savaged, that was one thing. Charles Monohan, as the police knew him, that was something else. His life, his death, his body . . . it all changed.

'How long was he in prison?' Lewis asked, musing.

'The sentence was four years,' I answered. 'I don't know how long he served. I haven't seen him since he went in.'

Kelly was counting on his fingers. 'He was with that third lot, wasn't he? Marvin—he went to jail as well. And Lindsay, but Lindsay skipped out. There were a couple of others . . .'

Graham was leaning back in his chair and regarding me sadly.

I said, 'I was one of them too.'

Kelly stared at me, his fingers still in mid-count. 'You?'

And his partner was pointing. 'George Verney. You were the journalist.'

'That's right.'

Kelly was nodding now. 'But you didn't get any jail time, did you?'

'No.'

I was guilty all the same, by association at the very least, and the two detectives considered me with new, unfriendly eyes.

Graham stretched in his chair, reasonable. 'He didn't go to prison, but then it's debatable if he committed any serious crime, and he did still lose his job and everything else. For the last ten years he's been quiet as a mouse up here working on our little paper. So don't be too quick with any ideas.'

Lewis wasn't convinced. 'But this changes everything.'

Graham nodded. 'It does. Just remember, though, a lot of people got burned back then, police as well as civilians. Not all of them deserved it, not by any means.'

And I detected in that the barest hint of a kindred soul. He was right, a lot of police had fallen under the Inquiry's sway, too, senior men; and unlike the two detectives, Graham was old enough to have known some of them.

'But you've kept an eye on him?' Kelly wanted to know.

'Sure I have,' said Graham.

'Charlie Monohan,' Lewis wondered, gazing at me. 'How many clubs did he own in the end?'

'He didn't own any clubs. He owned three restaurants, and that was it.'

'Oh, come on . . .'

'You were in partnership with him,' Kelly put in, 'and it was more than just restaurants.'

'We weren't exactly partners. We were friends and I invested some money in his business . . . but we weren't exactly partners.'

And was a cock crowing somewhere in town, three times?

'But you were still part of things,' Kelly insisted. 'And here's Charlie, dead outside a little nowhere town where you just happen to live.'

'Am I under arrest?'

Kelly considered me for a moment. 'Where were you last night?'

'At home.'

'Alone?'

'No.'

'Who with?'

'A friend. Do you want her name?'

'We will. Eventually.' He pulled up a chair and sat down in front of me. 'But first, how about you refresh our memories a little about those old days. Your associates, for one thing . . .'

He raised his fingers, ready to count again. One hand wouldn't be enough. Six fingers, that's how many he'd need.

21

'Let's see, there was you and there was Charlie and there was Marvin and there was Lindsay. There was some old guy, too, someone in the premier's department. I can't remember his name.'

'Jeremy Phelan.'

He nodded. 'And a woman. There was a woman, right?'

'Yes,' I said. 'There was a woman.'

But Charlie was the first.

The saddest thing was, of all of us, he was the only one who looked like a criminal. In the TV sense, anyway, and in the sense that when a jury got a look at him, after watching all that TV, they had no doubts about it either. He looked like a thug, a door warden at the sort of clubs he would later be convicted for owning. Something of a curse for a man whose dream was to run restaurants. And that's all it was, in the beginning.

'What was her name?'

'Maybellene,' I said. 'May.'

But first it was just Charlie and me.

And alcohol.

And Queensland itself.

FIVE

Alcohol and Queensland. And the restaurant business.

It took the combination of all three to bring Charlie and I together.

In any other state, in any other business, it wouldn't have happened. And if there'd been no wine in the back room, if I hadn't gone there that night, if Charlie hadn't realised who I was . . .

Lots of ifs and all of them pointless.

It was the early 1970s, and it was Brisbane. The disasters that would be visited on Queensland were, for the most part, still in the future, but all the groundwork had been laid, systems were already in place. Charlie and I knew nothing about the majority of them, not then. We'd both only just turned twenty. I was a cadet journalist working for a community paper. Charlie was working in a small Italian bistro his parents owned in Paddington. We knew some things, of course, the things everyone knew—that Queensland was different from the rest of Australia, that things worked in Queensland in a way they didn't anywhere else. But we didn't know why. Or more importantly, we didn't know who.

We were just a couple of years out of school, and what was politics to us? My little paper covered purely lifestyle issues and real estate. We had two food columns—a fine dining section, a staff position which was sought after, and a cheap eats section, which no one wanted at all and had fallen to me. So all I was after that first night was an inexpensive meal. All Charlie wanted was a good review for his parents' bistro. Beyond that we only had the one thing in common.

We had a flair for drinking.

Which put us in an odd position in the Brisbane of those days. To all appearances, especially to unknowing youths such as ourselves, it was a puritan town. Bars were allowed to open only from ten in the morning to ten at night, except on Sundays, when it got worse, a mere four hours of trading permitted. A few restaurants were licensed to sell their own drinks, but generally they were the expensive ones, and the rest had to survive on customers bringing their own. Even then, when it came to buying your own supply, there were no liquor stores or off-licences. Only hotels could sell the product, and only during the same hours as the bars. If you drank then, you drank to very restricted hours in limited venues, or you drank at home. Brisbane after ten p.m. was a ghost town of empty streets, haunted by a few unhappy drunks either wandering around with nowhere else to go, or carrying that last bottle home to the wife and kids. Sundays it was like everyone had left the planet.

Charlie's bistro did not have a full licence, but it was BYO, otherwise I would never have gone there at all. I took three bottles of beer with me that night, and I only expected to be there an hour. I had more beer waiting for me at home. It didn't seem unusual—I never questioned any of the restaurant laws at the time, I just made sure I always had my own supply. What bothered me more were the pubs and the bars, and the fact that they all closed so early. I didn't understand that at all.

But I ate my meal and was just finishing off the second bottle of beer and reaching for the third when Charlie emerged from the kitchen and came my way.

'You from the paper?' he demanded.

I looked up, startled. 'Yes.'

That's how much of an investigative reporter I was.

But really it was that Charlie himself was so alarming at first sight. He was in dirty kitchen whites and he was squat, all beef and muscle. His hair was cut prickly short on a square head that was already going bald, and his voice had a thin, whispering edge to it. I thought he might be a boxer. And I wondered why they had sent the dishwasher out to threaten me.

But Charlie had never hit a soul in his life, not then, not ever.

Still, people would always react to him that way. I don't know that he was ever aware of it himself. I certainly never saw him try to intimidate anyone physically. The idea would have appalled him. But the way things worked out . . . he was so right for the part he ended up playing. Not on his own behalf, perhaps. More for Marvin and for Lindsay and the others. He was so right for what *they* wanted.

But once he smiled at you, you knew it was all an illusion.

And that night Charlie smiled at me and shook my hand and sat himself down at my table.

'Thought I'd seen you round,' he said. 'What're you gonna say about us?'

So we talked.

About the meal for a little, but then more about Charlie.

Even in those first few minutes it was obvious that his body had nothing to do with the rest of him. He wasn't the dishwasher, he was an apprentice chef under his father, and in fact his father was ill and really Charlie was half running the place. Nor was he Italian, he was Irish Catholic, same as me. And he had plans for much bigger and better places one day.

'I'd want somewhere licensed, for one thing,' he said, looking at my bottle of beer.

'You want a glass?'

'Sure.'

So we drank the bottle. There was hardly anyone else in the restaurant, and Charlie was only called away a couple of times to deal with customers, but you could tell how much he liked striding the floor between the tables, and how people, after their first resistance, warmed to him. He was a natural with an audience, and in what was a rare moment of insight for me I understood that his real future didn't lie hidden away in the kitchen.

He kept coming back and sitting down.

'You know,' he said, when the beer was gone, 'the folks keep a few cartons of wine out the back. Strictly private supply.'

'Okay,' I said.

And so we drank a bottle of wine. The other customers drifted away. Charlie's mother poked her head out of the kitchen and said she was going home. So it was just me and Charlie.

And all that wine.

Maybe that's all it was at first. Genuine friendship would always take time, but there were other connections that could be instantaneous. And for all that I could sense the quick mind and gentle heart that dwelt perversely under all the muscle, and for all that he obviously saw something he liked in me, it was only when he went and fetched the second bottle of wine that we first considered each other in that certain, special way. A *drinker's* way. And it was really only after we'd emptied that bottle, and Charlie had asked me if I felt like a third—it was really there and then, in that moment. If I'd said no, I would have been making it clear that I wasn't serious when it came to drinking, that I would let things like the late hour or work the next day get in the way of the next glass, if the next glass was available. If Charlie hadn't offered that third bottle, he would've been telling me the same thing. And that would have been that. I doubt we would have crossed paths again.

But he did offer, and I accepted, and from there he didn't bother to ask, he just kept bringing out the bottles. Neither of us said, 'I should be getting home.' Neither of us said, 'I shouldn't be getting drunk tonight.' The question was never even raised. The understanding, magically and effortlessly, had been made. What we talked about all night, what we actually expressed about our views of the world, the things we agreed upon or didn't agree upon, the things that made us genuinely like each other, they mattered no doubt in the long term— even alcohol couldn't forge a bond where one didn't exist. But it was alcohol that got us started, and it would be there as long as the friendship itself. Later it would all become twisted, and both the drinking and the friendship would mutate into something darker. But for me the drinking would end only on the same day the friendship did. And for Charlie . . . for Charlie, I didn't know.

Either way, I wrote a good review the next day, and not long after that I found a job on a real paper, out at Ipswich. Charlie kept on cooking and his parents retired and the restaurant was all his. And with increasing frequency I would drop over to the place around closing time, for a late meal, and for a few glasses of wine, or a few bottles. We'd sit at a table, surrounded by upturned chairs, and look out the front window to the night and the quiet streets of Brisbane. There was nowhere else for us to go anyway. Everything was closed. There was always that one simple, baffling fact—after ten o'clock on a weekday night it seemed next to impossible for men like us to go out and get a drink. We'd talk about that, and about other aspects of the city, its strange ways that we were only just beginning to understand.

For one thing, Charlie had applied for a licence for his restaurant, and been turned down.

The body concerned was the Queensland Licensing Commission. It was overseen by a government minister, and staffed by representatives from the police, the alcohol industry, and other respectable members of the community. Except there weren't really any respectable members of the community—at least, no impartial ones. I asked senior journalists at my new paper about it. I told them about Charlie's problems, and they only shook their heads, amused, as they explained. There were just two groups on the Licensing Commission. Half of the members were hotel or restaurant owners themselves. They already controlled all the bars and the trade and had no interest in weakening the monopoly. The other half were police representatives, who had no interest in losing the kickbacks they received from the first half. A neat example, it seemed, of self-regulation.

And just a small demonstration of the way Queensland worked.

Charlie wasn't overly concerned. 'I hear,' he said, 'that for an extra fee to the right people, a licence can still be arranged. Apparently that's the only way.'

'Who are the right people?'

'That's what I gotta find out one day.'

It should have been harmless. We were just friends. Tossing back the wine. Dissatisfied with the way things were. Thinking about the future.

Of all things, it didn't feel like the birth of a crime syndicate.

SIX

Three p.m. and I sat in my car across the street and a little way down from the front gate of the Highwood State Primary School. The day that had started in darkness and dawned into blue skies had now turned overcast and cold. The light was already fading. Clouds shrouded the heights around the town, and later in the evening fog would probably creep down into the streets. Another night to hide away in front of fires, to sleep warmed by electric blankets. At least the power was back on. The fluorescent lights in the police station had flickered to life again around mid-morning. And Charlie . . . by now Charlie would be in a morgue in Brisbane somewhere, waiting for the knife.

I was exhausted, as if it had been days since I'd slept. The detectives had finished with me at noon, and not knowing what else to do, I'd gone home. I didn't know what I was hoping for but the house was frigid and empty, and even the fire couldn't seem to warm things. I ate food and drank tea and the cold within me wasn't soothed. Finally I'd crawled into bed and piled quilts over myself, but whenever I closed my eyes I saw things I didn't want to see. Charlie was in my bedroom. He'd heard everything I said to the detectives. Heard my lies and evasions. It didn't matter that they felt like the truth. Charlie knew better, and he kept me awake, his blank, idiot face asking an eternal question.

A bell shrilled somewhere in the school grounds, and then another. I watched the front gate. A small crowd of anxious parents waited there. Normally, in Highwood, most of the children, even the first graders, walked or cycled home from school alone. Or if they were farm kids, they caught one of the two school buses. But not today. Today there was a flock of mothers and fathers at the gate, milling restlessly. News had got around. I didn't know yet to what extent or in how much detail, but the air was unsettled, something horrible had happened, and if you had kids the first instinct, it seemed, was to get them home and get them safe.

The students began filing through the gates. Parents sought out their children and clutched their hands, led them off to waiting cars. Some stooped to button up loose jackets and tug down woollen caps—as if even the cold was somehow more evil today, more to be dreaded. Up the road a distance the two buses waited, and at each bus a teacher stood, making sure all the passengers boarded safely. And it was all unnecessary. No one was out to snatch children that afternoon, at least, no one who had anything to do with Charlie and the cement block of the substation—that was something which spoke of another sort of mind, another sort of cruelty. But fear was fear.

Parents with their children hurried past my car, and a few of them gave me short, uncertain stares. News would have spread, too, that I was somehow involved. It wouldn't help the atmosphere that I was sitting there in my car, watching. After all, I had no children, at that school or at any other. But then everyone knew that, and knew why I was there.

I waited. I'd given up trying to sleep back at the house, and resorted to pacing, sitting blindly in front of the television. Nothing stopped the thoughts ticking over, and my body yearned for heat. I realised that most of all I felt lonely. Lonely for myself, and for Charlie. Nothing, perhaps, was so alone as a death like that. A body left tied to a wall, naked and beaten. Whatever had happened to him, no one had stopped it, no one had tried to help. He'd had no friends when he died.

'You haven't seen him in ten years?' the detectives had wanted to know.

'No.'

'You weren't close any more?'

'We . . . we just didn't see each other.'

'Why not?'

'It all went bad. At the end there. You know how it was.'

'What about the others? You see any of them? Marvin? Lindsay?'

'I haven't seen anyone from those days.'

'You think any of them would do something like this to Charlie?'

'Why would they? And why now? It was all years ago.'

'What about you, then? Would you do this?'

'What reason would I have?'

'You tell us.'

I had no reason. I'd already done all the damage to Charlie I could ever have wanted to do. And the others? As far as I knew, they had no reason either. Charlie was harmless and it was all finished and surely no one cared any more.

'We'll be talking some more,' the detectives had said. 'Just as soon as we get the deal from the forensic team.'

And they let me go.

I waited in my car. The students and their parents had all melted away, and I was the only one left parked in the street. The afternoon deepened and fingers of mist crawled down the hillsides, pale grey amidst trees turned black. I huddled in my seat. Over time three or four of the teachers came through the gate. I knew them all, at least by name, and they all knew me, but none of them glanced my way. I waited. Finally the principal emerged, and pulled the gate closed behind her. I watched as she worked with the padlock. Like so many things in Highwood, the padlock wasn't really needed. No one had ever robbed the school, and anyone could easily step over the gate if they wanted to, no matter how securely it was fastened. But some years ago a few youths had got onto the sports oval with their motorbikes and torn up the grass. Everyone had known who they were, and they were made, to their great embarrassment, to reseed the damaged sections, but ever since then the front gate was locked at night. And it was the principal's duty to lock it. She was always the last out.

I watched. She seemed preoccupied, shoulders hunched against the cold and head facing the ground. She began walking away from me up the street. I started my car and followed her. Mrs Klump was her name. She was known to the children,

I'd heard, as Mrs Hump. There was nothing visibly misshapen about her back, but obviously the students had heard some sort of rumour, and since she was in charge of discipline at the school, in charge of punishment, some sort of threatening alias was required. And although in reality there was nothing at all of the witch about her, she seemed to go along with idea. She liked to dress in severe black suits, wore her hair tied back in a bun, and let her glasses hang permanently on a chain about her neck, although she hardly needed them, except for driving at night.

I pulled up beside her. She turned, saw it was me, then came over to the passenger window, her eyes full of concern.

'George,' she said, 'I was going to call as soon as I got home.'

'I couldn't wait.'

'Graham rang me this afternoon.'

'I know. I'm sorry about that. They needed to know where I was last night. And who I was with.'

We looked at each other for a moment. She was thirty-eight years old and widowed, and though to her students she was all austerity and cool command, she wasn't anything like that to me.

'Emily,' I said, 'can you come over?'

And I was surprised at my voice. I hadn't meant it to come out as nakedly as that, but the day had been long and endlessly cold, and I found that now I was even shivering. My self-possession was almost at its end.

In answer she opened the door, climbed in and kissed me warmly on the lips, and for all that everything was understood and settled, that was something she rarely did in public.

'Of course I can,' she said.

I'd heard it expressed somewhere that in reaction to death a human being would always reach out for the physical comfort of another, but it wasn't something I'd directly experienced before. Increasingly throughout the day, however, with the police and in my house alone, I'd been thinking of her. The urge was instinctive and irresistible. It wasn't for sex, exactly, nor was it just for companionship. It was the need for contact.

The need to feel living flesh, to wrap myself in it, to feel a heartbeat and breathing and movement.

I drove Emily home in silence. And while it was true that the need to talk was there, first it was just touch I wanted, wordless and clutching, tugging away the clothes to get closer to her skin. And though it did indeed turn into sex, it was a longing and vain attempt, like trying to grab onto life once and for all and keep it forever, or to burrow so deeply into her warmth that I would never fall out of it. Both were impossible, and in the end it had to be enough just to hold her, huddled under the covers of my bed as darkness fell outside, and to feel that at least someone and something stood between me and an end so desolate.

'He was your friend?' she asked finally, my head on her breast, and her hands moving in my hair.

'My best friend, once.'

'From those old times?'

'That's right. But I haven't seen him since.'

'You haven't seen anyone from those days, not that I've ever met.'

She was wondering, I knew, about my life before I met her. It was the one great unspoken thing between us, though she knew a little, as much as was public knowledge. Over the years she'd told me everything about her own life, and there'd been times when I'd been close to telling her in return . . . but somehow it had never happened. I didn't want her to know, to see me that way. There were too many things that seemed to have no place in the life I'd made in Highwood, and it had always seemed dangerous to dredge them up to Emily, as if they were evil talismans, still holding the power to mar and spoil even after so long. Keeping them secret had done another sort of damage, I supposed. And now one of them had turned up anyway. Worse than I could ever have imagined.

'Did he work with you on the paper?'

'No. He was a chef, I guess you'd say—well, he ran restaurants, anyway, very successful ones. Amongst other things.'

Other things indeed. But not now. I couldn't talk about it now.

'And do you know why he ended up like . . .' Her hand paused in my hair. 'Like that?'

'No idea. No idea at all.'

But I didn't want Charlie there in bed with us. Instead I sat up, pulled back the covers and stared down at her lean, pale body. I hadn't studied it like this for a long time, and it suddenly seemed such a vital thing. She lay there and watched me gravely. She could be shy about her body, and in our early days had preferred me not to see it. There were broad scars on her shoulders and back of which she was ashamed, worse than a hump, if her students had known. But there'd been too much between us for that to matter any longer. I ran my hand over her skin, trying once more to imprint it in my mind, to have the moment to keep. It seemed important to appreciate everything about her. As if she, too, might be gone in the morning. Another body in another empty room in another town.

I'd met her, like Charlie, through my work. One of my duties at the *Highwood Herald* was to cover all the school news. I recorded their sports carnivals, their fetes, the announcement of their school captains, the installation of new blackboards—things I would never have touched in my day, but this was the stuff of which small town newspapers were made. Emily was my contact. After my first year or two at the *Highwood Herald*, we knew each other well enough for me to invite her around for dinner without things seeming forced, and nothing had ever been forced from there.

And they were strange things, small towns.

Highwood was conservative in almost every way that mattered, possessive of its own, and protective. I once would've thought that the idea of a primary school teacher—a guardian of five and six-year-old minds—openly sleeping with an unknown city journalist, under no suggestion of marriage, would have been cause for at least comment, if not outright scandal. But it hadn't turned out that way. For one thing, Emily was a local girl, born and bred, and locals were always given a leeway that strangers weren't. More importantly, she was a hero. That is, her husband was. Leo—a local boy, a dairy farmer. He and Emily had been childhood sweethearts. Everyone knew them, and when they married at twenty-two, half the town was at the wedding. I'd seen the photos.

They'd enjoyed four years together. They were young and healthy and by the sounds of it they'd been the ideal country couple, involved in all of the town's clubs and societies and dance committees, its sporting teams and its volunteer groups. One of the latter happened to be the Highwood Volunteer Bushfire Brigade, an important body in a small town surrounded by forests. One summer, not long after their fourth anniversary, a bushfire swept down from the hills to threaten outlying houses, and both Emily and Leo had joined their crew and rolled off in a water-truck to fight it. It wasn't their first fire or even their biggest, but on a narrow firebreak trail the wind had turned on the crew just as they were running low on water. Everyone had dashed back to the truck and grabbed on to whatever they could, but the driver had barely got into gear before the wall of flame hit. And bushfires were notoriously fickle. Those in the cab came through virtually unharmed. Those clinging to the mid-section, Emily included, came through with burns of varying severity to their backs and legs and arms. One man had only got a hand to the rear of the water-truck, and he didn't come through at all.

There was a monument to Leo in the park in front of the courthouse. It was sizeable and sincere, but Emily laid flowers only at his grave, on their anniversary—I'd never seen her even glance at the memorial. But that was where Highwood surprised. Leo had died for the town and he was a hero, sure enough, but the cost of that fell mostly on his widow, and all of Highwood knew it. People thought she might pack up and leave, escape the memories, and they would have forgiven her that. But once she was out of hospital she went right back to teaching, went back to all the clubs and societies and everything about her old life, with the sole exception of the Fire Brigade. For that they respected her, quietly and voicelessly, but deeply. They wished her nothing but happiness. For years there'd been no other men in her life, but when finally she'd chosen to dally with an out-of-town journalist, it seemed there wasn't a soul, even the meanest, who was going to question her about it. They glared a bit more sternly at me, perhaps—I wasn't worthy of her, no one doubted that—but it was decided that after all she'd lost, what little she chose to take was firmly her own and no one else's business.

Most of this, of course, I discovered only after Emily and I were already an item, which was thankful, otherwise I might have felt the whole town in bed with us those first few times. Which was maybe why she'd picked me in the first place. I was an outsider and saw her just as a person, not as an object of pity, or respect, or anything else. Nor had I ever known her husband. Nor, to be honest, did I care about him. And while she had certainly loved him, and mourned him, in a town where she had to walk past his monument every day, and face all his friends and family and legacies, he was like a prison cell. So for Emily, I assumed, I offered some sort of escape.

And for me she was . . . I wasn't sure what she was. Except that, like the town itself, she was part of my second attempt at life. A decent life. Without Charlie or Marvin or Lindsay. Or Maybellene.

She was also my alibi. On the previous evening she had come over for dinner and we'd sat in front of the fire until half an hour past midnight, and then she'd gone home. If the time of death was one a.m. then maybe that cleared me for Charlie's death, maybe it didn't. I didn't care either way. All I felt was bad that, even to the least degree, the whole thing had involved her at all.

I stared at her on the bed, and it was too cold to be lying around naked.

'Can you stay over tonight?' I asked.

She nodded and the moment, whatever it had been, was over. She sat up and I swung my legs out of the bed.

'I'll get the fire started,' I said. 'And there's a bottle of red in the kitchen, if you want.'

'Good, I could use a drink.'

And there was a fractional pause that still caught us, even now.

It was true that I no longer drank, but Emily did. Just a glass or two at a time, at least around me. I didn't really know if it bothered her. I suspected that in her earlier days she and Leo had drunk much more, and maybe she still did, on her own time—she kept something like a cellar of wines in a cupboard at her house—so it was possible I was an inhibiting influence. It wasn't what I wanted, though. Alcohol had been my own disaster, not hers. So I kept wine in my house as well, and she drank it, and we pretended that it didn't matter to either of us.

It wasn't the truth. Sometimes I could taste a hint of the wine on her lips when we kissed. The memory it roused could almost be fond, but at other times it pricked a darker, sourer emotion, and for a moment I'd think of another woman entirely, and feel another sort of passion, much more painful and long suppressed. I'd have to pull away, and Emily would look at me, knowing.

'It's okay,' she'd said to me once. 'You don't have to keep all that control around me, George. You can let it go sometimes.'

But I couldn't. Not with Emily.

I watched as she dressed and headed for the kitchen. I listened to the rattle as she searched through the drawers for a corkscrew. I heard the pop of the cork.

And I yearned for all things lost.

SEVEN

The next day dawned with wind and rain and cold, as if winter never planned to leave. Mercifully my sleep had been dreamless. I'd woken a few times to the moan of air gusting about the old house, and later to the drumming of rain on the tin roof, and I'd stared up at the blackness, afraid. Each time, however, there'd been the warm presence of Emily, curled up next to me, and I'd sunk almost instantly back into sleep. She was gone when I finally woke, back to her own house to prepare for school, and the bed seemed cheerless without her. But on the bedside table the digital clock—reset from the power failure—told me it was nearly eleven, and through the window came a grey light, muttering with rain. The night had been survived.

And Charlie was still dead.

The shock of it, the disbelief, had receded. But the fact remained, and I lay in bed, wondering what it was I should be feeling now.

The reality was, until the previous morning I hadn't even known for sure that Charlie wasn't already dead. There'd been no contact between us, no phone calls or visits, nor did I know where he was living or what he was doing. I'd safely assumed that we would never meet again. Neither of us would have wanted it. The things that had gone wrong could hardly be made right by any apology or understanding—and for most of what had gone wrong, I was the one responsible. Charlie had made that clear. He had laid something like an actual curse on me, that last night in the hospital. If I'd been unable to deal with it back then, if it had driven me to run away . . . then what was the use of embracing it all over again now?

Only now he was dead. And it was here, virtually on my doorstep.

Was that my responsibility?

I didn't know. Apart from Highwood itself, what was there to link his death to me? And that could have been a mere accident, a chance of locality . . . it was possible. But somewhere inside me an old weight lingered, ready to press down again.

I dressed and ate, then drove back down into town, rain beating against the windscreen. Crossing the bridge I looked down at the creek and saw it swollen, red with topsoil. Up in the hills the streams and waterfalls would be flowing apace, but the hills themselves were lost in cloud. Unlike other times, I had no business up there today. Instead I drove to the police station. There were more cars than usual parked outside, and within there was a tense, urgent air. Phones rang and the floor at the entrance was muddy. The Highwood district police were all in attendance, familiar faces that looked harried and strange. There was no sign of the Brisbane detectives. I found Graham in his office, studying papers and drinking coffee. It did not seem that he had slept as well as me.

'What have you found out?' I asked him.

He regarded me wearily. 'About what exactly?'

'About anything.'

He put his cup down. 'Are you asking this personally, or as a reporter? I've already had some Brisbane media in this morning. We made page three down there, not that we've released all the details. We're pretending it still might have been a death by misadventure. Like he was some poor old homeless guy, just trying to get warm on a cold night.'

And if only it could have been something that sad and simple.

I said, 'I won't be covering this for the paper, for obvious reasons. Gerry can handle it. So it's just me.'

Gerry was the owner and proprietor of the *Highwood Herald*—officially my boss. In fact he was semi-retired and the reporting fell mostly to me, but he was still happy to run things if I was on holiday or in other emergencies. And this would qualify.

Graham still wasn't satisfied. 'Even personally I'm not sure how much I can tell you. You know the Brisbane boys have suspicions about you.'

'You talked to Emily.'

'Yeah . . . look, I don't think it was you. But those others don't know anything about you. Or about Emily. They're not just gonna take it on faith.'

I didn't answer, only watched him.

He paused. 'Are you sure Charlie made no contact with you at all? We've gotta assume there's *some* link to you, to bring him up here. It can't all be coincidence.'

'Maybe not. But then maybe it is. I hadn't heard a word from him, honestly. I'd tell you if I had. I don't think he would even have known I live here.'

'You never told him you moved up here?'

The memory of that last abortive phone call was in my mind.

'He might have known I came up ten years ago. He wouldn't have known that I settled here permanently. For all he knew, I could be anywhere.'

But Graham was shaking his head. 'The general opinion seems to be that it's related to the . . . involvement . . . all of you had back then.'

'Have you found any proof of that?'

'No.'

'I wouldn't believe it even if you had. None of us were like that. There was no need to be.'

'Maybe you don't think so.'

'I know so.'

He sighed and shook his head, shuffling some papers around on his desk. 'Like I said, I'm only assisting on this whole thing, George. It's a homicide investigation. I've been providing some manpower and they've kept me informed as a courtesy, but how the investigation goes, and what leads they choose to follow, that's not up to me.'

'I understand that, Graham. But he was my friend once. I need to know.'

Another sigh. 'All right. Officially, though, I'm only telling you this in the hope it might suggest someone or something to you, to help with our inquiries. And it's strictly confidential, you understand.'

I nodded and waited.

'Well, quite a bit has turned up so far. We found a car, for one thing. Halfway down the range, shoved into a gully. Keys were in the ignition.'

'It was Charlie's?'

'Actually, it was reported stolen two mornings ago. It belongs to a Uniting Church society down in Brisbane that runs hostels and halfway houses for recovering addicts and alcoholics. We rang them and mentioned Charlie's name, and they said he'd been staying in one of their hostels recently. He knew the place well and would've been able to get the keys if he'd wanted them. It would explain how he got up here at least. Anyway, we know it was him because we took his prints and they match the ones on the car.'

'Charlie wasn't a car thief.'

'Oh? So he only broke *some* laws . . .'

'I just mean it's odd.'

'A lot of this is odd. We got other prints too. There are lots of them around the substation of course, most of them from power workers we assume, and some of them are Charlie's. But do you remember all those cans and bottles?'

I remembered. The concrete floor of the substation, cans with beer frothed at their mouths, the empty bottles lying on their sides. 'What about them?'

'They're clean as a whistle. No prints at all.'

I thought about that and came up with nothing but phantoms.

'We'll want prints from you, by the way,' Graham said, neutral, 'just to be sure.'

I nodded. 'What about Charlie and the way he died?'

'That's not so good either. The pathologist did him last night and the Brisbane detectives got the first report this morning. He was alive when he was strung up against the switchboard, and all the burns to his back were made while he was alive. They were quite specifically done, enough to hurt certainly, and leave marks, but not to kill, because the current was so localised.'

'Jesus . . .'

'Yes. So obviously the desire was torture of some sort, not homicide. At least not at first. And whoever was doing it had to know a fair bit about electrical stuff.' He paused. 'Any of this suggest anything to you?'

'No.'

Graham pondered the wall.

I said, 'So how did he die?'

His gaze shifted back to me. 'The most serious burns, those associated with the fatal electrical charge, have an entry point at his genitals and exit points at his wrists and ankles, where they were attached to the metal framework of the switchboard. This is a different thing altogether. A major charge went through his whole body and completely fried his system.'

I remembered the blackened flesh around his wrists. But the rest . . . I hadn't even thought to look.

'So he was just . . . burnt . . . all those times on his back? And then he was given one big shock to finish him off?'

Graham thought, pushed at more papers. 'That's not the theory we have right now.'

'Well?'

But it wasn't something Graham wanted to tell me. 'What I mean is, he wasn't killed by the wires they were using to burn him with. Certainly whoever was doing this seemed keen not to do anything so drastic with the power supply that it would crash the substation, not before they were finished anyway. I say 'they' because the theory is there was more than one person there. All that alcohol, for one thing. A lot for one person to drink.'

'Charlie might have been drinking. He had . . .' I paused, looking for the words, 'a problem with alcohol.'

Graham nodded. 'We assumed that, from the hostel. And the pathologist said his liver showed signs of chronic abuse. And certainly there was alcohol in his system, a lot of it. That's part of what makes what they did to him so terrible. But there were two bottles of vodka there, and a dozen cans of beer. Charlie had only vodka in his stomach. And even then, we don't think he could have drunk both bottles.'

'You still haven't told me what happened.'

Graham debated with himself for a long moment, and gave in. 'The power boys say the substation finally blew because moisture was introduced into the switchboard and shorted the whole place. That moisture we at first assumed was alcohol, but it wasn't. It was urine.'

I tried to make sense of it, remembering the smell, entwined with the alcohol. 'Whose?' I said, baffled.

'Charlie's, of course.'

'I don't understand.'

Graham fixed me with eyes serious and tired. 'He was hanging there, right, up against the switchboard, and he's getting tortured. God knows how long, or what state he was in by the end of it. Meanwhile they're filling him up with vodka. A lot of it. Eventually, you know what has to happen. Think about it. He would have fought it, but in the end, there's only so long you can last . . .'

I thought, but the only thing that came was something monstrous.

Graham was nodding.

'We assume the people doing this to him knew this as well—had him arranged that way against the switchboard for that very reason, possibly, and kept making him drink. The urine goes straight into the switchboard and bang, he's got thousands of volts running through him, from his penis through his whole body to his extremities. It kills him. The substation shorts out. Whoever was there with him has had their fun now, and they get the hell away. An hour later, the power truck arrives, and you know the rest.'

He was angry, staring at me.

'They might have kept him there for hours, waiting for it, zapping him from time to time to keep things lively. He would have known what was going to happen, fought it.'

I shook my head, disbelieving. 'Charlie was . . . he had a brain injury. He wasn't fully aware any more. That's what I've been told anyway. I don't know how much he would have understood.'

'You think that makes it better?'

I couldn't answer. All I felt was nausea. Not like that, no one deserved to go like that. And he was old, he was weak and already long beaten. Why? Why inflict something so slow, so agonising? It was only Charlie. Poor, retarded Charlie. But Graham's eyes were still on me, and there was no sympathy in them, for Charlie or anyone.

'If this *was* any of your old friends, you'd better tell me,' he said, 'because maybe you don't know them as well as you think you do.'

EIGHT

I fled the police station.

A misty rain swirled along the main street and I walked headlong into it, my face to the sky. Tiny droplets stung my skin, cold and clear, and I breathed in gulps of wet air. In times past I would have gone straight to the nearest bar and blotted the whole thing out. I would not and could not go that way any more. Even the thought of alcohol only took me back to Charlie, a vodka bottle raised to his mouth by an unknown hand, the fire burning down his throat, choking and fighting and the pressure building in his bladder no matter what he did . . .

I walked.

Not far this time, for the main street of Highwood was not very long, and the offices of the *Highwood Herald* were only halfway down. Around me the town seemed strange and new, a mirage that had been fractured. That something like this could happen here made Highwood seem sinister, a backwoods community of secrets and violence. Was it someone from town, someone I knew? Was it someone watching me now? With the wind and the rain there were few people on the footpaths, but I felt their stares as I passed. I felt suspicious of everyone and they, too, were suspicious of me—they all knew, it was *my* friend who had died, *my* history that had crept up into the mountains. I was an outsider again, someone to be observed. Ten years. Ten years and I'd almost been accepted. But that was all gone again now.

I didn't want this. Why had Charlie come here? Why had he died here? There were substations all over the country, there were dozens of little towns just like Highwood—why this one? Why *my* town?

And then I remembered Charlie, his empty, crumpled face, and felt ashamed.

It didn't matter. No matter what Graham or the detectives might think, none of us from the old days was capable of anything like that. Charlie had been in prison since then. Who knew what sort of people he'd met in jail, or what sort of trouble he'd come across? That was where the police should be looking. There were killers in prisons. Psychopaths. People who could do the sort of thing that had been done to him.

People who had nothing whatever to do with me.

And Graham had mentioned a clinic, a hostel for addiction treatment. Maybe that was where the answers lay. Addicts could do anything. They could go completely crazy.

Nothing to do with me either.

But the weight was still there, pressing on my heart.

I reached the *Highwood Herald* offices.

As always, the counter was manned by our ancient secretary, Mrs Hammond. Her first name was Vivien, but with the exception of her dead husband, there was only one person who was allowed to use it, and that was Gerry, not me. A lifelong resident in Highwood, and at the paper, Mrs Hammond was one of those who, even before recent events, had never fully approved of my presence in town.

She was not alone. A man was leaning on the counter, talking with her. The conversation stopped as I entered. No difficulty guessing, then, what the topic was. And the man was not someone I was in any mood be seeing right now.

'Hello Stanley,' I said.

He looked as thin and bitter as he had the last time I'd seen him, and he smiled at me without any friendliness whatsoever. 'George.'

Mrs Hammond only disliked me with the basic suspicion that the old always held towards a stranger, perhaps, but Stanley Smith had much more personal reasons of his own. He loathed me. And though he rarely came down from his property up in the hills, the news that I was in trouble of a sort, especially of *this* sort, would have been more than he could resist.

'Gerry around?' I asked Mrs Hammond.

She nodded, lips thin.

I edged by them. Stanley shifted an elbow to make room, his smile still in place, the satisfaction in it palpable. 'Back in the headlines I see, George.'

I didn't answer. There was no point engaging with someone like him. His hatred wasn't even for me alone, it was for the whole system I represented. Or *had* represented. Instead I went straight on through and found Gerry in his office. He was staring at a computer screen.

'What d'you think?' he said, without turning.

I looked over his shoulder. He was working on a headline.

MYSTERY DEATH IN SUBSTATION—MAN ELECTROCUTED, TOWN BLACKED OUT.

'Admirably reserved,' I said, sinking into a chair.

He nodded. 'I thought about "The Lights Go Out In Highwood" or even just "Death Shocks Town"—but I don't know that anyone would really appreciate it.'

'It's no joke, Gerry.'

He looked over. 'I know that.'

He sat back from the screen and reached for a cigarette. Gerry was seventy-three years old and his fingers were stained a mixture of yellow from the nicotine and a grimy black from a lifetime of newsprint, even though he rarely smoked any more and the *Herald* no longer ran its own presses. There was a long dim room at the back of the building where the machines had once been, but only their memory remained, and only on hot days, when the walls sweated and the air held the tang of clattering noise and steaming metal. These days the paper was typeset on computer, and printed by contract out of town, two editions a week, Tuesdays and Fridays. The entire staff was just Gerry and me, Mrs Hammond, and sometimes a student from the high school, on work experience and disillusioned about it as well.

He lit up. 'You been talking to Graham?'

'Him, and a couple of detectives.'

'Should I report you as a suspect?'

'That's up to you.'

He gave a snort of disgust, puffed out smoke. 'Did you get

anything useful from Graham? I've got bugger-all so far. And all joking aside, this is still the first murder we've had in years.'

It was true enough, though Highwood had certainly known deaths before, even violent ones. The *Herald*'s archives, dating back over one hundred years, testified to that. In its day the town had been a mean camp of loggers and timber getters, bullock drivers and sly grog sellers, and more than once an axe had found a human target. But now we lived in more civilised times, everyone agreed. And though during my ten years in Highwood I'd covered assaults and robberies, rapes and domestic abuse, in all that time I'd reported but one other murder. And in that case the man had called the police himself, and waited numbly by the body of his wife for them to arrive. Not much of a story. But a story was the last thing on my mind.

'It was confidential,' I said.

'He was tortured then killed, that much is right, isn't it?'

'Yes.'

'Do you know why?'

'I don't. Neither do the police.'

He peered at his story on the screen. 'So far I've got just two paragraphs on the death, then the rest is all stuff about how people were late for work because their alarm clocks weren't working, or how the kids were sent to school without a hot breakfast. And for once we were the first paper on the actual scene.'

Gerry and his little paper were notable, in fact, for just one thing. The *Highwood Herald* was one of the last fully independent news-sheets in the state. Most other small town concerns had long since been bought out by one or other of the two big national chains, but Gerry despised both of them equally and had long refused to sell. Not that he was a threat to anyone else's circulation, and even in Highwood, everyone read the Brisbane paper for serious news. Still, I suspected that one of the reasons Gerry had befriended and then finally hired me, wreck that I was at the time, was because I was a fugitive, sacked and disgraced, from one of his syndicated enemies in the city.

And for that I'd told him more about my past than anyone else in the town, even Emily.

'Sorry,' I said again, 'but really, there are no theories yet.'

'You think not? I've been getting calls all day. The whole town is agog, I can tell you. If I could print theories I'd have ten pages.'

'What are they saying?'

'Most people seem to favour a gang killing. One report has it he was machine-gunned to death, not electrocuted. Someone else said the substation was regularly used as a drug pick-up, and that this was a deal gone wrong. Apparently there were piles of cocaine everywhere. Someone else said it was Nazi skinheads—one of the power workers has been quoted as saying there were swastikas in blood on the walls. People have a real bugbear about neo-Nazis around here, ever since those high school kids shaved their heads. Another version of that says it was Satanists who have been holding black masses out there, and that instead of swastikas it was upside-down crosses and 666 everywhere, and a goat's head on the body. Or else he was part of a paedophilia ring and did things to kids out there and some parent finally caught him and he was only getting what he deserved.'

'Which one do you favour?'

'You tell me.'

I was sick of the conversation. 'There was nothing on the walls. There wasn't anything.'

'Just lots of empty beer cans?'

'You heard that?'

'People haven't been completely uncooperative.'

'Well, yes, beer cans. And bottles of vodka.'

And that was all I could say. Gerry smoked on, thoughtful.

'I'm sorry about your friend,' he said finally.

'Thanks.'

'What're your plans?'

'I don't know. I don't know if there's anything I should do, or shouldn't do. I don't see if this is linked to me or not. I can't really see how it could be.'

'Something from your Brisbane days, maybe?'

'None of that stuff back then was anything like this.'

He shrugged. 'I had Stanley Smith in here a minute ago. He doesn't agree. He thinks this is *all* about the old days.'

'You know what he's like about that. Stanley is crazy.'

'A little, but he's still right about some things. Those times always had their ugly side, George. Maybe you never saw it, but don't kid yourself.'

I was determined not to think that way. 'It could still just be a coincidence. Charlie has had a whole other life since then, and it's not as if he died in my house or anything. The substation is ten miles away.'

It sounded like a wish, a prayer I hoped might be answered. What I needed most of all was for there to be no connection at all between me and Charlie's death. Apart from everything else, my position in the town and the suspicions of the police, the idea that I might be somehow responsible yet again, however remotely, for bringing destruction into his life . . .

Gerry was staring at me, dubious.

'It really might mean nothing,' I said, as if praying could make it true.

Gerry let it be. 'Well, I can hold the fort here for a while, if you'd like.'

'Thanks.'

'It's probably a good thing if you skip the paper for a while anyway. People might not believe your reporting would be totally unbiased.'

'As bad as that?'

'Didn't I mention it? The other favourite theory going around is that *you* killed him. An old enemy from the dark and doubtless criminal past that you ran up here to escape. People still haven't stopped wondering about you, you know. In fact the town is ready to rally around Emily again once you've been arrested and taken away. The trials that poor woman has had to suffer over the years with her men etc etc—you know the drill.'

'God . . .' I said. This was all getting too much.

'Don't worry. It might take a while, but things will calm down.'

I stood up. 'How about you run things for the next week or two, and then we'll see how things are going after that?'

He nodded. 'Hell, a murder in town, I probably would've been down here every day even if you didn't want me.'

I went out through the front office. Stanley was gone. Mrs Hammond was on the phone, and she paused when she saw me, her eyes narrowing and her hand going over the mouthpiece. There was no understanding in her at all, and I felt a hatred of my own take root. I banged open the door, looked up and down the main street. The rain had eased momentarily and knots of people had appeared, standing on the footpaths, talking with a hushed intensity. A few faces glanced at me and then looked away, frowning.

The hatred hardened. It really wasn't fair. Coincidence, it could all just be coincidence. Charlie could have died anywhere, nothing to do with me at all. It was possible. Maybe it was even likely. We hadn't spoken in *ten years*.

An old woman was coming along the footpath, staring at me. I stared back, angry for a second, on the verge of shouting, *ten years*. But she was tottering on a walking stick and I realised it was only Joan Ellsgood—meek, harmless Joan who had helped me once, and given me my first home in Highwood. I had friends in the town, after all, and it was something to remember.

The anger drained out of me.

'Hello, Joan,' I said.

'George,' she said, 'I was hoping you'd be here.'

Joan was as old as Gerry and nowhere near as robust. She operated, with her daughter, the Pine Hill guest house, one block back off the main street, overlooking the park. It was where I'd stayed for several months when I first came to Highwood, and Joan and I had become friends, though these days I saw very little of her. These days she rarely left her house.

'How's business?' I asked.

'Oh, Betty takes care of that these days. I'm retired.'

'You've earned it.'

She smiled, but she was uneasy.

'Is something wrong?' I said.

She looked up and down the street. 'I don't know. It's this terrible thing, out at the substation. They say the man was a friend of yours.'

'Yes, he was. But I don't know anything about it.'

'No, no, of course not. Except . . .' she agonised for a moment, then looked up at me. 'Except I was alone at the house the day before yesterday, Betty was out, and a man came, knocking on the door.'

She paused, and I waited.

Her eyes were wide and worried. 'I didn't think it was anything, you see, it's just that he said he was a friend of yours, and now this man out at the substation, they say he was a friend of yours, so I've been wondering.'

I felt myself go very still. 'What did he say, Joan?'

'He said that he'd been told you lived at our house. I said oh no, you hadn't stayed with us for years. I told him where you live now. I gave him directions. He seemed very relieved.'

I reached out, a drowning man. 'What did he look like? Did he have a . . . was one side of his face deformed?'

She nodded keenly. 'Yes, yes, that was him. I gave him directions, told him to go straight around, I told him it wasn't far.'

'What time was this, Joan?'

'Well now, let me think, it'd just gone dark . . .'

'Joan, what was the time?!'

She blinked at me. 'Six o'clock, it was about six o'clock.'

Six o'clock. Seven hours before he died, Charlie had been here in town and looking for me. That was it, then. My presence had brought him to Highwood, and at Highwood he'd been killed. The weight was back, familiar and crushing, and for a moment I felt as much a murderer as if I'd taken the gun myself and shot him in the face all those years ago, or put the electric wires to his skin just the one night before.

I felt like sinking to the footpath, but Joan was watching me fearfully.

'Have you told anyone else this?' I asked.

'I didn't know what to do. I didn't know if it was important.'

I took her bony arm and turned her gently.

'C'mon, Joan. Let's go and see the police.'

NINE

Brisbane's sole remaining major newspaper had this to say on the subject:

POLICE SUSPECT SUBSTATION DEATH LINKED TO INQUIRY

A police spokesman said yesterday that it is believed the death of former nightclub owner Charles Monohan is linked to his involvement with key figures investigated by the 1987 Inquiry into official corruption. Monohan was convicted in 1988 of taxation, licensing, soliciting and bribery offences, and served three years in prison. He was closely associated with the disgraced cabinet minister Marvin McNulty, who himself was convicted and imprisoned in 1988 on similar charges, as well as other figures who were investigated at the time. While police are not aware of any criminal activity carried out by Monohan since his release, it is considered likely that his death relates to his earlier underworld connections, and may be a payback killing. Police state that while they have no definite suspects at this time, investigations are continuing.

Investigations were continuing.
Charlie had been alone when he arrived in Highwood. That is, Joan Ellsgood had noted that the man who visited her arrived in a white station wagon which he'd left across the road, by the park, and which otherwise appeared to be empty. He had not given his name and she had not seen him drive away, but the car matched the one found abandoned in the gully, the one stolen from the hostel, and the police had no doubts. So there seemed to be only one conclusion that could be drawn—Charlie had come looking for me, and somewhere

between the Pine Hill guest house and my place, a five-minute drive in all, something had happened to him.

Or, from the police point of view, something had happened to him *at* my place.

I was called in to offer further assistance.

'You said Charlie didn't know you lived up here?'

It was Detectives Kelly and Lewis again.

'I said I didn't know for sure. Anyway, he was ten years out of date. I only lived at the guest house for a few months, after I first arrived here.'

'But you gave Charlie that address? Back then?'

'I tried to, but I don't know if he ever got the message. I did tell his wife.'

'You mean Maybellene?'

'Yes.'

'She's not his wife any more. They got divorced while he was in jail.'

'Oh . . .'

It was the first direct news I'd had of May since the end of it all, but it was no surprise, it was what I'd always assumed had happened. I'd heard it in her voice, the last time we'd talked. The finality of it. What else could the two of them have done?

'She still might have given him the address,' I said. 'And either way it proves what I've been saying. If I'd talked to Charlie in the last ten years, he would have known not to look for me at the guest house.'

'But he was still looking for you. For some reason.'

'I don't know what the reason was.'

'Been talking to any of your other old friends?'

'No. Check my phone records if you want.'

'We already have.'

It went on. They searched my house and found nothing. They combed the substation for fingerprints and found none that matched mine.

'But someone wiped those cans and bottles, didn't they?'

'It wasn't me.'

And they had plenty of other things to go on. History, for

one thing. They'd dug out all the old police files on the six of us.

'You and May had an affair, we know that, and she left Charlie for you.'

'Not for me. She might have left Charlie, but I haven't seen her since.'

'Doesn't matter. He'd still hate you. You might still hate him.'

'We never hated each other.'

'Oh really? He went to jail, you didn't. You took his wife away. You're saying that's not reason enough? To come up here looking to get his own back? And who knows what might have happened if he came barging into your house. An argument? A fight?'

'Why wait ten years?'

'Why not?'

'It didn't happen.'

And for all that they might speculate, they couldn't really suggest that it had. I'd been at the *Herald* offices when Charlie arrived in town, and then I'd met up with Emily, and though she'd left me alone half an hour before Charlie actually died, that still didn't leave enough time for everything that had happened out at the substation.

'What about the others?' I asked. 'If you're so convinced it was one of us.'

'We're looking into it,' they said.

'Well? What about Marvin? Where's he?'

'We're tracking him down.'

'And Lindsay?'

A sneer. 'Don't you worry about Lindsay. We know it wasn't him.'

'What about Jeremy then?'

'Not likely, he's in a wheelchair.'

I paused at that. Jeremy was in a wheelchair? But then he'd be old, of course—he was already old when I'd seen him last. Maybe that's all it was.

'And Maybellene?' I asked, quietly.

'We don't know. There's no Maybellene Monohan listed in Queensland anymore.'

'Her own name was Campbell.'

A smile. 'We know. Nothing there either.'

'I guess she's gone then.'

And in the end, that was what I'd always hoped.

But eventually the police ran out of questions, and let me go again. The town wasn't so forgiving. Joan's evidence had flashed around the community as fast as phones could be dialled. Highwood brooded on the news. For the next three days the weather remained cold and wet and people were stuck inside with nothing better to do than talk and wonder about the stranger in their midst. In the papers they read things about me that most had never heard before, or at least things they had long forgotten. All my associations, all my crimes . . . although there were officially no crimes and certainly no convictions, only things that sounded like crimes, and associations that had proved to be bad. And over it all hung that talismanic name—the Inquiry. That was what really decided people. The Inquiry was the hand of doom, still, even a decade after it had closed down. And one finger of it had curled up into the hills, after all that time, and touched me on the shoulder.

I was in exile again.

Emily stayed with me, the two of us hidden away in my little house. The phone rang from time to time. Sometimes it was Brisbane journalists. Sometimes it was anonymous callers, dark and suggestive but sounding familiar, like local teenagers. Sometimes it was one of the few friends I still had in town, offering support. It didn't matter. I had nothing to say to any of them.

I read the papers.

I read them with Emily, and over one long night I tried to explain what was true in the news reports and what wasn't about Charlie and me and the rest. I told her the whole story. I told her about the restaurants and the clubs and the casinos and the brothels, the way it all worked and the way it all fell apart. And I lied. I didn't tell her everything about Maybellene. I didn't tell her about the last time I saw them both, Charlie and May. I told her we'd just drifted apart during all the difficulties.

And she believed me.

'You were stupid, that's all,' she said. 'You didn't know what you'd got caught up in. I know you, George. You're not an evil man.'

'No. I'm not.'

She believed me. And if nothing else had happened, maybe that would have been enough. Maybe over time the town would have forgotten all they'd read and heard. Maybe they would have looked at Emily and trusted her belief. Maybe I could have just hidden away for a week or two and then gradually emerged, and life could have returned to normal. I could have forgotten Charlie. Gerry would have taken me back at the paper and maybe one day it might have been my paper alone, and Mrs Hammond could have retired if she couldn't bear it. Emily and I might have gone along as always. I might have kept my home. Grown old there . . .

Instead, Graham came knocking at my door one evening, looking troubled.

'How's the investigation going?' I asked him.

'For the moment, nowhere much. The fact is, since getting out of prison, Charlie lived life pretty much on the street in Brisbane—with his physical and mental problems he wasn't really employable, and according to the hostel his alcoholism became acute. No one can say what else he might have been up to. Or why someone might have wanted to kill him. But he doesn't sound like someone with enemies. Not those sort of enemies.'

'But there's still me, of course.'

'No one's saying you killed him, George. But you can't blame us for wondering about some other connection.'

'So why are you here?'

The troubled look returned. 'They'll be holding Charlie's body for a while yet. They do, in cases like this. But eventually they'll be releasing it.'

'And?'

'He had nothing when he died. He lived in that hostel. No property, no estate. His parents are dead and there aren't any other next of kin.'

'He had a wife.'

'You know we can't find her, and she hasn't come forward to claim him. No one has.'

I saw where he was heading.

'He's no relation to me,' I said.

Graham nodded sadly. 'I know, I know. And the state will dispose of the body if no one else will. But that's a cold way to bury someone. And I thought, seeing there's no one else, and you were his friend . . .'

'He had other friends.'

'He doesn't have any now.'

I almost hated Graham then. Why did he care, and why had he laid it at my door? If Charlie just got buried, then all this could be over, all this could go away.

Graham shrugged. 'It's up to you, of course.'

And the weight was in my very bones now.

I sighed. 'What does it involve?'

He studied me for a moment, then cleared his throat. 'It's probably better if it isn't up here, you understand that. Besides, his body is already down in Brisbane. And that was his home anyway.'

'I understand.'

'When was the last time you were there yourself?'

'I haven't been. Not since then.'

'Ah.' He nodded to himself. 'Well, come down tomorrow then. I'll get on to the officials, and we'll sort out the details.'

And he was gone.

I went back inside and sat. A funeral for Charlie. I considered what I would have to do, where I would have to go. I stared at the fire. Warmth filled the room. Emily worked quietly in the kitchen, making dinner. A curtain of rain swept across the roof, the night locked away outside. We were safe, the two of us. In that moment I could see and feel and hear everything that I'd gained since coming to Highwood, everything I had to lose, and a premonition of disaster swept through me.

I strove to ignore it. After all, I would only be away a matter of days. It was only a two-hour drive, it was only one funeral, only the one city, waiting for me down there. And besides, what choice was there?

Newspapers were scattered across the floor. One of them was open at the editorial page. It said:

The death of Charles Monohan, while disturbing in its manner, need not cause undue concern in the general community. He associated with violent and criminal elements that poisoned the very fabric of government at the time, and no doubt met his end through those same elements. Instead, his death can be seen as part of the final chapter of a sad and reprehensible period of Queensland's history, a period well left behind. No doubt relics of those elements still linger in the shadows of this state, but they are reduced now to preying on each other. They will not linger long, and it is no great loss to the rest of us.

I knew the editor who'd written that, or I'd known him once. I'd seen him at Charlie's restaurants, accepting Charlie's food and drink and company, sometimes paying, sometimes not. I'd seen him dining with Marvin. I'd seen him working out deals with Jeremy. And when finally the sky started falling, I'd seen him run away from them all, just as I had. Seen him run that little bit faster, in fact. He was an old, old acquaintance.

Brisbane would be full of them.

TEN

Seven days later I was on my way, winding slowly down the steep Highwood road, rain sheeting across the windscreen. The weather was terrible. A week of fleeting cloud and passing showers had culminated in one last drenching downpour. It was as if the mountains didn't want me to leave, or then again, were attempting to flush the memory of death and torture out of the town in a cleansing flood, and me with it. Water ran in streams across the bitumen. In places it had stripped the road to bare gravel, digging deep ruts that clutched at the wheels of my car. Sodden trees hung low enough to scrape against the roof. I peered ahead and ground the gears, my mood sinking with every curve.

There was only one end to this road.

Occasionally the forest parted to be replaced by guard rails that ran along naked cliffs offering misty glimpses out into the clouds. In clear weather there would have been a view eastwards, over the low plains and hills that stretched towards the coast. It was normally an impressive outlook, the countryside below carved up into farms and dotted with small towns, and far off, right on the eastern horizon, there could be seen a darkness that spoke of something much bigger. At night that darkness became an ominous orange glow in the sky. All of it was hidden now, but I knew what waited down there.

Brisbane. The Fallen City.

Or indeed, Queensland itself. In many ways the city and the state were one and the same. And I'd deserted them both, long ago.

But then it was said that an alcoholic never really left the bottle and, in a similar way, maybe no one ever really left

Queensland. Even in the act of desertion I'd never quite made it over the border to New South Wales. I had certainly intended to that final night in December 1989, when I reeled drunkenly to my car and steered it south through the city, the streets ablaze, on and on until the crowds and people and celebrations were gone. Highwood had not been my destination then. I'd had no destination, other than crossing the border into New South Wales, and Highwood was nothing more to me than a name on a road sign. I still had no idea why I took that road, or stopped where I did. When I woke next morning, I was only a few miles from the border and there was nothing stopping me, nothing to hold me back. Only Highwood itself.

But there I stayed.

It was not a thing I could ever fathom. Perhaps it was that while Highwood was geographically *in* Queensland, its soul was not *of* Queensland. A fine distinction, perhaps, but any distinction was a saviour then. Highwood was a mountain town, high and cold, while Queensland, everyone knew, was hot and tropical, its face turned towards the beaches. Queensland houses were supposed to be things of wood and corrugated iron, wrapped in wide verandahs against the heat. Highwood was a town of small brick cottages, closed in on themselves, chimneys prodding up. Unheard of anywhere else in the state, Highwood even sometimes received a light dusting of snow. By rights it shouldn't have been in Queensland at all. It was an accident of map making. The mountains were a different world, a fragment of the New South Wales tablelands that jutted north over the border.

But all the same, I remained a Queenslander.

And finally, perhaps, there was something in my heart that needed that assurance—just as a reformed alcoholic might need to know that somewhere in the house there was that one bottle, both a temptation to be resisted and a last resort if it came to the worst. Queensland was an addiction. Maligned and scorned by the rest of the country—an intellectual backwater, a redneck breeding ground for ignorance and bigotry and corruption, and it had earned the titles—but still, it infected the soul somehow. Demanded love of those it bore and bred, no matter how weary and sickened they might become of the place. Demanded loyalty, no matter how bizarre its government and its laws, no matter what political oddities were thrown up over the years.

And oddities there were. In my day, some people didn't even call it a democracy. There was a parliament, yes, but alone of the Australian states, Queensland had no upper house. Under generous inducements, it had voted itself out of existence years before. It meant that any majority party in the one remaining chamber could run the state completely free of scrutiny, and free of balances. That is, a certain core of the majority party could run the state. Long tradition had made Queensland a system operated almost wholly by the executive. The premier and the cabinet ruled Queensland. A scant few men, with unopposed legislative authority. Those same few men appointed their favourites as police ministers and police commissioners, and so controlled the law enforcement arm. They also appointed their favourites to the bench, and so controlled the judicial arm. There was no separation of powers. No supervising committees. No safeguards. Strong leadership, that's what Queensland was about in my day. Absolute leadership.

And there were elections, yes. But in the thirty-two years leading up to 1989 there was only ever the one winner. Poll after poll, Queenslanders kept voting the same government back in. It was monolithic and unassailable. Opponents of the regime, disillusioned by defeat after defeat, could offer many explanations for this. For one, the electoral boundaries were notoriously distorted in favour of the ruling party, who of course controlled the electoral commission. For another, the media had become increasingly cowed and uncritical over the years, and were far too friendly with too many ministers, and far too reliant on government patronage to dare make trouble. And the opposition themselves, long starved of seats in parliament, had become so withered and bitter and internally divided that they barely offered a serious alternative anyway. There was really only the one political force in Queensland, so how on earth, save by some great upheaval, could a new regime ever achieve government?

But all the justifications in the world could only excuse so much. The baffling thing was that, deep down, Queenslanders liked their rulers and wanted them to stay. Not once in those thirty-two years did the overall vote for the opposition ever top fifty per cent. Of course, it wouldn't have mattered if it had. Such was the bias in the voting system that even with fifty-five or sixty per cent, they could still be denied a majority of seats. But they never got close to those figures. Regardless of how blatantly the electoral boundaries were rigged, or how utterly unrepresentative the final allocation of seats in parliament might be, the fact remained—the majority of Queensland's population preferred the government they had.

So we went openly and willingly to our own disaster.

And the smaller lapses in the democratic system didn't seem to matter. The bans on public gatherings or street marches. The strict censorship of books and films. The constant war against unions of any kind. The freakish treatment of minorities like homosexuals or Aborigines. The Special Branch of the police force which spied on and persecuted the government's enemies with complete impunity. The increasingly frequent declarations of States of Emergency, with all their force of martial law. The use of rank and file police as political shock troops. The judges who quietly smothered investigations. The steady whisper of outrageous scandals concerning the use of public money and contracts.

None of it mattered. We kept voting for them time and time again, for three decades straight. We loved ministers like Marvin. Flamboyant. Entertaining. Certainly not tied down by anything as grim as due process or bureaucracy. And for the rest, it was just the way things went in Queensland. It was *different*, and meanwhile the climate was warm, the beaches were golden, the reef was a Wonder of the World, and taxes were low. Out west were some of the biggest cattle stations and coal mines in the world. It was a boom state. Tourists and investors came from everywhere.

So why complain? So what if the rest of the country loathed the politics of the place, laughed at it, dismissed it? As various government ministers liked to remind the voters, Queensland was a law unto itself. And if Queensland wasn't left to go its own way, free from southern harassment, well then, it could always secede from the federation. What matter civil war?

You had to love Queensland.

Thousands didn't, of course, and they headed south across the border in legions as soon as they were old enough to drive. But millions stayed and convinced themselves that nothing was seriously wrong. It was a betrayal, somehow, to believe that anything *could* be wrong. As if admitting that even one small fault existed would lead to an entire flood of admissions, and we'd all drown in it. It was a state of mass denial. Pilots joked about it to their passengers as they flew in from Sydney. Turn your watches back one hour, ladies and gentlemen, and your mind back fifty years. The worst thing was, Queenslanders laughed at it most of all. Defensively. Defiantly. Proud of themselves.

I would never quite understand it, but it was inside me all the same. So even when the Inquiry came, when everything imploded and I ran, the saving of my own skin the only thing on my mind, even then I couldn't bring myself to abandon Queensland. Instead I went as far south as my heart would allow, set myself up in the high hills, a noble exile, and tried to forget everything that festered and bubbled down below. The view was splendid from up there. I could see everything with clarity. With hindsight, the view just about stretched on forever. And for ten years, I had declined to descend.

Now, in rain and blindness, understanding nothing, I was creeping my way back down. And while an alcoholic might never leave the bottle, would he deliberately go back to his favourite bars to pass the time with his old drinking partners? Would he test his will to such limits?

My car groaned down the slope. Soon I was under the mist and cloud, and the rain was easing to a drizzle. It was already warmer. In summer, driving down the range could feel like descending into a steam bath, the change was that dramatic. The mountains themselves were to blame. They trapped whole air masses and kept them sweltering over the coastal plain, sometimes for weeks on end. Brisbane, caught between the mangrove waters on one side and the hills behind, steamed in its sink. In winter it wasn't so bad. Brisbane in winter was balmy and fine, and really it was no winter at all. But in summer . . . it might still be early spring and cold in the mountains, but Brisbane was a world away, and in that world summer could come early, and full blown.

I remembered the heat like a dream, a blur of drunkenness and hangovers and sweat-tangled sheets. Lethargic, for at times it seemed that the heat took on a moral quality as well, it sank into your limbs and your heart, made everything slow and confused. It was another explanation, perhaps, for the way things went in Queensland. It took effort to protest, to question, when you were stupefied by a long afternoon of sun and humidity. It was easier not to bother, to shrug and accept things as they were, to chant the refrain—that's Queensland for you.

Besides, I was as rotten as the rest of it. Me and my friends. We were part of the problem.

I drove. I was down in the foothills now, winding away from the range towards the little town of Boonah. Already the omens weren't promising. In Highwood the damp air had been bracing; down here it felt clammy and close. Away to the east, shafts of sunlight broke through the clouds. I switched off the wipers and rolled the window all the way down. In time I was opening the glove box and pulling out my sunglasses.

Brisbane, said a road sign, and I was only an hour away.

We were part of the problem, me and my friends, but by no means all of it. There were bigger syndicates than ours, people who ran more clubs than Charlie, government ministers far more famous and corrupt than Marvin. At times it seemed everyone in Queensland was involved. It was as if the law didn't matter because the police broke it more than anyone. It was as if democracy didn't matter because the government hadn't lost an election in decades and never would, the electorate was dazed, fast asleep, the media had given up even trying. Everyone knew it, everyone accepted it, anyone who hadn't had long since left town. It was Queensland, that was all. No one cared. All of us too drunk and fat and glutted to know what was really happening any more. Trusting simply that things would never change.

All ancient history now.

I passed another Brisbane road sign, then I was off the back roads and onto the highway. It rolled east over the hills. I opened up the throttle, speeding when the last thing I wanted was to hurry. The sun came out and moisture steamed off the bitumen. In my rear view mirror I could see the mountains, a grey line on the horizon, still swathed in clouds, but ahead of me the sky was glaring with light and haze and heat.

Brisbane.

By the time I hit the outskirts, sweat was itching on my scalp.

ELEVEN

The syndicate proper was born in early 1979.

By then I was working at the *Daily Times*. As a tabloid paper it was a slightly more relaxed concern than our broadsheet competitor, and we were suited to each other—my style as a journalist was relaxed as well. I'd drifted into lightweight features and the more social side of the news, and even though I was still very young, the editor liked me and the way I wrote, and was already talking about more money and a column of my own. Our offices, meanwhile, were in Fortitude Valley, and surrounded by pubs. I liked that as well. I'd moved into a flat just a short walk away in New Farm.

Charlie, meanwhile, had built his parents' little bistro into a serious restaurant. It was getting favourable reviews in the major papers now, not just the community weeklies, and not just in Brisbane. His photo had appeared from time to time, and he was marked as a restaurateur to watch. He was ready to open a second establishment, and it was agreed that I would go partner with him in raising the money. The only serious question, for both of us, was obtaining a licence to sell alcohol. And by now we both knew what a sham the licensing laws were.

For all its puritan facade, Brisbane in 1979 was a town awash with alcohol. The licensing laws might have fooled the teenagers we'd once been, or the out-of-state visitors who found Brisbane so lifeless, but for those who knew where to look, or who to ask, and who to pay, anything was possible, anywhere and any time. Behind closed doors, special clubs and bars were permitted to operate at all hours. And that was the least of it. Gambling was illegal in Queensland, yet casinos were permitted to flourish everywhere. Prostitution was illegal, yet brothels were permitted to flourish everywhere. True, none of it was casually visible, none of it open. Brisbane still *looked* like the moral town its government so proudly declared it to be, but underneath there was a different Brisbane. And it was my own New Farm, and next to it the Valley, that formed the nexus of it all.

Not that Charlie or I were yet very familiar with that world. We knew about it, we'd heard about it, we'd caught glimpses of it, but we weren't on the inside. The one trick eluding us was how to make the right connections, to meet the people in charge of it all. We would have found them ourselves eventually, no doubt. The whole point was that these people could be found by anyone who really wanted them. But as it turned out, the right person came directly to us. In the form of Marvin McNulty.

He was only a backbencher then, on the government side, but not in any position of power. Young and green and vaguely ludicrous, with an unimpressive background in private business, his arrival in parliament had been greeted with derision by the more sober political observers. No one was even sure exactly how he'd got there. Yet there was something fascinating about him, and somehow he never settled into obscurity the way everyone had expected. He kept on appearing in controversial places, and doing unexpected things, and everyone knew who he was. And while in 1979 no one would have predicted he'd rise to the ministry, in fact that feat was less than three years away.

For the moment, though, Charlie and I knew him mostly because his electoral office was close to Charlie's restaurant. Marvin was a big eater, and he liked Charlie's food. He would bring his staff along to the restaurant, after work, and hold brainstorming sessions around the table. They would drag on till late in the evening. Marvin would always be the last to leave, and often Charlie and I would be the only ones left there with him. So we talked. Drinking, once again, was the key. Marvin was a drinker, a serious one, and would join us in sessions long into the night. But like every other customer, Marvin was forced by the laws to bring his own alcohol. That was what grated, with him, and with Charlie and me. It wasn't convenient, and it wasn't civilised. So eventually Charlie explained about his difficulties with the Licensing Commission. And Marvin went to work.

In later years, when he was in the cabinet and considered something of a prodigy in government circles, he could have fixed a licence as quick as uncorking a wine bottle. In those days, however, member of parliament though he was, he still had to go through channels.

When he was ready, he called a meeting at Charlie's place. After hours.

Ironically enough, we met by candlelight.

Not by choice, but because the electricity was out. It was another of the accepted truths about Queensland—it was poorly served by its power system. Accidental breakdowns haunted the state, then as later, no matter whether you lived in the city, or away off in the hills, in a place like Highwood.

But just like the one caused by Charlie's death years afterwards, this power failure was no accident.

The basis of it all was an industrial dispute. At the time, the generation and supply of Queensland's electricity was a state-run monopoly, and all its employees were union members. The Electrical Workers Union—a notoriously strong and aggressive association, not afraid of occasionally holding the government to ransom. The government in its turn—never one to tolerate another power base within its realm—had a keen interest in breaking the stranglehold. As Marvin and Charlie and I met that night, an opening skirmish was being fought between the government and the EWU, over the issue of contracted workers being brought in to take the jobs of union members. The union had called a retaliatory strike, no maintenance was being performed, and so load sharing and short blackouts were rolling back and forth across Queensland as the arguments wore on.

Marvin didn't even seem concerned that he, a member of the government, was being forced to hold his own meetings in the dark.

'We're backing down anyway,' he said. 'Things will be back to normal by morning.'

We were seating ourselves at a table, a bottle of wine

between us. It was late and the restaurant was empty. Charlie was only running a reduced menu in any case, because of the power stoppages.

'The union has won then?' I asked.

'Fuck 'em,' Marvin replied, even though he wouldn't have lasted five minutes on a picket line. He was a sad physical specimen. Short and dumpy, with a big head perched on a narrow neck, topped by slicked-down thinning black hair. To complete it all he was almost blind and wore oversized, thick-rimmed glasses. 'But don't worry. This is just the start. We'll be ready in a year or two.'

'I didn't think it was your department.'

'It isn't. But you know, I've been hanging around the halls. Friends of mine are in there. Believe me, this was just testing the waters.'

I was hardly listening. I was a reporter, of course, but not that sort of reporter. I couldn't care less about power strikes.

We got down to business.

'You'll need to meet,' said Marvin, 'a man named Lindsay Heath.'

'Is he on the Licensing Commission?' I asked.

'Not exactly. He's sort of a . . . consultant. He's got a few businesses of his own. An accountancy thing. And a security company. But he was a cop once, so he knows how it all works, and who to talk to. He can set it all up.'

'And?'

'And there's the normal licensing fee to be paid. Plus another fee, to be allowed to pay the first one, if you know what I mean.'

'And how much is the second fee?'

Marvin smiled. 'That's where it gets nasty.'

So we talked money. It was only afterwards that it would even occur to me what a bizarre situation it was. A member of parliament and a journalist openly discussing the payment of a bribe, and neither one for a moment questioning the other's intentions. Marvin seemed not to even consider that I might actually report on what I was hearing. And I never considered that Marvin was actually guiding us through the pitfalls of his own corrupt administration.

In fact, Charlie was the only one who had even momentary doubts.

'And you're sure all this is okay?' he asked, when faced with the details.

Marvin was all sincerity. 'Charlie, of course it is. Shit, this is the way it works for everyone. And we're covered from every angle. That's why it costs so much in the first place. Everyone gets a cut. The police in the licensing division, the boys on the board—Christ, a percentage of it even filters up to the bloody commissioner. I know the man! It's standard procedure.'

But there was still the actual money. A lot of it. Charlie and I would be struggling to raise the excess we needed. Especially as it would more or less disappear as far as tax purposes went.

'Lindsay can help out with paperwork and stuff,' Marvin offered, 'but for the actual cash . . . this is where I come in.'

And he announced he wanted to be our partner.

We were amazed. What did Marvin need with a restaurant?

'Why not?' he said. 'I've got irons in the fire everywhere. I'm not gonna live on my fucking MP's salary, am I? And I like you guys. I wanna see this restaurant thing get going. I want a place I can feel at home, a place I can keep the bar open as long as I want. Shit, we all like a drink, so there's no problem there. And think of the trade I'll bring in.'

He was right. Marvin was perfect for someone like us. So we became a threesome. A foursome, really, because without Charlie or I quite realising it, Lindsay would end up an investor as well.

The overhead lights flicked on again as we were shaking hands on the deal.

'There you go,' said Marvin, looking up.

It was midnight. The power was back on in Queensland. It seemed a good omen.

Marvin drained his glass. 'So how about we head out and celebrate?'

'Where?'

'There's a place I go over in the Valley. The thing is, I told Lindsay we'd probably meet him there tonight anyway. I got my car outside.'

So the three of us drove across to the Valley. The power was on again everywhere, but even though midnight had only just passed, Brisbane looked as desolate as if it was four in the morning. Traffic lights flashed a neutral orange—switched off because even by this hour there was hardly any traffic. I stared at the dark windows of the pubs and restaurants, watched the occasional lone figure glide by on the footpath, and wondered, despite everything I'd heard, how people like us could really survive in this town. It was like battling against prohibition.

Which started me thinking. I turned and studied Marvin, propped up behind the wheel of his car and struggling to peer over the dashboard. We'd just agreed with him upon the breaking of the law. Yes, the law was ridiculous, but still . . . how far could something like this go? Surely not too far, not with a member of parliament involved. But there was something about Marvin. A certainty and a confidence, no matter how incompetent he looked. An indifference to legalities. Were we doing the right thing, involving ourselves with him, or with his friend Lindsay? This wasn't just about serving alcohol. This was about joining a system. A big, entrenched system that in its sheer scale was undoubtedly criminal. Even if we stayed at the bottom of it, what did that make Charlie and me?

Then we were in the Valley. Marvin parked his car beside a large building that appeared to be a gym. We climbed the stairs and knocked on a door. A man opened it, took one look at Marvin, and then . . . and then we were ushered into what, for Charlie and me, was our very first illegal casino. I saw people, heard noise, smelt beer and cigarettes, all in one warm, confused rush of cheap fluorescent light.

'Drinks are on the house,' said Marvin.

I felt the door close behind us, locking the everyday Brisbane out, and the real Brisbane in. At that moment all my doubts vanished. I knew I was on the right side of that door. I knew I was home. And I headed for the bar.

TWELVE

Twenty years after that night, and ten years after I'd been run out of town, I was back.

The grand exile returning at last, welcomed home . . .

Was I actually thinking that?

Maybe a part of me was. Why else would I have booked accommodation in the middle of New Farm, of all places? For all the apprehension I'd been feeling, a part of me must have wanted to be there, to see the old places again, and find out what had happened to them. After all, I could simply have driven down from Highwood for the day, I didn't really need to stay overnight. And especially not for the two nights I'd booked the room. And there was something packed away in the bottom of my bag that made me wonder even more about my motivations, about what I was really doing there.

I was expecting the city to be different, of course. In ten years any city would have changed, and Brisbane had been through the Inquiry and a colossal collapse of government in that same time. The laws, the culture, they'd all been transformed. I knew Brisbane wasn't going to be the same. But even so, I wasn't ready. And despite all my misgivings, I was still expecting, perhaps, to feel some sense of welcome, some sense of homecoming.

What I wasn't expecting was the aftermath of a revolution.

In fact it was really only after seeing the new Brisbane that I finally understood how profound a revolution it had been. Highwood had sheltered me from the truth. I'd lived through the Inquiry, perhaps, and lingered to see the old establishment topple into ruin, but I hadn't stayed to see the new world that would emerge. And when I saw what that new world was, I realised for the first time how little I'd understood Brisbane, outside the small circles in which I'd always moved.

That was the problem, for the Brisbane of my day was in effect two cities. There was the public face of Brisbane, a quiet country town, a million people strong, with a government whose morality declared that any sort of decadence—excessive drinking, gambling or sex—was something Queensland was better off without. The other face was the one I knew, the casinos and the brothels and the all-night clubs. Behind red-lit doors and windows painted black, they not only thrived, they thrived with official sanction, and for the official circle's pleasure. Everyone knew about them, maybe, yet they were enjoyed only by a certain elite, patronised only on a clandestine level, by a class that wanted life's more sophisticated delights, and yet didn't want them shared. It was as if they were held to be dangerous pleasures, too dangerous for the common man. They were only for those who were part of an understanding, a superior minority who could look at the rest of Queensland and realise that the rules which applied for the population at large didn't need to bother the few.

Charlie and I became part of the few, and it felt good.

But outside that select world, for all that I didn't realise it at the time, a resentment and a passion were building. For thirty years those in government and their friends had, in looking after their own interests, kept Brisbane frozen in time. The city was caught in the perpetual twilight of the 1950s, as though the '60s and '70s that had wrought so much havoc around the rest of the world had quietly passed Brisbane by. But it couldn't have remained frozen that way forever. Even if the Inquiry hadn't come along and split the state apart, something else would have given somewhere. But because it had all been dammed up and fettered for so long, it meant that when finally the regime did fall, decades of pent-up energy burst forth in a fury. It wasn't simply a generational change. It was an explosion.

For some it must have been joyful and liberating. For others, caught on the wrong side, like me, it was something else again. But either way the old Brisbane was levelled in the turmoil, and the city I drove into now was a new Brisbane, and it was nothing like the town I remembered.

There were *some* things for which I was ready. Gambling was completely legal now, and I knew about the big new casino and the gaming machines that had flooded the hotels and bars. I knew about the relaxation of the licensing regulations. I knew that many of the censorship laws had been abolished. I knew that street marches were permitted again, I knew it was now legal to be gay, I knew the electoral boundaries had been redrawn. I knew there would be new roads and new buildings. I knew about the efforts to clean up the river and decorate its banks. I knew about the new parks and theatres and galleries.

It was the people themselves I hadn't expected.

It was a Sunday, early afternoon. In my day Sunday afternoon was the epitome of all that was wrong with Brisbane. Nothing was open and nothing was happening and people stayed home to watch the football or cricket on TV, and the streets would be deserted. But now, as I drove towards the centre of town, the traffic on the main roads was heavy. Staring out my windows I saw people everywhere, eating lunch, or strolling about in the sun. The shopping strips had bloomed with cafes. In my time cafes in the modern sense had been a rarity. There had been pubs, and there had been restaurants, and that was about it. Visitors from the south had pointed out plaintively that there were no casual venues anywhere, that a relaxed drink or a decent coffee were an impossible dream. Now there were chairs and tables spilling out onto the footpaths in a way that had been strictly forbidden back in the early 1980s. Customers in loose summer clothes lounged about sipping coffee in all shapes and sizes and, for that matter, all sorts of wines and beer. Alcohol seemed to be on sale everywhere, in wine shops and off-licence liquor stores and boutique bars. All of them new.

Here and there on familiar corners I spotted the old pubs and restaurants I remembered, but even they weren't the same. A philosophical shift had taken place. The pubs I'd known had always been dark places, colonial, rejecting the sun, like caves into which you retreated to drink. The ones I saw now had opened themselves up, with broad awnings and outdoor tables. Picture windows had been knocked through the thick old walls, the narrow doorways widened, beer gardens extended and brightened with colourful sunshades and umbrellas. It was all light and glass, as if there was nothing to hide any more, as if heat and sunlight were no longer an enemy.

Woolloongabba passed by, and then I was in Kangaroo Point, up along the cliffs. Traffic slowed to a crawl, and I gazed out over the Brisbane River. Broad and muddy, it had always wound its way through the city, but it had never been like this. Now it was lined with boardwalks and new parks and marinas teeming with yachts. There were riverbank trails busy with bike riders and roller-bladers. Sleek ferries cruised back and forth, their decks packed. Along the cliffs themselves families were having picnics, watching climbers and abseilers go up and down the rocks. And across the river was the city centre. Not only were there plenty of new office and apartment blocks, but they looked grander, they'd been designed, not just thrown up like the cement piles I remembered. They had spires and ornaments, they gleamed in the sun. At their feet a whole new esplanade of restaurants and bars fronted the river. And people, people everywhere I looked. Ambling about, at ease, out of their homes.

I sweated in my car, somehow disturbed by it all.

I told myself it was just the crowds and traffic. Ten years in a small town and I wasn't used to it any more. I told myself it was just the heat.

And it *was* hot. Like an early heat wave had struck the city. My shirt was plastered to my back, and the air shimmered up from the bitumen. But no one else seemed to notice it. In the old days, Brisbane would have fallen into a torpor on afternoons like this. But now . . . it was as if the heat didn't matter. I saw shirtless bodies and bikinis. Eskies full of beer. Kids dashing about under their broad-brimmed hats. And for some reason I couldn't grasp, it bothered me.

It only got worse. I crossed the bridge into the Valley, and the first thing I saw was the building which had once housed my newspaper. It was gone. That is, the building was still there, but now it was filled with luxury apartments. And all the old journalists' pubs that once surrounded it had magically turned into cafes and bars full of youth and music. There was a new mall, new trees, new bookstores. A crowded market spilled people onto the road. The Valley had been something akin to a slum; now it seemed to be reborn and shining. Even the big Carlton and United brewery that had suffused the whole area with the stench of yeast and beer—even it had vanished. The site was all luxury apartments once again, and cafes, cafes. How could they all survive? How could people eat and drink this much?

Then I was turning down Brunswick Street into New Farm. New Farm—my beloved, dirty, half-crazed and occasionally dangerous New Farm—had disappeared completely. In its place was . . . I didn't know what it was. I inched down Brunswick Street in a traffic jam. In my memory it was a long seedy street of boarding houses, pawnshops and streetwalking prostitutes. They had all been swept away. The entire street, virtually from the Valley right down to the park and the river, seemed to be lined with cafes and art galleries, sushi bars and designer stores. There was barely a single building I could place. And then there was the park, which was still just a park, but had it ever been that full of people? New Farm Park had always been for the junkies and alcoholics. What were families doing there? What were people doing jogging there, or walking dogs, or playing cricket? And what about the junkies and alcoholics and boarding-house old men, and all the other folk that had peopled the New Farm I knew—where had they all gone? Where had all these fit bodies come from, all this wealth and tanned skin and good clothes?

So much change, and in so little time.

I wasn't prepared, hadn't expected anything like this. I drove and sweated and felt something like claustrophobia closing in, as if the whole city, all of its life and bustle, was directed against me. It wasn't just that I'd been away so long, it wasn't just that things were different, that there was nothing I recognised . . .

It was that things were so obviously *better*. Like any exile, I'd imagined, hopefully, that I might have been missed, that somehow the city might have suffered from my absence. But even at a glance it was clear Brisbane had blossomed without me. It had become what a city should be, what Brisbane should always have been. It was what Charlie and I had wanted it to be, back before we joined the system and went rotten with the rest of it. Everything was out in the open. All the things that had been kept unlawful, except for the privileged few, seemed to be anyone's now. And people had swarmed out of their houses and embraced it all. As if the old Brisbane, my Brisbane, couldn't be forgotten quickly enough.

I turned off Brunswick Street, searching. This was all a mistake. Bad enough that I'd come back to an alien city, but New Farm was the worst part of all. It had been my home, but I had no part in what it was now. I felt dated. Dulled. I belonged to the bad old days. A decade or so earlier I'd walked these streets as if I'd owned Brisbane. It might have been ugly and drab on the outside, but it was mine, I was on the inside, and I knew where the true heart of it lay. Now . . . now the only thing ugly and drab was me, and I knew nothing.

The heat was insufferable. I needed to get off the streets. I gazed around vainly for landmarks, and then at last there was the motel. Two stories of plain brick, somehow reassuring amidst all the madness. I parked and sat in the car a moment, wiping the sweat from my face.

One night, I was thinking.

Just one night and then I could get Charlie buried in the morning and be gone again. Who knew what I'd been expecting or hoping, but even after barely an hour in Brisbane, I knew there was no point in staying. There would be no welcome home. No fond remembrance. The new Brisbane had thrown me off and prospered. It didn't need me, and nor, I felt, did it want me back.

I climbed out of the car, dodged a couple gliding by on their roller-blades, and went to see about my room. The sun beat down on my head as I crossed the car park. The grand exile returning.

A man ten years out of time. Looking for somewhere to hide.

THIRTEEN

I slept the sleep of the hunted.

Cars moaned in the street outside, voices called and doors slammed, and all night an orange light tainted the room. For ten years I'd known nothing but the dark mountain nights of Highwood, the deep silence that could make your ears ring, but Brisbane knew no such quiet. I rolled in the sheets and sweated, starting awake at unknown sounds, and slowly the hours passed. I woke finally to daylight, a headache and an empty pizza box on the pillow beside me.

It was a sign of defeat, that box. I had certainly seen several Italian cafes along Brunswick Street, but still, I'd dialled for pizza and waited for it to come to my door. I couldn't bring myself to leave the motel room or to walk down those footpaths or to eat in public. The entire city available for just that one night, and I'd drawn the curtains and huddled in front of the television, preferring to think none of it existed.

And what did it matter?

It was the day of Charlie's funeral, and after that, Brisbane and I would be through with each other.

I rolled out of bed and fetched the newspaper that had been pushed under the door. I turned to the obituaries and found Charlie's funeral announcement. I knew what it would say. I'd placed it myself, and it had run for the past four days. Just his name, the time and the place. I hadn't mentioned anything about his family, or any details about his life, or by whom he was deeply mourned. I didn't know if he was deeply mourned by anyone—or if he was even really mourned by me. For now it was enough just to pay some of the old debt, and to get him underground.

In truth, not even that. The service was to take place at a crematorium. I wasn't going to bury Charlie, I was going to burn him. I couldn't see him in a cemetery, with a small flat gravestone in the grass that no one would ever visit. Let him become ashes. His life had gone up in flames anyway. I would scatter him somewhere, disperse all the ruin. I didn't know where. I couldn't think of any favourite place of Charlie's—no tree or hill or river that seemed fitting. Brisbane in general had been his favourite place, his only place. He'd loved the town, or at least he'd loved the old town. In the new Brisbane I had no idea what had become of him, or how he'd survived.

I closed the paper, looked around my room. It was plain. A bed, some chairs, a small kitchen, sliding glass doors that opened onto a balcony. Through a gap in the curtains I could see that the morning was glaring and blue. The city still waited out there, and the funeral was at nine. Not a fashionable hour but appropriate, so the crematorium staff seemed to think, for what was expected to be a small and brief ceremony.

In half an hour I was packed and in the car.

The crematorium was back across the river in the southern suburbs. Driving there I barely looked out the windows. I had steeled myself, I was no longer searching for the Brisbane I once knew. It was an anonymous city, a Monday morning with people driving to work, impatient and angry. Horns blasted and it was hot. It was any city. And there were other fears on my mind now, ones that I'd been suppressing ever since Graham had laid this cup before me. Charlie's funeral. It was one thing to organise it, and to attend. But the question I'd dreaded from the start loomed again now—who else would be there?

I had no way of knowing. In all the time since Charlie's death I had not heard from a single interested person, none of his old acquaintances, none of his old patrons. Were they all like me? Had they all long since abandoned him? The papers had marked him as a criminal, as someone the world would not miss, so would anyone come to bury such a man? Only his closest friends, maybe, those who had worked with him and risen with him and shared his fall. But I remembered what the detectives had told me. Marvin—they were still looking for Marvin. Jeremy was in a wheelchair. Lindsay—they hadn't said where Lindsay was, but of all of us, Lindsay would be the last one I'd expect.

Which only left Maybellene . . .

Would any of them have seen the funeral notice? Would any of them act upon it?

I arrived. The crematorium sat high on the side of a leafy hill, surrounded by remembrance gardens. I had attended funerals there before. There were only two other cars visible in the parking lot, and they were both empty. There was no one standing in the gardens or waiting in front of the chapel. For all I knew, the cars belonged to staff. For all I knew, I wanted them to belong to staff.

I got out and stood in the sun. The heat and humidity were rising with the morning, and the air, even up on the hill, was perfectly still. Out over the city a thin layer of smog hung in the sky. Brisbane, my Brisbane . . . all gone. I scratched at sweat in my armpits. I was wearing an old black suit that smelled of age. It hung loose on me. It was from my earlier days, when I drank all the time, and ate all the time, and never thought of walking if I could take a taxi and charge it to the newspaper.

No other cars arrived.

At five minutes to nine I walked across to the chapel and up the stairs. I peered inside, a twinge of nervousness in my stomach. Would there be *anyone*? But the chapel was empty. There was only Charlie. His simple coffin sat on its rollers in front of a cream curtain, and around him everything was silent. I retreated into the sunlight again, not knowing what I was feeling. Funerals had their place in the world. There was something about the dignity of death, with its respectful mourners and the hushed whispers of their conversations— grim, and yet still a due part of life. But I knew Charlie had died without any dignity, and it seemed there would be me and only me to witness it. No whispers, no respect. And yet privately I was glad it was only me. It would be easier that way. For me, always for me.

A man came round the side of the chapel studying his

watch, then saw me and introduced himself. He worked for the crematorium and would perform the service, as per our arrangement. His suit was a more subtle black than mine, and modern, and to his credit he pretended no grief. We discussed the details of the service itself and the collection of the urn afterwards, then he went inside and stood by the coffin. I waited on the steps. The sun shone and the heat built moment by moment. Then it was nine o'clock. So no one else was coming, *she* wasn't coming, and all this would be over in moments.

I turned to walk inside.

A small bus came labouring up the drive and turned into the car park, its windows full of faces. I paused and stared at it. It was the last thing I was expecting and could have nothing, surely, to do with Charlie. But it stopped at the bottom of the steps, and doors slid open. People were climbing out. At their head was the driver. He was young, with square glasses, and a black sports coat covering otherwise casual clothes. He was *too* young. He was no one that Charlie could ever have known.

But his hand was out to mine.

'We're not too late, are we?'

'For what?' I said.

He stared at me a moment, through his glasses.

'This is Charlie's funeral, isn't it?'

'Yes.'

'Then we're in the right place. Are you the funeral director?'

'No. I'm a friend of Charlie's.'

'Ah. Well, so are we.'

His passengers were filing past me, about a dozen of them, men and women. They were mostly older. In fact, very old. Thin faces and cheap clothes and shuffling steps. But there was something familiar about them, about their movements, their eyes.

'We're from the centre,' the driver was telling me. 'We had Charlie with us a lot over the last few years, and we always try to attend, when one of us goes.'

I understood. The centre. They were from the Uniting Church hostel, the hostel for alcohol abusers that Charlie had apparently been frequenting. That was what I was recognising in the faces, and of course they weren't that old at all, not much older than me and Charlie. They were just old before their time. It was in their stares, the cast of their shoulders, all the signs of a life's battle with alcohol, mostly lost. These were hard-core cases by the look of them, hollow and pained, with the air of the long-term homeless. For all that they were sober and erect and clean right now, it was something that could never be simply washed away. It went deeper than that.

The old ache flared. So the centre was that sort of place. A home for lost causes. That was where Charlie had ended up. And these were his friends.

'No,' I said, 'you're not too late.'

He followed his passengers inside and for a moment longer I waited in the sun.

No one else came.

So we burnt Charlie. It was small and it was quick. The man from the crematorium waited until we were all sitting down, and between us we only took up the front two rows. If he thought there was anything strange about the mourners that had gathered, either their number or their form, he did not let it show.

'We are gathered here to mark the passing of Charles Monohan . . .'

He didn't speak for long. I'd told him nothing personal about Charlie, and I hadn't asked for any special readings or music. I'd thought of songs we'd all once liked, or books we'd read, from which there might have a been a relevant passage, but there was nothing that seemed to mean anything now. It was a different world and we'd been different people, and none of us had ever been poetic. If it meant the ceremony would be stark and voiceless, then so be it. There was nothing to say, so let silence reign before the flames.

But the crematorium man asked anyway, after he'd finished his speech. 'If there's anyone who has anything to add?'

He looked at me and waited.

The old men and women looked to me as well. I looked back at them. They would have no idea who I was, but they might have guessed that alone of all the mourners, I at least had known Charlie before his fall. I didn't answer. I searched in their eyes for any sign of judgement, for the command, 'It is you who should speak', as if they somehow knew everything after all. Or the question, 'Where are the others? His real friends? Why are you the only one?' But there was nothing in their eyes apart from a mute and distant pain, and that didn't have anything to do with me.

I shook my head.

The crematorium man cast a glance over the chapel, then nodded to himself and lowered his eyes. For a time we all sat there in silence, giving witness to the coffin and a man's life. From outside came the sound of birds, and distant traffic. Then the crematorium man pressed a button and the curtains parted. The coffin began its slow roll through to the darkness, and I thought from somewhere behind me I heard a sob, or a groan, but it may have been no more than a cough. Then the curtains were sliding shut.

Goodbye, Charlie, I thought—but it was mechanical and it wasn't what I felt.

We all stood up. The crematorium man came over and we shook hands. I turned my head and blinked into the glare from the open doorway. Beyond the doors, out across the white gravel of the car park, I could see a woman walking away. She was framed like that in the light for a moment, just a dark shape, and then she passed from view, but my heart seem to catch.

It was Maybellene.

It wasn't Maybellene.

My hand was still in the crematorium man's grasp. He was saying something to me I didn't hear. I nodded, I said, 'Yes, yes. . .' and tore my hand away. I strode down the aisle towards the door, but before I reached it I stopped again.

Even if it was her, what was the point? What could we say? Would we be able to even look at each other?

Then my feet were moving again, and I was outside on the steps. I could hear voices behind me but there was no one in the car park. A car was disappearing down the drive, its brake lights flashing briefly. I couldn't see the driver.

A hand was on my shoulder.

It was the driver of the bus, the young man. His eyes were calm and sympathetic, watching me through those big glasses.

For a second he reminded me of Marvin. It was only the glasses.

'It's George, isn't it?' he said.

'How . . .?'

'I've been reading the papers. I'm sorry about your friend.'

It stung suddenly. Something like tears. It was sympathy I didn't deserve. 'I hadn't even seen him in years.'

The old men and women were filing by, as quietly as they'd filed in.

'Are you going to be in town long?' the driver was asking.

'Why?'

I was still watching the old men and women. I wondered how many times they'd done this before, and if they'd really been Charlie's friends, or known him at all beyond sharing a ward or a room. And did it matter? When it was their own turn to be in the coffin, at least they knew that someone would be there. The dying rounded up to mourn the dead. Any dead.

The young man was watching the old people as well.

'Charlie left some things,' he said. 'Nothing much, nothing important, but there's no one else to give them to except you. I thought maybe you'd like to come over and collect them. And maybe there are some questions you'd like to ask me. About Charlie.'

Questions about what? About the life he'd led after May and I had inflicted all the pain that was possible upon the man, and then deserted him? Why would I ask? I didn't want the answers. I never had.

I looked away westwards. From high on the crematorium hill I could see right over the south-west suburbs of Brisbane to Ipswich and beyond. Out on the horizon a low blue line marked the mountains. It was only a two-hour drive. The clouds were all gone up there now, it would be bright and clear and cool. I wanted to be there, not here in this heat and haze. Charlie was buried. My duty to him was done.

But I nodded, all the same.

FOURTEEN

The Uniting Church Dependency Hostel was situated in Bardon, a green and wealthy suburb miles from where any homeless alcoholic might be wandering the streets. This was quite intentional. The hostel wasn't like some of the centres that existed in the Valley or in West End—it wasn't a drop-in facility for the homeless to find a meal or a bed. The Uniting Church staff did indeed liaise with those sorts of places, and took referrals from them, but the idea at their own hostel was to detoxify their clients, get them sober or straight, educate them on survival strategies, and then either send them home or, if there was no home, set them up in one of the Uniting Church's halfway houses. The accompanying brief was to focus on clients that other detox units wouldn't take, or couldn't take—the long-term abusers with no money of their own, no family or friends to help, and not much chance of recovery.

All this was told to me by the resident psychologist, the driver of the bus, and his name was Mark. We were sitting in his office at the hostel. From down the hall came the rattle of the kitchen gearing up for lunch. The hostel consisted of an old wooden house, at the back of which a brick annex had been attached . . . all of it small, all of it simple. Most of the labour was volunteer and they had no aid from any government, federal or state.

'The original idea,' he was saying, 'was to deal both with alcoholism and with drug dependency. In the end, though, we tend to deal mainly with alcoholics. Heroin users do end up here sometimes, but we seem to have developed a reputation just for alcohol. It does make things simpler. The two groups don't get along. It might just be an age thing. The heroin users are generally younger, while the alcoholics are older. The heroin users think the alcoholics are pathetic and useless and that they'll never end up like that, while the alcoholics think the heroin users are punks and thieves, and that they were never that bad.'

He was smiling faintly, staring at a battered briefcase on his desk.

'Of course, we don't get many older heroin addicts because they all die so young, and we don't get many younger alcoholics because it takes a lifetime of drinking to get bad enough to be sent here.'

I, too, was staring at the briefcase. It was made of leather and would have been expensive when it was new, but it was no longer new. The handle had been stretched until it sagged, and the bottom corners were patched with masking tape. As if it had been carried, and set down, and carried, and set down, over and over and over again.

'Sorry,' he said. 'Maybe you already know all this?'

I looked at him. 'No. Not really.'

It was a lie. I knew plenty about it. But in a way it was the truth. In all my life, this was the very first time I'd stepped inside a detox ward.

'Is that Charlie's stuff?' I asked.

He nodded and pushed the case over towards me. I took it on my lap and looked inside.

'This is it?'

'That's all he had here. Our clients don't generally have much, and there isn't room for many personal belongings anyway. Some of them do have their own places, but if Charlie had one in recent years, we didn't know about it. He was either here, or at one of our halfway houses, or just somewhere else. He had clothes, of course, but they were really ours, donated from our second-hand stores, so after he died we put the useable items back in stock. That's all that was left.'

The suitcase was full of papers. Documents, it seemed, on the top at least. I shuffled through some of them. I saw bank statements and utility bills, mostly several years old. Terminated rental agreements for what looked like boarding houses. Social security forms. Medical prescriptions for drugs I didn't know. A tattered birth certificate. But there was nothing that looked personal, nothing in Charlie's own handwriting. I studied two of the uppermost sheets—recent bank statements. The balance was never more than a few hundred dollars, and on the last page it was a flat zero.

The psychologist was watching me. 'That last statement came after we'd heard about his death. We informed the bank and the government agencies, and everything has been closed.'

I said, 'He spent every cent he had the week before he died. Two hundred dollars.'

'He fell off the wagon. It was fairly typical, unfortunately. He disappeared for a few days and only showed up here at the end of it, broke again, and very ill.'

'You didn't try to stop him?'

'We can't stop anyone. We can advise, but they can leave whenever they want, and do whatever they want. Of course, if while they're gone we fill up with other clients and there aren't any beds left when they come back, then it's their tough luck.'

I nodded and dug deeper into the case. At the bottom there was a thick sheaf of yellowing newspaper. The top page bore a large photograph. A pang as sharp and palpable as a heart tremor ran through me.

It was me and Charlie. The page was from the society section, and the photo was of a gathering at one of Charlie's restaurants . . . his third, by the look, the one down by the river. Charlie was in the foreground, a glass of wine raised in a toast. He was in chef's whites and smiling, and it was only the smile that saved him, as usual, from the brute force of his own body. But he looked so young, so solid, so real—no scars on his face, no vague and empty eyes. They were bright, full of energy. There was nothing to connect him with the thing I had seen tied to the wall in the substation. And no matter how I stared, there was no hint of a future so terrible, so friendless.

In the photo he was surrounded by friends. Right behind him, at a long table, we were all there. I was at the nearest end, my glass also raised, smiling at the camera. A well-fed, cheerful man, young, with a whole life of success ahead of him. Charlie's best friend of all.

'Rising star of kitchen drinks to success' read the caption.

Fresh young restaurateur Charlie Monohan has recently opened the doors to his third establishment, and is now officially one of Brisbane's most successful chefs. In glamorous surroundings on the Brisbane River, Charlie has increasingly become host to a range of the town's social and political elite, including new government heavyweight and man of the moment . . .

Marvin was there, sitting next to me, his grin idiotic and his eyes huge behind his glasses, arms spread happily to the lens, his tie wide and hideous, sweat stains on his shirt. Lindsay too, across the table from Marvin, his back to the camera, shoulders stiff and uncomfortable. And Jeremy as well, fading off into the background, his head turned away from the rest of the group, aloof as ever. It would have been still early in the days of the syndicate, before Jeremy was really one of us. Was it 1981? Or 1982? I couldn't remember.

And wine, wine everywhere. It must have been late in the meal. A lunch, it looked like. Amongst all the plates and dishes there seemed to be six or seven bottles of wine, glasses of all shapes. A glow in all our eyes.

And at the edge of the photo, furthest from Charlie and me, the very end of the table was cut out of frame. The only thing visible there was an arm, slender and pale. It lay across the tablecloth and the hand was curled lightly around a wine glass. A woman's hand.

Was it our first meeting then? Our first real meeting with Jeremy, and trailing along behind him, sullen and reluctant, Maybellene herself? Had a photographer been there that day?

I couldn't remember.

I flicked to the next page. And the next. Dozens of newspaper clippings. Yellowed and crinkled, but intact. All about Charlie and his restaurants. The reviews, the awards, the expansions, the new openings, the celebrities, the socialites, the politicians. Sometimes Charlie was in the photos, sometimes not, but the captions all mentioned his name. It was his entire history.

Or most of it. I cut to the last page. It was dated early 1987. Only a month from the beginning of the end. And from there on in, Charlie's appearances in the media had nothing to do with food or wine or parties. All the coverage in the world perhaps, but nothing to cut out and preserve.

I let the pile fall back. I found it hard to look at the psychologist.

'Quite a career,' he said, his tone neutral.

'Do you know how it ended?'

'Oh, yes.'

'Did he . . . did he talk about it?'

'Not really. But some of us knew. It made it all the more sad. I mean, to go from that to what he became . . .'

I swallowed. 'What was he like? In the last few years.'

'Well, there were the head injuries, of course. That wasn't something he was ever going to recover from in terms of full social functioning. There was still a lovely man in there somewhere, but there was frustration, too, and a bitterness driving him.'

'Do you know what he did, after getting out of jail?'

'He drank.'

'He never worked again? In restaurants or anything?'

'Not that I know of. He went on the disability pension and I assume he lived in a few different places. Eventually he ended up here. It's hard enough at any time to make the transition from jail to the normal world, but for someone in his condition, and with his past, the odds were against him. If he'd had a family for support maybe, somewhere to go . . .'

He left it unspoken. Friends. If he'd had any friends. I felt my face reddening.

'Did he ever say anything about me?'

The psychologist thought. 'Not that I remember.'

'It's just that he was coming to see me, when it happened.'

'So I read in the papers.'

'I don't know what he wanted.'

'He didn't say anything to me. The police asked the same question. They asked everyone else, too, clients and staff, everyone that knew him. No one heard him say a thing.'

'But he stole the car from here.'

'Yes. We weren't sure at first that it was him. He was supposed to be away at St Amand's, but one of the other clients said Charlie was nosing around in the front office that afternoon. That's where we keep the keys. So we reported it, and then next day the police called with the news.'

'St Amand's? What's that?'

His eyebrows lifted. 'I thought you knew. There's another detox ward over there.'

'He went to another ward?'

'That's right. As I said, he came in sick one night, after a two- or three-day binge, but next day he transferred out. An ambulance came and picked him up. It was a few days later still that he came back for the car.'

'I didn't know that.'

'We told the police. I just assumed you'd know as well.'

'Why was he transferred?'

'It was his idea. We were surprised, though. St Amand's only takes paying customers—and we all knew Charlie didn't have any money. But it's a good ward. Far better facilities than we have here. So we thought good luck to him.'

'And where is this ward?'

'It's a part of St Amand's hospital, over in Hamilton. First class. On the other hand, the hospital doesn't really advertise the ward's existence. It's generally for private clientele, and not everyone wants the world to know they've got a drinking problem.'

I hadn't heard a word of any of this before.

'Do clients of yours often get transferred over there?'

He laughed. 'We're two different worlds. They're the top and we're the bottom. No, our clients never end up at St Amand's.'

'Except Charlie.'

'Except Charlie. But then he was a rarity in more ways than one. After all, he actually *had* been wealthy once. That's true of very few of our other clients. It's a myth, the ex-millionaire reduced to rags, "Once I built a railroad" and all that. Most of our clients started out at the bottom and they've stayed there.'

'So you think Charlie still had some cash stashed away from the old days?'

'It's possible, but unlikely. I was thinking more that maybe someone was paying for him. An old friend or something.'

'Did he ever mention anyone like that?'

'No.' He shrugged, lowered his eyes. 'But then you'd be more familiar with his old circles than I am.'

I was . . . and that was the whole problem.

Coughing erupted in the hall outside. An old woman staggered by, choking up volumes of phlegm in her throat.

I looked back to the psychologist. 'Does St Amand's actually cure people then?'

'There's no cure. Some people survive it, some people don't. In fact the latest research questions the very idea that any particular treatment is much better than any other. The truth is, none of them is very successful in absolute terms. So it comes down to what sort of quality of life you can maintain in the meantime. And that comes down to money again. Go over to St Amand's. The people you see there won't look anything like the people you see here, and they'll have nice furniture, and bigger TVs, and good coffee to drink. But money is the only real difference.'

We sat in his plain little office for a moment, silent.

I studied the briefcase.

'I can keep this stuff?' I asked.

'You paid for his funeral, and that's as close to next of kin as I think we'll ever get. The police have already been through it, and there's nothing they wanted, so . . .'

I thought a moment about the next question. 'There was his wife. Did she ever come here?'

He shook his head. 'I knew he'd been married, but he never talked about her, and she never came to see him.' He regarded me steadily. 'No one did.'

It stung again, and I was standing up. The briefcase hung from my right hand, the handle worn soft under my fingers. I thought of Charlie's fingers in the same position, lugging the case with him wherever he went, wherever that had been, in all those years. It felt heavy.

I said, 'If St Amand's is so good, why do you think Charlie left after only three days?'

The psychologist sighed. 'Don't ask me, George. Like I said, go and see for yourself how the other half live.'

I nodded, and carried the briefcase out to my car.

FIFTEEN

But memory played tricks.

There was no photographer present when I first met Jeremy. It wasn't a lunch, it was a dinner, a late one. Nor was the venue the riverside restaurant, it was at one of the others. And May wasn't there either . . . although there was a discussion about her. Not that I realised it at the time.

I was drunk, for one thing.

We were celebrating. Things were going well. It was three years since the foundation of our little syndicate, and we were a success. Both as a group, and as individuals.

Personally, I had my own daily column at the paper. I was known all about town, invited to social events, to launches, to everything. I was not a man who lowered himself to daily news events. Instead I cast impressions, told amusing stories, passed on anecdotes about the rich and powerful, stripped away pretensions. People fought to get my attention, to be mentioned by me, or to not be mentioned by me. Occasionally, to my editor's delight, there was even the threat of a libel suit.

I was a gossip columnist. Years later, I wouldn't remember a single word of what I wrote.

But meanwhile I was also an investor in three fully licensed restaurants, and that's what I would remember more. Charlie's restaurants. The original site, greatly expanded, in Paddington. Another in the city centre. And the third on the river. They were the places where I spent my nights, roaming between them like a nomad. All of us were the same, dragging our friends and our contacts and our colleagues along with us. There were no problems with the time, no problems with bookings, no problems with drinks. Not as a part owner, and not with Lindsay working away behind the scenes, soothing everything with the official bodies, even though we broke every single law concerning food and alcohol and opening hours. And not with Marvin bringing half the government through our doors, night after night. We were safe inside the system.

Nor was it a secret. Charlie's places were known for it, at least by those whose business it was to know, and the rest of the population, what did they matter? Charlie's prices weren't cheap, and they were paid by people who had no particular concern about money, or trifles like the law. Charlie himself was everywhere. He still oversaw the menus and the cooking, but his triumph was playing host. His ugly face was what greeted the patrons, everyone knew him, and he knew everyone in return. And an air surrounded him now. A hint of political connections and intriguingly shady dealings. It only added to the glamour, and Charlie was smart enough to play along, to act the benign gangster. He certainly looked the part. Maybe no one exactly knew that Marvin was involved, or Lindsay, or even me. But they all knew something was going on, and that was all that really mattered at four in the morning, when the bar was almost the only one still open in town.

On the other hand, when it came to actual cash flow, we were still small time. The real money lay elsewhere. So one night Marvin called a meeting to discuss some possible diversification. And by those days, when Marvin called, we all came. He was famous now. A cabinet minister. And the strange thing was, it was electricity that had put him there.

As Marvin had warned us three years before, the government was determined about breaking the Electrical Workers Union. So two years after their initial move, they once again tried to open the field to independent sub-contracting companies and non-union labour. Once again the union responded with strike action. Nine hundred workers walked away from their jobs. Linesmen, maintenance men, station staff. Everyone. Picket lines were manned, the offices of the sub-contracting companies were besieged. And once again, Queensland was wracked by power blackouts.

Both sides, government and union, knew that this time there would be no backing down. But this time, the government was ready. They declared a State of Emergency, sacked the nine hundred workers, and offered their jobs to all comers.

Mayhem broke out. The Minister for Mines and Energy, backed by the premier, declared that as the strikers had been formally dismissed, they no longer constituted a legitimate union, hence they were just a rabble illegally blocking the streets. An army of police was sent in, arrests began, and terrific violence ensued, a set of running brawls and pitched battles that headlined news all around the country.

At first it seemed the government had miscalculated. The state was crippled. The power would fail four or five hours every day, and the picket lines still prevented the new contractors from getting the system working again. Complaints mounted, even from government supporters like mining and tourism. The media woke momentarily from their long slumber and began to question the government's strategy. Other unions were threatening strikes of their own. The Maritime Union. The Federated Builders. Bus drivers and train drivers. After two weeks of chaos, with no sign of the union surrendering, and with the contractors wavering, the Minister for Mines and Energy was sacked. The union was on the verge of claiming victory.

And then, to everyone's amazement, Marvin, an untried backbencher and political lightweight, was appointed to the job.

Up until that point, my own interest in it all had been minimal. I suffered the blackouts with everyone else, watched the picket line violence on TV, and left the reporting of it to the more mundane journalists. I had no particular opinions about who should control the power supply. All I wanted was my beer kept cold. It was only much later that I realised how directly those few weeks would affect my life. And that if only I'd watched the TV screens a little more closely, I might have seen, caught up amongst the police and unionists, the woman with whom I would later fall in love.

Maybellene.

She was younger then, of course, and moved in a world utterly opposed to mine.

She was a university graduate, working on a masters thesis in sociology, and she had gone straight from her Catholic girls' school into political activism. Queensland infuriated her sense of justice. It wasn't just the government, but also the voting population that allowed it to stay there. The electricity dispute was the final straw. She'd been following it for the last two years, and originally she'd been talking with the union only for her thesis research, but by the time the final eruption came, she was in deeper than that. She was on the picket lines with them. After the State of Emergency was declared, she was arrested in the first round of police assaults, and spent her first night in custody. She was back on the lines the next day, and arrested again. She was prepared to fight until the end. But when the minister was dismissed she thought, like everyone else, that maybe the battle had already been won. After all, who was this Marvin McNulty?

Marvin, it turned out, was the man for the job.

I heard only rumours about how he secured the position. That he had friends in the right places, and money from somewhere undeclared. That he had direct links with the private contractors concerned, or some hold over the premier. That the old minister had been too squeamish, had been scared off by all the sound and fury, but that Marvin was going to be different.

He was. The assault on the picket lines burst out afresh. The contracting companies, who before had been vacillating, suddenly produced strike-breaking forces of their own, and hit back at the unions. The police rigorously stood by, or came in only on the contractors' side. Marvin flooded the media with his own propaganda about union rorts and corruption, cast visions of what a de-unionised power industry would be like—cheaper electricity, faster service, better maintenance. The union suddenly couldn't seem to get their side into the news. Public opinion, never very favourable to the strikers, began to slide. People wanted the lights back on, and they didn't care how. Another two weeks went by. The sacked workers were running out of money, and there was still no end in sight. Doubt set in. Where was it all leading to?

Then Marvin played his trump card. He initiated legal action directly against individual strikers, each of the nine hundred, suing them for financial damages to the state. The amounts threatened were huge. At the same time he offered an alternative. The suits would be dropped and they could all have their jobs back—as long as they signed new contracts which shut out the union, lowered working conditions, and which contained a cast-iron 'no strike' clause. Everything, more or less, that the government had wanted from the start.

And then he just waited.

The union understood the danger. They called for solidarity. The opposition in parliament called for solidarity. May, somewhere in amongst it all, called for solidarity. But it all began collapsing. Some of the workers started signing the contracts. The opposition fell to in-fighting over who was to blame for letting it go so far. Numbers fell on the picket lines.

In despair, May and some of her comrades turned to extreme measures. In a midnight raid they invaded the depot of the major contracting company, and set the whole place on fire.

That was the end. Whatever sympathy the union still commanded went up with the flames. Marvin declared a moral victory, and for all that the union could decry the fire and deny official involvement, they knew as well as Marvin that it was over. Hundreds of the sacked workers surrendered and signed the new contracts. Hundreds more quit the industry forever, and many of them the state as well. The power supply returned to normal and, from then on, although electricity remained a government enterprise, the work itself became increasingly the domain of sub-contractors and private suppliers. Police investigating the fire finally arrested one suspect who confessed to the crime, and named all the others.

May ended up in jail again. On arson charges.

All in all, it was one of the government's greatest triumphs of the era. It cowed all the other unions into silence, and left the opposition party in ruins. They would not even come close to power for yet another seven years. And it was all Marvin's work. No one laughed at him anymore. He was a political star now, he was the Minister for Mines and Energy. And though his fortunes would never be so high again as they were in those first few months after the dispute, it was no wonder he thought he was invulnerable.

So he called us to a late dinner at Charlie's place, and obediently we all came. Marvin even looked different. He was getting fuller and rounder with the years, more imposing, and while he would never have charm or style, he now exuded that intangible aura that always denoted authority. He announced it was time to go beyond the restaurant business. Clubs were the answer. Nightclubs. That's where the real money was. And if upstairs from those clubs there was room for some small gambling facilities, or perhaps some form of adult entertainment, well, that could be a nice sideline as well.

I knew what he meant. Casinos and women. It should have sounded ominous, but in the Queensland we'd come to know, these things were accepted. In those three years since linking up with Marvin, we'd seen how it all operated. We knew all the casinos and some of the brothels and we knew their owners, we drank with them, haunted their establishments. They didn't seem any different from the rest of us. Everyone in our world did *something* that was theoretically criminal. SP bookies, prostitutes, politicians, the police themselves. Even legitimate businessmen knew the score. If you wanted anything done in Queensland, there was always going to be someone you had to pay. And now we had a government minister on our side. What could go wrong?

I was drunk anyway, had been drinking since lunch earlier that day. But it seemed to me that if we could claim part of Brisbane's nightlife as our own, give ourselves even more places to go, and more sins in which to indulge, then why in heaven not. In fact, once again, Charlie raised the only concern. Clubs weren't really his style, and besides, he was already busy enough with the restaurants.

'No problem,' said Marvin. 'Lindsay can handle the day-to-day running. But you've got the name, Charlie. These clubs have gotta at least look legitimate, and the liquor licences are already registered to you, so if your name is on the door, all the better. Obviously I can't appear to be directly involved, and no one's heard of Lindsay . . . who else is there?'

So Charlie agreed. We all agreed.

It was a golden moment. Bottles were opened. We were in the midst of the first toast when a diner from across the room rose from his table and approached ours. He was lean and old and tastefully dressed, and I thought I recognised him vaguely. Marvin certainly did, and put out his hand.

'Jeremy,' he said.

The old man smiled. 'Marvin. Just thought I'd offer my congratulations.'

'Thanks.'

'The premier, I gather, is very impressed.'

Marvin waved a hand. 'Well . . . I try.'

'I was wondering, actually, if we could have a word?'

'What about?'

The old man's gaze drifted across the rest of us, and then back to Marvin.

'Go on,' Marvin laughed. 'They're all okay.'

The old man nodded calmly. 'It's about these . . . arsonists . . . of yours.'

'They're not mine, Jeremy. Thank fuck they came along though, hey?'

'Yes, but one of them I have a . . . special interest in. I'd like to help her.'

Marvin grew serious. 'They're in pretty deep, you know. It's out of my hands, really. The police are keen to see some jail terms. They're even fighting bail.'

'I know, but in this particular case, I can possibly chat to the police myself. She wasn't a ringleader. What I'm worried about is the company whose premises they attacked. I'd need to get them onside as well.'

'Ah . . .'

'And I'm told you have friends there . . .'

Marvin was nodding. 'Maybe we *should* cover this later. How about we set up a meeting? Actually, there are a few things I wanted to raise with you anyway.'

Again the old man looked the rest of us over. 'I thought there might be.'

And he was gone.

Which was how I first met Sir Jeremy Phelan, high-ranking career public servant, already semi-retired but sill consultant to the premier's department and various other government bodies. And that was the first I ever heard of Maybellene.

I didn't think much of it. I drank down my wine and reached for another.

But a few days later, when we were sorting out the purchase of our first nightclub, Lindsay reported that Jeremy was now an investor and partner, in return for various favours he'd performed for us in the areas of town planning permits and zoning restrictions.

And Maybellene, stewing in her holding cell, received an unexpected visitor.

SIXTEEN

I stood in the car park of St Amand's Hospital.

The name was familiar, even though I'd never been there before.

Had I heard someone speaking about it once? Or maybe I was thinking of the actual saint. My background was Catholic, after all. But I couldn't remember any particular saint called Amand, or what he might have done.

I stood sweating under the sun and stared up at the building. It looked like it might once have been a convent—stately and old, with two tall storeys of sandstone. The roof was gabled and towered, and boasted crucifixes as decorative works. Cowled nuns might have whispered down its hallways. The whole site was contemplative—set high on a hill east of the city centre, with sweeping views of the river and out to the shimmering glare of the bay. Ex-convent or not, however, the modern car park and the mirrored windows spoke of a more practical function. It was a hospital and obviously an expensive one. The humble little Bardon hostel would have fitted into its porch alone.

Where was it I'd heard about the place, and from whom?

The asphalt was burning hot under my shoes. I made my way across to the front doors and into the foyer. Conditioned air embraced me like winter. The interior was all polished floors and dark wood panelling. There was no emergency entrance, no ambulances parked outside, no bustle of activity. All was quiet and calm. An imposing staircase curved up to the second floor, wide doors flanking either side of it, but there was no indication as to where they led. I looked about for a list of departments or wards, but the walls displayed only artwork and gilded mirrors. There weren't even any 'no smoking' signs. It might have been the entry hall to an historic home. There was nothing else but an antique desk off to one side, staffed by a single woman at a computer terminal. And she was watching me, waiting politely.

I went over. I was going to ask where the detox ward was but somehow, in the surroundings, the term didn't seem appropriate.

I said, 'I'm told you have an alcohol dependency unit here. I was wondering if I could speak to someone from it.'

The woman smiled smoothly. 'Perhaps I can help. What is it you wanted to know?'

'I had a friend stay here recently. I just had a few questions about his treatment.'

'He isn't staying here at the moment?'

'No.'

'You're a friend, not a relation of any sort?'

'No.'

'Hmm.' She appeared to consider for a moment. 'Of course, as you'd realise, all medical treatments carried out here are strictly confidential. There's very little any of our staff could tell you. You'd be better off discussing this with your friend.'

'He's dead.'

'Ah. Could I ask his name?'

I told her and she typed it into her terminal. She considered the results for a moment.

'And could I ask your name?'

I told her that, too, and she picked up a phone, spoke quietly into it for a moment, hung up.

'If you'd like to take a seat, someone will be with you shortly.'

I went and sat on a high-backed wooden chair. Minutes passed. No one else came into the foyer and the receptionist typed quietly at her desk. There were muted sounds from distant parts of the building, but there was still no sense of location. I could have been sitting anywhere. If not for the computer, I could have been in any time as well.

The receptionist was right, though. This place wouldn't be

anything like the Uniting Church hostel. They wouldn't lightly discuss details about a paying patient. Even one who was past caring. But how had Charlie ever found his way in here? Where did he get the money from?

Finally a woman was coming down the stairs.

'Mr Verney?' she asked.

I rose and took her offered hand, shook it.

'My name is Angela,' she went on. 'Come this way.' She led me through a side door into a small room that held couches and armchairs, a television and a coffee machine, and a case of neatly arranged magazines and books. A waiting room. Angela herself was middle-aged and soberly dressed, but beyond that there was no indication of her function. Doctor, nurse, janitor. Patient, for all I knew. We arranged ourselves in the armchairs.

She said, 'You were a friend of Charles Monohan?'

'I was. You know he died recently?'

'Yes. We were sorry to hear it.'

'I'm told he was a patient here just before he died.'

'That's correct.'

'I was hoping you might be able to tell me something of his stay here.'

'What exactly was it you wanted to know?'

'Well . . . what he did while he was here, anything unusual that might have happened.'

Her manner to this point had been grave and sympathetic. It developed now to grave, sympathetic and regretful.

'As you would understand, discretion is a key concern in a hospital such as this—in any hospital, for that matter. Next of kin are entitled to certain information, but otherwise we have to respect the rights of any patient to deal with an illness in private.'

'I know he was an alcoholic, if that's what you mean. I know you have a detox ward somewhere in here.'

'Yes . . . but as we understand it, his treatment here had nothing whatever to do with his passing, so I don't really see any need to divulge privileged information. I'm sure that you were a close friend, as you say, but to me you could be anyone. Even a journalist, for instance.'

I controlled a smile.

'Have the police talked to you?'

'I can confirm that they have. And they, as we, are completely confident that our treatment of Mr Monohan was unrelated to later events. In fact, if it helps, I can tell you that in the three days he was here his treatment progressed very favourably. By his choice he discontinued treatment on the third day and left the ward. It was not on our advice, but patients are at all times free to do as they wish. Medically he was certainly well enough to leave.'

Medically he was well enough to leave. The treatment was not at fault. But then I'd never thought it was. Detox procedure was detox procedure, whether with money or without it.

'I wasn't really thinking about his medical condition,' I said. 'I was more wondering what state of mind he was in when he left. After all, he went straight from here to another facility and stole a car, then left Brisbane.'

'So the police told us.'

'Well, that's a little strange, isn't it?'

She thought for a moment. 'His was a serious condition. It affects the mind as much as the body. Non-sufferers such as ourselves can't be too judgemental about the behaviour of the afflicted.'

'Did you actually treat Charlie personally?'

'I'm more on the administrative side, but I'm always aware of how treatments are progressing.'

'You knew him? Talked to him?'

'Yes.'

'Did he say anything before he left? Did he give any indication of what he planned to do, where he was going? Or did you just let him walk out the door?'

'As I said, Mr Monohan expressed a desire to depart. Medically—both physically and mentally—there was no reason to prevent him. To say anything beyond that I'd be betraying the confidentiality that all our patients value so highly.'

'And that's all you told the police?'

'Our discussions with the police are also confidential. Rest assured, however, they were as convinced as we are that we had fulfilled our medical responsibilities to Mr Monohan, and the hospital bears no liability for his death.'

She was choosing her words very carefully, and I supposed I could see why. It was true, I could have been anyone. But still, she'd said 'discussions with the police', so there'd been more than one.

'Was this Charlie's first visit here?'

'As I've been saying, that sort of information is only for next of kin—'

'What about the fee? Can you tell me who paid his fee?'

'Why do you ask that?'

'Mr Monohan was destitute. He couldn't have afforded five minutes here, yet alone three days.'

'Well . . . financial records are, of course, as confidential as medical ones.'

'But you don't take cases who can't pay, I assume?'

'We are part of a large organisation. Other parts of that organisation perform extensive and valuable charity work. St Amand's, however, does not.'

'So did you tell the police who paid for him?'

Exasperation made her smile. 'Mr Verney, these are all questions I can't answer. All I can say is that we cooperated with the police fully. I'd suggest you talk to them if you have an interest. They already have all the information from us that could possibly be relevant. So if there's nothing else . . .'

She'd risen and was indicating the way to the door. I could think of no other questions—none that she would answer, anyway. Information flowed only in official channels. I rose from my chair.

'Once again,' she said as I passed by her, 'I really am sorry about your friend.'

And it seemed perfectly genuine. Nor was there any reason why it wouldn't be.

I paused. 'What about the other patients? How many do you have up there?'

'That varies.'

'How many did you have when Charlie was here?'

'I'm afraid I can't tell you that.'

'I don't suppose you could tell me who they were either?'

'That would be breaking the most fundamental code of all.'

'Of course. But did you tell the police?'

She only shook her head at me, lightly scolding. I nodded and headed on past her, out through the foyer and into the steaming afternoon. I walked over to my car, and then turned back to look at the hospital. The upper storeys were shaded by their deep verandahs. I could see windows, but they were all closed and only reflected the sky. The verandahs themselves were deserted. I didn't know if the actual detox ward was up there or somewhere else in the building, but still, those windows were not meant to be seen through.

I opened my car door and felt the air roll out of it, stifling.

Privacy. Necessary, no doubt, in an alcohol detox clinic that catered to the wealthy. Who knew what sort of important people frequented a place like St Amand's? Still, somehow Charlie had got in there, and he had seen whatever there was to be seen, and met whoever there was to meet. And three days later he was dead.

There had to be a meaning in that somewhere.

It was police business. Nothing to do with me.

Even if it was, the police had been there ahead of me. They weren't fools. Whatever they needed to know, they would know already. I'd done my best for Charlie. I'd buried him. I'd talked with those who'd seen him last. There was nothing left for me to do except pick up his ashes from the crematorium. Then I could leave Brisbane and go home.

I turned away from the hospital and climbed into the car, felt the vinyl seat mould itself stickily to my back. The steering wheel seared my fingers as they touched it, and suddenly I remembered.

It was Jeremy of course. That was where the elusive memory lay. St Amand's and Jeremy. The two went together. There was something he always used to say, a glass of wine trembling in his hand, his pale eyes full of hunger. Something I never really understood at the time.

What was it exactly?

Then it all came back to me. It was at the opening of our first club, when I'd sat down with Marvin and Jeremy, and, somewhere else in the room, May had been there too . . .

I put the car in gear, suddenly not sure where I was heading.

SEVENTEEN

Sir Jeremy Phelan was, amongst other things, an alcoholic.

In the end it emerged that all of us were. Drinking was the focus of our lives, the flood which swept along everything else we did. But Jeremy was the only one of us who, at the time, made the admission openly. The rest of us were still lost in that tangle of semantics and rationalisations that was the haven of all drinkers. But Jeremy answered to a sterner truth.

He was a Catholic, of course. But then again, so were we all. Nominally, at least. For a brief period during the Inquiry, the papers tried to read something into that. But Jeremy was the only one who would have actively claimed the faith. And even then, as something of a heretic.

And either way, drinking lay deeper at the core of him. That, and women. Much younger women.

He was married. He came from old pastoral stock, and his wife was the same, a grand figure of a woman who had long since left him in disgust. Everyone in government and media circles knew about both the departed wife and the young mistresses, but it was never commented upon publicly. Everyone knew, too, that his knighthood had been purchased directly with a donation to the government's party funds, but that was never commented upon either. Many knighthoods of the era were bestowed the same way.

None of it mattered. Like so many others, Jeremy was deep within the system, and a completely protected species. Government was in his blood, cabinet ministers hung on his family tree and there was barely a section of the Queensland public service that hadn't felt his touch over the decades. Which was not to say he wasn't public spirited. For one thing, he volunteered his services as a guest lecturer to the University of Queensland, speaking on law, on government, and on administration. As a reward he was given an honorary doctorate. And on the level of more private incentive, there were all those young female students to profit from his wisdom.

Maybellene, however, was something special.

She was brilliant and she hated him. He stood for everything about Queensland politics that she loathed. She harassed him during his lectures. Asked him exactly the questions that no one else in the state dared. Admittedly he could brush them all aside—he had a lifetime's experience beyond hers—but he was intrigued just the same. There was something about her. Something vulnerable behind all that intelligence and anger. Something lost. Something, Jeremy decided, that called out for guidance. His particular guidance.

Maybe it was Catholicism serving as a link. Later, Jeremy would tell me she reminded him of a wayward novitiate, using all her faith and passion to fight against her vocation rather than with it. And it was true that May was the sort of student who, in an earlier age, might have been drawn, in some troubled way, towards a nunnery. In that same earlier age, Jeremy himself might have been a bishop. A worldly bishop. Layered in red, unctuous and unholy, and an exploiter, a manipulator, of men's souls.

So it was that in the aftermath of the great electricity dispute, with Marvin triumphant, with the union routed and all their allies scattered, with Maybellene disgraced and in prison, so it was that Jeremy arrived in her cell, to tempt her in the wilderness.

His timing was perfect. May was suffering a crisis of belief. Her cause had collapsed, riddled with division and faint hearts. Her comrades had betrayed her, were less than her, were despicable. Her studies were in tatters. The university wanted nothing more to do with her. And looming ahead, at the behest of an all-powerful government she had no hope of defeating, lay jail time.

Jeremy saw all this, and knew what blandishments to whisper. He was an old man, he told her, he'd seen how the world worked. Some things would always be, and it was worse than futile to battle against human nature. Queensland itself was an example of human nature. Greed and selfishness and stupidity . . . it was all there. The thing was to understand it, to mould it, not fight against it blindly. He could show her the real way of things, he said. The side of suggestion and influence, where friends would not desert her. Where there was no weakness or doubt. Where there was a use for her brilliance, not a grave for it. Come and work with me, he said. If Queensland must be a state of mindless voters and fools, then what was the point in trying to save them all? They weren't worth it, they never would be. Come and work with me instead, and see what it's like to make what you want to happen actually happen.

And as a token of good will, with a wave of his hand, Jeremy showed her just a glimpse of what powerful friends could do for her. He set her free. All charges dropped.

In a dream May walked out of prison that same day. Her soul was in turmoil. For a week she struggled with herself. She went to one last union meeting and witnessed only anger and recriminations and division, all of it useless. She read newspapers singing Marvin's praises. She listened to people on buses, thanking heaven that the power was back on, and to hell with unions. And with that she gave up on Queensland. She took the job, and moved into Jeremy's house as his personal assistant.

All of which passed without public comment.

And none of which I knew at the time.

My first real meeting with Sir Jeremy did not take place until our new club was ready to open. The club was in the Valley, one street across from Brunswick. The syndicate, plus a few close friends, had gathered to inspect the premises one last time, and to have a few drinks before the first official patrons arrived. I was wandering around on my own. Downstairs there was a long bar, tables and chairs for dining, a dance floor and a stage—for bands, for girls, whatever we wanted. This was where we'd spent the money. On carpeting, on furnishing and on lights. It was the public face of the club. But it wasn't where we expected to make the money.

That was upstairs, in the casino. Not that it really looked like a casino, not in the sense of glittering lights and plush surroundings. There were roulette tables, and blackjack tables, and a few gaming machines flown in from the south, but it didn't seem quite real. The furniture was cheap, the windows were darkened, lighting was basic, there was no decoration on the walls, and there didn't seem to be room for more than ten or twenty people. The bar was serious, though. Fully stocked, and drinks were free, of course, to all players. And once it was filled with people and noise and smoke, it would be a casino, sure enough. But that first night it felt like a private room under someone's house. It felt like a toy.

I went back downstairs. Marvin brought Jeremy over to me, and formal introductions were made. I knew a little more about him now, and was more aware of the air that surrounded him. Aristocracy, a studied, polished mastery. Tall and gaunt and venerable, he made an interesting contrast to Marvin—all brash and loud and utterly graceless. I was puzzled, even in that first moment, about what the two might have in common. Or why, indeed, Jeremy was getting involved with any of us. He was almost three times my age.

'I read all your columns, George,' he said.

'Thanks.'

'Of course, you don't know nearly half of what really goes on in this town.'

'No? And you do?'

He smiled, and there was a glint of something not at all aristocratic in his eyes. 'Oh, yes.'

I liked him.

They moved off, and I headed for the bar, nodding at people. The crowd was building, but I knew everyone, it was only close friends and insiders in attendance. The door to the casino was wide open. Later on there would be a doorman and a stricter security policy. True, the police and all the relevant authorities had been paid and notified, but even so, there were protocols to observe. The high life wasn't available to just anyone.

I leant on the bar and stared about, nursing my drink. I had some friends of my own arriving a little later, and for the time being I was content just to watch the others. Lindsay was roaming about looking serious. This was really his night, for all that Charlie's name was over the door. Charlie himself was entertaining a group of familiar faces at one end of a table laden with complimentary wine and champagne. Laughter rolled across from him. Marvin was still leading Jeremy around the room, continuing the introductions. Music played softly . . . but later it would be much louder, I would be drunker and, upstairs, cash would start flowing over the tables. I sipped my drink, satisfied. The night was assured and it all felt as it should.

Movement caught my eye and I glanced at the stairs that led to the casino. A woman was coming down, a woman I'd never seen before. She was young, and frowning to herself, severe. I studied her in surprise. It wasn't just that she was a stranger and yet was obviously exploring the place as if fully invited, it was that she didn't look like anyone else in the room. The other women—the wives, the investors, the staff—tended towards the glamorous. There was a lot of gold and white and waves of blond hair. Tanned skin. Rings on fingers. This woman wasn't anything like that. She was pale, wearing a straight black dress and flat black shoes, and there was no jewellery. Her hair was short and dark, lightly curled above a round face free of make-up. And she looked utterly unfriendly.

I watched as she stared around the room, not noticing me. She hesitated, then went to the champagne table, the far end from Charlie and his friends. She stood there alone for a moment. Did she even know anyone here? She studied all the wine and glasses. Her arms were crossed and her fingers drummed against her side. Then abruptly she reached out and picked up a bottle of champagne. It wasn't open. She unwrapped the foil and examined the cork. There was a certain bafflement coming from her, as if champagne was an unknown thing.

Frowning again, she untangled the wires around the cork, and then started tugging at the cork itself. It didn't move. She glanced around the room, tugged at the cork again. I was on the verge of pushing myself away from the bar and going over when Charlie loomed suddenly at her side. She reared back, startled by the look of him. But Charlie smiled his smile, said something I couldn't hear, and she relaxed. She offered him the bottle. He shook his head and instructed her instead, showed her how to hold the cork and twist the base of the bottle until the cork started to give. Then she jammed her thumbs under it, pushed, and with a pop the cork sailed across the room. She laughed, and her entire appearance changed. Charlie laughed. Champagne bubbled up, and they both reached for the glasses.

I shoved away from the bar, went over to where Marvin and Jeremy were finally sitting down at a table.

'Any idea who that is with Charlie?' I asked Marvin.

Marvin glanced over and shrugged. It was Jeremy who nodded. 'She's with me,' he said. 'My personal assistant. Her name's Maybellene. Though I think she prefers May.'

Marvin considered her again, interested this time. 'Ah . . . so she's the one. Hope she was worth all the trouble.'

'Oh, she is.'

Marvin guffawed. 'I'll bet.'

Jeremy shook his head gravely. 'It's not like that at all. This is purely platonic.'

'Why? What's so special about her?'

The old man thought, watching her. I watched as well. She wasn't laughing any more. She was sipping on the champagne, listening to Charlie, and a wariness had clouded her face again. A resistance. Even to Charlie.

Jeremy sighed. 'I don't really know, but there's something in that girl. If she could just get over those scruples of hers. Would you believe she was almost a teetotaller when she came to me. I've only just got her started on red wine. I think there's a drinker in there somewhere. Drinking should help.' He looked back to us. 'Speaking of which . . .'

'Shit, of course,' said Marvin, sitting up. There was a freshly opened bottle of red wine on the table, and Marvin took it up and poured three glasses. Marvin and I drank immediately, but Jeremy merely sat for a time, silent, and studied his glass. Finally he slid out a thin hand and lifted the wine. His eyes held an intensity as he did so, and I noticed the faintest of tremors in his fingers.

His gaze rose, caught mine watching his hand.

'My apologies,' he said, his voice dry. 'But I'm an alcoholic, you understand.'

Then he raised the glass and drank. It was only a small sip, but something in his eyes seemed to die with it, and at the same time there was a minimal relaxing of his pose, a breath of . . . what was it? Abandon?

He looked at me again. 'And it's been some time.'

Marvin nodded. 'That's right, you've been away for a while, haven't you? St Amand's, was it? Supposed to be a great place.'

Jeremy nodded, considering his glass, still raised before his face. Then he gave a distant smile and looked at us. 'Here's to St Amand. Patron saint of the lost weekend.'

'Hail to the detox ward,' Marvin added, and clinked his glass with Jeremy's.

And we all drank.

EIGHTEEN

I found myself back in the motel room in New Farm, unpacking for another night.

I had an extra briefcase with me now. Old, stuffed with papers.

And an urn full of ashes.

I set it on the coffee table and stared at it for a time. Outside, the afternoon was growing late, the sky fading orange with the haze. A briefcase and an urn. A man's entire existence sat before me. All the houses and cars he'd owned, the fine furniture, the wine cellar and the restaurants and the clubs . . . all gone, and the remains no more than could be carried in one hand. Was it right that they had come to me, me of all people? Was it what he would have wanted? He had died on his way to find me, but what was he after?

What was so urgent after all these years?

I took out my wallet and dug through it until I found a card. The paper was crisp, with a name and number printed on it. I picked up the phone, dialled, and waited as it rang. I reached out and rested a finger on top of the urn.

'Detective Kelly here,' said a voice.

'It's George Verney.'

'George . . . how are you?'

'I'm fine. I cremated Charlie this morning.'

'Damn—was that this morning? I meant to go.'

'It was in the paper.'

'So who showed up? Any old friends?'

'No one.'

'No one at all? We actually need to know this, George.'

I thought of a woman, outlined for a moment in a doorway. 'Only some old alcoholics from his hostel, and one of his counsellors.'

'Marvin wasn't there, for instance? Or Maybellene?'

'No.'

He sounded disappointed. 'Loyal bunch, weren't you.'

'I was wondering if there was any news. On the investigation, I mean.'

'Our inquiries are still ongoing.'

'Am I still a suspect?'

'We're not ruling anyone out.'

But it sounded like a no.

I said, 'After the service I went over to the Uniting Church hostel. They said they'd been talking to you.'

'That's right.'

'And you know Charlie stayed in St Amand's Hospital?'

'We have that information.'

'You've been up there? You talked to the doctors?'

'Yes, we talked to them.'

'So . . . did anything in particular happen to him while he was there?'

'That's stuff I can't go into, George.'

'I just want to know if it's related to his death, that's all.'

'Sorry.'

'Well, do you know who paid his way in there? Charlie was broke.'

'We're looking into that.'

'But you must have an idea?'

He sighed. 'I've said all I can say.'

'You haven't said anything.'

'I think that's the idea.'

We hung on the line, silent.

He said, 'You gonna be in town a while, George?'

'I don't think so.'

'And where are you exactly?'

I hung up.

Official channels. They had it under control. It was their business. Police business.

115

But my head was full of memories. And I was in Brisbane for one more night.

Lightly, not wanting to think about what I was doing, I flicked open the phone book. I turned it to the letter P, ran my finger down the names. There was no entry for him, but then his number had always been unlisted.

I took a breath. I got up and went through my luggage. It was there, tucked away at the bottom of the bag, under all my clothes.

A little black notebook.

I studied the cover. It had a brittle feel, delicate. It was an item I had kept with me for ten years, never really admitting to myself that I was doing so. But nor had I ever actually thrown it away, even after I'd thrown away everything else. And when I was packing for the return to Brisbane, I'd taken it out of its cupboard and stashed it in the bag without really admitting that to myself either. How could I admit it? It had only one purpose, that little book, and it was a life I'd sworn I'd never go back to. Not even for the sake of burying Charlie.

It was an address book and it was full of phone numbers and addresses—all the contacts I'd ever made in those far-off days before the Inquiry, dozens of them, from all walks of life. It was my old self in its most compact form. And now it was time to open it again.

I sat by the phone, carefully parted the covers, and stared at the pages. It was like time travel, looking directly ten years into the past, more than ten years. My handwriting seemed somehow bigger, old-fashioned, not mine at all. But everything was still there. Names and places and numbers. Offices. Restaurants. Bars. Page after page of it. It was as if I could even smell the beer again. The long heady rush that filled my days . . .

It wasn't good. It was a minefield. Every name and location meant too much, or worse, meant nothing at all. How much did I remember and how much had I forgotten? I didn't want to know.

And then, jammed between some pages at the end, was a single, terrible piece of paper. Scribbled on it was the name of the Royal Brisbane Hospital and the number of a room. There was no date on it, but I didn't need a date. I would always know the date. The words were written on 2 December, 1989. The day I fled Brisbane. And I'd written them while on the phone to Maybellene, all her tears and horror coming at me through the line. The writing was in pencil. Jagged and hurried. I stared at it for some time, remembering only May's voice. And the thing she was telling me.

I blinked. I stuffed the paper back between the pages. Instead I found the place where, long ago, I'd written down Sir Jeremy Phelan's unlisted home number. Then I picked up the phone again, and dialled.

Would he be there?

He was in a wheelchair now, the detectives had told me.

They hadn't told me where that wheelchair was.

Would he even be in Brisbane? The last I'd heard of Jeremy, he was in Sydney, and that was over a decade ago, during the Inquiry. He was smarter than the rest of us. Older and wiser. He decamped as soon as the Inquiry began, and remained in Sydney for the duration. And he survived it all unscathed, without charge or prosecution. Perhaps he always would have, even if he'd stayed in Queensland. He wasn't like the rest us; he was establishment. Old Brisbane. Doubly a protected species. Certainly his name was mentioned in connection with our syndicate, but only remotely, and as far as I knew no attempt was ever made to extradite him out of New South Wales. Anyway, they already had Marvin and Charlie, two of the ringleaders, and the third, Lindsay, had disappeared from the country, so maybe enough was enough. Those of Jeremy's senior years and stature could be forgiven, it seemed. As it always was, with the gentry.

I'd never heard of him since. In truth he could be anywhere. Still in Sydney, or another city, or locked away in a nursing home somewhere. He'd be over eighty now, and his lifestyle had hardly earned him a healthy old age. On the other hand, his house in Brisbane had always been the ancestral home, and I doubted he would simply have sold it. So perhaps whoever lived there now might know where he was.

I waited, my hand tight around the receiver.

The phone rang and rang.

And clicked up.

'Hello?'

It was a female voice. I explained that I was after someone who had once lived at this number, long ago, his name was Jeremy . . .

'Oh,' she answered, 'this is still the right number. I'm Jeremy's personal assistant. Whom shall I say is calling?'

I was speechless for a moment. I was fifteen years in the past. As if time had stood still, and Maybellene was living with him again.

'George,' I said faintly. 'Tell him it's George Verney. I'm a friend from years ago.'

'Just a moment.'

I waited. I looked at the little black book. May's phone number was written in there. Would her number still be the right one too? But no, that had been the number for the house Charlie and she owned together. That was gone. Eventually she'd moved into a flat on her own somewhere. I flicked to the page. There didn't seem to be a number for it, not even an address, and I couldn't remember why.

The new Maybellene was back.

'Jeremy can't come to the phone, but he says come on over tonight and he'll open a bottle of wine.'

'Um . . . I'll come, but I don't drink any more.'

'That's okay. Neither does he. You know where we live?'

'I know.' And then I asked, just to be sure, 'And your name is?'

'Louise.'

And time moved on again.

NINETEEN

Jeremy lived near West End. In my time the area had been something of a ghetto for a mixture of communities. Aboriginal, for one. Then European migrants, Greek and Italian for the most part, and later Asian, and finally also a cheap quarter for university students. However, there had always been a wealthier section, on the high ground that overlooked the river—a line of grander homes that had never housed migrants or students. Not quite mansions, perhaps, but they were still impressive, with deeply shaded verandahs and leafy gardens. If they had a certain air of decay about them, all the more appropriate, for most of their residents were in decay as well. Old widows, old families, old money from the very founding of the state. True influence might have passed them by, but the memories lingered.

It had never been my part of town, West End, but I could still note how it had changed. The main street had once been a crowded strip of delicatessens and tailors and fruit stalls, busy with people from a variety of races. It was a place apart, the one section of the city that had seemed to be genuinely alive, even in the old days. Indeed, if there was a centre of resistance to the government and its policies back then, West End was it. There had been collectives and legal centres, radical bookshops and protest groups. And in small rooms above the shopfronts, the Italians had run their own casinos—card games for the most part, but they were strictly small scale and no part of the system. The Inquiry had safely passed them by, if it knew about them at all. And yet now, ten years later, it didn't look as if any of them would still be there. As in New Farm, a middle-class revolution had swept through the suburb, scattering cafes and bars and a bland sense of space. The new Brisbane marched on. And West End, without the old enemy to fight, perhaps, seemed to have dwindled.

I drove through, up along the ridge towards Highgate Hill, to Jeremy's house. It was positioned high on the southern slope, hidden behind a tall fence that was choked by an overgrown hedge, exactly as I remembered. It was early evening when I pulled up outside, heat still hanging in the air. I sat for a moment in my car experiencing, once again, a shift in time. Charlie and I had arrived there at similar times on evenings such as this, bottles of wine under our arms, for dinner with Jeremy and Maybellene. With May, really. We were both courting her—at least, I thought we both were, but Charlie was already the winner, if I'd had the eyes to see it.

I got out, pushed open the gate and went in.

Nothing had changed at all. The yard was shaded by the same ancient Moreton Bay figs, the ground was still thick with rotting leaves that muffled sound. The house was there, too, over a century old, and wrapped in creepers. Beyond it the ground dropped away into a gully, all wild with weeds and vines, and though there was a view to be had southwards, Jeremy's back verandah was enclosed, and I'd never known him to look out the windows. Still, this was the house, unaltered, where, at the age of thirty, I'd finally fallen in love. And the memory of May was everywhere.

I rang the bell.

In the old days that was enough. Jeremy would yell from somewhere deep inside to come on through, and usually the door was off the latch. But there was no yell this time, and the door appeared to be locked. I noticed that the windows were barred, something else which was new. And when the door finally did open, the woman standing there wasn't Maybellene, and for all that I'd half expected she might, this woman looked nothing like her.

'You must be George,' she said. 'I'm Louise. Come in.'

But then again, there was something about her voice. And though physically so different, her hair red rather than May's black, and a sharp freckled face compared to May's softer features, there was still something in her that took me back. An air of reserve. Or of sternness.

I followed her inside, and we threaded our way through the artefacts.

For Jeremy, as befitted his class, was a collector, and it was in collecting that he most expressed his missed vocation for the priesthood. In his older years he had haunted church demolitions and renovations and auctions, salvaging religious pieces. Altar pieces, crucifixes, statues—the rooms of his house were crammed with them. There were also antique copies of the Bible, folios, Latin manuscripts, spread out in display cases. And on the walls were Madonnas and icons and stations of the cross. All objects of worship, and all long rejected by a more practical Church in its contemporary age. The iconography of a more devout time. The direct representation in pagan stone, here on earth, of the godhead.

He also had another collection, not generally on display. It was nineteenth-century pornography, sheet after sheet of faded sepia images, obscenities from a century ago. Explicit perhaps, but somehow made chaste by the years, by the lack of colour, by the absence of movement. Jeremy considered that the one collection reflected the other. That if you looked at the faces of the men and women arranged in their poses, they had expressions every bit as detached and otherworldly as the faces of the painted saints and Madonnas. Or the marble figures of Christ, racked upon the cross . . . every bit as sacrificial and cold as the naked bodies wracked upon each other. And the eyes of all—men and women fucking, or saints and saviours praying—always raised in a distant ecstasy to Heaven. The sense of the divine was the key, it seemed. It was the reason Jeremy dismissed both modern pornography and the modern Church. One dwelt inanely on the details of the genitalia, the other dwelt pointlessly on the details of the day-to-day physical world. They both lacked abstraction, and transcendence.

Transcendence . . . this from a man who haunted casinos and brothels, and who wallowed in the fleshiest of pursuits. I'd never understood it, or him. And now the rooms looked unused, like a museum. Dim lamps shone in the corners, and the blinds on the windows were down. And though it might have been a warm evening outside, inside the air seemed to hold no temperature at all.

We reached the dining room.

'George.'

And it was with Jeremy himself that time had most visibly moved on. Hunched in his wheelchair, he was a distilled version of his old self—leaner, bonier, more shrunken. And when he reached forward, his hand outstretched, I saw there were bruises on his arms, and the shape of what appeared to be bandages on his shoulder, under the shirt. And on the shirt itself, leaking through, a spot of blood the size of a ten-cent piece.

'Jeremy,' I said, and shook his hand, the weight of it no more than a sheet of paper.

He smiled the old half smile at me, ghostly on a face so thin. 'You look younger, George. You even look healthier.'

'You look like you're dying.'

'I am.'

We let go each other's hand. His voice had dwindled from its old clear smoothness; now it had a tone of effort about it, breathless.

He gestured. 'You've met Louise.'

'Yes.'

'Well sit down then. Dinner won't be long.'

The table was spread with lace and decorated with silver, and there were three places set—Jeremy's at the head, and one on either side of him. A bottle of white wine, already open, sat there between us. There was also a carafe of water.

'Wine?' Jeremy inquired.

'I don't drink any more.'

His head dipped. 'So I heard. Oh well, there's water for us. Louise?'

Louise nodded and took up the carafe. There was only one wine glass on the table, and just the two water tumblers. Louise poured our water, then lifted the wine and filled the wine glass. Without a word she raised it briefly in toast to Jeremy and myself, then put it to her lips.

Jeremy was staring at her, fondly, an old expression, the way he'd looked at another personal assistant once, when she was learning to drink.

'Well,' he said, turning his faded eyes to mine. 'So another one has found his way home.'

'I'm not back for good. And this isn't home.'

He smiled. 'That's what they all say.'

'Who's they?'

'Oh . . . others.' He waved the thought away. 'How have you been, George?'

'Do you know Charlie's dead?'

'Yes, I know. The police were here.'

'You weren't at his funeral.'

He glanced down at his chair. 'I don't leave the house these days. Did you see the bars on the windows? People thieve around here now. I may as well have gone to prison like everyone else.'

There was a querulous edge in his voice, self-pity, and that wasn't like the old Jeremy.

'Did anyone else attend?' he asked.

'No one.'

'No one at all?'

'Maybe . . . I thought maybe I saw May. I don't know.'

'Ah . . .' He addressed Louise. 'Maybellene was one of your predecessors. A long time ago. But then I lost her to a friend of George's here. To Charlie, in fact. And then others.' He looked back to me. 'No. I don't think it would have been May.'

'Have you seen her?'

'Have you?'

'No.'

'But you want to, of course.' He shook his head. 'May is a lost soul, George. I couldn't save her. Neither could Charlie. Or you. She won't be back.'

'Where did she go?'

But he sounded forlorn. 'I don't want to talk about May . . .'

'What about Charlie? Did you ever see him after he got out?'

'No . . . I heard he came back to Brisbane, but he never

contacted me.' He coughed faintly, a wet sound in his throat. 'But I knew you'd be calling around. Once I saw that funeral notice. I told Louise you would, didn't I, Louise?'

She nodded, and drank from her glass, a long steady swallow. Something flickered in me at the sight, and was gone.

'How long did you stay down in Sydney, Jeremy?'

Yellow stubs of teeth gleamed in his smile. 'Not as long as I meant to. I was back here even before the trials were over. Not even a year.'

'You didn't have any trouble?'

'The police didn't care. No one did. The new government would hardly want my services, not them, so what danger was I? Who was I going to influence or corrupt? No . . . it was all finished. So they let me come home.'

I looked around at his house, at the art on the walls, still the same pictures in the same places that I remembered from years before. I hadn't come home, and neither had Jeremy. This house was the past. A refuge in history.

'Time for the soup,' he declared.

Louise drained her glass, and rose from the table.

I observed her while we ate. She said nothing, only watched and listened, but by the time the main course arrived she had almost finished the bottle of wine. Wafts of the alcohol, sweet and cloying, drifted over the meal. When she leaned across to slice Jeremy's meat for him, I could see him drawing in breaths of her. Was that how it was then? Had he taught her, too, as he had taught her predecessor? She didn't appear at all drunk. A certain languidness had suffused her movements and there was a liquid wideness to her eyes, but that was all. The minutiae of alcohol. Only an ex-drinker would even notice them. A thirst stirred in me, the old thirst, and it wasn't for water. Or simply for alcohol either. Maybellene lingered in the air like the wine.

We talked meanwhile, Jeremy and I, but about very little. Long sentences seemed to exhaust him. If I'd taken him outside, into the wind and sun, he would have crumbled to dust. He had not touched his glass of water, nor eaten more than a mouthful or two of his finely mashed food. And from time to time his eyes would cloud over and his attention wander, as if he was battling with sleep. Or with pain.

He asked me about Highwood, and about what I'd been doing up there. The idea of the *Highwood Herald* seemed to amuse him. The old condescension was still there. The implication that he still knew things I didn't know, and never would. Only his health had betrayed him. Looking at him now it was hard to imagine him in the clubs and at the bars, gliding about, tall and urbane and convinced of his inner dignity, even when surrounded by vulgarity. I remembered him scattering a table of blackjack players once, like a raging Jesus at the temple, as if they were an insult to him. I couldn't remember what it was about. Only that, from time to time, he would look around and seem to hate what he saw.

'Why did you bother with us, back then?' I asked. 'You didn't need the money.'

'Neither did you.'

'Maybe not . . . but it was all new to me, all those people we met, the things we did, so of course I fell for it. But you already had all that. Why bother with us?'

The question didn't seem important to him. 'Why does a king fuck his kitchen maid? Why does a rich man hire a ten-dollar prostitute? It's human nature, George.'

'To do what?'

'I don't know . . . to wallow. To be lower than you need to be. To *choose* to be lower. Otherwise, how can you be sure you're superior? Inferior people, George, don't have the choice.'

He was smiling again.

'And that's all it was?' I asked.

'To tell the truth, I don't remember. I was drunk most of the time.'

The smile faded, a vagueness creeping into his eyes.

None of this was to the point.

I had yet to ask him the thing I'd come to ask.

I said, 'Just before he died, Charlie spent three days at St Amand's detox ward.'

He arched an eyebrow. 'The old alma mater? My my . . .'

'I know. That's why I'm here. I thought maybe you were the one who got him in there.'

'No. Why would I do that?'

'I don't know . . . it's just that you were such a regular patient.'

'Twice a year, every year. They kept me alive, those people.'

'Have you been there recently?'

He breathed the barest suggestion of a laugh. 'I don't need detox any more. Even one drink would kill me now.'

'When was the last time you went?'

'Years ago.' His eyes lit for a moment. 'Do you know why I really went to Sydney?'

'To avoid arrest?'

'I went there to kill myself.'

I blinked at him. 'Why to Sydney?'

'It's a place to die, that's why. It's a toilet of a city. They would have taken my body and thrown it in the gutter and that would have been that. I didn't want a state funeral, George.'

'But you didn't kill yourself.'

'I almost did.' He nodded at the glass in Louise's hand. 'I was going to drink myself to death. Not over years, I was going to do it in months.'

'Why? Because of the Inquiry?'

And there had, after all, been suicides.

Jeremy was disgusted. 'The Inquiry didn't matter. Or it only mattered because it meant everything was finished with, everything was shut down. No . . . I was sick to death of myself, George, sick to death of me. That's all.'

He almost sounded drunk, and I wondered if he was taking something. Painkillers, perhaps, for whatever was wrong with him.

'So what happened?' I asked.

'I had a room, in a very nice hotel. I had them install a full bar for me there, and restock it every day. I called in women even though I couldn't do much with them.' Another glance at Louise. 'It was better than drinking alone. And it seemed to be working. I grew ill, then very ill. The hotel was worried. They wanted to call in a doctor. You can understand I hardly wanted one. But of course, they didn't want a dead public figure on their hands, not with all that wine and so many women around. That sort of thing happens too often as it is.' He started to laugh, and that descended into a cough which racked his entire body.

Louise paused, glass halfway to her lips, and watched him carefully.

The spasm passed. Was the spot of blood on Jeremy's shirt larger now? His eyes were shining with tears. 'It got awkward. I was soiling myself, vomiting blood, the room was an awful mess. Finally they asked me to leave. And the truth was, I was in too much pain to argue. Too much pain to even hold a single drink down. My plan was falling apart. You have to have some strength to kill yourself with alcohol and, as it turned out, I was too weak.'

He was ignoring both Louise and me now, staring straight ahead down the table to where, in a large golden frame, Satan tempted Jesus in the desert. It was his favourite painting. His theme on the whole world, and the role he had always played.

'Still, I might have made it. But then I had a visitor. An unpleasant visitor. I thought Marvin had sent him at the time, just for cruelty's sake. But Marvin didn't send him. Marvin had too many troubles of his own . . .'

'You're not talking about Lindsay, are you?'

'Lindsay? I thought he went overseas? No, it was no one you know.'

'I knew Marvin's friends.'

'Not all of them, you didn't. And not this one. He wasn't one of us, George. He was from altogether lower stock. It was bad for him to see me like that, a silly old man pissing himself on the floor. He laughed at me. He wanted to watch me die. I couldn't have that. Not from him.'

And there was an anger rising in his voice, a trace of the old pride.

'Jeremy,' I said, worried, 'I don't know who you are talking about.'

'It doesn't matter.' He thought some more, shook his head. 'I sent the women away, sent away the alcohol, and came home. I went straight to St Amand's. They fixed me up, as much as they could anyway, but that was it. That was the last time I went there. That's what you asked, wasn't it?'

'You never needed to go back?'

'I never drank again. What was the point if I couldn't go through with it? Why carry a gun if you don't have the nerve to use it? It's ironic, though. After all these years, it's not even the drinking that's killing me.'

'What is?' I asked.

'Leukaemia.'

I stared. I'd assumed his liver was the problem, that the damage done over his lifetime was too great to be recovered. But cancer of the bone marrow? What did that have to do with Jeremy, with his decades of sin and indulgence?

He was grinning at me. 'You remember what we used to say?'

And I did. We'd talked about it all the time, deep in our drinking. The way death would come, and the power that drinking gave us over death, that any addiction gave its victim. For when death came, every alcoholic and addict knew at least one precious thing—it would come in the form of the beloved. Drinkers would die by their livers, smokers by their lungs, and junkies, perhaps, by their very blood. But that was where the power lay. You chose your own end.

'If only it was that simple, George.'

'I'm sorry,' I said.

'It's all right. It'll be another funeral for you to attend.'

He turned to Louise, who had finished the wine.

'Time for the red?' he asked.

TWENTY

Alcohol . . .

How much was it to blame, in the end, for the mess my life became?

And how could I lay blame anyway, when it was my choice if I drank at all?

It was an old mystery. I was, for instance, finally, a failure as a journalist—but did I fail because of the drinking, or drink because of the failure? Or were the two always fused, failure and alcohol, right from the start? Did the potential alcoholic, even in his youth, peer fearfully into the future and, not liking anything that he saw there, reach for the bottle?

No one knew. It was true, I had never visited a detox ward in my life before, but I knew plenty about the treatment of alcoholism. I'd read about the medical theories and treatment regimes, I'd studied them, furtively, all throughout that long first year in Highwood. There were drugs to cope with the convulsions of detoxification, therapies to learn, behaviour patterns to avoid, self-help groups to join, but the root problem remained ephemeral. Was it a disease or not a disease? Was there a cure or was there no cure? Was there a genetic predisposition? Was it a learned response? Was it a cultural malaise? The answers were unlimited and contradictory. No one knew for sure.

Was I even an alcoholic?

Ah . . . that was the question. Asked in a million hearts on a thousand agonised mornings, right around the world. And always in mine.

If you answer yes to one or more of these questions, then you may have a problem.

They always started like that. The self-help books, the pamphlets, the warning notices. Always questions. In the dry wasteland of sobriety, they baked like rocks under the sun, and one by one, over the years, I'd turned them over and studied them bleakly, a prophet maddened by thirst, looking for signs.

Question—Did you take to drinking from an early age?
Answer—Yes.

It started at fifteen. It was a bottle of Bundaberg rum one summer night, with friends from school, in someone's back yard. I didn't enjoy it at all, I gagged on the taste of it, was deathly sick afterwards, nor did I drink again for several months. Indeed, I never went back to rum. But there was a hint of something in there before the sickness hit, a golden promise opening in my mind. The next time I stuck with beer, and from there I didn't look back. The promise blossomed. It was as if the pores of my brain were opening in a vast relief, coming truly alive for the first time. Within months my tolerance soared and I was sampling vodka, gin, bourbon, tequila . . . anything, as long as the rush was there. I would never know what it was exactly. But in an otherwise unremarkable youth, drinking was my chance to shine. It was my special field of achievement. I could drink more than most of my acquaintances, and drink longer, and apparently suffer less the next day. I wasn't the hardest drinker by any means, but I was harder than most. And as a teenage male who had no great ability at sport or academic pursuits, that was something to savour. I was good at it, I received praise from my peers, and as sad as it would seem to me later, I'd discovered a talent and I was on my way.

Question—Does the world seem better when you drink?
Answer—Yes.

Oh yes . . . especially in those early years. With that first flush of drunkenness, a whole new vista of possibilities would open, as if the night could go anywhere, as if all the normal rules were in abeyance. It was exciting, full of the unknown. Which was the tragedy of alcohol. After all, the possibilities were always there, drunk or not, and any night could go anywhere, drunk or not. But somehow I could never see that.

Some people's minds just didn't flow when they were sober—it was only alcohol that could fire them up, liberate them. It was like that for me, and for the people I drank with. Sober we bored ourselves, drunk we were inspired, lifted to another realm that was hazy with truth and beauty. It didn't matter that usually the nights went nowhere and involved nothing more than getting drunker and drunker and finally passing out. The feeling was enough. Escape. And transcendence. Jeremy wasn't the only one who understood the word . . .

Question—Do you drink more than forty standard drinks a week? (Or fifty drinks, or sixty, or four a day, or six a day, or whatever the current threshold was thought to be.)

Answer—Yes.

Yes of course, of course, but who cared? It was never how much you drank, it was how long, and in what sort of style. Three hours, six hours, all night, two days straight. And who was still standing with you after all that time. They were your real friends. The ones who never went home, the ones who shared the dream, the passion to never let a session die. A person who counted their drinks, who exercised moderation, who thought about the morning after, they were lesser beings. They were to be avoided.

Question—Do you organise your day around drinking?

Answer—Yes.

I organised my whole life around drinking. Why else pick journalism as a career? Not that I was actually drunk when I chose it, but by the time I was seventeen, I knew what sort of life I wanted. Something hard-bitten and lived fast, with a drink always at hand—that's what I *thought* journalism would be like. And in a way I wasn't completely wrong. Whatever else might be said about life in the press, there was always someone to have a drink with. Always. Other reporters, the editing staff, political contacts, business contacts, entertainment contacts, they all drank. Pubs appeared like magic next to newspaper offices; they had cheap lunches, cheap dinners, happy hours set just as the paper was put down and the day's work was done. No doubt it was different now, but in the old days the whole newspaper world was high on alcohol fumes. No one seemed to be married, not happily anyway, and no one seemed to want to go home, and there was always some issue to discuss, something to mutter over, someone to hate and abuse—and there was always a bar nearby, or our own restaurants, and then finally the clubs . . .

Question—Do you need alcohol to get through the day?
Answer—Yes.

Though I didn't need it to get out of bed, at least. Then again, I was seldom up before ten or eleven in the morning, and during lunch I might have a drink or two, and throughout the afternoon, if the occasion demanded, I would slip out for a beer. It was all part of the workday, but still, I was seldom drunk before nightfall. The night was where I did my drinking, the night was for the real conversations, the real friends, for Charlie and Maybellene and all the others, and I would no more spend time with them sober than I would try to write my columns without a computer terminal. It would have been possible, perhaps, but the very idea . . .

Question—Does alcohol ever adversely affect your ability to work?
Answer—Yes.

But then nor could I have worked without it, and besides, I was still a success, wasn't I? I had a photo next to my name, I was someone. I received fan mail in the letters to the editor. I was invited to theatre first nights, movie premieres, private boxes at the races. I dined with actors and government ministers and TV executives. It was all a glittering drunken haze. Failure? Failure was a dark shadow at the back of my mind, somewhere I never slowed down enough to examine.

Question—Do you ever wish you could stop drinking?
Answer—Yes.

At least sometimes I did, as the years went by and I found myself suffering through deepening hangovers that never quite seemed to clear. Or when I noticed that the words did not come as fluidly as they once had, that there always seemed to be a fog in my mind, and that I was fatter, and my heart would thump wildly merely from walking up a flight of stairs. Occasionally on those hungover mornings I would lie in bed and wonder about my life and where it was headed, and the prospect would not be all that pleasing. But it was only a nagging worry, and it would pass by the time I'd had a hot shower and the first coffee of the day. And true, sometimes I'd look back at my last ten or fifteen articles and realise that every single one of them was droll and wry and utterly, utterly trivial, and a dim suspicion would form that the serious business of the newspaper was going on without me—but that too passed, if not with the shower and coffee, then with the first drink at lunch.

Question—Do you avoid people who do not drink?
Answer—Yes.

Well, not exactly avoid them, perhaps, but nor did I seek them out. At the paper, for instance, I was vaguely aware that some people did not drink, didn't automatically go from the office to the nearest pub, but then who were they? I didn't know and didn't care. Some of them were my fellow journalists, but I hardly even read the rest of the paper, barely knew what they wrote. True, sometimes a serious political story would be broken by the *Daily Times*, and once in particular I was blearily surprised to notice that an investigative journalist on staff had actually won an award for a story covering some scandal. But he was no one I knew. He was thin and dry and dull. I patted him on the back and offered him a drink and then forgot about him. Scandals came and went every day, this was Queensland after all. Besides, I already knew everyone there was to know. I drank with them all the time, didn't I? I had all the friends I needed.

Question—Does alcohol adversely affect your sexual activity?
Answer—Yes.

But if erections were harder to come by when I was dead drunk, it was no surprise to anyone. And there was still plenty of sex. Alcohol provided the bodies, for all that it hampered the actual event. I had drinking partners everywhere, and my sexual partners were my female drinking partners with their clothes off. The sex was blurred admittedly, as were the relationships themselves, starting and ending from one drinking session to the next. But so what? Later there were the nights at the brothels, the private parties where who it was didn't matter any more, it was just bodies and noise and rolling around, skin against skin. And then finally, when Maybellene and I gave in to ourselves, alcohol and love curled together into such a dark ecstatic pleasure that we barely needed sex at all, so it didn't matter that we were hardly ever capable.

Question—Do you constantly seek out other heavy drinkers?
Answer—Yes.

Haven't I already said? It was what brought us all together, and what held us together. Money, greed, ambition, power—those things floated around as well, for Marvin and Lindsay in particular, but still, that first step into the underworld was in search of a licence to serve alcohol, and alcohol would always remain the focus, even when prostitution and gambling came along on the side. First and foremost we did all those things because *we* wanted to drink. *We* wanted a place that never closed, where we could always go at any time of night, so that the night never needed to end. If to achieve that we had to break laws and own the clubs ourselves, it didn't seem too high a price to pay. At the time, it didn't seem to be any price at all.

Question—Has alcohol destroyed any of your close relationships?
Answer—Yes.

But surely that was at the end, only at the end, when the world was falling apart anyway. It wasn't just the drinking, it was the Inquiry, the trials, the convictions, it was Charlie finding out about Maybellene and me, it was Charlie taking up a gun and . . .

Question—Do you lie to yourself about the effects of your drinking?

All right, all right, enough.

They never ended, the questions.

But you could answer them all, as honestly as possible, and still . . . was I an alcoholic? Should I have stood up and declared, as the AA faithful did, that I had no power over drink? That drink, indeed, had complete power over me?

The odd thing was that on all the questionnaires there was the one query to which I could always answer no. Maybe it was that question alone that kept the illusion intact. That convinced me that even if there was a problem, it wasn't out of control, I could deal with it. The question was 'Have you ever sought medical help because of your drinking?'

Never.

Even when I finally quit drinking, I did it on my own. I attended no AA meetings, visited no detox wards, underwent no therapy.

Which raised yet another question. Was it possible for an alcoholic to quit drinking with no outside help at all? Indeed, did the fact that I quit drinking with no help mean that I was never really an alcoholic in the first place? What was the definition?

It could circle in on itself infinitely.

But at the time, even in my most wretched moments, I could never say those four simple words.

And even after ten years of sobriety, when I knew I would never drink again, I still couldn't say them.

So the question remained.

TWENTY-ONE

At Jeremy's dinner table, Louise was opening her third bottle.

An hour had passed since the meal, and Jeremy himself was increasingly drifting away. The man I knew appeared only for moments, then faded again, replaced by the invalid.

He was watching Louise, his breathing laboured.

I watched her, too, as she worked on the cork. This bottle, like the others, had come from a cellar beneath the house. I recognised the label and the dust that encased it, and I knew what it was worth. No one spoke as she filled the glass and then downed it smoothly. The wine made dark stains on her teeth, and the room was filled with the smell of earth.

It was perverse, but I was fascinated by her. She didn't drink like other people I'd seen since I became sober. Not like Emily, or anyone else in Highwood. Maybe it was closer to what I was myself once. The wondering came even though I didn't want it . . . what was the alcohol doing in her veins, in her mind? I felt echoes of it, memories. Rings of pleasure, expanding and expanding. My mouth was dry. What was going on here anyway? For whom was she drinking? Jeremy? It was his wine, and it seemed to be for his pleasure rather than hers. Replacing his withered system with one young and fresh and flung open to the wine and all it could do. But it couldn't only be that, surely, not just prostitution in some other form. The way she took the liquid in . . . there had to be a link there of her own. Maybe that was the art of Jeremy and his women. Finding the ones in which the flaw already lay, and then merely providing them with the means.

I didn't know. A rich man might indeed buy a ten-dollar whore.

But did he convince himself that she enjoyed it too?

Louise's glance lingered on me a moment, moved away.

It was getting late. Jeremy seemed exhausted. And yet St Amand's was still as elusive to me as ever. I needed to know more.

I said, 'I went up there, you know, to the detox ward, but they wouldn't talk to me.'

And Jeremy's head inched around. 'Of course they wouldn't.'

'You've been there, though. I was wondering what it's like inside.'

'Little rooms, George, lots of little rooms.'

'But what about the treatment? What would Charlie have gone through?'

He sighed, mustered strength from somewhere. 'Don't get any strange ideas, George. A detox ward is a detox ward. St Amand's is very comfortable, but they don't do anything unusual there. Charlie was electrocuted. The hospital had nothing to do with that.'

'I know, but it can't just be coincidence. Something happened in there.'

'You won't ever find out. Confidentiality is the whole point about a place like St Amand's. That's what you're paying all the money for.'

'Isn't any doctor the same?'

He was displeased. 'How much would the average doctor have to tell? Routine diseases, that's all. That's not what St Amand's is about.'

'Alcoholism is routine.'

'The patients aren't. Not at St Amand's. At St Amand's the Queen herself could be having her stomach pumped, and no one would breathe a word.'

'So they're discreet . . .'

'No, George. You say it like it's nothing. But think about what discretion means as a therapeutic tool. Why do you think we Catholics are so ready to confess all our deep and dark sins to total strangers in a booth? Because we like the priest? No . . .'

He dug laboriously in a pocket, pulled forth a set of rosary beads. They might have been white once but were yellow now. Jeremy held them out to me like they were an explanation. His hands shook, and Christ trembled on the cross.

He said, 'It's because the priest can never tell anyone. You could have killed his own mother, but if you tell him about it in the confessional, not only will he not tell anyone else, he will deny to himself that even *he* knows. Because when you confess you're not really talking to a person at all, you're talking directly to God. The priest is only a conduit, a human face on the divine.'

His hands sank to the table, and his fingers slid over the beads.

'They have a marvellous mental agility, priests. That's what I mean by discretion. Not just a promise to withhold private information, but a spiritual imperative that makes it impossible to do otherwise. It's a liberating thing, when you know you have that at your disposal. You can say anything. You can do anything. You can confront the truth. That's what St Amand's offers.'

He was lost in the beads. Louise drained another glass. I noticed her fingernails were painted, just the lightest shade of red, barely above skin tone. Her lips as well. Her eyes met mine again. I was almost intoxicated by the atmosphere of the room, with the memory of drinking, like phantom pain. I picked up my own glass of water and drank, tasting nothing.

Jeremy looked up from the beads. Sweat had broken out on his face. 'Have you ever been through alcohol withdrawal?'

I thought of night and rain and water dripping from trees.

'Not in a detox ward,' I answered.

Jeremy reached out and pulled the bottle of red wine to him. He peered at the label, or beyond it, into the depths of the wine itself.

'It's a terrible thing. Your body is collapsing without the drug. Your mind is collapsing as well. And sometimes, if it's especially bad, everything comes out. It can be like a religious conversion, a revelation, a Road to Damascus. Every weakness, every crime, every shame, big or small—they're all laid in front of you, and they get more unbearable with every passing hour. All the cruel and vicious things you've done in your drunkenness, it's a version of hell. It's either go back to the drink, or go mad, or deal with it somehow. The doctors have drugs, they can sedate you, they can stop the physical convulsions, the hallucinations, and later they'll start the counselling, but for those first few days, sometimes it's just you, all alone . . .'

A tremor passed through Louise, and her throat worked momentarily. Her eyes were still wide and shining, but they were focused on nothing. Jeremy tilted the bottle and refilled her glass. The shaking in his hands sent wine spilling onto the white cloth.

Jeremy looked at me. 'When all *that* is happening, if you have secrets worth the telling—and believe me, the patients in St Amand's have those sorts of secrets—then you want people around you who hear but do not hear, who see but do not see, who will act but who will never remember or repeat. You want a confessional, George. You want a priest. That's what you get at St Amand's. And that's what you pay for.'

My head was full of wine. I could feel it pulsing in my veins as Louise raised her glass yet again and drank.

I said, 'And what sort of secrets were you keeping when you went there?'

But Jeremy shook his head, sank back into the chair. 'You're a friend, George, but you're not my confessor, or my doctor. It's none of your business.'

I needed to move, to breathe a lighter air. I rose, headed for the bathroom. Once there I dashed cold water on my skin, stared at myself in the mirror. It was an old face, tired, flushed with heat. But the eyes were clear. I was not drunk, had not touched alcohol in ten years. I never would again.

I went back out. Louise was standing at Jeremy's side, her hands on his shoulders, as if massaging them. His head was sunk again, old and shivering. She moved back to her seat as I resumed mine, and as she lowered herself she swayed for a second, reached out a steadying hand. So smooth it was hardly noticeable at all. She had drunk almost three bottles, and it hadn't even been three hours. Jeremy leered at me sidelong, bent over, an evil dwarf.

'Better?' he asked.

'What sort of people might Charlie have met while he was in St Amand's?'

'So that's what you're thinking . . . it was someone he met in there.'

'He was alone and penniless and yet he spent three days in that ward, at whose expense we don't even know. On the third day he suddenly checked out before his treatment was complete, immediately stole a car and drove to Highwood, where he was killed that night. What am I supposed to think?'

'And why do you want to know?'

'He was my friend.'

'Oh? I heard that bullet gave him brain damage. I heard he was a derelict, George. Did you take him in? Did you and May say you were sorry for everything?'

'He wouldn't talk to me.'

'A guilty conscience is a bad motivation. The worst.'

'It was your place, Jeremy. You knew everyone else who was in there. All the regulars. Was there anyone who knew Charlie? Anyone from the old days? Anyone who might . . . I don't know . . . not have wanted to see Charlie again?'

He shook his head, stubborn.

'Who else went there, Jeremy?'

His voice was distant. 'Kindred spirits.'

'Like who?'

'I can't say. One of the things you sign upon entering the ward is a contract that you will never discuss anything that you see or hear. That's the deal, George. That's why it works.'

'But you weren't like that. You told everyone you were an alcoholic. You didn't even keep your visits secret. So what would it matter?'

'It was different then. I told everyone because I was ashamed.'

'Of being an alcoholic?'

'No,' and it was a whisper. 'Ashamed of wanting a cure.'

He was gazing longingly at Louise. She had finished the third bottle now, and was gazing back. I might not have been in the room. Something flamed in their eyes.

'Kiss me,' said Jeremy.

She rose and, swaying ever so slightly, leaned over him and gently touched her mouth to his. Jeremy sighed and closed his eyes while she hovered there, watching him, a fiery angel. I thought of the three bottles of wine swirling in her blood. I thought of Emily, the taste of alcohol faint on her lips. I thought of Maybellene, of drinking whole mouthfuls from her,

her hair lightly touching my face. Then Louise turned her face away, took one aimless step, and vomited onto the floor.

We watched. It was a simple cough at first, a mouthful of wine, then her knees gave way and she was hunched on the floor, retching repeatedly. The smell of it flooded the room, but still, she was quiet about it, almost refined. When it was finished she stood for a moment, considering us both. Sweat sheened her face and her eyes shone as if with great joy or relief. Then she was gone.

'All right,' Jeremy breathed. 'If you have to know . . .'

I hardly remembered. 'What?'

'I know who paid for Charlie.'

'How can you know that?'

'Think, George. It could only be one person. He came here. Before you. Only a few months ago. He's not well. He's sick, George. And deluded. He thinks he suffered the most, but he doesn't know what the word means. He came and saw me and we talked about everything. You never knew it, no one did, but St Amand's was his escape as well. It still is, and he still keeps it secret. He wasn't like me. He never told anyone.'

'Who?'

'It was sad. He was always ashamed of the wrong things. And he was ashamed, too, about Charlie. He wanted to find him. That's why he came here. He thought I might know where Charlie was. He thought he could help. He was like you, George. He was leaving it far, far too late.'

'Who are you talking about?'

From the bathroom came the sounds of more vomiting. It didn't sound dignified now. It sounded painful and hard, broken by gasps for breath.

Jeremy tilted his head to the sound. He smiled. 'It was good to see you again, George. Thank you for coming. But I think you should go now.'

'Who?' I demanded.

The smile was serene, a death mask. 'Marvin, of course. Who else?'

TWENTY-TWO

The Marvellous Marvin McNulty.

He haunted my dreams that night, back in the New Farm motel room.

What did you call such a man? A confidence trickster? A political operator? A visionary? A fraud? Not even Marvin himself could decide, even in his own book.

Nor could the public. They loved him, they hated him, laughed at him, stood in awe of him. They voted him in with derision, voted him out with regret. They sent him to jail, then they couldn't wait till he got out again. It was like schizophrenia, but they wanted him around, one way or the other. All that mattered was that Marvin entertained. The people of Queensland were his audience, and they were fascinated by the show he put on. His only problem was that he really arrived on the scene too late. If he'd started five years earlier, he might have climbed all the way up to premier, and with Marvin at the helm, who knew what might have happened to us all?

But could he have made it anywhere else other than Queensland? Would he even have *tried* it anywhere other than Queensland? After all, a state with sound and sensible government would hardly have attracted men like Marvin. Not if decision making was reasoned, policy cautious, and accountability a prime concern. A state in collapse, however, a political party with no fear of ever losing power, a browbeaten media, a compliant police force, an entrenched air of secret deals and unexplained cash flows . . . that was when the Marvins of the world took notice. That was when the small-time con men and shady entrepreneurs suddenly saw that the main chance for a fast operator was in so-called legitimate government. That was when the circus really began.

Such was the government of Queensland of my day, and such a man was Marvin McNulty. Of all things, a used-car salesman.

That was literally where he started. A small used-car lot in the suburbs that he ran with a friend. It was the late sixties. Marvin was only eighteen. He showed me a photo once, him and his partner in front of their car yard. They were laughable. His friend was a dour, grim-looking boy from the bush, and Marvin . . . Marvin was a bony, pimply youth with his slicked-back hair and monstrous glasses that swallowed half his face. They never changed, those glasses, and the lenses seemed half an inch thick. His green eyes bulged through them like baby watermelons. But there was the brain behind them, and meanwhile those eyes and those glasses were his winning edge. The sheer size of them entranced you, they never seemed to blink and you couldn't look away. So you hardly noticed his bad teeth or thinning hair, you hardly noticed the ludicrous body his head sat on—all legs and arms when he was younger, all *belly* and legs and arms when he was older. All you saw were the eyes.

And all you heard was his voice. It was deep and earnest and almost seemed to be crying out against his appearance. You had to take what that voice said seriously, because no one with those eyes and that body could possibly be anything but trustworthy, desperately and hopelessly so. A kid like that, trying to sell used cars (the customer would think), it's too sad—and so they would buy a car off the sorry boy, just to give him a break. Later they would invest in his idiot projects, just to give the sorry boy a break. Later still they would vote for him in elections, maybe for the same reason. And like everything about Marvin, it was pure connivance. He took the public's instinctive pity and worked it like a seam of gold. Not that it was an original strategy. Half the Queensland government was running on the same ticket, even the premier, for Queenslanders were always wary of the more sophisticated types—they *liked* their representatives to be awkward and stumbling. They mistook it for honesty. So much so that the

Queensland parliament sometimes bordered on a sideshow collection of the ugly, the misshapen and the incoherent.

Meanwhile the cars Marvin sold were lemons, one and all, and his business went bust. Undeterred, he and his partner formed an enterprise named McNulty and Co, indulging in property speculation. They got caught up in one of the bayside property scandals that plagued Brisbane at the time, and promptly went bust again. Next they went into insurance brokerage. They grew bored with that, veered into swimming pool construction, grew bored with that as well, then started dreaming of theme parks for tourists. It was the mid-seventies by then, and Queensland tourism was booming. Brisbane may have been the most bland city in the country, but there was still the weather and that long coastline of beaches, and the glory of the reefs. Tourists were flocking up from the south. The only problem was, you couldn't charge money for the weather or the beach. So everyone was dreaming about theme parks, and everyone was building them, and Marvin joined the throng. Marvin always joined in everything. Whatever other crimes he may have been accused of later, originality was never one of them.

Then again . . .

McNulty and Co's theme park was to be called The Big Hill, and its aim was to be the hilliest golf course, hopefully, in the world. They'd got hold of a worthless and incredibly knotted piece of country behind the beaches north of Brisbane, all ridges and steep gullies, and on it they wanted to build eighteen holes of madness. Near-vertical fairways, greens perched on ledges or hidden in hollows, par fives that were five hundred yards long, three hundred of which was straight down and which you needed a cable car to descend. Marvin could already see the T-shirts, the novelty pens, the celebrity tournaments. He'd never played a game of golf in his life.

But the money rolled in. It was such a fool of an idea from such a strange man, investors could smell a hit. Then, to everyone's surprise, just before construction was due to begin, McNulty and Co sold out to a wealthy southerner, recently arrived in Queensland and bedazzled, perhaps, by the sheer craziness of the place. Several months later, torrential rain caused most of the landscaping to collapse in a landslide, and the government surveyors announced the site was unstable and unfit for any public use. The whole deal folded, and even after the dust of legal action had settled, McNulty and Co came out holding the cash. No one ever found out about Marvin's relationship with certain figures in the state surveyor's office. Or the amount of money he paid them to doctor the initial reports.

All in all a minor enough incident, but it must have been that first brush with the elasticity of official procedures that gave Marvin his inspiration. Government! The real money obviously wasn't to be made in bribing official bodies, it was to be made in *controlling* those official bodies. Within another two years he was a member of the ruling political party, had secured pre-selection for a safe seat, and was duly elected into parliament at the tender age of twenty-nine. It was all so unlikely that the voters had no choice but to believe he was some sort of boy wonder—anything else and they would have felt like fools themselves. Where he got the money for it all, no one really knew. Even his Big Hill windfall would barely have covered the money he was rumoured to have thrown around the party structure. But no matter how deep his debts might have been, it wasn't a problem now. He had a steady MP's salary to rely on and, more importantly, he was in government, it was the late seventies, and the Queensland cash-cow was just getting into full swing. As he would later admit, the first thing he did after being sworn in was to send his secretary out to buy him a new wallet.

The second thing was to move into his electorate, a technicality he hadn't bothered with until then. And his new electoral office was, of course, right around the corner from Charlie's little restaurant.

And so it went. A few years later came the meteoric leap to Minister for Mines and Energy, during the power dispute. No one knew what he'd said to convince the premier he could handle it, what strings he had to pull, but even his own party was shocked by him. And it was too good to last. Mines and Energy was a rich portfolio, ripe with kickbacks and incentives from big business and mining, and for all that Marvin had outclassed the striking electrical workers, it was deemed too high a reward. The more senior ministers, alarmed and protective of their own rackets, made sure he was demoted in the next reshuffle. For the rest of his career, Marvin was forced to wander the minor ministries. Minister for Education, which was baffling given that he didn't have one; Minister for Small Business, for a man who'd failed at every commercial enterprise he'd tried; and finally, Minister for Local Government, when his only interest in local councils was the circumvention of their zoning laws.

In all they were a disappointment, even though he turned a personal profit out of each of them, and even though he remained a star to the public, out of all proportion to his actual power. Still, maybe that disappointment explained why he threw so much of his time into the syndicate. True, towards the end there was talk of handing him the police ministry, which showed how crazy things were getting by that stage. If he'd got there, maybe he could have gone the rest of the way as well. Marvin certainly had no doubts he was destined to be premier. But then the Inquiry came along and kicked the whole business out from under him.

So the syndicate remained his true love.

I never knew exactly how big it was in the end. That was Lindsay's business. Apart from the restaurants, we owned two clubs outright, with their attached casinos, of that much I was certain. But we also had investments in others clubs and bars, and even connections with several dedicated brothels. Meanwhile we all had roles to play. Marvin was unquestionably in charge, for all that Charlie was the figurehead. Lindsay, of course, was the financial manager. Jeremy was the elder statesman, our patron, so to speak. And Maybellene, to everyone's surprise, left Jeremy's employ after a year or so and took up a position working for Marvin as his political advisor and general assistant—despite the fact that he'd been the very man responsible for her ending up in jail. Jeremy was philosophical about losing her, however. May had learnt his lessons too well, that was all.

And me? Public relations for the syndicate? Media liaison? Marvin's tame hack in the press corps?

They were some of the names I was called whenever I was mentioned at the Inquiry, or when they drew up the power structure of the syndicate on a whiteboard for a jury to see, where somehow Charlie, not Marvin or Lindsay, always ended up in the centre.

They were wrong about Charlie.

But me?

Was Marvin behind my success? He was friends with my editor. He gave me a lot of material for my pieces. He got me into places I couldn't have reached on my own. Parliamentary bars, back-room parties and dinners, chartered fishing trips with the elite. Maybe some of my best lines came from him as well, and he didn't seem to care that I credited them as my own. But he never *told* me what to write. Although, as it turned out, I was often attacking his political enemies in my articles, it was never organised, never contrived. It just . . . happened that way. And besides, it was nothing serious, just a rumour here, an insinuation there. I was not a political observer, I was a social commentator, a light-hearted one at that. No one took any notice of these things. Marvin wasn't running me, I wasn't his direct line into the city's second major newspaper . . .

But why all the defences?

I was never charged with anything anyway.

Meanwhile Marvin went to jail, not merely for his dealings with our syndicate, but for a whole glut of crimes—misused expense accounts, misappropriation of funds, bribery, attempting to pervert the course of justice, tax evasion, to name a few. But the prosecutors didn't even bother pressing all the charges at their disposal. The thing was, everyone still loved him. He still entertained. There was no doubt about his guilt, so once it all started to unravel, Marvin saw that his best shot was to throw up his hands cheerfully and confess. He'd made a fortune, but then he'd been generous with it as well. Charities, donations, huge parties, all sorts of extravagance. And what was it all, really? Wine, women and gambling—who could condemn a man for that? After all, other ministers had been more corrupt than Marvin. Older, more senior, and far more respected men. And those other ministers had been grasping about it all. Mean. What's more, they couldn't even own up with any style. Most of them denied the whole thing completely.

So in his way, Marvin was seen as forgivable. And when his sentence was finally handed down, he waved to the media from the dock and cried, 'See you in a few years, boys.'

And God help us all, they applauded him.

Five years later, true to his word and with time off for good behaviour, Marvin emerged a model prisoner who'd earned an arts degree in prison and of whom the warden himself couldn't speak highly enough. The papers splashed him across the front page. Marvin 'The Marvel' McNulty was back in town. Even up in Highwood I read the headlines and shuddered. You could almost feel the journalists wetting their pens and waiting for the copy to flow.

But Marvin surprised everyone. He disappeared.

That is, he didn't reappear. He didn't launch any bold new enterprises, though no doubt people would have invested. He didn't even throw any parties. He simply retired, a private citizen, and was never heard from again.

The Marvellous Marvin McNulty.

In my New Farm motel room I woke to the heat of noon, and the memory of his laughter in my head. I hadn't known he was an alcoholic.

I lay in bed and thought about his bad suits and sweaty armpits, his devouring eyes, his gargantuan appetite, for food, for cigars, for drinks, for money, for everything. Yes . . . that alcoholism would be part of it all made sense. But Marvin surrendering himself to a detox ward like St Amand's, Marvin admitting to a problem and seeking treatment, that was harder to fathom. I looked back and tried to remember any times he'd disappeared suspiciously for a week or two, ever looked sick, ever stopped drinking, even for one night, but the memories were all a blur. A drinking bout that had carried on for years. And Marvin's face was always there, hazy, beer soaked, eyes blazing. If he'd been seeking help, I never saw it.

And where was he now?

I swung my feet out from the under the sheets and consulted the phone book. There was no Marvin McNulty listed. Expecting even less, I tried his old number from my little address book. It was no longer connected.

Still, he'd appeared at Jeremy's house, so chances were he was somewhere in town, and in a place as small as Brisbane, someone would know where he was.

I lay back in bed, pondering. The media would know. They would have tracked him, kept the file open, even though he had proved so disappointing. But there was only the one major paper left in town, and there was no way I could call them up and ask. I could imagine the hilarity it would cause. The contempt. 'He was *your* friend, George, why are you asking us?'

That was if they remembered me at all.

Which left the police. They would have tracked him as well, and for the same reasons. And besides, they'd told me themselves they were looking for him.

I dialled the number. Detective Kelly did not seem excited to hear from me.

'I thought you were going back to Highwood,' he said.

'The sooner the better, believe me.'

'So what do you want?'

'Any news?'

'Didn't we talk about this yesterday?' He sighed. 'What do you want, George?'

'Have you found Marvin yet?'

There was silence on the line.

'Well?' I said.

'Why are you asking me that?'

'I just want to know where he lives. You guys must have kept some sort of record.'

But there was an intensity in Kelly's voice I hadn't been expecting. 'The question is, George, why do you suddenly want to know? I thought you people didn't speak any more.'

'We don't.'

'Then why the sudden interest?'

'I want to speak to him now, that's all.'

'You still claim you haven't seen or spoken to him since the old days?'

'I've already told you, no.'

Kelly was silent for a time. 'Okay, sure, we know where he lives.'

'So have you seen him?'

'No. He isn't home.'

'Oh . . .'

'It seems very strange to me that you should be calling about Marvin, George. Especially right now.'

I was a little alarmed at his tone. 'Look, I want to talk to him about St Amand's, that's all. I've heard Marvin booked in there from time to time.'

But that only interested him more. 'Who told you that? The hospital?'

'Not likely.'

'Then who?'

'I heard, that's all. Did *you* know that?'

A pause. 'Yes, we did.'

Neither of us spoke for a moment.

'Is there something you should be telling me?' I asked.

'I'm not sure if this will be news to you or not, George, and that's what's got me curious.'

'What, for Christ's sake?'

'Marvin was officially reported missing yesterday afternoon. Just after I talked to you. By his housekeeper. In fact, she says he's been missing for weeks. To be exact, since three days before Charlie died. Which is something, don't you think? And now here you are again, as soon as we learn this, all keen to know if we've found him or not.'

I went to respond, couldn't think of anything to say.

'What's your address there, George?' he asked.

'Why?'

'I think maybe you should stay put after all. And we'll have another little talk.'

TWENTY-THREE

They took me for a drive.

It was both of my old friends, Detectives Kelly and Lewis, and the car was unmarked. And like old friends, their suspicions about me seemed to have come visiting again too.

Lewis craned round to look at me while Kelly drove.

'You expect us to believe you don't know where we're going?'

We were going, they'd told me, to Marvin's house.

'I've never been there,' I said. 'I don't even know what suburb it's in.'

'Of course you don't.'

'Why are we going there anyway?'

'We want to show you something.'

And from there we drove on in silence. The car was air-conditioned, but heat gathered out on the streets. It was the third sweltering day in a row, and even the new Brisbane seemed to be wilting. We drove over the bridge and along the cliffs, then across Highgate Hill and down into Yerongpilly. The river met us there once more, having looped about on itself, and luxury houses stretched along the waterfront, interspersed with parks. We pulled up outside a bungalow that was mostly hidden by trees and a high fence. Kelly switched off the engine and we sat there.

'That's Marvin's place,' he said.

I stared at it.

'You know what it's worth?'

I shook my head.

'Half a million. At least.'

Which was a lot, for Brisbane. River frontage was prime—

if you could live with the periodic floods that swept down from the mountains. In the big one of '74, this house would barely have had its roof above water.

'Not bad,' said Lewis, 'for a man who was bankrupted by the Inquiry.'

'How did he afford it then?' I asked.

'You don't know?'

I kept my voice patient. 'No, I don't know.'

'Six months after he gets out of prison, some old grazier up north dies and leaves one-third of his estate to Marvin. Says Marvin was a dear friend of the family, like a son. It's all for real, the family doesn't complain, and suddenly Marvin's a millionaire again.'

'Lucky Marvin.'

'You remember any grazier friend of Marvin's, from the old days?'

'He had lots of friends.'

'Oh, I bet he did. Marvin didn't even go to this guy's funeral.'

We all stared at the house.

'So what else did he do with his money?' I asked.

Kelly answered. 'Nothing. As far as we can tell, he's been a recluse ever since. Not that we watched him every day, but if he was doing anything in public, business or otherwise, we never heard about it.'

Lewis was grinning. 'But now we know he's been working on something in private instead.'

They glanced at each other, amused, but did not elaborate.

Kelly went on.

'He lives there alone. He has a housekeeper who's hired to clean the place on Mondays and Fridays. She's worked for him five years, and she tells us he's almost always home. If he's ever away he lets her know, and leaves a forwarding number. He's worried about the place being robbed, or burning down or something. Turns out that the forwarding number is usually for St Amand's. She says he must have been there six or seven times since she met him.' He paused. 'Was he that bad, back in your day?'

'I don't know,' I said.

A shrug. 'Either way, this particular time there was no forwarding number, and he's not at St Amand's right now.'

'You're sure of that?'

'We're sure,' said Lewis. 'The hospital was reluctant to discuss most things, maybe, but they couldn't wait to assist us on that point.' He reached into the glove box and pulled out a set of keys. 'C'mon inside.'

The front gate, which had to be unlocked, led to a small yard, shaded by trees and ferns. The front door was double bolted, and Lewis fiddled with the keys for some minutes before we got through. Inside the air was very warm, tinged with the smell of tobacco, and more faintly with alcohol, but everything was tidy and neat. I looked around for signs of Marvin, but in the end it could have been anyone's house. A wealthy anybody, at least. The living area was spacious, well furnished and tiled in slate. The entire further wall was glass, opening to a sloping lawn that ran down to a pool, the pool itself overhanging the river. Thick shrubs and trees marched down either side of the yard, and even the far side of river was dense with bushland. I thought about where we were and worked out the bushland was probably the back of the St Lucia golf course. It was a secluded view, private from anyone, and very exclusive.

Lewis inspected the answering machine by the phone. There were no messages.

Kelly continued on as if he'd never paused.

'According to the housekeeper, Marvin does almost nothing but drink. She comes in on her Mondays and Fridays and this place is a mess of empty bottles, ashtrays and cigarette butts. He cooks for himself, but he doesn't clean, so the kitchen is a pigsty as well. Mostly there's no sign that anyone has been in the house but him, although occasionally she thinks there must have been guests. Spare beds slept in, strange clothes lying around, empty bottles of stuff she knows Marvin doesn't drink. Several times she's cleaned up what has obviously been a sizeable party, and several other times she's come across women staying in the house, even in Marvin's own bedroom, but the impression the housekeeper gets is that Marvin didn't always know them very well. Much younger than him, for one thing. She suspects they were prostitutes.'

I felt myself sweating. Not a window in the house was open. Out beyond the pool, the river was as flat and still as concrete.

Kelly smiled. 'She's not a judgemental person, this housekeeper. She thinks Marvin must just be lonely. He's always very friendly and considerate towards her, his untidy personal habits aside, so she likes him. She's worried about him.'

Lewis took up the story. 'Friday two and a half weeks ago she arrives to find the place is particularly bad, like a real binge has been going on, for days. Marvin isn't here, but she cleans up anyway. When she comes back the following Monday, the house is still as spotless as she'd left it. No sign of Marvin, and no sign that he'd been home any time between. That was unusual, but it wasn't until she came round the following Friday that it really gets strange. Marvin still isn't there, but there's one empty bottle of scotch on the table, one glass and one used ashtray. Plus the bed has been slept in. But no Marvin. She calls St Amand's, and they say he isn't there. They wouldn't tell her even if he was, maybe, but she says that in the past he left instructions to allow her calls through. So now she's really wondering. She searches through the house to see if any of Marvin's clothes or things are missing. She can't be certain, but she doesn't think anything much is. Another ten days go by, still no sign of him, so finally she decides to call the police, yesterday. Missing Persons. Soon as they type in his name, of course, a red flag goes up, a criminal investigation, wanted for questioning about your friend Charlie's death, all that—so they send her straight to us. We bring her back over here, and we go through the house.'

'Funny thing is,' Kelly concluded, 'we've been round here a few times in the last couple of weeks anyway, knocking on the door, looking in the windows. We just never came when she was here. We left a stack of messages on his phone, too, but when we checked, ours were the only messages there. And all they did was freak out the poor housekeeper.'

Why wasn't someone opening a window? The two of them were in suits, but the heat didn't seem to be bothering them at all.

'Into thin air with Marvin,' Kelly observed, looking at me.

'I don't know anything about it,' I said.

'Like I said before, it's odd though. Before any of this is even public, you ring up and suddenly you just have to talk to him.'

'It's a coincidence.'

Lewis snorted. 'Charlie dying and Marvin disappearing are just coincidences?'

'That's not what I meant.'

They studied me for a moment.

'Relax, George,' Kelly said. 'We don't think he's dead or anything. For one thing, his bank accounts are still being used. Places here and there around town. He's just gone underground, that's all.'

'Why would he want to do that?'

'That's the question, isn't it? Why would he want to disappear so completely that he won't even tell his beloved housekeeper? What could have happened?'

It was stifling. 'Did St Amand's tell you when Marvin was last in the ward?'

Kelly put on his best expression of innocence. 'Why would that matter?'

I felt myself getting angry. They had to know all this themselves already. 'Maybe he's not there now, but maybe he *was* in there when Charlie was.'

He gave me a slow clap of hands. 'Well done, George. You could be a detective.'

'So was he?'

'Yeah, he was in there.'

It was like relief, cool water on my brow. Maybe it all made sense after all. 'And did he pay for Charlie?'

'No. He didn't.'

And the sense was gone again.

'Then who did?'

'Charlie paid for himself. Cash. On arrival.'

'That's impossible. He didn't have any money.'

'The hospital said he had plenty. A bag full of it. They thought it was all a little strange themselves. He hardly looked the wealthy type, after all.'

'He was homeless.'

'He was rich once, George. Who knows what he had stashed away?'

'It still might have come from Marvin.'

'Maybe, but we don't think so. The two of them arrived at different times, for a start—Marvin in the morning, Charlie that afternoon. Marvin paid his own way with a credit card. There's no link. Besides, it makes more sense if Marvin had nothing to do with Charlie getting in, if they just met in there by accident.'

'More sense? It makes less sense.'

'Depends on your point of view. For a start, they'd have to be pretty good friends, Marvin and Charlie, for Marvin to hand out so much cash.'

'So? They *were* friends.'

'You think so?'

'Time to show him the opus?' Lewis inquired.

'Oh yes,' Kelly answered.

I stared at them both, baffled. They led me down a hall into the wing that contained the bedrooms. One of them had been made into an office. I'd seen offices of Marvin's before—rooms full of ashtrays and files and plans and phones ringing—but this was nothing like any of those. It was almost empty. There was just the one desk, set under a window overlooking the lawn and the river, and one chair. A computer sat on the desk, and there was a small bookshelf set against the wall. It was hard to even imagine Marvin in the room. It was too small, too simple.

'This is the answer to the big mystery,' said Lewis, tapping a pile of paper that sat next to the computer and the printer. 'What he's been doing all this time.'

'Marvin, it seems,' said Kelly, 'is writing a book.'

I looked at the pile of paper. It was maybe a hundred pages thick, the paper covered with single-spaced typing.

Marvin? A *book*?

'What is it? I asked.

'His memoirs. His whole story. The life and times of Marvin McNulty.'

'Sort of, anyway,' added Lewis, flicking through the pages.

Kelly pulled out the chair and offered it to me. 'We had a good read of it last night. His version of events is, to say the least, pretty subjective. And he's not telling everything, not by a long shot.'

I sat in the chair. There was a small selection of books on the desk, propped up between two book ends. A dictionary, a Windows 95 manual. I examined the little bookshelf, four shelves high. There were novels and texts and histories, mostly Australian. Books of which I'd heard, but never read. Maybe it was what you needed to get an arts degree.

This was what Marvin had been doing?

Lewis was sorting through the typed pages. 'It's all over the place, really. But you're all in here. You, Jeremy, Lindsay—even May.'

Kelly said, 'Find one of the bits about George.'

Lewis sorted through some more pages, then handed one to me. 'It's not long after the Inquiry has started, and Marvin's just been sacked from cabinet.'

They both watched, smiling, while I read.

It was like we'd lost a war or something. People were running. I went out to survey the city one last time, and I came across George hiding out in a bar. He was white as a sheet and terrified and didn't want to be seen with me, not any more. Poor old George, he was worried about his job at the paper, and looking for courage in a bottle.

'Kiss the job goodbye,' I told him. 'What did you think this all was? A tea party?'

'What if I get charged with something?' he wanted to know.

Fat fucking chance of that. Not fat boy George. Fucked almost as many of our girls as I did, had a ball with them all, free of charge, but he never had a clue really. George was always strictly gloss.

'How's May?' I asked, and that sent him trembling all over again, for he was fucking her too, of course, on the sly, and to hell with Charlie. I dug it in a little. 'Hey, if Charlie goes down he'll be out of the way for you two.'

That made him squirm. George and Charlie were supposed to be best buddies.

'Charlie won't go to jail, will he?'

'Course he will. So will I.'

'Just for running a few clubs?'

Honestly, he was a simpleton.

'The walls are down,' I told him, 'and this town is gonna burn.' Then I left him to it.

Later I heard he'd run off into the hills, but that was no surprise.

I put the page back on the desk. The detectives were still smiling.

'He can actually write okay,' Lewis suggested, 'don't you think?'

My face was burning. I mustered a reply. 'Like you said, his version is pretty subjective.'

Except it wasn't. I remembered that meeting with Marvin. It was the last time I saw him in private. And he was right, I was scared, I didn't know what was happening, and drinking seemed to offer the only escape from it all. That and Maybellene. For the two years between the start of the Inquiry and the final collapse, they were the only two things I had.

Lewis was still flicking through the pages. 'There's more like that, but he doesn't really talk about you much. The really interesting stuff for us is in the last chapter. The last chapter he's written so far, anyway. It doesn't look like he means it to be the end.'

'Interesting stuff about what?'

'About Charlie, of course.'

And he handed me another page. The last page.

Prison was fucking terrible for a man like me. All that time, and there's nothing you can do with it, you can never act. That was the worst. I was a man of action, I never looked back, never regretted. But in prison you can't look forward, it's a dead-end road, the future. You can only look back. It's a test you've got to pass. Deal with the past somehow. Otherwise you'll go mad.

That was Charlie's problem. I only met him once in prison. He was a mess to look at, his face was all scarred and he couldn't speak properly. They were just transferring him through our section. They usually had him in special sections, 'cause his brain was gone after the gunshot. But he was having other troubles, too, someone told me. Getting violent, picking fights, screaming about stuff, like he didn't deserve to be there. As if any of us did.

I don't think he recognised me at first. 'Charlie,' I said.

He stared at me, and it wasn't the old Charlie. He started yelling. 'Get away from me!' He spat in my face. It was hatred, pure hatred. He even went for me, but I had a few friends there, and they held him off, got some guards to drag him away.

Like I said, his mind was gone. He was looking for someone to blame. As if it was all my fault, everything that happened. Everyone always thought it was my damn fault.

Christ, it wasn't my fault. Charlie wouldn't have got anywhere without me. I was doing him a favour. It was his own life. I didn't force him into anything, I didn't steal his wife, I didn't pull the trigger. And what did I get out of it all?

So hey, fuck you too, Charlie.

And that was all there was.

'It doesn't sound like they were friendly to me,' said Kelly.

'Sound likes Charlie was an angry man,' his partner added. 'We thought he might have just been angry at you, over the Maybellene thing. That's why we had you pegged for a while, if Charlie was heading up to Highwood to sort you out. But we don't think that any more.'

'Not now that we know Marvin and Charlie met up in St Amand's. And that they felt this way about each other.'

I needed air. I wanted out of this house, away from this book, away from these men.

'What do you mean?' I asked.

'What we're telling you is, if you do see your friend Marvin, you tell us straight away. For your own sake. He's dangerous.'

'Marvin? Dangerous?'

Kelly sounded almost sad. 'Don't you get it? We think Marvin killed Charlie.'

TWENTY-FOUR

The police drove me back to the motel.

It was only much later, when everything was finished, that I tracked down and read the rest of Marvin's unfinished memoirs, only much later that I understood the way it had all become warped in his mind. It was a wandering, disjointed account, jumping between styles and arguments and excuses, and made almost no sense in the end. I suppose most of it was written while he was drunk. But for the time being, all I had were those two stark pages, and they had seared themselves, ugly, into my brain.

'Marvin wouldn't hurt anyone,' I said to the detectives.

'Why not?' they replied. 'He was obviously pissed off at Charlie, and God knows, Charlie loathed Marvin. Stuck in a detox ward together, who knows how bad things might have got between them?'

I thought of Charlie's body, tied against a wall. 'Not that bad. Never that bad.'

'We've seen worse, George. People do unbelievable things.'

'And why up there? Why in Highwood? Why was Charlie looking for me?'

'Maybe we'll never know. Maybe Marvin had him fired up about old times, so Charlie was looking to settle things with you too, like we first thought. Maybe they went up there together to see you for some reason, and things got out of hand . . . anything's possible.'

'I don't believe it. It's crazy.'

'It's the best we've got so far.'

They dropped me on the street outside my motel, the sun blazing in the sky.

'What are your plans now?' Kelly asked me.

'I don't know.'

'Go home, George. If anyone finds Marvin, it'll be us. Then we'll know, one way or the other. But you got nothing more to do here.'

Lewis was digging in his wallet. 'Tell you what, if you're looking for something to do on your last night, why not check this out?'

He handed me a card. Above the address was a stylised picture of a cocktail glass balancing on a crouching woman's back.

'What's this?'

Kelly was frowning, but Lewis only grinned, boyish and cruel. 'It's your sort of place, George.'

And they drove away, leaving me alone on the footpath, in the middle of New Farm, my old home and a foreign land.

He was white as a sheet and terrified . . .

I studied the card again. It meant nothing. I looked up at the mirrored windows of my motel room. There would be no relief in there. Only more stifling air and Charlie's ashes on the coffee table.

His face was all scarred and he couldn't speak properly . . .

Sweat dripped out of me. I needed something to drink. It could only be water. What I really needed was a dark, cool bar and droplets of condensation on the rim of a beer glass, golden and foaming, and Lord if only . . . but it could only be water. Tasteless, useless water.

My feet were moving.

Go home, George . . .

And why not? Why stay? Marvin was gone, for whatever reason, and there was nowhere else to look, no one else to ask. My car was there, it was only a couple of hours.

Later I heard he'd run off into the hills . . .

I walked away from the motel, away from the shame and the temptation. I didn't know where I could go, what I could do, but I walked anyway, if only to hold down something that was swelling in my chest.

Could Marvin have done that to Charlie?

It was inconceivable. After all those years that we'd drunk

together, laughed together, wandered the night. Marvin had no standards, no morality, everyone knew that, but something so cold, so merciless? No. I *knew* the man.

George was strictly gloss . . .

I didn't know him at all.

I walked. Heat beamed off the ground and down from the buildings on either side. It was only a block across and I was into Brunswick Street. It was busy, traffic jammed back in both directions, and the footpaths were crowded with people. I stood still and looked up and down. Cafes and bars, galleries and bookshops, none of them recognisable. I had a choice of going left or right. Left would lead me up into the Valley, right would lead me down to New Farm Park and the river. I turned right.

I felt increasingly unsure of everything. A sneering, contemptuous Marvin. A bitter, hateful Charlie. Strangers to me. And what was I now? What had happened to me? Was I really that much of a coward? The others had all come back at least, whatever else might have happened to them. At least they'd had the courage to confront Brisbane.

I could barely look it in the face.

Driving through the town had been bad enough. Down on the footpaths, the hatred for it came back like weariness. Change was everywhere, in the buildings, the smells, the noises. Everything felt brand new. The dark little second-hand shops were gone, the grimy takeaways, the corner stores and the pawn merchants, the narrow delicatessens. The prostitutes were gone, the drunken old men shuffling along the pavement or sleeping in corners, the paranoids from the halfway houses. The police station was still there, but the brothel which had once existed across the road from it was not. And of the dozens of boarding houses and cheap hotels that had once lined the street, barely two or three remained, and it didn't seem that even they could remain much longer. Jackhammers rattled death knells. The only real familiarity was the heat, and that was an old enemy, not an old friend. And without the old refuge of alcohol, the heat was unbearable.

I stomped along, dizzy with it, feeling as if every eye was upon me, full of scorn. It wasn't just that all the old buildings were gone, and all the old people—it was the new inhabitants that disturbed me most, the new generation. So young, so confident. Late lunchers and afternoon coffee drinkers idled at the tables of the cafes and watched me go by, safe in their shade. Stylish waiters lounged in dim interiors. Mobile phones trilled, and music I didn't understand thumped from passing cars, and from inside shops. It was vibrant, alive, but for me it was all distorted. It was a world that had replaced my kind. There was no reason to hate people for being young and bright, but I did. I wanted my world back. Where things moved in secrecy and back rooms, where there was no glamour, no grace, only a sweaty drunken rush, and only for the few.

Except even that world had been an illusion. I hadn't belonged there either.

. . . *he never had a clue.*

It ached like pain. I walked, as if walking itself would be distraction enough. But this wasn't the forests of Highwood, walking wouldn't help me now. I came to New Farm Park. It was not as crowded as when I'd seen it two days earlier. Today people had withdrawn from the sun, into the shade of the trees. There were only a few elderly couples having afternoon tea, a man sleeping with a newspaper over his face, a dog owner watching his animal chew on a stick it was too hot to chase. I walked across the grass, alone in the sunlight. The park felt much smaller than I remembered, its rose gardens somehow thinner and drabber, the grass tinged with brown. In my time the park had been the one fresh and beautiful spot in a suburb half derelict—now the suburb itself was shining and new and it was the park that looked worn out. A police car cruised by on the road that circled the lawns. Its occupants watched me indifferently. I came to the wall of grey rocks and boulders that marked the river bank.

The river was much wider than it had been back at Marvin's house. Here it was spreading out as the swamps and sandbars of its mouth drew near. Not a breath of wind ruffled its surface, and nothing moved. At low tide I knew the mudflats would be exposed, but the tide was in now, perhaps just turning, and the water was poised, high and sluggish, with nowhere to flow. Twenty yards off the bank three yachts hung limply on their pylons. No one was on board. I waited. Finally, off to one side a lone figure in a kayak appeared, labouring towards the ocean. I watched him, the dips made by his paddles stretching out behind like footprints in mud. I could hear his breathing across the water. Heat pooled in my head. Out across the river, and beyond the roofs of Woolloongabba, there was a haze in the south-western sky, low on the horizon. The suggestion of shadow and cloud. Maybe a storm was building in the mountains, maybe over Highwood itself. But a change was hours away from Brisbane, if it ever came at all.

A man stirred in the shade of a tree behind me, came my way.

'Do you have the time?' he asked.

I told him. He was wearing a watch and studied it, as if to check, hovering.

'My name's Justin,' he said. 'What's yours?'

I told him that as well.

He looked up and down the river, hesitant. 'Do you have Jesus in your life, George?'

Oh God . . .

I turned and walked back the way I'd come.

The ache was still in my chest. How could memory be physical like this? I left the park, trudged along Brunswick Street again, taking the opposite footpath. A few blocks along I came to an imposing stone mansion set back from the road amidst a large garden. It was the residence of Brisbane's Catholic Archbishop. It appeared unaltered, as timeless as the church itself. I didn't know who the Archbishop was now, but I'd met one of his predecessors once, a man long since dead. It was at a dinner with Marvin, in the days when bishops mixed with government ministers and neither bothered much with their respective congregations. All of us Catholic, all of us lapsed. Just beyond the residence I turned into a side street. There was a church there, not a cathedral or anything grand, simply a church. And next to the church was the block of flats in which I had once lived.

It was a dark, brick building, three storeys high, two apartments to each floor. I'd rented the forward flat on the top level. It had big rooms and high ceilings and had cost hardly anything—no one with money had wanted to live in this part of New Farm in those days. Even the church next door had been more of a curse for the rental agent than a boon, because of the noise. Sunday mornings I had always woken unwillingly to the endless tolling of bells. Sometimes there would be a choir. I would hear their soaring voices begging the Lord for deliverance, and from the depths of my Sunday morning hangover, I would echo their plea. For silence. For mercy. Suspecting even then that salvation was not something I had earned.

It would be expensive to rent there now. The garden had been remodelled and the small lobby redecorated and a security door installed. I looked up at my old windows and saw the tops of pot plants and white walls behind. The walls had been brown in my time, half panelled in wood, and darkness was the way I remembered it. I'd possessed very little furniture and no plants. And suddenly I remembered myself and Maybellene, together on a couch in the middle of an otherwise empty living room, the hint of dawn coming through the windows, a bottle of wine on the floor. The apartment had felt as vast and cool as an auditorium, and May's whispers seemed to echo, close to my ear.

He was fucking her too, of course . . .
The ache sharpened around my heart.
I'd left the couch and all my other furniture when I fled Brisbane, abandoned it for the agent to do with as he wished. Perhaps some of it was still there.

And that couldn't be borne.

I turned and went back to Brunswick Street. The afternoon was lengthening into evening, and the cafes were filling up, but the heat still held the air breathless. I walked blindly for twenty minutes, shouldering my way through pedestrians and around tables on the footpaths, just putting distance behind me. I stared at the ground straight ahead and met no one's eyes. Laughter seemed to follow me along, careless and innocent and piercing. And when I looked up I was at the other end of Brunswick Street in the very heart of the old Brisbane I'd once known—Fortitude Valley—a heart that seemed to have been removed by surgery and replaced with something pink and new and pulsing to a different beat.

There was no escape. I faltered and gazed about at all the new people and lights and noise, the hopelessness growing inside me. The building that had housed my newspaper was square across the road. Apartments now, but there was no mistaking it. There was the top floor corner window, where the editor's office had been. Where I'd been called, finally, knowing what would happen and dreading it.

'Pack your bags,' was all he'd said to me, and I'd stood, waiting, as if there might be something else. He'd looked up at me, amazed I was still there, and anger had flared. 'What did you expect? Christ, George, what the fuck were you thinking?'

And I'd left then.

He'd had more worries on his hands than one wayward journalist. His hands were hardly clean themselves. Too many friendships with too many suspect people. And the paper was losing money, the day of the afternoon tabloid was passing, and they'd lost the whole jump on the Inquiry business to their morning competitor. Within a year they were gone. Another victim, in their own way, of the whole disaster.

It was enough, it was too much. I needed somewhere to hide. The old hotels were still there, but the public bars and tiled walls were gone, and I couldn't trust myself in any of them anyway. The cafes all seemed too small, too open, too full of people. I reeled through the traffic and moved into a mall where a guitarist played on a stage and where transplanted trees dropped leaves onto paving stones that had just been a naked street in my time. I saw a restaurant that had a long room running back from the front doors. I knew it, possibly, from my own day, though it was hard to tell when everything else was so different. But more importantly, the back of the room was empty. I took a table in the far corner. I ordered iced water and drank it thirstily, glass after glass, until my stomach started to cramp. It satisfied nothing. I ordered a bowl of pasta I didn't want, just so I could remain there. Across the mall I could see a bar full of people sitting with their drinks, talking, smoking. There was no need for them to order food. A drink in front of you was an allowance to sit forever, undisturbed. Everything in this world was better when you drank.

Tension ticked in me, minute by minute. People came and went in the restaurant, always in groups. I was the only person seated alone. I stared at the table, at the floor. My pasta arrived and I picked at it, but there was a nervous pit in my stomach, I had no appetite. The cold water went straight through me and came out in my armpits and on my back as sweat. Every time I looked up someone seemed to be looking back at me. I moved seats, to face the wall, but a mirror hung there. I saw a sunburned face, flushed with moisture, a tight, clenched mouth. I moved back again. I was going mad. What was I waiting for, why was I here?

George and Charlie were supposed to be best buddies.

It was too late, too late.

A man approached my table, not a waiter. I looked up at him, confused. I recognised him from somewhere. Then I had it—he was the Christian, from the park.

'Still alone?' he said.

What was this? Was he *following* me?

I lurched up. 'Get away from me.'

I dropped money on the table and almost ran out into the street.

It was dark now, and more oppressive. People were everywhere. The sky above was lurid and starless. I didn't know which way to go, didn't think I could face the walk back to the motel, not down that street, not like this, and what would I do when I got there anyway? Then there was a giant flash of blue from high above. I stared up, baffled. Thunder rumbled, and a curl of air whispered along the mall. The diners at the cafes paused momentarily, glancing at the sky, and the blue light flickered again. In that moment all I saw were their upturned faces illuminated in the corpse glow of the lightning, hundreds of them, pale and open mouthed and staring, and there swept over me a sick loathing for everything Brisbane had become.

Then fat drops of water were smacking onto the paving stones, thunder rolled and, startled, the crowd began to move.

TWENTY-FIVE

The downpour cleared the streets.

I sheltered under an awning and watched it. Thunder muttered and sheets of lightning flickered between the buildings, but there was no real violence in it. It was no more than a passing spring shower. Still, the drops on my face were icy cool and something uncurled in me. I sucked in breaths of wet air, and remembered other Brisbane storms. Dark lines of them marching down from the hills, dropping hail and fire, winds sweeping at their feet. This was not one of those storms, perhaps, but I felt as if the old city itself had come to my rescue. If only now it would rain all night.

Spring storms did not work that way. After half an hour the first rush eased to a light rain, then to a drizzle and then was gone altogether. The thunder and lightning faded into the northern sky. I emerged from my shelter to a mall that was shining and wet and mostly empty. Down one end people still gathered in the windows of the cafes, but I walked to the far end where there were only trees dripping and the pavement steaming from the day's stored heat. Cars swished by, and brick walls glistened. I went on beyond the mall and back into the Valley streets, up towards the train station. There was almost no one on the footpaths here, and the cafes had not reached beyond the mall. Instead there were clearance houses and souvenir shops, video arcades and stairways leading to nightclubs. Empty and wet like this, it was almost like the Valley of old. Robbed of crowds the discount stores seemed cheap and vagrant, and the nightclubs as seedy as the ones I remembered from ten years before. Maybe inside they were still the same, maybe only the owners and the names had changed.

And it was all so small. Just four or five city blocks had contained most of the sin and corruption that would eventually bring a government down. As I walked I listed off the buildings I still recognised, the doorways that had led to the gaming dens and the parlours where women waited and menus offered sexual services. There'd been no big signs or bright lights or semi-naked girls loitering outside, no touts calling at passers-by. It was never a Kings Cross or a St Kilda, but it had been blatant enough. A government minister had once bizarrely asserted in public that there were no brothels or illegal casinos in Brisbane. Amused journalists had pointed out that over twenty advertised almost openly in the daily papers, and insisted on taking the minister on a short tour of the Valley that showed up a dozen. The minister publicly expressed amazement. Privately some of the casino operators observed that the same minister was one of their most regular customers, and in higher circles he was told to keep his fat mouth shut. The journalists were told the same thing by their editors. All those ads were worth money to the newspapers. What were they trying to do—fuck up the whole system?

Marvin was in hysterics.

But it was nothing to laugh at. In its small way, it was the beginning of the end.

The thoughts did not seem so bitter now. I sat on a bus stop seat and stared around and strove to remember what it was like, and who'd owned what. There had been the two major syndicates which together had controlled most of the prostitution and gambling in Brisbane, and there had been the smaller, individual operators. Situated between them, the smallest of the syndicates, or the largest of the private operations, there had been us. Either way, almost everyone had used the Valley as their headquarters. From where I sat now, the nearest police station had been just out of sight around the corner, and its proximity had been a benefit rather than a disadvantage. Each syndicate paid into the police funds for protection, and the money filtered all the way up to the police commissioner. That he was corrupt was widely enough known, even to people outside the system, but he had the ear of the premier, and had always proved invulnerable to investigation or removal. He would not fall until the premier himself began to totter.

That was the history, it was what you could read in the papers, but it wasn't what I remembered. Instead I remembered how Charlie and May and Marvin and I, and sometimes Jeremy, would roll out of one of Charlie's restaurants at one or two in the morning, and walk the Valley streets, drunk and knowing that the city was ours. How we'd walk up some narrow flight of stairs or through some closed doors and find another world, crowded and hot, full of cigarette smoke and beer fumes and men, and a bar that never closed. Police cars could be parked right outside and it wouldn't matter because the car would be empty and the police would be inside, enjoying the drinks and women that were their due. Or if it was a casino, then the police might be at the tables, and if their losses were too big, the proprietor would stroll over and have a quiet word to the dealer, and chips would magically reappear.

I remembered another time, when the five of us had wandered further afield and come across a newly opened club in Woolloongabba, we noticed that there were no police around and that the women were nervous and the owner was worried and then, to everyone's amazement, the police suddenly appeared on an official raid. They bundled off the owner and the girls, along with all the towels and sheets, but left us and the other customers alone. What the hell was all this, Marvin wanted to know. The police officer apologised for all the trouble, but informed us that the establishment was in direct competition with a major syndicate brothel around the corner, and that it had refused the takeover bids and the veiled threats, so the police had been asked by the syndicate to shut the rival down. Of course there was no need for our night to be ruined, the officer went on. As he'd said, the approved club was just around the corner.

It never happened to one of our own, of course. Marvin had the right connections, and Lindsay, in charge of the actual clubs, kept in touch with the bigger syndicates and trod on no toes. There was, after all, more than enough to go around.

I remembered how good it felt, being on the inside of it all, knowing that there were some laws for the little people, but that they didn't apply to me or my friends. I remembered the excitement of stepping through those secret doors off

Brisbane's quiet country-town streets into a life that was fast and drunken and heavy with sex. It was an excitement all the richer for its veneer of illegality. In Sydney anyone could visit a far wider range of clubs of far more sophistication, but that was Sydney. Brisbane was the moral town, the town of law and order and decency. The spice of sin in Brisbane was so much the greater, the seedier, the dirtier. Primal, in a backwoods sort of way. I found it intoxicating.

I remembered the rooms, gold with the haze of alcohol, couches and dim light, bad music playing from somewhere hidden. The lazy pace, the drugged stares, the hypnosis. And the women, in all states of dress and undress, slumped in chairs, lounging in doorways, waiting for you to catch their eye. I remembered May, in a room somewhere some night, swaying drunken on Charlie's lap. Around them were other women, most of them topless or naked, and it was dark and a beat was thumping and bodies were entwined in the shadows. I remembered May's eyes, locked onto Charlie's, her hands unbuttoning her blouse, shrugging it from her shoulders, all the while whispering as the women watched and I watched. I remembered taking one of the other women in desperation, staring up at her face and seeing only May, wanting only May.

I remembered how year by year the clubs got bigger and brighter, full of more people and more money and more police. I remembered wondering just how big and far and wild it could all go. And I remembered one night seeing a strange man stalking about in the shadows of one of our places. Narrow faced, with square glasses that had eggshell-thin lenses, a man not drinking, not using the women, not gambling—just watching, seeming to observe everything and everyone. I knew him from somewhere, some earlier time, and distant alarm bells sounded. Had he worked at my paper once? He certainly didn't any more. But, as always, I was too drunk to really bother about who he was, or what the alarms might mean.

Fool. I was so far beyond genuine newspaper work that I couldn't even spot an investigative journalist when he was jotting down notes right next to me at the bar.

That's all it took, in the end. The serious elements in the media shook off their thirty-year lethargy and almost casually, certainly with no belief that anything serious would happen, they began to report what everyone already knew. They listed some of the venues, some of the names of the owners, noted that the police appeared to be involved. Just a few feature articles, but a ripple ran through the state. Then came an hour-long piece on a national current affairs television show. 'The Moonlight State' it was called. Another ripple, perhaps a small wave. But that was all. In the end they'd barely scratched the surface, and besides, it had happened before. None of us was worried. All that was needed were a few official denials, a few suppression orders, and it would all die down again. But inexplicably, the government panicked. To this day no one knew why. The premier was aging, some said, losing his grip. Others said the police minister was running wild and had no idea what was really happening under his authority any more. There were all sorts of stories. But the result in the end was that an Inquiry was announced.

An independent Inquiry.

Even then it might not have mattered. There had been inquiries before, and they'd been safely managed, the terms limited. But something was in the air this time. The Queen's Counsel appointed to run the Inquiry was, to everyone's surprise, apparently in deadly earnest. The long-suffering elements of law and order saw a sliver of a chance. Lawyers rolled in, whistle-blowers rolled in, all the long-silenced enemies of the system burst into song and the initial panic of the government disintegrated into angry confusion. The terms of the Inquiry ballooned out from a simple question of brothels and casinos to involve corruption within the whole police force. From there it sprang to their political masters, and finally to the entire Queensland political structure. It was wildfire, no one could stop it, only stand back horrified. Desertions began, papers were burnt, ministers were suspended. Harried witnesses saw themselves being abandoned, started buying immunity by informing, and suddenly the whole invulnerable edifice was shuddering, and then collapsing, awfully, into chaos.

It amazed me even now.

I looked up and down the street. It had all happened here. A different world and a different time. A different culture even.

Prohibition was gone. Gambling was legal now. There were big casinos in every major Queensland city. Poker machines in every bar and club. Liquor licences were handed out almost for the asking. Pubs and bars could open virtually any hours they liked. Even the cafes had beer and wine. It was all out in the open and anyone could have it, no elites, no secret societies, everything properly taxed, properly monitored. What need, then, for an underworld? What need for men like Marvin or Lindsay? Or for the rest of us, the hangers-on, the drunkards, the dupes and the fools.

Prostitution remained the only riddle. Ten years of new governments and new laws, and they still hadn't worked out what to do. To legalise brothels or not to legalise them. To arrest the streetwalkers or not, or the women working from their homes, or their pimps or their customers—the laws seemed to change every year. As if it was really any different from drinking or gambling, as if there was really even a choice about whether it should exist or not. Of all the old Inquiry sins, only prostitution was still in the shadows, and as always, I assumed, it would be thriving there. Someone would be running it, paying the money, making the money. The only difference now was it would be someone I didn't know.

I saw a cab rank a short way up the road. There was one taxi there, its driver sitting smoking behind the wheel. I seemed to remember that smoking in cabs had been outlawed since I'd left. Even for drivers free of any passengers. Some vices went out, others came in.

I got up and walked to his window.

'Going somewhere?' he asked.

I didn't even bother with euphemisms. 'I've been away for ten years,' I said. 'I was wondering where the brothels are these days?'

He looked at me, considering. 'Who says there are any brothels any more?'

'What?'

'Brothels are illegal,' he told me, indifferent.

I sighed. In the old days the cab drivers didn't hesitate, they'd take you right to the front door of the nearest club and gratefully take the kickback.

'I'm not a cop or anything,' I said.

He laughed. 'I can see that.'

He looked at least fifty. Old enough to have it seen it all happen, the rise and fall.

'Come on,' I said, entreating.

He tossed away his cigarette. 'Of course, I could drive you round for a while along certain streets, and if you see a place that *you* think looks like that sort of place, then I could drop you off.'

Ah. So that's the way it was now.

Different ways, but still the same.

'So you getting in?' he asked.

'No. Just curious.'

I started walking again. I felt better somehow, reassured. The world still rolled along after all. Maybe it was all I'd needed to realise, after hours of pointless wandering and brooding. We weren't the only ones, we weren't unique or anything terrible. It all still went on. Legally or illegally, what did it really matter? We weren't demons. Not me, not May, not Charlie. Not even Marvin, wherever he was. Other things had gone wrong, yes, but they were personal things, personal betrayals, and they could happen in any walk of life. It had nothing to do with the evils of crime, nothing to do with the Inquiry.

Except Charlie was dead. And Marvin was missing. And May would be forty years old by now.

I walked, turning corners, the streets to myself.

Go home, George.

And it was good advice. To some things there were no answers.

I stopped in front of a flashing sign. It showed, in neon, a cocktail glass balancing on the back of a crouching woman. Below it, the front of the building was jet-black glass. Ultra-violet light leaked out of the doorway.

I took out the card that Detective Lewis had given me. It was the same.

It was a strip club. Something we'd never bothered with, fifteen years before. They existed, they were legal, even in those days, but the money wasn't there. Cheap rooms with tables and chairs strewn out in front of a stage, the only audience young boys too nervous, and old men too poor, for anything else. Watching dancers who were only one step up from working topless bars.

Perhaps they pretended to a little more class now, but even so . . .

Why did Detective Lewis want me to come here?

A car pulled up behind me. I turned and watched two men climb out, both in suits. They didn't so much as glance at me, just marched straight through the door.

But I stood transfixed, the night around me, the storm and rain and the long hot day forgotten in a moment. He was ten years older, the hair was thinner, the stomach bigger—but I recognised the face, and without even thinking I was reaching for my wallet and following the men through the door.

One of them was Lindsay.

TWENTY-SIX

Lindsay Heath, the Invisible Man.

The money man, the bagman, the accountant, the working manager, the one who kept all the wheels turning, night by night.

I hadn't seen him since the day the whole thing first hit the papers. As far as I knew, no one had, not even Marvin. He vanished—interstate, some said, overseas according to others, to England, to Spain, to anywhere. And behind him he'd left a pile of paperwork which clearly placed Charlie as the legal guardian of the whole enterprise—Charlie's name on all the licences and leases and pay cheques, Charlie's bank accounts full of unexplainable and untaxed money. Charlie himself was hardly pleading innocent. He'd broken the law, he knew that, had always known that, and he was prepared to admit to what he thought was fair. The licensing dodges, the bribery, some of the responsibility for the clubs. But his name, and his name alone, was on *everything*. Stuff he never even knew about. All Lindsay's little schemes and sidelines. And there were a lot of them, stretching back through the years.

He'd started out, not surprisingly, as a policeman, following in his father's footsteps, and already knowing, no doubt, all the tricks. His law enforcement career was brief but typical of the day, rolling quickly through the key sections like the old Consorting Branch, which extorted money from prostitutes, and then into the old Licensing Division, which extorted money from everyone else. Like Marvin, however, Lindsay saw soon enough that the real rewards were not to be found in petty bribery. He quit the force and set himself up as ostensibly a security specialist, but actually as consultant to a host of illegal interest groups. For a fee he would broker deals either with the police force or, later in his career, directly with the government. He represented SP bookies up and down the state. He represented gaming companies that wanted to sneak dubiously legal slot machines into clubs and pubs. He represented property developers who needed approval for criminally destructive projects without the scrutiny of any environmental agencies.

He represented anyone. And as so many of his interests coincided with the fields in which Marvin was working, it was only natural they formed a relationship. They rose hand in hand, one of them in public, the other in private. Eventually hundreds of thousands of dollars were flowing through Lindsay's fingers each week and on to Marvin, to other political figures, to public servants, government boards, councils and, of course, the police—and a percentage of it all was his to keep. No one knew just how rich he was. Certainly not me. Most of it I learned only at the Inquiry, and I was appalled. To me he'd always just been the man who knew how things worked. Perhaps outside the law, strictly speaking—and weren't we all?—but one of Queensland's key criminal figures? That I didn't know. He wasn't the only consultant of his type in the state, nor was he the biggest, but if anything placed the rest of us squarely on the uglier side of the underworld, and doomed Charlie to prison, it was Lindsay.

What had the detectives told me about him?

Don't you worry about Lindsay. We know it wasn't him.

But I'd never thought to ask them how they knew. I'd assumed they'd had word of him in Argentina or somewhere— somewhere safely out of reach and suspicion. Never would I even have conceived that he might be back in Brisbane, that I would come across him walking the streets, entering a strip bar. He was like an apparition from history.

And for the first few moments, an apparition was all he might have been. By the time I paid the cover charge, got past the front desk and entered the club, Lindsay was once again nowhere to be seen.

I stared around the room. It wasn't what I was expecting. There was no stage, no tables, no spotlight set up on the back wall. Instead it was a confused space of different levels and dim lighting, with deep couches and high booths and rooms opening off to the sides, all focused around a central pool of light, a revolving dance floor. Music pulsed from a console, and there was a naked woman on the dance floor, draped about a steel pole. No one was watching her. In the dimness all around were what seemed to be dozens of other women, all of them in lingerie, some of them with men, some of them alone, moving restlessly. And off in the booths, and glimpsed through doorways, naked women swayed privately over tables and couches, or the laps of the men who sat in them.

I stood in the doorway, unsure what to do. None of the men appeared to be Lindsay, but it was so dark. Women watched me, waiting. I couldn't simply stand there. A bar ran along one side of the room and automatically my feet took me in that direction. I was at the counter before I even remembered I no longer drank.

'Yes?' said the barman.

'Iced water,' was all I could say.

He nodded, scooped ice into a glass and slid it my way. I reached for my wallet again and he shook his head. 'No charge.'

I sipped water and leant on the bar, feeling flushed with heat, as if the storm had never come. I gazed around, trying not to let my eyes linger anywhere, and yet searching. He was in here somewhere . . . in whatever this place was. Nothing like anything from my day, that was certain. This was something less than a brothel, but more than a strip club. I felt strangely innocent. I was seeing nothing I hadn't seen before—admittedly not for a full decade, and that alone would perhaps have made me an outsider—but it was more than that. There was a new culture operating here, a new understanding I'd missed out on. So close to sex, and yet not sex. More languid somehow, less cheap, but also more distant, more aloof. I didn't get it at all.

A woman edged up to me. She looked young and serious, jet-black hair curved over half her face, her lace underwear glowing faintly in the neon light. There was nothing about her that reminded me of the working girls I'd known in the old days.

'Hi,' she said, a brief smile.

And I didn't know the routine any longer, the rules.

'I'm just here to meet a friend,' I said.

Her eyes held nothing but good will. 'Male or female?'

'Male. Um . . . so what's the deal here?'

'Up to you.' She nodded towards the woman revolving on the platform. 'The entertainment is complimentary. If you'd like something more personal, however, then we could go to a booth.'

'And?'

'Thirty dollars for half an hour, fifty for an hour.'

'And?'

'I can touch you, but you can't touch me.'

'I see.'

I was sweating, uncomfortable. Even if I'd been looking, I couldn't do this sort of thing now, not sober, not so much older. I wanted her to go away. She was too poised, too cool. It had always seemed easier in my day, almost thoughtless, just a roll on a bed somewhere in the drunken careen that was the night. I peered through the shadows. Lindsay wasn't anywhere. I noticed that the woman who was draped around the steel pole had a pubic mound that was perfectly shaven. The skin there looked as smooth and soft as if a razor had never touched it, as if hair had never grown. And suddenly I remembered from one of my own nights a beefy country girl tugging at her hefty chunk of pubic hair and shrieking with laughter at the very suggestion.

'I'm just going to look around,' I told the woman next to me.

She nodded. 'I'll be here.'

I moved off, glass of water in hand, and worked my way through the crowd. There seemed to be plenty of men, but even more women. The men were mainly in suits and looked like business types, but it was not like my time. The suits were of a better cut now, the lapels narrower, the ties thinner, the haircuts shorter. And for the women, the lingerie was less garish, the high heels more subdued, and there was no eye shadow, no outrageous waves of hair. I couldn't remember, had I realised how tasteless we all were back then? It didn't matter.

The music thumped. I couldn't see Lindsay. I edged along walls and peered into booths. Naked thighs slid along the zips of black suit-pants, men stared up as breasts swung before their eyes. Why? To what end? I still didn't understand it. Men glanced sideways at me and I moved on. Women approached me and smiled, and I moved on. A hallway led to more booths and rooms. In the darkness it was like a maze. Could sex be happening in here somewhere? Would anyone see? Was there an extra charge you could pay?

I wound up back at the bar. A new woman was dancing on the revolving floor. The first woman I'd spoken to was walking away with another man.

I ordered more iced water from the barman.

'You don't drink?' he asked.

'No.'

'You might want to pick yourself a woman then.'

'Why?'

'They won't like it if you don't spend money one way or the other.'

'Oh.'

I scanned the bar behind him. All the old bottles, the old companions, glistened there as if I'd never left them. I could always order a drink, leave it sitting on the counter. I could trust myself that far, surely. Hold a drink in my hand again, feel the weight of it, hear the ice clink against the side . . .

And then there he was. Across the room a curtain in a doorway swung back and he came through. It was him, there was no doubt. Older, much older, more then ten years' worth. But it was him. He glanced about the room, his expression harried, his eyes darting over me as if I wasn't there, and then he hurried straight across the floor and disappeared through another curtain. The women all ignored him.

And I understood. He owned the place. That's why Detective Lewis had sent me here. He knew I would meet Lindsay. It was just a game, a parting joke to play . . .

I turned back to the barman, pointed to the curtained doors.

'Does Lindsay Heath own this place?'

'Sure he does. Why?'

'I need to talk to him.'

The barman shrugged. 'He should be back out later.'

'Please. I need to talk to him right now.'

He went to a phone that hung on the wall. He picked it up and spoke into it. After a time he looked at me.

'Why do you want to see him?'

'I'm an old friend. From years ago. George.' I had a sudden fear he wouldn't remember me, or wouldn't care, wouldn't want to see me anyway. A flash of inspiration came. 'Tell him I'm looking for Marvin McNulty.'

The barman spoke into the phone again, waited, spoke some more and then hung up. He nodded at me. 'Just wait a minute.'

I turned and faced the second doorway again. Around me the music pulsed and the women sauntered to and fro, but I was hardly aware of any of it. Time passed. A minute. Two minutes. Five. What was taking so long? Finally the curtain parted and two suited men emerged. They looked like bouncers, young and clean-cut and bulging. They came over to the bar, and the barman nodded towards me.

'This way, sir,' one of them said.

I followed them across the floor. They paused at the curtain and parted it, waiting for me to go through. Beyond the curtain all the luxury and carpeting ceased. I was in a bare cement hallway, and suddenly my arms were pinned behind my back, and an arm was around my neck.

'What the—'

'Hold fucking still,' a voice hissed in my ear.

I was in shock. I didn't understand what was happening. Even if I'd wanted to, I couldn't move. My feet were almost off the ground, and the grip on my neck was tight enough to be choking. I could feel nothing but the raw muscle holding me, and hands as solid as bricks moving over my body, inside my shirt and pants. It dawned on me, amongst it all, that they were looking for weapons.

'I don't have anything,' I gasped. 'I'm just a friend.'

'Oh, really?' the voice in my ear said.

I was lowered minimally and shoved along the hall, my arms still locked behind me. This was crazy. We came to a door and one of them moved ahead to open it. I was pushed through. I caught a glimpse of an office—a desk, chairs, filing cabinets, an overflowing ashtray, all cheap. Then I had a bouncer on either side of me, each holding an arm, and there was Lindsay. His eyes were narrow and surrounded by deep, fleshy bags, and there was no recognition in them.

'You must be fucking suicidal showing up here,' he said.

'Lindsay,' I got out, 'it's me. George. Remember? Charlie. Marvin. All of us.'

The eyes peered at me, and for a moment I thought I had it all wrong and that I'd never known him and he'd never known me, no matter how clearly I knew otherwise.

'Well, fuck . . .' he said. He shook his head. He stared some more and laughed. 'Let him go, fellas. This isn't him.'

The grip on my arms disappeared.

Lindsay was still laughing. 'George, you dumb bastard. I was about to fucking kill you.'

And, legs gone weak, I sank into a chair.

TWENTY-SEVEN

I'd never liked Lindsay.

It was a drinker's suspicion, possibly, of a non-drinker. Lindsay drank, but he wasn't like the rest of us. There was no love affair with the alcohol, no shining path opening in his mind the way it did in mine, no drunken night extending off into infinity. He was a money man. And the money was always the reason he was with us.

He sent his bouncers away, patted me on the back. 'It's okay, George. Take a second.'

But there was no friendliness in him. He'd never liked me either.

I gulped in air. Lindsay sat behind his desk, stared at me a moment, then shook his head and reached for a cigarette. Up close he was harder to recognise than he'd been from a distance. He'd taken off his jacket and his shirt was wrinkled and sweat-stained. He looked unhealthy, pale and overweight, and tired. His naked scalp shone. There was a coarse, veined sheen to his face, and his eyes were sleepless. He cupped his hands around the lighter, sucked in, then snatched the cigarette away from his mouth impatiently.

'What was all that about?' I asked when I had my breath back.

He exhaled a tight jet of smoke. 'We thought you were someone else.'

'Who?'

He shrugged.

'I gave my name.'

'So we got it wrong.' The cigarette tapped against the ashtray. 'What are you doing here, George?'

'Me? What are *you* doing here? What are you doing in Brisbane, in *Australia* even?'

'What does it look like?'

'But when did you get back?'

'Years ago.'

'I didn't hear anything.'

'I hardly made any public announcements.'

His voice was different too. When I'd known him, he'd had the calm and steady air of the ex-policeman. Now he sounded hoarser, less convincing. And irritated. Like a harried public servant, lower management, after a lifetime's career in a cramped little office that reeked of tobacco, dealing with a client he had no interest in seeing.

'And they let you come back . . . after everything?'

'Why not?'

'Why not?!'

'I fixed it, George. That's all that matters.'

'But then . . . why come back at all?'

He stared at me like I was mad. 'Why wouldn't I?'

'Jesus, a million reasons.'

'I didn't see it like that.'

I couldn't believe I was having this conversation. This was Lindsay . . . I'd even heard a rumour once that he was in *Iceland*.

'But where were you all those years?'

His gaze moved away, restless. 'Around.'

'That's it? Around?'

'Well, what about you? I heard you hid out in the fucking mountains.'

I gave up. Wherever he had been, he was back. I looked around the room. 'And you're still . . . in the business?'

He relaxed a little. 'More or less.'

'I didn't see your name on the door. They'd never give you a liquor licence, surely?'

A thin smile. 'I've got partners.'

'Silent partners? Like Charlie?'

I was still in shock, perhaps. Lindsay was the one with two bouncers waiting outside, not me, and I wasn't fooled by his appearance. He was not a man to insult lightly. Though I'd never seen it—or at least, I'd never come close to it until a moment before—I knew he was capable of violence. How much, I didn't know. There were stories of beatings in his police days, and worse. And for all its amateurish, chaotic ways, people *did* get killed in the Brisbane underworld of the '80s. No one I ever knew, and nothing had ever suggested to me that Lindsay was involved in anything like that. But on the other hand, as I'd learned in the Inquiry itself, he was involved in everything.

He only shrugged again, breathed in smoke. 'I had nothing against Charlie.'

'It didn't seem like that.'

'It was just the way things went. We all made money for a while there. You too, far as I remember. And Charlie.'

'He's dead, you know.'

'Yeah. I know.'

'I didn't see you at the funeral.'

A shake of the head. 'What are you doing here, George?'

'The police think it might be someone from the old days who killed him.'

His interest was barely polite. 'Well, it wasn't me.'

'They think it was Marvin.'

'Why would Marvin do anything to Charlie?'

'Why would anyone? Charlie was harmless.'

'Someone didn't think so.'

I stared at him, not knowing what I wanted from this. My head was still spinning. What did it mean, Lindsay being in town? And if the police thought Marvin and Charlie had reasons to hate each other, what about *Lindsay* and Charlie? Of all of us it was Lindsay who Charlie had reason to hate. And whereas it was impossible to imagine Marvin doing anything like that, Lindsay . . . Lindsay was something else. If Charlie had come out of the past, full of anger and blame, nipping around Lindsay's heels, what would Lindsay do?

Don't you worry about Lindsay . . .

I said, 'The police told me they *know* it wasn't you. How do they know that?'

'They know where I was that night. And it was nowhere near Charlie.'

'You've talked to the police?'

'Course I have.'

'They told me to come here, you know.'

'Who did?'

'Detective Lewis.'

Lindsay considered this for a moment. 'He's an arsehole.'

I looked around the office again, at the filing cabinets, the boxes of alcohol, the rosters and pay-sheets piled up on the desk, and it was all as familiar as yesterday. 'They don't mind that you're back in the trade?'

'This is all legal, George, it's not like the old days.'

'Where are the bedrooms? Upstairs?'

He was scornful. 'You don't get it. Brothels are illegal. For the moment anyway. Next year they got new legislation coming through and they reckon maybe then we can set something up. But right now, this is it.'

I was scornful myself. 'So no one is running women any more?'

He smiled. 'It's supposed to be single girl operations only, no collectives, no management. It's trickier than it used to be. That's why these places do so well now.'

'I never thought you'd end up running strip clubs.'

'It's not that bad. It's all more upmarket. It's corporate. You can't hold a business lunch in a brothel, but a business lunch with lap-dancing and a steak, everyone thinks that's fine. We have a kitchen upstairs, that's all, no bedrooms. But if it's sex you're after, well, things can be arranged. Why? You after a woman for the night?'

'No.'

'You've changed then, from what I remember.'

'So have you.'

He nodded. 'Things were crazy back then, it was always gonna fall apart.'

But there was a certain bitter satisfaction in his tone. As if he'd triumphed in some way that I didn't understand. And maybe he had. Almost everyone else, from our syndicate and from all the other syndicates, had gone broke or gone to prison, and yet Lindsay had survived—reduced admittedly, older and smaller, but still in business. Though I couldn't see that it had brought him any joy. Ten years had not treated him well. Nor could I see how he'd arranged it. The authorities had wanted him more than anyone.

'Did you ever see Charlie after the inquiry?' I asked.

He shook his head. 'From what I heard about him, I don't think he would have got past the front door of any of my places.' He looked me over. 'I'm a little surprised you got in.'

'What about Marvin?'

'That's right, you said you were looking for him.'

'So are the police.'

His didn't answer. His eyes were following the curls of smoke above his head.

'He's been officially reported missing.'

That caught his attention. 'Missing?'

'His housekeeper reported him missing yesterday.'

Lindsay blinked. 'The fucking idiot.'

'Who—the housekeeper?'

He gave me a disgusted look. 'No, not the fucking housekeeper.'

It sunk in. 'You know where he is, don't you?'

He was stubbing his cigarette out angrily. 'Why do you want to see him anyway?'

'Because of Charlie, of course.'

'Marvin didn't have anything to do with it. Electrocution, for Christ's sake. That's hardly Marvin's style.'

'Do you know that for sure?'

'It wouldn't make any sense, I know *that* for sure.'

'Marvin and Charlie met up in St Amand's detox ward just before Charlie died. And since then, Marvin's disappeared. There must be some connection.'

He was taken aback. 'A detox ward? Marvin?'

'A detox ward. With Charlie.'

'Marvin didn't say anything about any detox ward. Or about Charlie.'

'You've talked to him?'

Lindsay pondered his ashtray for a moment, made a decision. 'He came to see me a couple of weeks ago. He just said he needed to lay low for a while and did I have somewhere he could stay. I said sure. I guess he forgot to tell his housekeeper he'd be away.'

'But what's he hiding from?'

'Who knows? None of my business. None of yours either.'

'But Marvin must have said something.'

'He didn't, and I didn't ask. I was just doing him a favour, for old times' sake.'

'But you must have some idea.'

'You don't get it. Marvin and I aren't in business any more. I hardly ever see him. He calls me up sometimes if he wants some girls for a party or something, but that's about it. So this time he calls up and needs a place to stay, and I got a house I'm not using right now, so what's the harm?'

'But haven't the police asked you where he is? They asked me.'

'To hell with them, I'm not their fucking errand boy.'

'You lied to the police?'

'I withheld information.'

'That's a big favour, just for old times' sake.'

'Believe me, it's as far as I plan to go. To hell with Marvin too. I'm not his fairy godmother.'

I realised he was furious. It was something to do with Marvin. What was their relationship now? In the old days Marvin had been in charge. Lindsay managed the money, certainly, but it was Marvin who decided what clubs we opened and when, Marvin who brought in the special friends and guests and entertained them, Marvin who would call Lindsay out of the office and let him know that *this* friend was to get everything for free, and *that* friend wasn't.

But Marvin went to jail and lost it all, and here was Lindsay. Prospering, it seemed, all on his own. What need would he have to help Marvin?

I said, 'Can I get a phone number, or an address?'

'He doesn't want to see anyone.'

'Well, could you call him at least, and let him know. He can ring me if he wants. I'll give you my number.'

'Maybe,' he said, but it was mostly a refusal.

'C'mon . . . you don't think it's *me* he's trying to avoid?'

'No offence, George, but why the fuck would anyone hide from you?'

'Tell him I just want to talk about Charlie. That's all. And I won't say anything to the police. About you *or* him.'

His eyes blazed, and suddenly Lindsay didn't look old or tired at all. 'Not if you have a brain, you won't.' Immediately he cooled, leaned back again in his chair. 'Why do you wanna get involved in Marvin's mess anyway? Wasn't once enough?'

'You know what Charlie was doing up in Highwood, don't you?'

'Getting himself killed?'

'He was looking for me.'

He nodded, but his gaze still held, undecided. 'What do you do these days, George?'

'I work on the paper, up at Highwood.'

'Nice town, is it?'

'Very nice. A little too quiet for you, though, I'd think.'

He didn't smile. 'You wanna know why those two guys were so heavy when you came in?'

'Why?'

'Marvin did say a few things. He said the police might be looking for him, and he didn't want them to know. No problem there. But he said someone else might be looking for him too. Someone he *really* didn't want to meet.'

'Who?'

'A friend. An old friend.'

'Like I said, he doesn't mean me.'

'I know. He told me who it was.'

'Who?'

But Lindsay appeared not to have heard. 'So I'm sitting here,' he said, 'and I get a call that some guy is in the bar looking for Marvin . . .'

My eyes strayed to a security television screen in the corner. The picture flicked between an overhead shot of the foyer, and a long shot of the bar. It didn't show any of the booths. I watched as a man handed over money to the bartender. Lindsay would have been able to see me there, but the definition and the lighting weren't good. I could have been anyone. The man at the bar could have been anyone. The television made him seem ominous, a dark shadow in black and white.

'But I gave my name.'

'Exactly.'

'I don't understand . . .' And then I did. 'This person's name—it's George?'

Lindsay nodded, waiting.

'But George who? I don't know any friends of Marvin's called George. Except me.'

He stared at me, wondering. 'You really don't know?'

'No.'

'Fuck, what were you doing back then?' He sat up abruptly, all business again. 'Well it isn't my job to tell you.'

'But . . . is this anything to do with Charlie? Is this the man who—'

'No idea. Marvin didn't say.'

'But he was worried?'

'He was shit scared.'

We sat there. On the closed-circuit TV screen, the man walked away from the bar and vanished into darkness.

Lindsay was watching me. 'I've never met this guy myself, you understand, but I've heard some stuff about him. And like you saw, I wasn't taking any chances. The thing is, if someone comes round, I can always look after myself. You, George . . . you sure you don't just want to go back to your little town?'

And suddenly I wasn't sure. I was disturbed. It was Lindsay himself, partly. Even balding and old, he was harder than I remembered, and colder. Maybe everything about the old days had been harder and colder than I'd realised, if I'd ever been sober enough to notice. I was sober now, and I thought of other men like Lindsay, even harder men. I thought about a man who had taken the time to string Charlie up and apply electrodes to his back, to pour mouthful after mouthful of vodka down his throat. Did I really want to know who that was?

Later I heard he'd run off into the hills . . .

I leaned across the desk and took up a pen, wrote down my motel's name and my room number on a blank pay-sheet.

Lindsay sighed. 'I'll call him tomorrow. From there, it's up to Marvin.'

And despite the heat I felt a chill inside, committed to something I knew could only be bad.

Lindsay noticed perhaps. 'You want me to get you a drink?'

'I don't drink any more.'

'No women, no drink. You given up living, George?'

'Not yet.' I rose from my chair, as if everything had been said.

Lindsay didn't stop me. He took up another cigarette.

'I'm assuming you won't come back here. If you're not buying anything I'm selling, then why bother? And there's no "old times' sake" between you and me.'

'I won't be back. I still can't believe you're even here. Why didn't you just stay away? What's so special about Brisbane?'

He paused, lighter in hand. 'Money, George. What else? This is still one of the biggest sucker states in the world. It always will be. But if you can't see that already, even after all these years, then I can't explain it to you.'

I didn't know what he meant, and didn't care.

I put my hand on the doorknob. I said, 'What if I had been this other George. What would you and your two boys have done with me?'

Lindsay smiled, and I saw in that smile a pit opening, both to the past and the future, where nothing I'd believed was true or had ever been true. It was a smile that welcomed me into the world of the way things *really* were, if I wanted to enter it.

I was gone before he had a chance to answer.

TWENTY-EIGHT

It was Maybellene who blinded me.

To the way things really were.

It was a criminal world, a cheap and banal world, full of exploitation and even violence, and I should always have known. But May was part of it, and I was in love with her, and that's all I really remembered. Maybellene, and the drinking.

I wasn't the only one. In a way, with the exception of Lindsay, we all fell for her. In theory she was the least important person in the syndicate, she had the smallest amount of money invested, had no direct connection to any of the operations. But in other ways, she was the centre around which we all revolved. Jeremy doted on her like a grandfather, Marvin was smart enough to exploit her intelligence for his own ends, Charlie simply worshipped her, and I . . . I held her darkly in my heart, waiting.

None of us could have said exactly why. Perhaps it had something to do with the way she'd come to the syndicate. So reluctant and distrustful. The rest of us had never given a thought to the ethics of what we were doing, but May had started out differently. In the austerity of her Catholic school, the teenage May had developed an earnest and burning sense of morality. Not Catholic morality, morality of a deeper sense. One that involved fairness. She could see even then it didn't operate in Queensland. Part of her wanted to escape. To Sydney, or Melbourne, or somewhere overseas. Anywhere. But Jeremy was right. She may never have joined a convent, perhaps, but her sensibilities were of the missionary kind. The young May couldn't bring herself to walk away from a crusade.

And so she couldn't abandon Queensland. What place in the world, after all, needed her help more? Staying in Brisbane was her first act of self-sacrifice.

Hence university and the political studies and the activism. But it all went wrong. The crusade went nowhere. The people of Queensland didn't want to be saved, her fellow missionaries all betrayed the cause, and she ended up alone in a prison cell. All that concern and outrage and desire to improve things, thrown back in her face. The world *wanted* to be the way it was. No wonder it turned to bitterness. No wonder that when Jeremy came sliding in, arch manipulator of the young that he already was, he found her so easy to turn.

But there was a price, and from that moment on there would be a fatal division in May. While betraying all the beliefs of her youth, she could never embrace the opposite philosophy either, Marvin's philosophy, or Jeremy's. She did what they wanted of her, but for all that they might whisper in her ear that theirs was the only way, the right way, she was never completely convinced, could never quite forgive herself. So she was left with no beliefs at all, only an anchorless cynicism. One of us but eternally an outsider, holding as much disgust for her new life as she was disillusioned about her old. And that was what gave her power. She wasn't there for the money or the greed or the indulgence. She shared none of our laziness or self-congratulation. She was alone in her vacuum, cold and clear, and so formed a single, bright point in the muddy haze that was our world.

But the doubts remained, deep within.

Which is why, possibly, she resorted to alcohol. It silenced her conscience, stifled all the questions that ate away at her, cast the golden glow, just as it did for me. But she knew, too, that it was an illusion. From that first bottle of champagne I saw her struggling to open, the dilemma was never resolved. Whether to sink into the safety of oblivion, or face herself in sobriety. She would battle with those first few drinks, terribly at odds with the temptation, because once she'd had the one or the two, she knew it wouldn't stop. It was in those moments—when some higher sense of purpose in her strove with a blacker passion—that I fell in love with her. She went through it every time before she drank, and I watched it every time with a sort of breathless expectation. Nor did I ever encourage her one way or the other. Any other friend, I would have paid for the drinks and poured the first one down their throat . . . but not with May. She appeared so naked, so exposed, poised on the verge of that choice. In the end she almost always chose the alcohol, but it was never a settled thing, even after years. She would look at that first bottle with something like dread and something like longing, and the struggle for her soul would go on.

Charlie watched her too.

While May's agony aroused a fascination in me, it aroused only sympathy in him. It was a marginal thing, for of course none of us would ever have encouraged someone *not* to drink. But whereas I would welcome May's first glass with a toast of my own, Charlie mourned it with a momentary sadness. Maybe he saw, as I didn't in those early days, how different May was from the rest of us, that she could have done so much better than sink into our world. I didn't agree. I thought May fitted our world exactly, expanded it, fulfilled it. For when the alcohol was singing in her, she was free from any constraint or doubt at all. And free, she was far wilder and more dangerous than any of us. That's when her contempt for Queensland, for its hypocrisy and stupidity and suffocating small mindedness, was all set loose. In those moods it was May who drove us out into the streets, to the clubs and the casinos. May who called for champagne or cocktails instead of just wine and beer. May who never wanted the night to stumble to an end. May who would parade through the brothels as if she owned them, then drag Charlie off to a room to play whore for the evening.

And what a figure she cut. In a world of false brilliance and thin glamour, her very plainness was striking. The simplest of clothes and hair, a body that was lean and straight—surrounded by the rest of us, men and women alike, soft and overweight and overdressed. Everyone was aware of her, confused by her, unsettled by her. She didn't fit any of the patterns, never sank into any of the usual complacencies. No matter how much she drank, her face never lost its intensity and severity, its anger. To me she was a glowing streak through the night, leaving all the other women, as fiery and beautiful as they supposedly were, tumbling behind in her wake.

And yet it could turn black. As if this life was not the life she wanted at all, and even drunk it would come to her suddenly, turn her cold and furious. She would round on us all, rage against Jeremy and Marvin and the way they had sunk their claws into her. And in those moments, to my dismay, it was Charlie who would take her home, or take her out for walks through the empty streets, to sit in parks or bus stops and wait with her until the mood passed. It was Charlie she held, Charlie to whom she cried, to whom she apologised—for what, I didn't even know. But later I would understand it was the decency in him that she was clinging to. The innate thing that made Charlie, despite everything he did, a good man. He understood something about her I didn't, or maybe he saw the life she could have been living instead. In loving him she was choosing a man who did not applaud her failings, a man who saw more than the darkness in her, a man who, if she had ever sought to change, to rebuild herself, would have done his best to help.

I was none of those things. I didn't want her to change. I was excited by May just as she was, excited by the conflicts within her. And there were times, I knew, when she was excited by me. I wasn't like Charlie, she knew there was no moral base in me to hold her back. She knew I was self-centred and dissolute, that I cared nothing about the problems of Queensland or the world at large. She *liked* that. With me, she was the most free of her doubts, the most free to sink as deep as she wanted to go. So I was always the one to whom she turned for support when it came to action, to demanding more drinks, to choosing yet another place to go when the one we were in had shut down. I was the one with whom she laughed and mocked and hated and abandoned everything else. Marvin and Jeremy too, but mostly me.

It was another battle within her, forever being fought out between the two men in her life. At the time I couldn't believe she would choose Charlie. I was the one always at her side while Charlie was off sweating in his kitchen, or entertaining his customers. Charlie was always the one wondering if we really needed to stay out another hour, if we really needed to find another bar. And yet I was missing the things that really mattered. The things that were said when she and Charlie were out in those parks and bus stops. Charlie did have a moral base. He offered her a foundation, not one that would hold her back, but one that would hold her together. He offered her the hope that maybe she hadn't betrayed everything of her past, that maybe she hadn't lost everything the old self had been. He could still see those things in her, and so when she was with him, they still existed.

I had no hope to give. I knew I was spiralling downwards. I prayed that May was too. I wanted us both to go down together.

That was what I called love.

She chose Charlie, and I was best man at their wedding.

It was May who broke the news to me, and her tone was almost questioning, as if there was something perhaps that I should say. It wasn't that she wanted me to stop her but, as with her drinking, as with everything about her life, she was debating with herself about which way to go. And for once I broke my own rules and pushed her. I told her to get married, congratulated her, drank to them both, despite the empty wind blowing in my heart. Because Charlie *was* good for her, even I could see that, as much as it gave me no joy. Whether she was good for Charlie was a question I didn't even ask. I was thinking only of how it could be borne from my point of view. And I decided it was bearable. Nothing need change. It would still be the three of us, and even if there were levels of her that only Charlie could reach, well, there were levels that were purely mine, a link between us that alcohol inflamed and not even Charlie could join. I would settle for that.

But by then we were drinking all the time, and as Charlie's business kept growing and he got busier, more and more it was just Maybellene and me. Of course, not *just* May and me. It was a whirl of people. Jeremy and Marvin and Lindsay, and dozens of others as well. Journalists, politicians, political workers, pundits, socialites, gamblers, police and prostitutes. It was *never* just Maybellene and me. And yet we were always there, the two of us, at whatever party or function it was. Charlie would be late, if he came at all, and May would go home with him or home to him, and I would go home alone or with someone else. But we were the one constant for each other every night. Only friends, but with a tinge that was more than friendship, an unspoken acknowledgement that something possible had been refused. And the cruellest thing was that when a distance began to grow between Charlie and May, when the restlessness fermented inside her and the suspicions grew inside him, it was to me that Charlie came with the questions.

After all, Charlie said, I saw more of May in some ways than he did himself—had I noticed anything? Had she said anything? Done anything? She seemed so unhappy. He wasn't angry or jealous, only pained. It hadn't even occurred to him that it might have something to do with me. And there was nothing I could tell him. There was nothing to tell, not then.

But something *was* working at May, the dissatisfaction that lay curled in the core of her. Maybe it was inevitable, a delusion to think that Charlie's love was really enough to solve anything. Or maybe, once again, it was the alcohol that was to blame, for though she still fought the battle every night, she also lost it every night. She was drowning. There was still the lifeline to Charlie, but it was stretching thin and meanwhile there was me, down in the depths by her side. She knew, had always known, that I would only be bad for her, but somehow it was ceasing to matter. Her tears and apologies to Charlie were happening more and more and I knew I was one of the causes now. Seamlessly, night by night, things began to change. Our hands touched in ways they hadn't before, or our sides met, leaning against bars, goodnight kisses lingered seconds longer than they should have. And that look in the eye, that unspoken acknowledgement between us, became more of a challenge, a question of what choice might be made after all. Even so, I would have found that final step impossible to take, it could never have been me that reached out for her. As if, as always, I had to leave May out there alone on the brink and let her, her alone, make the choice. To walk away from me, or to drink from my poisoned cup.

So in the end it was May who looked up at the end of one long night without Charlie, drunk and swaying and deeply unhappy, defeat like tears in her eyes, and said, 'I give up, George. I don't want to go home.'

And thus the addiction started, rooted in sadness. Pleasure wasn't the word to describe it, neither was sex. Sex, amidst all the drunkenness and exhaustion, hardly seemed to matter. It was more the surrendering to self-destruction, the two of us tortured by our own flaws, and yet standing naked before each other, not physically, but spiritually, all the pretences and hope gone, one and the same. We were like a confessional, there in bed together. The face of God for each other, impossible to hide anything, and better, far better, to merge our failings together.

Everyone knew. Jeremy. Marvin. Lindsay. They read it instantly in our faces. Only Charlie couldn't see it—or couldn't let himself see it. Would we ever have told him, confronted him with it? I didn't know. We never talked of plans, May and I, never talked of any future. Perhaps we couldn't even imagine one. May always went home to Charlie in the end, racked with guilt and tears, and he forgave her without admitting the truth, and she always came back to me again. Still, maybe we would have said something one day. Or perhaps Charlie would have. It couldn't have gone on like that forever.

But around us, beyond the golden glow of the drinking and each other, the real world went on, and it was a world of cheating and lies and crime. It couldn't go on forever either. And when, inevitably, the Inquiry rolled over us all, everything changed. The glow evaporated and suddenly it was serious and stone sober, and Charlie was in deep, deep trouble. And for the first time in their relationship, rather than May needing Charlie, it was Charlie who needed May.

Even more than he needed me, his best friend.

TWENTY-NINE

It was all there in the night.

Crowded rooms and white limbs and sucking mouths, handshakes and laughter, breasts I couldn't touch, drinks that, whenever I reached for them, faded away, insubstantial, and Lindsay, leaning over a bar, handing me a phone. It was Marvin on the line, but when I picked it up it wasn't Marvin, it was Charlie, and his voice hurt, it was like a slow electric shock, and I dropped the phone, moaning, and a woman with no pubic hair lowered herself over me, warm and wet and not May, and then a real phone was ringing and I woke to the light and heat of a Brisbane morning.

I stared. The lights and the television were all switched on and I didn't know why. I was still miles away and ten years younger, suffering after another night spent sodden and fucked and forgotten. Pain danced through my bones, as familiar as a hangover. If there'd been a dishevelled female body snoring next to me, her name lost somewhere seven drinks ago, then the memory would have been complete. But I was alone and I had not spent the night taking discount sex from prostitutes. Or from May. Or from anyone. That was all years ago. The phone rang on.

Marvin, I thought, reaching for it.

'George?' said a woman's voice, and it took me a moment to recognise it.

'Emily?' I rubbed sweat from my face, blinking at the television.

'Are you okay? You sound dreadful.'

'I'm fine. I was asleep.'

'Asleep? It's ten o'clock.'

'I was up late.'

There was a pause from the other end. I could picture Emily, sitting in her neat office at the school, already long out of bed and at work on a crisp Highwood morning. I felt obscurely guilty, as if she somehow knew my dreams of the night, could see the erection that was dying as we spoke, or had finally heard all about the life I'd kept so hidden from her.

Maybe she even thought I'd been drinking.

'I'm fine, really,' I repeated, forcing energy into my voice. 'I was just up late, watching TV.'

And why was I lying?

'Good,' she said, sounding relaxed again. 'How's it all been going down there?'

'I got the funeral out of the way.'

'Was it as bad as you thought it might be?'

'Pretty much.'

'Did anyone else come?'

'No. Not from the old days.'

'That's sad.' But there was relief in her voice too. 'How have you found Brisbane after all this time?'

'Different.'

'You haven't seen *anyone?*'

'No.' I still didn't know why I couldn't tell her. 'I'll probably stay a few more days yet, though. Now that I'm down here.'

'Oh.'

'But not too long. Don't worry.'

'Good. I think Gerry would like you back. The novelty of running the paper on his own is wearing a bit thin. And anyway, I miss you.'

'I miss you too. I miss Highwood.'

She laughed. And then she stopped. 'Um . . . there was another thing.'

'What?'

'Joan got a phone call at the boarding house. It was for you.'

And the last of the sleep was gone. I sat up. 'Who from?'

'She didn't say. The caller, I mean. It was a she. Joan knew you were in Brisbane, so she gave the woman my number, and she called me.'

'You never got a name?'

'No. She asked for you and I said you were in Brisbane. She wanted to know where, but I said I wouldn't tell her that unless she said who she was. When I asked again, she just hung up.'

I didn't speak. A hope had flared and died in my chest, left me without air.

'Was that all right?' Emily wanted to know. She sounded upset. 'I thought I shouldn't give your address to just anyone, not after what happened to Charlie.'

It might not have been Maybellene. There was no reason it would have been her. No reason at all. I kept my voice calm. It wasn't Emily's fault. The woman hadn't left a name.

'It's fine, Emily,' I said. 'It was probably nothing.'

'I mean, it seemed odd that she tried to get you at the boarding house. You haven't been there for so long.'

'Yes.' And there were only two people it could be, two people who might try a number ten years out of date. Charlie was one of them and he was dead. The other was May. I'd given her that number the very last time we'd talked. She'd never called me back. Oh no, it wasn't anything important at all. 'But, Emily, if she calls again, you may as well tell her where I am.'

Emily was silent. She knew who we were talking about.

'Okay,' she said finally. 'I'll tell her.'

'It's okay, really, everything is okay.'

'Have the police found out anything about Charlie yet?'

'No. Not yet.'

'Be careful then,' she said, and I was remembering how good Emily had been to me, for so long.

'I will,' I said. 'And I'll be home soon. For good.'

'I've got a class, George, I'll have to go.'

'Emily . . .'

'Call me when you get home.'

And she was gone. It felt as if far more had been said than we meant to say, but I didn't know what exactly. I sat on the bed. Out through the window the sky was bright and clear, the haze of the last few days washed away by the evening's rain, but the humidity had already returned, and it would build for the next day or days or weeks, pooling over the city until another front came through.

The TV was switched to the mid-morning news. They, too, were talking about the weather. Last night's storm had been worse than I'd thought. Parts of the city had been blacked out and even twelve hours later the power still hadn't been restored. People were complaining, and a government minister was holding a press conference asking people to be patient. There was a restructure happening in the industry, and these sorts of delays would soon be a thing of the past.

Some things in Queensland, it seemed, never changed.

The phone rang again.

I picked it up, knowing it would be Emily, to unsay something, whatever it was that we'd said.

'He wants to see you.' It was Lindsay, his voice like gravel in my ear.

'What?'

'You got lucky. Marvin wants to see you. Today.'

'Where?'

'My place over at Redcliffe. It's on the beach.' He gave me the address and I fumbled for a pen, wrote it down.

'He's waiting for you,' Lindsay went on. 'And one more thing. Take this any way you want, but Marvin says to make sure you're not followed.'

'You're kidding?'

'*He* wasn't, that's all I know.'

And Lindsay was gone.

I stared at the coffee table and at Charlie's ashes, contemplating two different voices on the phone, and what they'd each told me. My head was full of May. I wanted to call the boarding house and get Joan on the line and find out if there was anything she might have missed, anything to tell me who the caller was, *where* she was. But Marvin was the important thing. Marvin was the key. Not May.

I showered and dressed and started on the long drive out to Redcliffe.

It was the last part of town I would have looked for someone like Marvin. Or Lindsay, for that matter. I doubted the police would think of it either. Which was possibly why Lindsay owned a house out there in the first place. Maybe he hadn't left the country after all—maybe he'd hidden the whole ten years out on the peninsula. Redcliffe was not even part of Brisbane proper. It occupied, all on its own, a headland at the northern end of Moreton Bay. It was a city in its own right, and historic, for it was at Redcliffe, in 1824, that white settlement was first attempted in what would later become known as Queensland. The idea was to set up a penal colony a safe distance from Sydney, hundreds of trackless miles to the south. Moreton Bay was selected as the general area, and the first boatload of convicts and soldiers opted for the Redcliffe site on the assumption that it had plenty of potable water, fertile land, and a safe anchorage for ships. They were wrong on all counts and after a year the settlement was abandoned in favour of a new site fifteen miles or so to the south-west, on the banks of a large river. Both the river and the new settlement were named after the current governor back in Sydney, and the city of Brisbane was born.

Redcliffe survived, however, and I drove through the sprawl of Brisbane's northern suburbs, heading for the bay. For Marvin's sake I kept looking in the rear view mirror to see if I was being followed. I felt ridiculous doing so, and even if I was being followed I had no way of knowing it. The roads were all major and busy and the streams of cars behind me were completely anonymous. I had an idea that maybe I should be taking a more tortuous route—doubling back and making odd turns to see if anyone stuck to my tail. But I was getting lost enough as it was amidst all the new arterials and bypasses, and if anyone was keeping track of me through it all, then I wasn't going to shake them anyway. Shake them? Shake who? Deep down I couldn't really believe in the whole idea. Charlie might be dead and Marvin in hiding, but some things still seemed beyond the possible. This was still only Brisbane.

I found myself in Sandgate and then made my way on to the bridge. It was long and low and narrow, running for kilometres across the bay to the head of the peninsula, for Redcliffe remained an awkward place to reach, eternally cut off by the ocean and rivers and marshlands. The tyres of my car thumped over the cement sections, and I gazed across the water to where distant container ships plied along the channel, and yachts searched vainly for a breeze. Then I was across. The road curved around, following the headland. On my right was the water, on the left was a line of fast-food shops and aging holiday units. Further inland I knew the town was a mix of working-class suburbs and more expensive estates built on reclaimed swampland, but near the water the old beach town of Redcliffe lingered on, ramshackle. A place for families on limited budgets to visit, perhaps, where there was little to do but swim, or fish, or drink.

Today the town sweltered and slept. The bay shimmered with the heat and on the beach the water was sandy green, lapping against the stones. A few small children paddled there under the gaze of their parents, but there were no crowds. Most of the holiday units had vacancy signs out. The cafe lifestyle of the new Brisbane had not reached as far yet as the peninsula, and the holiday season was weeks away. It was unlikely that Lindsay could really have spent ten years out here unnoticed, but on the other hand, Marvin had been here two weeks, a famous face, an ex-minister wanted by the police, and no one had heard a word.

Marvin. I was close now, and Marvin was here. What was I going to say to him? After all the police had told me, after reading those two stark passages from his book, I wasn't sure of the man waiting for me. Not the old Marvin—could the old Marvin have written those words? Had he always thought that way? When I met him now, would the sneering contempt still be there? I didn't know. Old or new, there **was** only one thing of which I was still certain. He couldn't have done that to Charlie. I wouldn't even have been there if I thought otherwise.

I turned onto the esplanade and slowed, counting the house numbers. There was a small rocky rise, and the road curled inland for a moment to skirt it. On the rise itself were three or four houses, all of them big, and they were the only ones on the entire strip that had actual beach frontage. I saw the number I needed. It was on a high security gate, the house behind barely visible, set up on the rise and back from the street. I parked across the road, walked over and studied the gate. There was an intercom, and I pressed the buzzer.

Nothing happened. I looked up and down the street. There was no traffic. Down at the bottom of the hill there was a park that fronted onto a short jetty. An old man slept, nodding on a bench. Another man, his belly protruding from under his T-shirt, was unpacking a fishing rod from the boot of his car, studying the flat glare of the ocean. Heat poured down from the sky and bounced back at me from the footpath. In winter Redcliffe could be cold and dreary, and the winds never seemed to stop. In summer it baked, airless, and even the bay didn't seem to help.

'Yes?' said the intercom, and there was no mistaking it.

'Marvin?' I said. 'It's George.'

'Look at the camera.'

I looked around. Atop one of the gateposts was a small security camera. I stared up at it. 'C'mon, Marvin, it's just me.'

'No one followed you? No one's watching?'

Jesus . . . but there was no joking in his voice, and the distant chill went through me again. I studied the street. The only visible life was the two men in the park. The old man had woken up and was saying something to the fisherman. It was too far away to hear, but they both laughed.

'Not a soul,' I said into the intercom.

'All right, come on up.'

There was a click, and the gate started to roll open. I walked through, a few steps up the drive. It was made of pebbled concrete and was fringed by dense shrubs and bushes. At the top there was a double garage with both doors shut, and above that loomed another two storeys of the actual house. It looked closed and empty.

Behind me the gate banged fully open. It hummed for a moment and then started to close slowly. On impulse I walked back down the drive and peered out at the street again. I only had a few seconds, then had to step back inside before the gate closed. A car glided by slowly. It was full of teenage boys. They stared at me, vacantly hostile, and rolled on past.

Then the gate clicked shut and I was locked in with Marvin.

THIRTY

He wasn't the man I remembered.

The garage door rolled up, and I saw the thick glasses and the wide bulbous eyes that would always betray him, but otherwise . . .

'Christ, Marvin,' I said. 'Put that down.'

It was a rifle of some sort, and the barrel was swung unsteadily in my direction. Behind it swayed a thin old man, barefoot, dressed only in shorts. The big belly of his political days had shrunk to a soft round ball on his waistline, blue veined, and the rest of him was all wrinkles of pale skin. Bony arms and legs. A gaunt, unshaven face under wisps of sandy hair.

'George,' he said, staring past me. 'George, get inside, quick.'

I looked back down the drive, saw only the gate and the empty street, but there was a sense of urgency flowing from Marvin like infection. I backed into the garage, and he rolled the door down, slammed the bolt. He sagged against the wall for a moment, the rifle drooping towards the floor.

'George. Thanks for coming.'

In the warmth of the garage I smelled sweat and alcohol. He was so small. His glasses barely clung to his head. Where had it all gone? The girth, the massive charisma, Marvin the Magnificent . . .

'I've been looking for you,' I said. 'So have the police.'

'Not any more. I rang the housekeeper, said I was on holidays, said I just forgot to tell her, you know. Fucking stupid of me. Told her to call off the cops.'

'Um . . . I don't know that the police will just forget about it, not now.'

'Well . . .' His eyes darted here and there, huge through the lenses. 'So what? It's not the fucking police I'm worried about. Come on, come upstairs.'

We crossed the garage. Four cars could have fitted in there, but it was empty now. At the back there was a door and stairs heading up. We passed through and Marvin latched the door behind us. Then it was one flight up into the main body of Lindsay's house. I was ready for glass walls and ocean views, but instead we entered a dark space that seemed to have no windows at all. The air was heavy with stale cigarette smoke and the smell of scotch. Lamps glowed dimly in the corners. I could see that the entire lower floor of the house—kitchen, lounge, dining area—was one open room. The wall facing the bay was indeed all of glass, but there was a system of exterior storm shutters and they were pulled down tight. It could have been midnight in there. Midnight, and hot.

'Jesus,' I said. 'How can you stand this?'

'Air-conditioning's gone.' Marvin had propped the gun up against a couch and was pouring a drink, scotch and ice, the ice coming from a bucket that was mostly filled with water. 'Can't open the windows, though. The house is supposed to be empty. Just take your shirt off. You'll be okay. Here, have a drink.'

'I don't drink any more.'

He blinked up at me, seemed to wince. 'You gave up?'

'Years ago.'

'Oh. Oh shit.' His mouth worked, at a loss. 'I was hoping we could have a few. For old times' sake. You sure?'

'I'm sure.'

'It's no fun drinking alone, George.'

Sweat was beading in my armpits. 'I'll have some water then.'

I went to the kitchen. It was a mess of dirty plates and frozen-dinner containers. My fingers felt grime wherever they touched. I found a glass, cleaned it out and filled it. There were empty ice trays in the sink. I tasted warm water, went back to the living room. Marvin lifted his glass to me and grinned. He must have lost forty kilograms. The scraggles of hair on his chest had gone grey. And he was drunk. Woefully drunk.

'Cheers,' he said.

'Marvin, I'm here because I wanna know about Charlie.'

The grin collapsed. 'I don't know anything about Charlie.'

'C'mon. I know you and him met up in St Amand's. The police know too.'

'They do?'

'They think you killed him.'

He goggled. 'Me? They think it was *me?* I never touched him.'

'Who did then?'

'No . . . George, you don't want to go into that. Please.'

'Why are you even here, Marvin? Who are you hiding from?'

'Fuck, George. Stop. Slow down. Just fucking sit a minute. I haven't even seen you in ten years. Sit down, sit down.'

I sat down. It was a white couch, streaked with cigarette ash.

The grin flickered again, desperate. 'What've you been doing all these years, anyway?'

'I've been working. In Highwood. Where Charlie died. Don't you already know that?'

'I . . . I've never been up there.'

'But Charlie has. He came up there, looking for me. Right?'

'George . . . are you really sure you don't want a drink?'

It was almost pleading, his eyes magnified a hundred times. I thought of Marvin in his prime, big and loud and confident, hectoring journalists at his press conferences.

'Just tell me,' I said.

He hung for a second, agonised. Then something in him gave up. He fell into a chair. 'All right, then, all right. But shit, George, what's the rush?'

'You and Charlie were in that ward?'

'Of course we were.'

'Why? How did Charlie even get in there?'

'I was trying to help him.' He gulped from his glass, stared into it. 'I felt terrible, you know, about all that stuff years ago. I didn't mean it to go so bad for him at the Inquiry. It was

Lindsay's fault, not mine. I thought he'd get a suspended sentence at most. Really.'

But that deep compelling voice he'd possessed of old, the voice that could convince you of almost anything, was long gone. I didn't believe him. I'd read those pages from his book.

'You didn't seem very worried about Charlie at the time,' I said.

'But later, George, I thought about it later. It was a long time there in jail. A fucking long time. And a lot harder than I thought it was gonna be.' He looked at me, his restless body going still for a moment. 'You know what I've been doing since I got out?'

I knew, but shook my head.

He puffed himself up, almost recognisable for a moment. 'I've been writing a book, can you believe that? A book! I've been putting it all down. Everything! Well no, not *everything*. That's the whole point, after all. Not *everything*. But enough. And it's fucking good. I can write, I can really write. I should've been a writer from day one. I could've made a packet.'

He deflated again, sank back in the chair.

'But it's hard. Writing's hard. You have to bring it all back. All the old memories. I'd need a drink to get me through. A lot of drinks.'

I said, 'The police know about the book.'

'They do?'

'They've read it. They know that the last bit you wrote was about meeting Charlie in prison.'

'They know that?' He giggled, a strangled sound. 'That's right, that's as far as I got. I was stuck, George, stuck right there, meeting Charlie in prison. I can still see the way he looked at me, his face all blown in. He was never gonna forgive me.' He brooded for a moment, looked up. 'I read a lot in jail. I did a course. Literature. I read all the greats. I read the Odyssey. That's me, I thought, that's us. We got the gods angry, George. Too high, too fast. So they destroyed us and sent us away and now there are trials, trials to overcome, if we ever wanna get back home.'

And truly, only someone like Marvin would have the nerve to see those tawdry days of ours in Homeric terms.

'All we did was break the law, Marvin.'

'George, we *made* the laws.'

I let it be. 'What about Charlie?'

'That's what I'm saying. I was stuck on Charlie. I had to get Charlie out of my head. He was like a curse, that face of his. Fuck Charlie, I thought. That's what I wrote down. But it didn't work. I couldn't get out of it that easy. It's a trial, George, it's all a trial. So I start drinking, the drinking works sometimes, you get ideas, beautiful ideas when you're drunk. So I drink and drink and drink. I get some girls in and we drink some more. And then, fuck, I've got it. I've gotta *help* Charlie. That's the answer. It's a penance. I've gotta put it all right. All I gotta do is find him. Find poor old Charlie, how hard can that be?'

'So where did you find him?'

'That's the weird thing, that's the fucking uncanny thing. I've got no idea where to look. I'm drinking with these women and I've got no idea. So I think, hey, I'll go back to the little place Charlie used to own over at Paddington, that first restaurant of his. I dunno why. I was drunk. I was remembering how much fun it all was back then, boozing on with Charlie and Jeremy and shit, even with you, you were there all the time, and that fucking amazing Maybellene . . .'

He stopped, peered at me.

'You heard anything about her?'

'No. Not for a long time.'

'No,' he pondered, 'I suppose not.' He brightened again. 'But we were all friends, right?'

I thought of the pages from Marvin's book. 'Sure. We were all friends.'

'That's what I told the girls. I told them all about it. I say, we'll go to Charlie's old place for a meal. Same as always. So me and the girls go, but can you believe it, I can't find the place. The cab drops us off, and I've got all this alcohol, and we're wandering around Paddington, and the girls are getting pissed off at me 'cause they're hungry, and we're going down all these little streets, and I can't find the fucking place.'

'It's gone, Marvin, long gone.'

'Is it?' He laughed. 'Of course it is.' He fumbled around on the floor for something, came up with a pack of cigarettes. I watched while he lit one. In the old days Marvin had smoked cigars. Now the ashtrays held only thousands of cigarettes, burned all the way down to the butts. He sucked at the nicotine like he could never breathe in enough.

'Anyway, the next thing I remember, I'm alone and sitting in a park somewhere. The girls are gone and it's just me and this little park, I don't even know where I am, it's the middle of the night. So what, I think, it's as good as anywhere. The wine's all gone but there's still a whole bottle of scotch, so I think, what the hell, I'll knock that off. I get drinking and that's it for the night, as far as memory goes. When I wake up I'm coughing blood and I'm in this little detox ward that I've never even heard of. Some place for fucking derelicts.'

'The Uniting Church Dependency Hostel.'

'That's it. Turns out someone found me on the footpath just a few doors down from the place. It was just luck. Somehow I'd wandered all the way down into Bardon. Not many bums on the streets of Bardon. Maybe they thought I came from the hostel. So they dragged me in there.'

'And Charlie was there too.'

He nodded, eyes shining. 'That's the damn thing, I wake up and in the bed right next to me, coughing his own guts out, is fucking Charlie. It's like a miracle. I went looking for Charlie and bang, there he is. I mean, it's like a sign from the gods, it's some sort of answer. Can you see? Can you see what I was thinking?'

'Yes. I can see.'

'Charlie, I say, we gotta talk. We gotta sober up both of us and talk. And Charlie looks terrible, he looks like an old man, he looks about seventy. Why should I talk to you, he says. He hasn't forgiven me. But this is the chance I've been waiting for. I can fix things. So I talk him round. I really can help him, after all. I've got money. I've got friends. We can get out of that little dump and go somewhere proper, where everything is the best, where we can get our lives straight.

And I can see him thinking, maybe, maybe . . . there's still that little bit of . . .'

He ran out of words, looked at me wearily.

'Okay, George, so you don't drink any more. But do you remember what it's like? That little bit of hope you have, that one day you'll kick it and get your life back again, all the bullshit aside. I had it that day, for real. And I could see Charlie did too. You only need one friend to help. We could've helped each other, gone through it together.'

He sighed, got up and poured another drink.

I said, 'I talked to the psychologist at that ward. He said he didn't really think there was any hope for Charlie.'

'Maybe not, but you know how it is. That first bit of sobriety and you think, just for an hour or two, that maybe you could make it.'

He sat down again, swallowed fresh scotch, long and hopeless.

'Anyway, I can't stay at that place, so I leave and book myself in at St Amand's. I'll send for you, I tell Charlie, and that's what I do.'

'Did you pay for him?'

'Who else would?'

'The police said Charlie paid with cash. And you paid with a credit card.'

'Christ, I didn't want Charlie crawling in there like a charity case. I sent him round the money. Fuck, I got money. That's not the problem. But I wanted him walking in there under his own steam, like he had the right.'

'The police will be interested to hear that.'

But Marvin didn't care about the police, he was back in the detox ward. 'So there's me and Charlie in the lap of luxury, we're gonna do this together. A couple of days go by and we're feeling better. Charlie, well, Charlie was never gonna be completely okay again, you know, but at least he's talking to me. Shit, we're going through detox together—in detox you gotta talk to someone, and me and Charlie are it for each other. I'm telling him about my house over on the river, I'm telling him about how nice the kitchen is, what a shit cook

I am, and Charlie's saying he hasn't cooked in years. There's a gleam in his eye. I mean, who knows? It might've worked.'

Cigarette smoke curled in the air, stinging my eyes. I thought, fleetingly, about ironies. That it would be Marvin, of all of us, who would think of taking Charlie in and giving him a home.

'So what happened?'

Marvin was staring inwards, back into the past.

'We might have made it,' he whispered. 'It was such bad luck . . .'

'Marvin, what *happened*?'

He considered me sadly. The blue of his eyes was washed out now almost to white.

'We weren't alone in there,' he said.

THIRTY-ONE

Marvin was up out of his chair, filling another glass. He was already so far gone. For all I knew he'd been sitting in this room drinking continuously for the last fourteen days. He looked like he had. He smelled like he had. I could see at least twenty empty scotch bottles, just in a glance. And yet it hadn't prostrated him or knocked him out. He seemed beyond simple inebriation, as if he'd found some ecstatic sort of drunkenness without end or unconsciousness.

I said, 'What do you mean, you weren't alone?'

He paused a moment, surveying a distant fear that seemed to hang somewhere above my head. Then he sagged. 'You should have a drink, George, really, you should. What's the use of giving up anyway?'

'You feel better, for one thing.'

He ladled scraps of ice bitterly. 'I never do. I sober up and I start remembering everything. I remember my first day in parliament, sitting in that big office up on George Street, after the swearing in. I'm looking out the window at the city, I'm smoking a cigar and I've got a woman on her knees sucking my dick, and I was thinking I am gonna own this whole fucking state, I'm gonna run all these morons into the ground. Christ, it felt good.'

'You had it good for a while.'

'I was kidding myself . . .' He walked over to a window that was covered by blinds. He tilted one open slightly, revealing a line of bright sunlight. He squinted through it, out towards the bay, eyes roving. I waited. If I strained my ears I could just hear the suggestion of small waves tumbling onto sand.

'You know any history, George?'
'A little.'
'They landed just down there on the beach, you know.'
'Who did?'
'The first settlers. This whole damned state started right outside this window.'
'I didn't know it was right here.'
'No one remembers. I'm not sure there's even a monument anywhere. I've been down there a couple of times, at night, when it's dark and there's no one around. It's the only way to get some air. I've been thinking about them, rowing up in their little boats. If they rowed up now, while I was sitting there, I'd say turn round, boys, go find some other place, somewhere nice, there's only a hellhole waiting for you here . . .'
'They were convicts, Marvin. It was supposed to be a hellhole.'
He nodded. 'The guards used to whip their backs down to the spine. There was nowhere to escape, just the bush and the blacks and starvation. For a while, George, this was the very last place on earth.'
'It was a prison.'
'It was a useful dumping ground, that's all it was. They wanted to keep the streets clean down in Sydney. Queensland started out as a hole to hide the fucking sewage.'
He let the blind snap shut, came back over to his chair. Marvin, who as a minister of the Crown had proclaimed Queensland the development capital of the world.
'Marvin,' I asked, 'who else was in St Amand's?'
But he was still thoughtful. 'I studied some history too, while I was in jail. Queensland history. You'd think I might have done that before I became a minister. Better late than never. And it's funny, you know. For twenty years Brisbane was a military prison and took all the crap that was dumped here. Then the big pastoralists from New South Wales and Victoria moved in, and they ran Queensland like one giant paddock for their sheep. Then later the same people ran it as one great big open-cut mine. It's always been like that here. Now we're just one big fucking beach. The whole world comes and sits on our sand. That's the weird thing, George.

We got nothing but lots of land, lots of minerals and lots of coastline. That's all anyone wants from Queensland, and in the meantime they just want us to get out of their way and let them take it.'

'I don't care about any of this.'

'Nobody cares. Queensland is like a beautiful girl with lots of money. But stupid. For some reason she just loves to open her purse and bare her big pink arse to the world and say "Fuck me over, please!" to all comers. And trust me, the fuckers come running.'

'Marvin, I'm only interested in Charlie . . .'

'You're a fool, George. You're not listening.'

'Who else was in St Amand's?'

Marvin didn't respond. His eyes were closed.

I said, 'Was it someone called George?'

He shook his head, forlorn. 'You don't want to know, you don't . . .'

'Lindsay told me you were hiding here because of someone named George.'

'Fuck Lindsay.' His eyes opened. 'You know how he did it? You know how Lindsay survived? He turned fucking police informer, that's how.'

'Lindsay?'

'Big fucking Lindsay. He was a cop himself, of course, that's why. They never really leave the club. So his mates got him immunity and hid him away for a few years and pumped him for dirt on everyone else, and then when the rest of us were fucked and gone, they let him come back. Now he's their door into the whole industry. He's a fucking stooge.'

'I can't believe it.'

'No one would. No one else even knows. Just me.'

I thought of Lindsay, the fury in him at the very mention of Marvin.

'So why did he help you? Give you his house?'

Marvin spat into an ashtray. 'Because if I told everyone else about him, they'd fucking lynch him, that's why. So like it or not, he still does what I say.'

And again, none of this mattered.

'Who is this person?' I said. 'Who's George?'

He was surprised. 'You mean you don't know?'

'Lindsay said he was a friend of yours once.'

'A friend . . .' Marvin seemed to marvel at the word. 'Oh no. Never that. Not even years ago. We were business partners, that's all. You really don't remember him?'

'You were partners?'

And suddenly I was thinking of the name McNulty and Co, and remembering a photograph I'd been shown once, long before. The young Marvin, in front of his little used-car yard, and standing beside him, another youth . . .

'You mean right back at the start?' I said. 'The car lot? You mean *him*?'

Marvin nodded silently.

I was incredulous. 'But that was thirty years ago.'

His eyes held something like panic. 'Leave it, George.'

'But who is he? George who? I never even knew his name.'

Abruptly Marvin was laughing. 'It's Clarke. Clarke with an E.' And there was a trace of hysteria there.

'But you split from him decades ago. Before you and I even met.'

'No . . . we never really split. I did try to, once, but he wasn't someone you just walked away from.'

'I don't understand.'

'You never did, George. You were in a fucking world of your own.'

'Are you saying you two were still partners? Even when you were in government?'

'We weren't really ever partners, not even at the start. You didn't know me then, but I was nothing, George. I was a joke. A little weed with big glasses. You couldn't survive like that in the sort of world I was in. Used cars, all those other rackets. People are always owing you money, or coming back to you pissed off, wanting refunds. What was a little guy like me gonna do? So I linked up with Clarke.'

'Because he was bigger?'

'Bigger. Harder. You name it. He could intimidate people, believe me. And more than that. When he went after people who owed us money, he didn't just talk to them.'

'He hurt people?'

Marvin was looking very small. 'If he had to. And it's not as if I objected. But I wasn't always comfortable with it, George. That wasn't my style.'

'And later? What happened later?'

'I tried to end it, after that golf thing. I was sick of all that small-time stuff anyway. I threw all my money into politics and told him to go his own way. I didn't need that sort of help any more. He wasn't that happy . . . but he went. For a while anyway.'

'But then he came back?'

'Oh yes.' Marvin leaned forward, intense with old memories. 'Remember the power dispute?'

'I remember.'

'Clarke saw it coming. After that first round of strikes he knew the union was fucked. So he comes to see me. He's got a plan, and he needs someone in government to help him with it, and who better than his old friend Marvin? I'm not all that keen, but Clarke is hard to refuse. He puts it nicely, but he knows stuff about me, things I've done that would get me kicked out of parliament, if anyone knew about them. So what choice do I have? And anyway, it's not as if I'm not gonna get something out of the deal as well.'

'Which was?'

'We know the union is gonna lose sooner or later, right? So Clarke is putting all his money into electrical contracting companies. Staff. Maintenance. Materials. By the time the second strike comes around, he's one of the biggest electrical sub-contractors in Brisbane. He's got debts and bugger all contracts and he's not gonna last long unless something drastic happens, but he's ready. Meanwhile I'm setting things up with the Minister for Mines and Energy, letting him know that Clarke is waiting to get his people in there as soon as the union is out of the way. So the whole thing goes ahead, the government commits itself. Strikes, chaos. And Clarke's in the middle of it all.'

'And you end up as the new minister.'

'That was the beautiful part. Halfway through the strike it looks like the union is winning. So me and Clarke go to the premier. We tell him that unless the old minister goes and I'm appointed in his place, Clarke is gonna pull out of the whole deal. The premier threw a fucking fit. He needed Clarke in there. Clarke was one of the key players, he was making all the running, copping all the shit on the picket lines. And suddenly he's threatening to just walk away and leave the government with its arse hanging in the air. The premier's own job was on the line over those strikes. So damn right he appointed me.'

I was remembering the rumours that had filtered through, even to me, that Marvin had friends on the other side, that he'd convinced the premier *somehow* . . .

I said, 'And then you two together finished off the union.'

'Shit yes. I gave Clarke carte fucking blanche. Police, special laws, you name it. We'd just been holding back till then, until the old minister was in too deep. But once I was running things, we let loose. The union imploded and Clarke ended up sub-contracting for half the fucking south-east power grid.'

Another thought dawned on me. 'That's how Jeremy got May out of jail. It was Clarke's place she burned down, wasn't it? It was Clarke that Jeremy had to talk to, to get the charges dropped. That's why Jeremy came to you that day.'

Marvin was nodding. 'Favours, George. It was all about doing favours.'

'So why didn't I ever know about him?'

'Jesus, we didn't exactly make it public.'

'And no one ever caught on?'

'Oh, a few people knew, but no one did anything. No one asked any questions. No one important, anyway. Hell, all the ministers had the same sort of deal going, their own special friends, bigger stuff than me and Clarke. That's how Queensland worked. We could do anything in those days. You could award contracts to whoever you liked, there was no tendering process, no supervision. You could rezone land just by ministerial decree. Suspend building codes, suspend environmental reports. There wasn't even such a thing as native title or land rights, and we had the green movement locked away on fucking drug offences. Anything you wanted done, you could do. As long as you had a mate in the cabinet.'

'And you were his.'

'I was his. I funnelled a truckload of money his way. Not just the power thing, lots of other schemes as well.'

'And took kickbacks from him in return, I suppose.'

'Of course. That was Queensland, George. Anyone who complained . . . you just said that they didn't understand the Queensland way of doing things. You called them a communist or something, or said they came from down south. And people fucking bought it. Mention the good old Queensland way and the whole population would stand up and salute. Even when they were being robbed blind. And the idiots kept voting for us, so what the hell were we supposed to do?'

He gulped at the scotch, clutched after another cigarette. I found myself increasingly repulsed by him. There wasn't anything left of the old Marvin at all, the force and the conviction. He'd become something malign and feeble.

'Why wasn't Clarke part of the syndicate, then?'

'That's the one thing we didn't agree on. That was my baby alone. He thought it was small time, the clubs and girls and all that, he couldn't see the point. And he was right. But that's the joke, George. It was the clubs that brought the whole thing down. They were the most trivial part of it all, drinks after hours and the odd whore or two, they were nothing. But that's what got us all caught. It's what they got me on, anyway. They didn't get him. When the Inquiry came along it was me and only me who got screwed.'

'We all got screwed.'

His eyes bulged at me. 'We all got screwed . . . are you crazy? Who got screwed? I did. Charlie did. Maybe even you did. All the clubs and casinos and their customers did. All the money-grubbing fucking police did—and the commissioner was the most money-grubbing of the lot—but so what? Who were any of us? We were nobodies. No one who really mattered even got touched.'

'The whole government fell, Marvin.'

He sneered. 'The government. Sure, the government fell— but why? Because the police took money? Because a few brothels were open? Christ, it happens everywhere, it's nothing. But the idiots in this state were dumb enough to think that was as bad as it got, and after they voted us out they were dumb enough to think they'd solved the problem and nabbed all the bad guys. What bullshit.'

I shook my head. 'Everyone knew it was more than just the little things. Everyone knew the government was corrupt on a massive scale . . . even the stuff you're talking about, big business and industry and government contracts, people at least suspected it was going on.'

'Yeah? Did the Inquiry even touch people like that? No. They named a few names, but not a single one was ever investigated. Even when the new government came in, they couldn't afford to get people like that offside. They ran the bloody economy. So they all got away clean. Shit, George, that's where *all* the problems came from. All the corruption, all the crap. Big business, big money. Who the fuck else could afford to buy a government? Not your local brothel owner, that's for sure. Big money. It was always about big money. But oh no, the Inquiry didn't bother with that. The Inquiry was all about morality. About scapegoats. It was a fucking witch-hunt.'

He was getting breathless, fresh sweat breaking out on his chest. It was like watching a schizophrenic, moods swapping between exhaustion, rage, resignation.

'So I go down,' he said, 'you go down. Charlie goes down. We all go down. Except Lindsay, the prick. But Clarke . . . Clarke walks away. Goodbye Marvin, he says. The partnership's over, you fucked it up, I can't deal with you any more. I'll see you right about money when you get out of jail, but otherwise, you keep your mouth shut. And off he goes as if nothing ever happened. He's still got all the sub-contracts, all the other interests I fed him, he keeps the lot. Him and everyone like him. All those bastards that fed off us. The Inquiry didn't even slow them down.'

He fell silent at last, disgusted.

And I thought that maybe he was right, maybe it was only big business and big money that could afford to buy a whole government . . . but that government had to be for sale in the first place. People like *Marvin* had to be there in the first place. And that was Queensland's tragedy.

I said, 'What does any of this have to do with what happened to Charlie?'

Marvin looked up, regarding his dark angel once again. 'That . . . that was the curse, George. The gods aren't finished with me yet.'

'You said you and Charlie weren't alone in that detox ward. So was it Clarke who was there? Is that what you're saying?'

He nodded, wary.

'And you're saying that, for some reason . . . it was Clarke who did that to Charlie?'

And the nodding was feverish. He drank, but his glass was empty, and he studied it as if he could bear no more.

'But you said you weren't in Highwood yourself.'

'No. I wasn't there. Never there.'

'Then how do you know?'

'The substation, George. It happened in that substation.'

'What about it?'

'You think Charlie ended up there by accident? You think whoever killed him just stumbled across that substation by chance? Hidden away in that forest?'

Marvin's hands fell down between his knees, and the glass rolled onto the floor. He didn't seem to even notice.

'Don't you see?' he implored. 'Clarke knew exactly where that substation was. He knew exactly how to get in and what to do in there. He built it. He installed it. It's his fucking place, George. It was the first fucking contract he ever got.'

THIRTY-TWO

So now I knew.

A man. A name.

But it didn't feel like knowledge. It felt like an unlearning of something rather than the discovery of any truth. Three men had met in a detox ward, and one of them was dead and one of them was in hiding. And I still couldn't see any reason behind it at all.

'But why?' I said. 'Why do that to Charlie?'

The fear was back in Marvin. It was always there, deep beneath the drunkenness. Maybe it was only fear that was keeping him awake.

'I don't know why,' he said. 'Honestly I don't. I hadn't even seen Clarke since the Inquiry. He got some money to me after I came out, just like he promised, but that was it. He didn't want anything else to do with me.'

'You didn't try to start up the partnership again?'

A sour laugh. 'When I was a minister I had some use to him, maybe. Not any more. And he didn't need bad publicity like me. He keeps a low profile, that's why he gets away with as much as he does. You ever see his name in the papers?'

I thought, shook my head. I'd never heard of George Clarke at all.

'You see? Even after the union was dead, on the face of it nothing had changed. The government still ran the power supply. But what you didn't see was all the cut-price sub-contracting that was going on, to little companies here and there. To build a new substation, to maintain a section of the grid, to manage staff. Anything, as long as it was cheaper. And a lot of those companies were Clarke's companies, but you didn't see his name anywhere. You didn't see his face.'

I thought again of the one photo I'd seen, long ago. I'd only ever been looking at Marvin. The figure next to him was taller, heavier, with a blunt, blurred face. Unsmiling. But there was nothing there, no feature to remember him by. And there was still no connection to Charlie.

'But what was Clarke doing in the detox ward?' I said.

'He . . . he was sick.'

'Drinking?'

Marvin nodded, puzzled. 'That's what I don't understand. He always drank, but he never had a problem before. He could handle it. I mean really handle it. Like I said, he was a hard man. He grew up tough, out west somewhere. He could drink me under the table and not blink an eye. He was proud of it, you know. It was part of the way he beat people down.'

'Are you sure alcohol was the problem? It wasn't for drugs or something else?'

'It was alcohol. He came in as drunk as you can be and not be dead. And he reeked of vodka.'

'Vodka?'

'It's funny. People think it doesn't smell. I think it smells the worst. And it's a mean smell. An ugly smell. It was his favourite.'

'Marvin . . . you know what they found? In the substation where Charlie died.'

'Oh yeah, I know. If I didn't know it was him before, I knew it when I heard that.'

'So what happened in that ward?'

Marvin's eyes cast about the room. 'I couldn't believe it when they wheeled him in. He was a mess. I mean a real fucking mess. Maybe it wasn't just alcohol, maybe it was drugs too, who knows what? But he was screaming. A man like that, crying like a baby.'

'You'd never seen him that way before?'

'No. And I don't want to see it again.'

'But you and Charlie had some sort of contact with him?'

'More than that, a lot more than that. When I saw who it was and what sort of state he was in, I made sure I stayed by his side. I was trying to help the bastard. So once the doctors had him drugged and the rest, me and Charlie spent the night with him, in his room. I don't think he even realised it was us, not at first, but I didn't want him left with just anyone. Not even the St Amand's staff, and they're the best. Clarke was raving, George. Saying all sorts of things. And when a man like that is spilling his guts, you don't want just anyone hearing. God knows, he's done a lot of things he wouldn't want anyone knowing.'

'Like?'

'Like there are some things you still don't talk about, George. Things that are dangerous, even now. I told you, he didn't always solve things just by talking. That union didn't go quietly. And Clarke wasn't the only one after all that sub-contracting work. He had competitors. For a while, at least.'

'But that was all in the old days.'

'It isn't just the old days, George. I mean, the old days aren't really over. They go on and on. That's the whole point.'

'I don't understand.'

'Open your eyes, George. Watch the news.'

'What?'

'You lose power after the storm last night? At that motel of yours?'

'No. I know other parts of the city did, but—'

'Other parts of the city. That's the thing. There's always some part of the city, or some part of the south-east, losing power. You know what I'm talking about. All these problems with the power grid. It's been in the papers. Poor maintenance and understaffing and constant interruptions to the supply. The whole industry is a fucking mess. Even worse than it used to be.'

And a collection of news items and articles surfaced in my memory. About a crisis in the power industry, about a breakdown in staff and infrastructure, about the need for drastic reform. It had been simmering away in the back pages for months. Not that I'd really been paying attention. Any more than I ever had, when it came to the truth about power in Queensland.

'And Clarke?'

Marvin laughed. 'That's what's so funny. We were always second-rate, me and him. All those scams we ran. And nothing changed. I was second-rate in government, and he's still second-rate, the way he runs things. No matter how tough he thinks he is, he's still shoddy and he's still cheap and he's fucked up once too often. Laws have been broken. Public money has gone missing. The government is sick of it all. It's launching an investigation. Contracts are under scrutiny. All the *old* contracts, and how they were won in the first place. And sooner or later, a lot of it's gonna come back to him.'

'I thought you said people like him were untouchable.'

'Not anymore. Not when the lights start going out. Even in my day, we couldn't have stood for that. You've gotta give people their television. First fucking rule of politics.'

'So Clarke is being investigated. Is that what he was talking about in the ward? Is that the reason his drinking has got so bad?'

Marvin was grinning at me. 'Not just an investigation, George. It's an inquiry.'

I paused a moment at that. 'An inquiry?'

'An inquiry. That's the word they're using. That's the word eating away inside Clarke's head right now. Another inquiry. Only worse than the last one. This time he's in the middle of it. That's the hilarious thing. It's an inquiry into *him*. And he's not gonna walk away this time. This time he's gonna end up in jail. That's what driven him to drink, George. That's what he was raving about, in that fucking ward.'

'But what's that got to do with Charlie?'

A malign glee had lifted Marvin for a moment, now he crumbled again.

'Nothing. It's got nothing to do with Charlie. Me? Maybe they'd call me to testify, sooner or later. I signed a lot of papers for Clarke back then. But so what? There's nothing they can do to me any more.'

'Then what happened in that ward?'

'I don't know. It got late. Clarke fell asleep eventually. They'd drugged him. I still don't think he'd even recognised us by then. So I went to bed. I'd done what I could. The problem was I left Charlie there in the room, Charlie wanted to stay . . .'

'Did Charlie know who Clarke was?'

'I'm not sure. It's hard to tell what Charlie knows now. But something about Clarke got Charlie interested. He wanted to stay, that's all I know. And something must have happened, 'cause next morning Charlie is shaking me awake. He's transformed. He's freaked out. He's getting out of there, he says. Right that second.'

'Leaving the ward?'

'I didn't know what the fuck he was talking about. But he said he was going to Highwood. He said he was going up there to find you.'

'Why?'

'I don't know. I was half asleep. By the time I was out of bed, Charlie was out the door.'

'But he'd spent the whole night with Clarke, right?'

'Right. So I go in and see Clarke. He's still groggy, he can hardly stand, but he's freaking out as well. He recognises me this time, sure enough, and he's not happy. I'm the last person he wants to see.'

'What did he say?'

'He wants to know where Charlie has gone. I don't know why. But something happened between them. Clarke must have woken up after I left. Him and Charlie must have talked. I don't know what about. But something was said, something a lot worse than anything I heard the night before, something that set Charlie off, something Clarke didn't want him to know. 'Cause Clarke wanted Charlie back, and fast.'

'What did you tell him?'

'I told him Charlie normally lived in that little detox place in Bardon, and that's probably where he'd gone. But I said something about Highwood too. I don't remember.'

'Did you mention me?'

'Shit, George, think! It wasn't the time to be talking about Charlie going to see a journalist—even if that journalist was only you. Clarke was furious enough as it was. He wasn't even properly sober, and he was angrier than I'd ever seen.'

'So Charlie went off to Highwood, and Clarke wanted him back, but you don't know why?'

'No. And Christ, George, if I'd known what was going to

happen I wouldn't have said anything at all. You believe that, don't you?'

'What'd Clarke do?'

'He got up and left. Straight away. Fuck what the doctors said, he wasn't hanging around.'

'He was going after Charlie?'

'I didn't *know* George. What was I supposed to do?'

'What *did* you do?'

'I checked out. I didn't want detox anymore. Things were too fucked up. I needed a drink. I went home.'

'The housekeeper didn't see you.'

'I was only there one night. First thing next morning I get a call from Clarke.'

'The next morning . . . this is after Charlie was already dead?'

'Right. I don't know where Clarke is calling from, but he still sounds drunk and he still sounds mad. He tells me he's found Charlie and Charlie refused to cooperate, and so he's had to deal with Charlie. I still don't know what the fuck he's talking about. But then he says that I'm next, and that I'd better be more helpful, if I know what's good for me. Then he hangs up.'

'He's dealt with Charlie . . . that's what he said?'

'But I didn't know what that meant until I saw the midday news. Highwood. And that fucking substation. That's all I needed to hear. I got the hell out of there.'

'He as good as told you he killed Charlie?'

There were tears in Marvin's eyes. 'And I'm next, George. That's why I'm here. I don't even know why. I don't know what started it all. But it doesn't even matter what that was any more. Clarke knows that I know it was him up at that substation. A man like him isn't gonna just let a thing like that be. Not if he can find me.'

But I wasn't interested in Marvin.

'What could it be?' I pressed. 'What could he have told Charlie that would set Charlie off like that? And why would Charlie come looking for me anyway? We hadn't talked in years.'

'Who knows? Maybe Clarke let something slip. About the old days, or about something that's happening now. Something

Charlie thought was too important to keep quiet. Maybe Charlie thinks you're still some sort of hot-shot journalist who would want information like that. I don't know. Charlie is all messed up. I just know that, all of a sudden, he said he had to see you.'

'But he hated me.'

Marvin was weary with it all. 'He didn't hate you. He thought you hated him.'

I froze. 'Charlie said that?'

'He talked about you a lot in that ward. You and Maybellene and the whole fucking mess. He thought it was all his fault. He said he'd always wanted to talk to you two, to apologise for everything, but he thought you'd tell him to fuck off if he even called. He said if he could ever find some way to put it right, he would.'

And God, I didn't need to be hearing this.

'There was no way to put it right,' I said. 'He must have known that.'

'Charlie wasn't himself any more, George. The alcohol had got to him, and the gunshot, and all that time in prison. He was like a little kid. He just wanted everything to be okay again. The poor fucking idiot was so guilty.'

I could barely answer. 'It wasn't his fault . . .'

'Forget it, George. This isn't just about Charlie. It's about *Clarke*. I don't know what happened in that room while I was asleep, but something did. Something was said. And Clarke is a man who sober wouldn't breathe a word about his life to anyone. He sure as hell never broke down like that, back in the old days. But now everything is fucking up for him and he's drunk himself into God knows what sort of hell, and he's let something out. Charlie was the problem. Charlie didn't know the rules, he didn't even know what he was playing with.'

He had another cigarette ready, flicked the lighter repeatedly, over and over until it fired, and the cigarette trembled in his hand.

'Forget about Charlie,' he said. 'It's too late for him anyway. I'm the one in trouble now. And it wasn't even my fault, George. Believe me. I was trying to help.'

And he was right. It was too late to help Charlie. I forced myself to think about Marvin, studied him as he sat there, pathetic and fearful. I looked around the room. Dark and hot, oppressive as a jail cell, with an ocean and sun and sand only metres away. He was afraid all right. Only a frightened man would do this.

'So your solution is just to hide out here?' I asked.

'I don't know. I don't know what I was thinking. I suppose I thought if I stayed out of sight long enough Clarke would realise I'm no threat to him, that I'm not gonna talk to anyone, not about Charlie, not about anything. God knows I won't. But I don't know if that'll be enough.'

'What about the police?'

He shook his head wildly. 'No, no, no. I make a move that way and I'm dead for sure. You think the police aren't still onside with someone like him? He always had friends there in the old days. He had cops on his payroll. You don't think he hasn't still got one or two of them lined up? The Inquiry didn't get them all, George, no fucking way. No, I gotta make him see I can be trusted, that's my only chance. I gotta stay hidden and stay silent. And even then . . . even then I don't know. I used to think he was reasonable, you know, a businessman first and foremost. Now I don't know. Look what he did to Charlie.'

'I have,' I said, toneless.

Marvin was staring about, his foot tapping helplessly. 'And there were empty bottles everywhere at the scene. That means he's still drinking. That's what scares the shit out of me, 'cause I saw what he was like drunk.'

I thought of the photo again, but it was pointless.

'Tell me what he looks like,' I said.

'Why?'

'Why not?'

'You don't need to know. You won't ever see him. Why would you? You're nothing to him.'

'Still . . .'

He sat up, alarmed. 'For Christ's sake, George, stay out of this. Don't go looking for this guy. Don't do a damn thing. Go home to Highwood and forget about it all. That's why

I'm telling you all this. If everyone would just forget about it, then maybe I'll get through this alive.'

But right then I couldn't maintain any sympathy for Marvin or his life. It wasn't his fault, he'd said, and maybe I even believed that . . . but for all he'd told me, he hadn't told me anything. Not the answer that lay at the centre of it all.

Something that made Charlie steal a car.

Sent him running to Highwood, where he knew I lived.

'What has this all got to with *me*, Marvin?'

'Nothing. Nothing at all. It was only Charlie. He was confused. Just shut up and lay low, George. Go home. That's all you have to do. That's all any of us has to do.'

But he couldn't meet my eyes.

I stood up. 'Okay . . . I'll leave you to it then.'

'No! I mean, not yet, George. Don't go yet.'

He swayed up quickly, grabbed the scotch bottle, spilled liquid into a glass.

'Have a drink,' he begged, the glass held out before him. 'Come on. We can still talk. About other things. We can drink all day, like old times, I've got plenty of bottles.'

'Not if you won't tell me what's really going on.'

He clutched the glass miserably, a small man, old and alone and mostly naked.

'*I don't know*. I've been stuck here for two weeks, I'm going mad. Please. Don't go yet.'

'You said yourself I should go home.'

'Tomorrow then. You can go home tomorrow. There's spare beds upstairs.'

But I couldn't stay. I'd had enough. Of the dark, of the heat, of the smell—of Marvin himself. I wanted air. I wanted to understand what it all meant. And in that room, with the thing Marvin had become, that was impossible. Because he was still as much to blame as ever, despite all the self-pity and fear. No matter how indirectly, Charlie was still dead because of him. And Charlie hadn't even hated me. He'd wanted to fix things between us, he'd wanted to say he was *sorry* . . .

There was a pad by the phone, and a pen. I wrote down my number at the motel.

'I'll leave this,' I said. 'You can call me if you need to.'

Marvin's face started to collapse. 'Jesus, George, you want me on my knees? Stay a while. I've never asked you for anything before.'

'You asked me for plenty.'

He staggered, spilling scotch. 'What are you talking about? We're friends, George, we were always friends.'

And I was disgusted now, with him, with myself, with everything we'd done together.

'Call me,' I said, and headed for the door.

He came after me. 'Just an hour or two, please.' But the alcohol had him now, his legs gave out, buckling beneath him. He sank into the couch. He sat there, confused, looking up at me. His glasses had fallen off and his naked eyes seemed tiny, like rats' eyes, not piercing or hypnotic as they used to be, just desperate and trapped. 'Only one drink. One drink won't kill you.'

'I'm sorry, Marvin,' I said, and turned away.

'George,' he called, as I walked back towards the stairs and the sunlight. 'You weak bastard. One drink, what's one fucking drink?' And he was starting to cry.

I didn't answer.

Because I was sick of alcohol, of everything it had done to my life, and was still doing. Because right then I wanted a drink more than I'd wanted anything. Because I was an alcoholic. Because I had no power over alcohol. Because one drink was everything, and it was never the last.

'I told you,' I said finally, 'I gave it up.'

But I was already in the stairwell, and nobody heard me except the walls.

THIRTY-THREE

I stopped drinking on Sunday, 3 December, 1989.

It was the day after a new government swept to power in Queensland for the first time in over three decades. The day after two years of Inquiry and scandal culminated in one great final public blood-letting. The day after Charlie tried to kill himself.

I woke to find myself in a motel room, fully dressed and on top of the bed covers. I had no idea where I was. I lay there, tasting dead alcohol on my breath, my head full of that pulsing thickness that only time or more drinks could clear. No thoughts came, no memories. It was a moment of waking unconsciousness, without a date or an hour. Finally I pulled myself upright, went to the window, and threw back the curtain. I was expecting the glare of a hot Brisbane day, some suburban car park by the highway, perhaps, but instead I looked out into a grey world of slowly curling fog and the dark shadows of trees. A silent, still world, dripping moisture. It wasn't Brisbane. I stared, lost. And then it all came to me, a road sign glimpsed in the dark, headlights carving through the night, and back and back to the hospital, a rush of memory that had been just waiting there to unravel, and in moments I was reeling for the toilet and vomiting up sick yellow strands of bile.

It was my first look at Highwood.

I would never know how it happened—how it was that, in my deepest, most drunken moment of misery, I took the turn that led me to sobriety. All that had been in my mind that night was escape. Escape from that hospital room, from

May, and from Charlie's single, staring eye. I'd stumbled blindly down the hospital steps, thinking of nothing but running as fast and as far as I could. South. I'd go south. Get out of Brisbane and Queensland and the whole disaster it had all become. I had no reason to stay. I had no job, no friends. There had been Maybellene—and only Maybellene, really, for the last two years—but now even that was over, ended in the most dreadful fashion I could have imagined. South, I thought, south into oblivion.

It was the logic of alcohol. I was drunk and had been for days, for weeks, and there was a quality I'd finally learned about drunkenness. When I'd been younger I'd thought that drinking expanded the night, opened the horizons, but I knew better now. The more you drank the more the world shrank in on you. It was almost a visual thing. A blurring of distance. In the early stages that was welcoming. Bars became glowing, warm homes. Faces loomed large, time faded away. But as you drank more and the world wrapped around tighter, it became claustrophobic—people became distant, blurred figures, passing you by. Thoughts stayed trapped in your head. Talking turned into an effort, meanings impossible to convey. In the end your whole world could become no greater than your own skull, and by then you were trapped, a distorted, speechless mind, capable only of looking out upon reality in a way that was no better than hallucinating. It *was* hallucinating.

That's the state I was in, and had been in for days, when I climbed into my car outside the hospital. South, drive south—it loomed like a vision, the only thing that seemed real. That and drinking, drinking still more. I had a bottle of wine in the car, and swallowed from it steadily as I drove back through the Valley to New Farm and to my flat, looking out upon a nightmare. The election had been lost and won. The streets were jammed with cars and crowded with revellers from the victory parties, from the nightclubs and bars, people running across the road, yelling incoherently. The sky flickered with fireworks. Thirty years' repression was exploding outwards and the town had turned hideous before my eyes, a city of madmen, a whirl of destruction and revenge, and all of it at my expense. I was one of the downfallen and the city was howling its joy at the demise of my kind. Fists banged randomly on my windows. Then I was through it all and down into New Farm and into my flat.

I was there only moments. The rooms were dark and empty and smelled of misuse, and it no longer felt like any sort of home. I gathered clothes, two more bottles of wine, left my key in the door and was on my way again. Speed was all I could think about. South. Sydney. I could be there in twelve hours, and in Sydney I could lose myself completely, never be seen again. I wanted to vanish from the face of Queensland. I steered around the Valley and skirted the northern edge of the city centre, aiming for the western freeway. I caught one last glimpse of Parliament House and its annex glowing orange in the spotlights. It looked like a castle besieged, the last few fragments of the government trapped inside, the mob rioting outside with flames in their hands. It was the fall of an empire, the last battle was lost, and for a moment I didn't feel alone. All over Brisbane there would be people like me, frantically packing bags, destroying documents, melting away into the night, beaten men, scattering to the winds. I didn't care about any of them.

Then I was on the western freeway, Brisbane was falling behind and it was just me and the wine and the road. I drank and stared into the arc of the headlights and from time to time an image of May or of Charlie would knife through the stupor and I'd find myself reaching for the bottle. I drank great mouthfuls, felt it sweep over me in waves, and every wave took me a little further away from the pain. The freeway became the Cunningham Highway. It would take me past Ipswich and through the hills and then up over the Dividing Range and across, finally, into New South Wales. Cars and trucks streamed towards me, lights blazing in my face as they passed. My own car swerved from side to side, straying at times into the oncoming lanes, and it occurred to me that I could die this way and that death wouldn't be so bad. But it didn't seem important either way. Speed was the thing. I couldn't stop for anything.

Maybe that was part of it. Maybe I realised that, drunk as I was, I might crash, or be pulled over by the police and detained. The thought was unbearable—not injury, not death, but delay. The idea of being trapped in Queensland a moment longer. And then I saw the sign to Highwood, left off the highway. A minor road, a back road. It ran, I knew, through a few small towns and then up into the mountains. I'd never driven it before, but it was another way into New South Wales, I knew that much. A slower way, but a quieter one too. No other cars. No crashes. No police. At least, later I assumed that's what I was thinking. I didn't remember next morning and never would remember. But the road sign remained in my mind, a second of perfectly clear focus, and I remembered nodding to myself as I slowed and turned off. Yes, I was saying, yes. And swilling from the wine bottle.

From there it all became vague. Back roads, narrow, fringed by tall grass or overhanging trees. Small towns flashing by in a blur of darkened houses and isolated streetlights. No one was on the footpaths, no one was still awake, no one was celebrating or mourning out here; the election might never have been fought. I seemed to be the only person on the road, the only person in the night. I faded in and out of awareness. The car was driving itself. Odd-shaped hills loomed up in the night. Then the forest closed in, the trees making fantastic shadows in my headlights, and the road turned and began to wind and climb. And it started to rain.

Good, I remembered thinking, good. Wash my tracks from the road, wash the dust of this state from my heels. Tears of self-pity. But the border couldn't be far . . .

And from there I remembered almost nothing. Driving rain. The car slipping on muddy turns, the wipers beating, the bottle rising to my lips and falling, rising and falling, trees, darkness and a noise that seemed to grow louder and louder in my head. And then one last clear moment of recollection—the car stopped, askew on the road, the rain hammering on its roof, and through the streaming windscreen a shining neon sign that I stared at, spellbound. And after that nothing at all.

Later I would be told that at two-thirty in the morning I woke the motel manager by hammering and yelling at his door. He couldn't understand a word I was saying, but he saw the state I was in, so he opened a room for me and threw me on the bed.

I was five kilometres from the border.

And the name of the establishment, illuminated in great golden letters that the manager later admitted he'd simply forgotten to turn off that night, was The Last Chance Motel.

Not that I knew any of this that first morning. Indeed, I knew nothing for most of the next twenty-four hours. After that initial awakening, I undressed and collapsed back into bed, still drunk, and slept feverishly for the rest of the day. Down in Brisbane the new premier was making victory speeches and the new era had begun, but I was oblivious. Sometime in the evening the manager woke me by knocking on my door; in the kindness of his heart he had even brought me a meal. I thanked him, paid him finally for the room, and booked it for another night. It was an automatic thing. I had no plans. My head was still full of noise. After he'd gone I ate a little, but vomited it up again immediately. I went back to bed. Another night passed, nightmare ridden, my head and my arms and legs all aching madly, my skin crawling with insects. Rain drummed on the window. Voices talked to me, May, Charlie, haunting half dreams. I cried, doubled up in a ball, utterly wretched, until somewhere in the depths of the night I fell unconscious again, and dreamed of nothing.

It was on Monday morning that I woke finally, ill and sore, but sober again, the noises gone. In its way, though, this was even worse. I lay there, stark and aware, without even the filter of alcohol to protect me, and studied the ruin of my life. If immediate suicide ever swung close, it was then. But it's the nature of the body to crave life, and in the end it was my body that could lie in bed no longer. I rose and showered and, without hope but with the need for simple motion, I left my room and went out into the day. Had it been a bright and sunny sky I might have made it no further than the door, but Highwood, too, seemed bent on saving me. It was another cool, foggy morning.

Feeling invisible I slipped from the motel car park out onto the main street of the town. It was almost nine o'clock, but the streetlights were still on, haloes in the mist, and windows glowed orange. I walked. People moved here and there, but it was all muted by the fog, and no one noticed me. Shops were opening their doors, setting out displays, the first customers chatting quietly. Breakfasters dined in a cafe. Outside a newsagent the Brisbane papers were thumping down in bundles from a truck. Those papers bore headlines of the weekend's events, but for all the convulsions that had gripped the state, up here on the border and in the clouds it was too far away to matter.

I walked on, past the park and the courthouse precinct. I wasn't going anywhere. I thought of breakfast, but my body seemed ethereal, not in need of food. I walked, limbs moving but my mind vacant, all decision held in suspension. The fog swirled in thicker and I passed by a school. A few cars were paused there under the trees, headlights gleaming, parents dropping off children. A teacher waited by the gate, ushering kids through and talking with mothers and fathers. Laughter rang out and I faltered. Unhappiness swirled up immensely. The whole town . . . it all seemed so secure, so warm, so safe. It was something I would never have, somewhere I would never belong, but the wanting was there, sudden and overpowering. To be whole, to know what the future would bring, day to day, without the excesses and degradation and the hangovers. To live a measured life, a proper life. To stop drinking, stop failing, stop hurting. Why wasn't that possible?

I turned, almost went back. I'd passed two pubs down the street, and if it had been opening time I would have marched right down to one of them and drowned myself again, just to blot out the question. But it was an hour before alcohol would be available anywhere. I turned again, tortured, not knowing what to do. The teacher by the gate was watching me now. It was a woman. Later I would wonder if it was Emily I saw that day, and if even then she played a part in my salvation, but in truth I was aware only of a female figure, no face, no age, it could have been anyone. But she was watching me, suspicious, and I couldn't stay. I kicked myself back into motion and headed up along the street, away from town, away from the shops and the bars. Instead I was heading up into the mountains, and towards the New South Wales border once again.

I didn't feel invisible any more. I felt like a monster come creeping into town, acutely visible to anyone who might see me, the disease in my head as obvious as if it was of my skin. I walked on. At the top of the street there was another park, and on the further side of it the forest closed in on the town, blanketing the hills that rose all about, looming dimly in the fog. There was a sign announcing the boundaries of the Highwood National Park, with maps showing the walking tracks that threaded their way through the bush to waterholes and lookouts. I paused at the sign. I saw that there were miles of trails and that, between the mist and the forest, I could disappear in there forever. Furthest of all, I saw, eleven kilometres from town, was a site called Redemption Falls. It would suffice, I thought. Then I plunged into the wilderness.

Redemption Falls. Last Chance Motel. Omens so banal even a fool like me couldn't ignore them.

I walked, hour after hour. Eleven kilometres. Up and down, through gullies and streams and over ridges, all of it on muddy, slippery tracks. I became soaked and streaked with mud. Blisters rose on my feet, burst and bled. Cramps speared up and down my legs. I drank cold mountain water and retched it up again. Chills swept through me, followed by sweat. I was a man who hadn't walked a single mile by intent for years, a man who hadn't eaten in two days, a man coming off months, years, of solid, body-leaching drinking. But somehow it seemed impossible to stop. The motion and the pain in my feet and legs kept thought at bay, kept the craving at bay, and that was all I wanted.

It was late afternoon when I reached the falls. The track came to an end and a small stream plunged over a sheer escarpment. I stood on the edge. Part of my mind realised that I was standing on the very southern rim of the Border Ranges. I could see a sprawl of further mountain ranges, deep valleys and forests, all of it grey beneath shreds of cloud and rain and mist. It was New South Wales. Even as I watched, the water of the stream was tumbling from Queensland into a new state. A single leap and I could follow it. A hundred, a hundred and fifty metres to the rocks below, and I'd be rid of Queensland at last. The spasms racking my muscles were almost enough to pitch me over, but my mind was exhausted, empty of either guilt or despair. I stood staring dumbly out for a mere few minutes, then turned and headed back. Motion, I thought. That's all that matters. Keep in motion.

Night fell early, and rain followed. The mountains closed in around me. I stumbled along in the darkness. I fell over rocks and roots, crawled in mud, groaning in something like terror. Awareness drifted off and all I knew was the placing of one foot in front of the other, and the searching out of the trail, an infinitesimally paler path that led through the surrounding blackness of water and forest. It stretched on forever, and I knew that I would die alone and lost and that, no, death wasn't what I wanted.

When pinpoints of light finally appeared through the trees I started to cry. I lurched through the park and down the street, past the school and the courthouse. People stopped and stared at me, but they meant nothing. I had walked twenty-two kilometres. And I was alive.

I saw a small diner that was still open. I fell through the door and demanded food. There were no other customers, and the girl behind the counter was cleaning down the stove, but there was a heated bay which held the leftovers of the day—a meat pie, some wrinkled chips, a sausage dripping grease. I bought the lot. She showered it all with salt, wrapped it in paper, and I carried it like treasure back to the motel, limping and muttering to myself. Once inside my room I spread it all out on the bed and ate until it was gone. Then I brushed the paper and the crumbs aside, cast myself headlong on the bed, and slept.

And lost another day.

Not to a hangover but to a complete revolt of my body. When I woke again I could scarcely move. It felt like my muscles had been individually ripped from their bones. I lay there in suffering all day, blankly watching television and ordering room service. The manager looked at me strangely when he made the deliveries. Just what was I doing in his motel, what was I doing in Highwood? In fact I was turning his room and his town and his mountains into my own personal detox ward, but I could hardly tell him that, I didn't know it myself. All I knew was that as the aches eased through the day, the misery lurking at the back of my mind started to press forward again and my throat cried out for a drink. If I stood still it would all catch up with me. So the answer was still the same—motion. Motion and physical pain, to pre-empt the pain I feared far more.

Next day I rose at dawn, stiff and creaking, and set off for the falls again. My luck was holding and once again the day was overcast and grey. This time I took food with me, and water, and I bought a torch in case darkness caught me again, but it was still a death march. I supposed the terrain I was covering was beautiful. Mountain gums and stands of temperate rainforest, rocky gorges plunging away to noisy streams, wide placid waterholes, it was all there. I even passed several other parties of bushwalkers, staring up, taking photographs. But I had no eye for the scenery. I was focused on the path, step by step, and after the first few miles the protests from my legs and feet consumed me. By the time I reached the falls I was panting at the stabbing in my chest. It wasn't long after midday. I glared out at the view.

I don't need you, I said to New South Wales, not yet anyway. Not yet. And I turned and started home.

It was dark again by the time I arrived, stumbling along behind my torch beam. I saw the lights burning in the windows of the bars, thought longingly of one long, delicious glass of beer—but I knew where that would lead, and what lay at the bottom of that glass. I forced myself instead into a cafe and ordered scalding hot soup. It satisfied me on a different level, a deeper, earthier level, and the smile of the waitress, too, was a boon.

The next day—before I had a chance to recover or think or plan—I did it all again. I walked to the falls and stared down at New South Wales, and thought, *I can survive*.

And I kept on doing it.

It was something beyond reason, and it wasn't a cure. It was a short-term measure. A holding pattern. I wasn't dealing with anything, or confronting anything. But that close to the brink any distraction was a precious one, and I stuck to it instinctively. All the aches and blisters and blood, they were an atonement of sorts, the purifying flame of the Inquisitors. I deserved them, and over the weeks they burned away the jagged edges of my life, made it seem endurable again. And somewhere amidst it all I found myself daring to form the thought—I would never drink again.

But it wasn't a cure, and the walking couldn't go on forever. It was Highwood itself that told me when it was time to stop. For two weeks the weather had held miraculously cool and wet, and I don't remember ever seeing the sun. But finally one morning I stepped out of my room to a bright blue sky and a warm breeze, and a town for once fully revealed. Green was the impression, green everywhere, forested hills rising steeply on all sides, the red roofs of houses creeping up the slopes, treetops on the high ridges swaying in the wind. I thought of the falls, and the hateful, torturous track that led to them, and couldn't imagine it in sunlight. And then I felt something crumble in my mind, a wall dissolve. I didn't need to walk that day. That part was over. Nor did I need to drink. At least not at that very moment. For the moment I didn't *need* to do anything.

I stood there, wondering. In the car park the motel manager was washing his car.

'Beautiful day,' he called.

I nodded.

'Heading for the falls again?'

'No. Not today.'

He turned off his hose and considered me. He was round and middle-aged and, as I would later learn, had taken up the motel after retiring from the stress of a Brisbane accountancy firm, having already been through one heart attack. Last Chance was a reference to his own life, not to mine.

'Finished with all that?' he asked.

'I think so.'

And I was right. I would not seek Redemption Falls even once in the next ten years. Nor did I miss them. They might have saved my life, but the memory was not good, and as time passed I would have no more desire to revisit the falls than

I assumed the motel manager would have to revisit the intensive care ward. Some remedies were too painful.

'Well,' he said, 'you're looking a lot fitter for it all.'

'Compared to when I got here, that isn't saying much.'

'No. So what now?'

'I don't know.'

He leaned on his car, thoughtful. 'You know, as good as it is having a long-term customer, you're really wasting your money staying in a motel week after week.'

'You want me to leave?'

'Christ, no. But if you're staying in town, there are plenty of guest houses that have long-term rates. More comfortable, too.'

Was I staying in town?

'I've got a friend who runs one,' he went on. 'Lovely old lady. It's called Pine Hill guest house. I can point the way, if you want to have a look at it.'

And so I moved in with Joan and her daughter.

It wasn't over, though, no more than it was ever over for an alcoholic. Two weeks of walking or two weeks in a detox ward, anyone could emerge sober from that. But once you were back in your old life, back with your old friends, that was when the battle began, when the habits of a lifetime clustered around, drinks in hand. No more doctors, no more clinic walls or, in my case, no more endless movement. I had to stand still and fight it squarely, and it was by far the hardest thing I'd ever done. Frustration and longing turned me short-tempered and mean, and it was Joan and her daughter who bore the brunt of that, and who forgave me for it, who put up with me being rude to the other guests, with me stomping around their house, sleepless, at all hours of the night. And it all would have been in vain if I'd gone back to Brisbane. That, too, was what saved me. My old lifestyle, my old temptations—Highwood, blessedly, was free from them all.

Later, it was Joan who introduced me to her friend Gerry, editor and proprietor of the *Highwood Herald*, and that was the real beginning of life reborn. Within weeks of the new year's arrival, and indeed the arrival of the new decade, I was spending my days talking with Gerry down at his office. In two months I was on the payroll, a working journalist once again. It was a job more humble than even my very earliest years, on the little Brisbane community papers. But I was older and wiser now, and I had sense enough to grasp the chance.

There was only the one wound beyond recovery.

One night, a week into the new year, I finally called the hospital and asked for Charlie. A nurse spoke to me at first, then came back on the line and reported, as I'd known she would, that Charlie had refused to talk to me.

'How is he?' I asked.

'They've managed to save the eye.'

'And the rest?'

'Are you family?'

'No . . .'

'I can't really discuss that with you, then.'

All I could do was leave the address and number of the guest house, and ask her to give it to him.

That same night I called May.

'Where have you been?' she asked, her voice distant, and after I'd told her there was nothing but silence.

'Charlie won't talk to me,' I forced myself to say.

'George, what did you expect?' And then, after a time, emotionless, 'They'll be transferring him back to a prison ward soon.'

'How is he . . . I mean, you know, with you?'

'I haven't seen him.' Her voice fractured momentarily. 'He won't see me.'

'May, I'm sorry.'

'George,' she said, and I could hear how close the tears were, how frantically she was striving for control. I knew every nuance of her voice, had heard it in all its forms of pleasure and anger and love, and my heart seemed to be breaking apart all over again. 'George, I can't talk to you.'

And she hung up.

I raved at Joan and her daughter that night, and threw their home-cooked dinner across the table. I stormed out and found myself heading for the bars, for the numbing blackness I knew only drunkenness could give. But halfway there I stopped, my fists clenched, and forced myself around. Loathing every moment of it I went back to the house, apologised to Joan, and helped clean up the mess. Then I lay awake in my room all night and spoke the mantra in my mind, over and over and over.

I will not drink.
I will not drink.
I will not drink.
I recited it for the next ten years.

And not for anything, not for Charlie's death, not for all Marvin's fears and desperate pleading, not for anything or anyone would I change my mind now.

THIRTY-FOUR

Back at my New Farm motel I took a long, long shower . . . to wash off the stink of the day, to clean away the touch of Marvin and, most of all, to rid myself of the ancient stench of alcohol. Yes, I'd stopped drinking, but sometimes it hardly seemed to matter. When everyone else still went on as they always had, when the world I thought I'd left behind was still there, when the events of those days still dictated my life, when Charlie was still dead anyway. What was the point? Who had I helped and who had I saved, apart from myself?

And what did I do now?

Should I call the police, my friends the detectives? I knew perhaps who had done those things to Charlie, but I knew nothing really, beyond a name. George Clarke. A businessman from the old days, an electrical contractor, a big one, a man who drank vodka, a man lost in alcohol, caught in the web of yet another inquiry. What would they do with a story like that? And I couldn't even tell them why it had happened. All they'd really care about would be that I'd seen Marvin. Marvin was the one they wanted. And even if I told them where he was, even if they went and arrested him—what would Marvin himself tell them? Marvin was the source, the only witness to it all, but he'd say nothing, not if he saw silence as his only chance. He'd deny it all. Still, at least he'd be in custody. He'd be safer than where he was now. Unless I believed everything Marvin had told me. That even the police were not to be trusted.

I didn't know what I believed.

This was unknown territory for me, where people acted

in ways I didn't understand, did things impossible for me to even conceive. If it was all true, then what did a normal person do with such knowledge? Loneliness washed over me as the shower water ran cold. According to the courts, I had associated with criminals for most of my adult life, and yet I felt innocent. Naive. Someone who'd walked all his days with his eyes closed. Charlie was dead and that should matter somehow. It did matter, but what could *I* do? I was no avenging angel. And the enemy was a face I'd seen once in a photograph years ago. Even if I tracked him down, my blood would freeze in the presence of someone who could do the sort of things he'd done.

No solutions came. I got out of the shower and dried off, sat on the bed. I stared at the urn of ashes, still sitting on the coffee table. Tears pricked in my eyes suddenly. He'd wanted to say he was sorry, with his twisted face and his mind that would never be quite right again, an ugly man made even uglier, a punch-drunk boxer, a little simple, half dead with drinking. He'd wanted to see me . . .

And all I'd been able to do was bury him.

Not even that. All I'd done so far was burn him, and his ashes surely weren't meant to sit on a motel coffee table forever. They deserved some sort of final resting place. I didn't know where that would be. I was still waiting for inspiration, a sign. I didn't think it would be in Brisbane, even though that had been his home. But where, then? What place was of any meaning to Charlie, in a state which had turned so wholly against him?

No inspiration came.

I went through the phone book and dialled up the Uniting Church Dependency Hostel. I asked for Mark the psychologist and caught him just as he was on his way home. He remembered me.

'So, you're still in Brisbane,' he said.

'I've been seeing old friends. Some of them were Charlie's friends too.'

'I didn't see them at the funeral.'

'They're not friends any more.'

'What can I do for you, George?'

'Charlie's ashes. I've still got them sitting here. I don't know what to do with them.'

'You're asking me?'

'You knew him better than I did for the last few years. I thought you might have some idea about what he would have liked.'

'I knew part of him, but it probably wasn't the best part. I don't think he would've said I really knew him. You're the one who was with him when everything was right in his life. That makes you the best judge. Besides, you have to take some responsibility for this. You can't pass it on to a stranger.'

I closed my eyes.

'Listen, George,' he said. 'Charlie is dead. It doesn't mean a thing to him what you do with his ashes. Obviously it means something to you. Burial is for the living, that's part of how we come to terms with death. What you do with his ashes you do for your own sake. Think about how you regarded Charlie, what he had in life and what he deserved, and how you can exist with it all. And see what happens.'

'I hope something does. I can't carry him around forever.'

'Have the police come up with anything? I'm guessing that part of your problem is that his death hasn't been explained or resolved yet. You might be holding onto his ashes until you have some answers, someone to blame, and can finally let him go.'

Answers, I had answers, but no explanation.

And I had someone to blame, but no reasons.

'No,' I said. 'The police haven't come up with anything.' A thought struck. 'But do you mind if I ask you some questions?'

'Not at all.'

'You never told me that you had Marvin McNulty in your ward.'

'Did we?'

'The night before Charlie moved out to St Amand's. Marvin was found in the street just near your place and someone carried him in. He was only there overnight.'

A thoughtful pause. 'I remember someone like that, but not the name. I didn't even get a chance to talk to him. He wasn't a proper client and he was gone so fast. That was Marvin McNulty? The politician?'

'What was left of him.'

'Did he see Charlie?'

'He did. Marvin was the one who got Charlie into St Amand's.'

'Oh . . . I see.'

'He still has plenty of money, if not much else.'

'Well, like I said, it was a lucky thing for Charlie.'

There was no luck about it. More like a curse, as Marvin had called it, the three of them meeting like that. Charlie and Marvin . . . and Clarke. But there was no face when I thought of Clarke. Why had he been there, on that particular night? Marvin was afraid of him, and yet he'd been wheeled into the ward screaming, Marvin had said. Crying. What state of mind did that to a man? And what had angered him enough to hunt Charlie up into the hills, set electric wires to his naked flesh? What would make someone do that?

He's still drinking . . . and I saw what he was like drunk.

I said, 'Have you ever worked in a place like St Amand's?'

'Not really.'

'I'm just thinking . . . alcoholism for those sort of people, for the wealthy, people in authority, is it different to alcoholism amongst the poor, like at your place?'

'Well, it's not something I have a lot of experience with, but I guess it's a matter of context.'

'How do you mean?'

'Well, for a start, a wealthy alcoholic can far better maintain the illusion of normality. A destitute alcoholic spends almost all his limited income on drinking, so has very little left for food, clothing, housing and the rest. So he'll look a mess, have poor accommodation or none at all, fall prey to sickness due to malnourishment, a whole host of related issues. A wealthy alcoholic will drink just as much, but can still afford a nice home, nice clothes and good food. He'll be drinking a better quality of beverage, too, which helps, perhaps, to a very minor degree. Alcohol is a poison no matter how you look at it, of course, but the cheaper drinks generally contain more chemicals and impurities.'

'What about psychologically?'

'Again, context is the thing. The destitute alcoholic can't help but know he's destitute, and so his self-esteem is low, throwing him back to alcohol to drown the problem. More than likely, though, he won't deny he has a problem with drinking, because the evidence is so palpable. He'll have all sorts of excuses for it, of course, but the basic acceptance is there. The wealthier person can deny that he has a problem, as his life is still outwardly successful. But of course the relationship problems, the health problems . . . they'll all still be there. He'll see a bum in the street and he won't for a second believe there's any similarity between the two of them, but somewhere inside he knows the only difference is his own money, and that'll scare him even more, that he could share an addiction with someone so obviously lower than he is.'

'What if . . . what if he's a man who's used to being in control? Who needs to be in control?'

'There's going to be conflict. Alcohol and self-control don't go together.'

'Could there be a breakdown at some stage?'

'Under enough pressure, yes. Exclusive detox wards are full of the rich and powerful for that very reason.'

'And if he did break down, what would happen?'

'Loss of control would be an obvious symptom. What form it takes is the question. It could be suicide, violence, obsessive behaviour. Lots of things.'

'And if there were people around during the breakdown, people who saw him at his worst, completely out of control, how would he feel about that?'

'He'd feel humiliated. No one likes to be seen that way. Of course, if he was in treatment then that humiliation would be used as a positive thing to help with a broader understanding, but if he's not in any sort of care then the humiliation will be purely negative. Which means more drinking, more dysfunction. It's all circular until it's broken by a genuine acceptance of the problem, and treatment.'

'What if he told those same people highly embarrassing private things during the episode? How would he feel about them? What would he want to do to them?'

There was a long pause on the line.
'Just who are we talking about here, George?'
'No one.'
'Marvin McNulty? Is that who you mean?'
'No.'
'But this has something to do with what happened to Charlie? Up in St Amand's?'
'Maybe.'
'I thought the police didn't have anything.'
'They don't. Yet.'
Another pause.

Then, 'Forget everything I just told you. I was talking about inclinations and moods on quite an abstract level. What was done to Charlie was pretty extreme.'

'More than just alcoholism?'

'Alcoholism is a nasty condition, and can certainly lead to violence, domestic violence in particular, but to pursue someone for miles to torture and kill them on some sort of psychological vendetta, I don't think you can lay all that on alcoholism. Definitely not. You'd be looking for other causes there.'

'I thought so.'

'You seem to have something quite specific in mind.'

'No . . .' no, I was just wondering . . .'

There was another doubtful silence. 'Okay, George. Just don't try to apply anything I've said to any actual person in particular. It's never that simple.'

'I know.'

'And, George, if you are thinking of anyone in particular, then stay away from them. Like I said, what happened up in Highwood . . . that's an unstable person.'

I thanked him and got off the line.

Charlie's ashes waited mutely on the table.

I was only wondering, it was only what Marvin had told me. But even if everything Marvin told me had happened the way he said, was there any sense in it? Was Clarke anything like that? It was impossible to say. I knew nothing about the man.

And without knowing there was nothing I could do.

Pack up, I thought. Pack up, get in the car and you can be home having dinner with Emily in two hours' time. Leave them all to it, the police, Marvin, everyone. You can't change anything anyway.

But I didn't pack. Instead I stayed in my room until it was evening, then I went out into the alien city and walked its bright streets. I wasn't so fooled by it all now, all that electricity. I thought of power failures stalking up and down the country, and of how quickly darkness would fall if it happened here. I watched the shining youth of the present parade the footpaths, and they all seemed shallow and inane. They laughed as if they had no need to bother with me, or with any of the shadows of the old city, even though we were all still here, watching and remembering. What was an old man dead in a substation to them? They were the future, and in the future there were never any sins or cruelty or bodies hanging on walls.

Finally I ate in a cafe and watched, waiting, as the night passed by and midnight approached and the crowds thinned on the streets. Doors were closed and lights were switched off. The last wanderers faded away. Then it was just me and the footpath. Me and Brisbane. My Brisbane. I walked the deserted streets alone and thought of Marvin hiding behind his shutters, of Jeremy waiting amongst his artefacts and wine, of Lindsay counting money in his club. Of another man, somewhere, who'd been one of us all along, even though I'd never known it. And now we were all back in town. It was a new town, perhaps, but it had yet to pay the debts of the old.

Just like me.

I went back to the motel. I lay on the bed, awake, not knowing what I was doing, or what I was expecting. Something, that was all I knew. I thought of calling Marvin again and didn't. I thought of calling Jeremy again, or even Lindsay, and didn't. Sleep came hovering in the early hours, while sirens cried distantly in the night.

The phone rang.

I picked it up. 'Hello?'

'Who's this?' asked a male voice.

'George,' I answered, not even thinking.

I listened to nothing. The sound of hoarse breathing.

'Marvin?' I said.

The voice laughed, chilling and totally unknown to me. 'Wrong number,' it said, and the phone clicked down.

I lay awake, unknown fears chasing through my mind, and it wasn't until the sky lightened with dawn that I slept. Then the phone was ringing again, and the sun outside was telling me it was something like noon. It was Detective Kelly.

'We found Marvin for you,' he said.

'He's not missing,' I replied, groggy. 'I saw him yesterday.'

'Really? And how was he?'

'He was fine.'

'Well he isn't any more.'

THIRTY-FIVE

A party of early morning joggers found Marvin at dawn. He was sitting on the beach at Redcliffe right in front of Lindsay's house, at the site where the first white settlers had landed, soldiers and convicts, in what turned out to be the founding of Queensland. His rifle was in his hand and a hole was in his temple and he was staring out to sea. By his side was an empty scotch bottle and in his pocket was a long suicide note, in his own writing, in which he confessed to the torture and murder of his old friend Charles Monohan. The note stated that the two had met in the Uniting Church hostel, gone to St Amand's together, then checked out together and gone on another drinking spree, ending up in Highwood, where they had argued about old grudges from the Inquiry days, which led in turn to violence and the substation. Since then, said the note, he had been in hiding, agonised with remorse, and he was sorry for everything he'd ever done. There were no suspicious circumstances. The only strange thing, it seemed, was that no one could find his glasses.

'But it all fits, George,' said Detective Kelly over the phone. 'St Amand's confirms that Charlie and Marvin left around the same time and that they both seemed agitated. Marvin even mentions you in the note—says they were going up to Highwood to see you, to talk about old times, and that this was what got them arguing, settling old scores and so on. Things got ugly, and Marvin took over and headed for the substation.'

I was sitting up in bed, numb with disbelief.

'But I just saw him. Yesterday.'

'So you said. And why didn't you tell us, George? You knew we were looking for him.'

'I was thinking about it, but I didn't know . . .'

'It might've helped. Once we had him under arrest we could have got a counsellor in, kept him under suicide watch.'

'But Marvin didn't do anything. Not to Charlie.'

'George, it's all there in the note.'

There was so much wrong with this I hardly knew where to start.

'Look,' I said, 'Marvin didn't kill Charlie. He was scared. Someone else killed Charlie, and Marvin was worried he was next. That's why he was hiding.'

'And who was this someone else supposed to be?'

'His name is George Clarke, he worked with Marvin, back in the old days.'

'I've never heard of him.'

'Ask some of your superiors. People who were around back then. They might remember. He's a big sub-contractor now for the power companies. And he was in the ward with them that night.'

'And why would he kill Charlie?'

'I'm not sure. Marvin didn't know exactly. But Clarke was in a bad way, and he told Charlie something, something important, I think. He killed Charlie to shut him up.'

'This is what Marvin told you?'

'Yes.'

'Sorry, George. I've got the records from St Amand's right in front of me. Marvin and Charlie ended up in rooms next door to each other. Otherwise the place was almost empty. There certainly isn't any George Clarke on the list.'

'He was there.'

'No, it was just Marvin and Charlie. We've always known that.'

'But . . .'

I didn't know what to say. Who was lying? Marvin? Or had Clarke used another name when he'd gone in? Did he have friends at the hospital, people who would doctor the records, deny he'd even been there?

Kelly had no doubts. 'Why do you think we were so sure

it was Marvin in the first place? Why do you think we wanted to find him so bad?'

'You didn't look very hard. I found him easily enough.'

'From Lindsay, we know. Sure, we checked with Lindsay as soon as we started. But he wouldn't tell *us* where Marvin was, swore blind he hadn't seen him. And frankly we had no reason to disbelieve Lindsay at the time. He's normally so . . . cooperative.'

'What's Lindsay saying now?'

'Nothing. Reckons he was just lending an old friend a house for a private holiday and had no idea Marvin was in trouble or suicidal.'

'You must know that's garbage.'

'Of course. We just figure that Marvin had some hold over Lindsay that prevailed over Lindsay's commitments to us, and now Lindsay is keeping his mouth shut.'

'But Lindsay knows Marvin was scared. He mightn't know it all, but he told me himself he knew Marvin was hiding from Clarke.'

'Well, Marvin was hiding from us, wasn't he? He could have spun Lindsay any old story to get the house, but in the end it was us he wanted to avoid. Hell, if Marvin wanted to get Lindsay's house and make sure Lindsay didn't tell a soul about it, this "scared for his life" routine is exactly what he would have come up with. See, it all fits.'

'But why would Marvin tell me the same story? Why lie to me?'

'You're Charlie's friend. Maybe he felt guilty.'

'But I saw him. He was terrified.'

'Terrified. Guilt-ridden. It can look the same, George. And he shot himself, that's pretty clear. Forensics will take a while to confirm it, but we don't really have any doubt. And the note seems genuine. It's his writing.'

'But it's all wrong.'

'Tell me why.'

'The substation. What about that? Clarke built it. Him and Marvin had a deal going back when Marvin was Minister for Mines and Energy, and that substation was Clarke's first contract. That's how Clarke knew it was there. That's how he knew what to do with the circuit boards.'

'You just said it yourself. If Marvin was part of the deal, then he knew where the substation was, too, and how it worked. Sounds to me like Marvin was just trying to shift the whole thing onto someone else, and this old friend of his fitted.'

'But why? If he was about to kill himself and confess . . . why bother?'

'I guess he wasn't thinking suicide when you saw him. But maybe all the lies got to him in the end, and he just wanted to come clean.'

I thought for a moment, completely at a loss. It was wrong, I knew that, but what did I have for proof? All I had was Marvin's own story and, really, it might have been made up on the spot, just to convince me that someone else was to blame. Marvin was a natural liar, the entire state knew that. There was still Marvin's own condition, his desperation, his fear, but had I misread even that? Could that have just been a tortured soul? Even at the time I'd known that Marvin wasn't telling me everything, not even nearly.

But it was terror in those tiny eyes. Real terror.

'I know it's wrong,' I said, 'but I can't think of anything that would convince you.'

Kelly sighed. 'That's a pity. I was hoping you would.'

'You were what?'

'I'll tell you the truth, George. I don't think this wraps it up either. I think it's pretty weird, if you want my opinion. But other people here think it's been wrapped up. In fact, my superiors have told me this wraps it up and that I have plenty of other work that needs attention. So what am I gonna do?'

'But Marvin was an ex-minister, he was famous. Surely someone is going to investigate his death more closely than that?'

'You don't get it. The suicide looks dead right. He was disgraced, he was an alcoholic, a long-term failure who'd killed an old friend in a stupid argument and was being hunted by the police. Suicide in that situation makes perfect sense. His mental state could hardly have been healthy. That house was a mess and he must have been drinking two or three bottles a day. And that's the other thing that clinches it. We found vodka in the house, the same brand that we found at the substation.'

And my world seemed to turn over. 'What?'

'The vodka. It's only circumstantial, of course, but it does help place Marvin at the crime scene. That still leaves all the beer cans, and who drank them, but I guess we'll never find an answer to that. Maybe a third party was involved.'

I was barely listening. He didn't understand, he didn't know.

'Detective Kelly,' I said, 'Marvin didn't drink vodka.'

And we sat silent on the line.

'You're saying Marvin never drank vodka at all?'

'Not that I know of. He only drank scotch.'

'But you hadn't seen him in years, people's tastes change.'

'I was in that house yesterday. I saw scotch everywhere, but I didn't see a single bottle of vodka. Where did you find it anyway? Was it stuck in a cupboard somewhere, or was it in the open?'

'It was in the living room. One bottle. Empty.'

'There was no vodka there yesterday.'

'Could you swear to that?'

Could I? I pictured the room, the darkness and the heat and the smell, Marvin's pale face sweating before me, and bottles everywhere . . . could there have been one that wasn't scotch? But I'd seen those bottles lying on the concrete floor of the substation, at Charlie's feet. There was no way I could have seen one of them again and not recognised it. Instantly.

'I can swear.'

'So what are you saying?'

'Don't you see? Clarke drinks vodka. Marvin told me that himself.'

'Marvin told you that this Clarke person drinks vodka. And then we find a bottle in his living room. That doesn't sound a little too neat to you, George? A little too easy?'

'He wasn't making this up. Trust me. Clarke tracked Marvin down, just like he tracked Charlie down.'

'But I'm telling you it was suicide. Maybe Marvin just

drank vodka sometimes and you didn't notice the bottle and it all happened the way the note said it did.'

'But you said yourself you don't believe it.'

'I don't *disbelieve* it. I just don't think it's everything, that's all. And what you're talking about, well . . .'

I searched through my mind for something else. This was madness.

'Joan Ellsgood,' I said. 'She said Charlie was alone at the boarding house. She didn't say Marvin was with him.'

'Marvin could have been waiting in the car. It was parked some distance away.'

'Did he mention it in the note?'

'Why would he?'

'What about his book, then? Marvin's book. You've read it. He must have mentioned Clarke, the sort of things they used to do together. That might explain some of it.'

'I don't remember reading about anyone called Clarke.'

And I could hear Marvin saying *not everything*. He hadn't written about *everything*.

'Besides,' Kelly was saying, 'the book fits with what we've got. Marvin is rehashing all that ancient history, brooding about the old days, then he meets up with Charlie. They've still got unsettled business between them, they argue about it and bang, it all goes wrong.'

'But Charlie wasn't mad at Marvin any more. Marvin told me that.'

'But he would, wouldn't he? Part of the lie.'

'What about fingerprints, then? You didn't find any on the bottles at the substation—what about the one at the house?'

'We're not fingerprinting anything at the house. It's a suicide. A bottle of vodka didn't kill him.'

'I bet you wouldn't find any prints on the bottle.'

'What would that prove? Anyway, I'm not in charge of this crime scene, George—there is no crime scene—so I don't think I can just tell them to start printing everything. Not without a reason.'

'Jesus.'

'You'll get to put all this in a statement at least. You'll have to make one, seeing you were the last one to see him alive. You aren't leaving Brisbane today?'

'No.'

'Good. Someone will be over to talk to you. They've got senior guys looking at it now, seeing it's Marvin and all. But without something harder than what you've given me so far, no one's gonna take much notice.'

I remembered it then.

I said, 'You haven't told me what time Marvin died.'

'Somewhere around two in the morning, supposedly.'

I remembered a cold laugh, a voice I'd never heard before.

'Someone called me around that time last night. A man. I thought it might have been Marvin, but whoever it was just laughed and hung up.'

'So?'

'So hardly anyone knows I'm here. And none of them would make a call like that.'

'Wrong number?'

'That's what the person said. But you have to go through the motel switchboard. It's unlikely that's a wrong number. And Marvin had my number written by his phone. I wrote it there myself.'

'I don't get you. We could check the phone records and see if it was Marvin that called you, but what's the big deal? If he was about to kill himself, he might've called you, then changed his mind and hung up.'

'But I know it wasn't Marvin on the line. I think someone else was in his house. Between the phone call and the vodka bottle, you could prove that.'

'It's a bit of a stretch, George. And anyway, the whole point is Marvin killed himself. This isn't a murder investigation.'

'But if someone else was involved, there could have been some sort of duress. What about footprints? Were there footprints near him on the beach?'

'A dozen joggers standing around his body? You bet there were footprints.'

'Can you at least check the phone records for me?'

He thought about it. 'Okay, I'll look into it. The bottle thing, too, if I can.'

'What about George Clarke?'

'I'll ask around about him, but that's all. You're only giving me hearsay, George, and I can't start an investigation on that.'

'He's already under investigation. Marvin said the government's been holding some sort of inquiry into his business practices.'

'Hardly my department, George, but like I said, I'll ask around.'

'Thanks.'

'Stay put in the meantime, and someone will be over to see you.'

We got off the phone. I climbed out of bed, went to the window and looked out at the bright Brisbane day. Marvin was dead. Twenty-four hours ago I'd been with him, and now he was dead. Twenty-four hours ago I'd listened to him fearing for his life, and now he was dead. He'd begged me not to leave and I had, and now he was dead. Sitting on his beach, waiting for that first boat to arrive, staring out blindly. *Turn around, boys, there's nothing waiting for you here . . .*

No one had found his glasses.

I realised I was watching the street, watching it for cars, for people. No . . . not people. For one person. One man.

Marvin didn't drink vodka. And he'd never been anywhere near Highwood. And it wasn't Marvin who'd called in the dead of night.

But my number was on the pad by his phone. I'd written it under my name. I looked at my own phone. Who else had I given those details?

I opened the phone book and found the number of Lindsay's club. He'd said they were open for lunch, for the businessmen and their steaks and their lap-dances. I dialled, got reception, and was put through. I waited, staring out the window. The street was empty.

Lindsay came on.

'I take it you've heard,' he said, and he did not sound friendly.

'The police just called.'

'Don't ask me if I got a place you can hide—I've done helping old friends.'

'You think I need a place to hide?'
'You tell me.'
'What have you said to the police?'
'Nothing. Marvin wants to kill himself, who am I to stop him?'
'You know it wasn't just suicide.'
'I don't know a thing. I told the police that, I'm telling you that.'
'You said different the other night.'
'I think you're mistaken.'
'It's a nice deal you've got with the police, by the sound of things.'
'Get the fuck off my case, George.'
And none of this was to any point.
'Did you call me last night, around two?' I asked.
'No.'
'Did you give my number to anyone but Marvin?'
'No.'

But was there a moment's hesitation before he answered? I said, 'Did anyone else come looking for Marvin?'
'What makes you think someone did?'
'Someone found him somehow. Who knew where he was but you and me?'
'They must have got it from you, George, 'cause I didn't say shit to anyone.'
'Neither did I.'
'Maybe you didn't have to *tell* them, George. You're the one that went out there.'
'What do you mean?'
'Enough, George. Are we through here?'
'I guess we are.'
'Then don't call me again.'
He hung up.

I stood there. But I hadn't told anyone. All I'd done was drive out there. And there'd been no one following me. No one who saw me. Only . . .

I took up the phone again, dialled Jeremy's number, and it was picked up on the second ring.
'Jeremy?'

'No, it's Louise.'

'Louise, it's George. I need to talk to Jeremy.'

'You can't,' and there was an edge to her voice. 'He's not here any more. Something's happened.'

I felt myself clutching the phone in a wave of panic. He was dead. Like Charlie and Marvin before him, someone had appeared at his door, a man with a bottle of vodka in his hand, he was rounding us all up . . .

'What?' I asked, faint.

'He's in hospital, George. Since the night after you were here.'

'What happened?'

There was a pause, and I heard the clink of glass against the mouthpiece. She was drinking. 'It's the leukaemia. The doctors say this is it, George. No more remissions.'

'The leukaemia? That's all?'

'What do you mean, that's all? He's dying!'

But I was almost laughing. 'I'm sorry, I'm sorry. How bad is it?'

'He's barely conscious . . . but, George, he was hoping you'd call. He said he wants to see you.'

'About what?'

'I don't know. But there's something he wants to tell you. He seemed pretty worried about it.'

'Tell me where he is.'

I wrote down the name of the hospital and the room number. The Royal Brisbane. I stared at that a moment, wondering about the way fate was working here.

'Listen, Louise, you didn't call me last night, did you?'

'No. Why?'

But I only said goodbye and tossed the phone aside.

I looked out at the day. Thank Christ for leukaemia, I thought. Thank the Lord for something as natural as cancer. I needed to keep my head clear. Clarke wasn't everywhere.

A police car came along the street, slowed in front of the motel. I could just make out the driver. He was looking up at the motel, as though checking the number. I watched as the car parked at the opposite kerb. More detectives. Senior men come to interview me, as Detective Kelly had warned.

But what could I tell them other than what I'd already told Detective Kelly himself?

The door opened and a plain-clothes detective stepped out. He turned and looked up at the motel. It was only for a moment, then I was reeling away from the window, tripping over the couch and falling to the floor. My mind was ice and my heart was thudding and I lay dead still on the carpet. Had he seen me? He hadn't looked directly at my window, he wouldn't even know which window was mine, surely. If he hadn't seen me then I could hide, I could run, I could do something.

It was seconds before I realised why these thoughts were racing through my head, before I realised why the sight of the detective's face had sent me backing away instinctively, thinking without reason of escape. It was seconds before I realised what it all really meant.

Because I'd seen him before.

Not like this—not getting out of a police car, pulling on his suit coat and grimly scanning the street. No. Instead I'd seen him as a harmless looking middle-aged man, dressed in a faded T-shirt and shorts, pulling a fishing rod from the boot of a car, and gazing out at the ocean from a Redcliffe beach. And not following me, not watching me, not concerned with me at all.

THIRTY-SIX

I lay on the carpet, the couch between me and the window.

I waited for the knock on the door.

Was it locked? I peered up. Of course. It was still locked from the night before, the security chain attached. He couldn't just walk in. But it was only a chain, a thin chain.

I listened. Blood hammered in my ears, beating with my thoughts. The fisherman was a police detective, the fisherman was a police detective. And he'd been waiting outside Marvin's place. But how was that possible? The police hadn't known where Marvin was until this morning.

My body already knew the answer. It's why I was on the floor, why I'd found myself there even before there'd been time to think. The police in general hadn't known where Marvin was—only this policeman in particular had known. And he hadn't told any of his colleagues.

Knuckles rapped on wood. I lay frozen, staring across the room. There was a fish-eye lens in the centre of the door, but I wasn't going to move, wasn't going to risk a sound. I waited. The knuckles rapped again, imperative.

'George? You in there?'

A police voice. Official.

I waited in silence, listening for every movement, every noise. A car idled by in the street, then suddenly changed gear and roared off. Silence again.

Another three knocks.

'George? It's Detective Jeffreys here. It's about Marvin. I was told by Detective Kelly that you were expecting me.'

Did he know I was in here? He couldn't know. The

windows were mirrored. Impossible to see through in bright midday sun.

I waited. Detective Jeffreys. A senior man, Detective Kelly had said. He'd taken over the investigation. He was in charge of finding out what had happened to Marvin. But if he'd already been there, even before I was . . .

Or had he been?

Make sure you're not followed.

The thoughts were racing. The other detectives knew about my motel. If this Detective Jeffreys was looking for Marvin, he could have found out from them where I was staying. He could have waited across the street, followed me when I pulled out, and I would have led him straight there. When I'd seen him out at Redcliffe he'd only just been opening the boot of his car. He might've parked only moments earlier. He might have been right behind me all the way. A policeman who was looking for Marvin, but who didn't tell anyone else what he was doing. And now Marvin was dead. It was Clarke's doing, I knew that. But if Detective Jeffreys . . . what if he didn't just work for the police?

You think the police aren't still onside with someone like him? You don't think he hasn't still got one or two of them lined up?

And I'd led him straight there. All he would've had to do was wait till I was gone. Put in a call to Clarke, tell him Marvin's address. And wait.

Charlie had already been dealt with. Now Marvin. I was the only one left who knew anything about it all.

I waited on the floor. There were no more knocks. No more words.

Was he still out there? And what did he want with me? Would it be just to talk, to find out exactly how much I knew? And if he found out just how much I knew—what then? Would he take me down to the station, where there were other police, where we could both be seen?

Or was there another man waiting somewhere? Nearby, perhaps. Clarke himself, a glass of vodka in his hand, his mind still half rotted with the alcohol. Waiting to tie up the last loose end. All he needed to do was sit there until Detective Jeffreys brought me to him. Then the detective would leave and it would be just me and Clarke in the room. I would be face to face with the man who had taken Charlie to the substation, who had come calling on Marvin in the middle of the night. Or perhaps Detective Jeffreys would stay. Perhaps he was always there.

And suddenly I was thinking of beer cans scattered on a cement floor. Bottles of vodka for one man, cans of beer for another.

There was still no sound. Was he gone? I remained motionless, counting seconds. Sixty. One hundred and twenty. One hundred and eighty.

Surely he was gone. I crawled around the couch, my chest to the floor. From this level I could see the building opposite and the tops of trees and a spread of roofs leading off to the beautiful warm blue sky, a normal day out there, people living without cares . . . but I couldn't see the street. I lifted myself slowly. There was the police car, but it was empty, it hadn't moved. Where was the detective? I lifted myself further and looked straight into his eyes.

He was standing in the middle of the street, arms on his hips, staring up at my window.

I dropped to the floor again. Could he see through the windows? I lifted myself slowly again. He hadn't moved. He was studying my window, frowning. His suit coat was open and beneath it a white shirt spread over a large belly. He was bigger than he'd looked when I'd seen him the day before, and nothing seemed relaxed or harmless about him now, but it was the same man. I stared straight down at him, safe behind my glass, then he turned around, walked back to his car.

I felt a surge of elation which immediately died. He'd stopped again. He glanced up at my window once more, then came back towards the motel. He *had* seen me. But no, he was heading across to the main entrance of the building, the reception office. What could he want there?

The manager. He was looking for the manager. He was a police officer, all he had to do was show his badge to the manager and ask to have my room opened. The manager wouldn't hesitate. They could be up here in moments with the key. The chain was still on the door, but once they saw the chain they'd know for sure I had to be inside somewhere.

I got to my feet, adrenaline surging. I stared down at the office. I had only seconds, a minute or two at most. Get away, that was the thing, get to my car. But my car was two flights down in the garage, the police car was parked right across the road from the driveway. There was no way I could drive out of there before they came out of the office. The detective knew what I looked like, he knew my car.

On foot then. Just get out and run. But it was the same problem. There was no back entrance that I knew of, all the stairwells opened out to the front. I'd be on the street, out in the open. He'd spot me in seconds. Find a linen closet, then, a storage room, anything, a hole to hide in. But that was ridiculous too. Rooms like that would be locked, and I didn't even know where they were to start with. I'd be stumbling around the hallways like a moth. It was only a motel, there was nowhere to hide.

The manager! He'd be there as well when they opened the room. He wouldn't just hand the key over, he'd come up and open the door himself. The detective couldn't do anything if the manager was standing there, a witness. But then what was the detective telling him, down in the office? That I was a criminal, a dangerous felon, someone who had to be apprehended and dragged away? Would the manager do anything to stop that, no matter what I said?

Call Detective Kelly! Get real police over here. I clutched at the phone, my other hand fumbling at my wallet. But Detective Kelly couldn't be here instantly. It would take ten minutes, fifteen. Anything could have happened by then. Would he believe me anyway? This was his fellow officer. It didn't matter, he was my best chance. I found the card, punched in numbers. My hands were shaking. I hit the wrong buttons. I swore and dropped the card, bent and picked it up. I went to dial again and my fingers froze on the first button.

Down on the street, the detective had emerged from the office.

He was alone. He stared up at my window and then back at reception, shaking his head. I could sense the anger even from a distance. It hadn't worked. The manager wasn't coming with the key. Maybe the manager was out, maybe there was no one in the office. It was a small enough place, there was no regular room service. The desk wasn't attended every second.

It didn't matter. All that mattered was that the man down there didn't have the key. He was walking back to his car. I watched him, hardly breathing, the phone still in my hand. He opened the door and climbed in. I watched. He didn't close the door. He sat there with one foot anchored to the road. He looked up at my window. He reached into his coat and pulled out a pack of cigarettes, lit one up.

Dread descended again. He wasn't going anywhere. And sooner or later the manager would come back. He'd get the key eventually.

I looked down at the phone. I hung up and then dialled again, Detective Kelly's number. Maybe I had enough time now. The tones rang as I watched out the window. The man down on the street flicked ash onto the bitumen and scanned the footpaths. The phone clicked up.

'Kelly's desk,' said a female voice.

'Is Detective Kelly there?' I was almost whispering.

'Not at the moment. Can I take a message?'

I thought feverishly. Was there a message I could leave? Could I explain everything to this woman, make her believe me and send someone? No. Maybe I could make something up, then, an emergency, report a crime in progress or something, get police sent anyway. But even if the police came, what then? He was a superior officer. He could send them away. They'd go soon enough when they saw nothing was happening. And if I came out, delivered myself to them, he would take over. He couldn't do anything right there and then, perhaps, but later. No matter what happened, he wasn't going to simply disappear, and no matter what happened, I couldn't just slip away unobserved. It would be the two of us again in the end. And then Clarke, waiting for me somewhere. Vodka pulsing in his veins like a disease.

'Sir?' said the woman.

And in a flash I had it.

'Is a Detective Jeffreys based there?'

'Yes he is, but . . . let me just check . . . no, I don't think he's about either.'

'I have an extremely urgent message for him. Is there any way you could reach him, right this instant?'

'Well, if he has his phone with him. Or if he's near a radio, maybe.'

He was near one all right, within a foot of one.

'This is important. Tell him George Verney called. He's looking for me, urgently. Trust me, he'll want to get this message. Tell him. . .' I cast about for an address, a convincing one, and that came in a flash too. 'Tell him I'm at Lindsay Heath's club in the Valley. I'm waiting here right now with Lindsay. He'll know exactly what I mean. Have you got that?'

'Yes, sir. But I can't guarantee he'll get this immediately.'

'Just send it. Please.'

I hung up and let the phone fall to the floor, my eyes not moving from the police car out on the street. Would it work? If the message got through, it should. It would sound natural enough to the man waiting down there. He would know that Detective Kelly had already told me to expect him. True, Kelly hadn't mentioned Jeffreys' name, but Jeffreys himself wouldn't know that. Nor was there any reason why I should be suspicious of him, or in hiding from him. After all, I'd made no sign that I'd noticed him, there on the beach at Redcliffe, I'd scarcely glanced his way. So in his mind there was no reason for me to act in any way underhanded. And bringing Lindsay into it made sense as well. It was natural enough that I would go and see Lindsay, and the police knew all about his club, it was safe territory from their point of view.

I watched, time standing still. The detective finished his cigarette, flicked it across the road. His eyes moved continuously.

It was agony. Didn't he have a phone with him? How long did it take to get a call over the radio? But then suddenly he was leaning back into the car. I couldn't see what he was doing. Was there a phone in there, sitting on the passenger seat, ringing? Had the radio squawked his name, was he responding to it? All I could see was one foot, still resting on the bitumen. Then he leaned back out again. He stared up at my window, his face set hard. His hand scraped across his chin. The call had come through, in one fashion or another, but he hadn't bought it, not completely. Some instinct was warning him. All he had to do was try the manager one more time.

Abruptly he swung his leg in behind the wheel, pulled the door shut, and within moments the car was speeding back off down the street. I leant against the window, my face to the glass, and watched until it disappeared around the corner. He was gone.

My legs were shaking, relief sending me sagging against the wall. I had time, I could get out now, disappear. And let Lindsay handle the shit when they found me nowhere near his place. They wouldn't believe him now anyway, no matter what he told them, even the truth.

Tyres screeched.

From the other end of the street came another car. It was dark grey, a luxury sedan. It sped up, u-turned, and parked exactly where the police car had been.

I stared at it, sickened. It was just a car, it could have been any car, but it wasn't. The detective had gone and this car had immediately taken its place. The vigilance hadn't lapsed, just changed hands. I hadn't fooled anyone.

I felt exhausted. Nervous energy jangled in my limbs, but there was no more surge, no more survival instinct. Only fear, cold and draining. I didn't have a thought left.

And yet it wasn't a police car, not even an unmarked one. No police drove cars like that. Nor could I see the driver. The doors did not open and the windows were black. I could no more see who was inside than whoever it was could see me, and yet I could sense the presence in there, staring up, just as I was staring down—two watchers hidden by tinted glass, confronting each other across fifty feet of heat-shimmering air.

It was *him*.

I backed away from the window, the fear sinking in like paralysis. I was right, Clarke had been waiting nearby while his tame policeman did the groundwork. And now that his watchdog had been called away, he'd taken up the job himself. And tinted glass wouldn't fool him, nor would any message. He wanted to see me, and he would wait forever until he did.

From the street I heard a car door open, then softly clump shut.

I stood there, blank. I turned my head from the window to the door. The chain hung from its catch, but that wouldn't stop him. Marvin had been hiding in a fortress, and still this man had got inside. Nerveless I took four steps to the door. I set my eye to the lens.

Sweat prickled on my forehead. I blinked. I couldn't see anything. The lens was cracked, its view distorted. I could see the short hallway and then the stairs descending, but everything was askew. A square of glaring sunlight made it a tableau of shadows, black and white. And in the middle of it all, something moved.

A man was ascending the stairs.

He was a silhouette, only a refracted, tilted figure, rising slowly. The face was a blur. He was right in front of the door now. He seemed to swell, shudder, and shrink again. Then an arm stretched out, angular and thin in the lens, and I felt strangely delicate knocks come through the wood, grazing my cheek like the touch of a spider.

I waited, eyeball straining, mere inches from a man I knew had come to kill me.

Then he leaned close. Through the fractured glass I caught a glimpse of pale skin, and one eye, black as a stone, a swath of dark hair.

He spoke. A low, soft voice that echoed faintly in the corridor, hollow and pitched only for me to hear. 'George?' it said. 'George, are in you in there?'

Something blazed in my chest, and once again my body reacted faster than my mind, my fingers were fumbling at the chain, sliding it free, and I was tugging open the door, because that voice, I knew that voice, and then the door was open and I was clutching the startled figure and it wasn't a man at all, it was a woman, and I knew exactly who she was, I'd been waiting for her since the whole mess began.

It was Maybellene.

THIRTY-SEVEN

Maybellene and Charlie and me . . . maybe it was as predictable as these things always were, affairs and betrayals and the eternal triangle. At least May and I, we did try. We stopped cheating on Charlie from the day he received his first summons to appear before the Inquiry.

Everything else had stopped anyway. The parties, the invitations, all the frenzied acquaintances, they were gone in the space of the first few weeks. Our clubs were shut down, everyone's clubs were shut down, there was nowhere to go, no night left to explore. The Inquiry kept expanding. I lost my job. Marvin was stood down, so May lost her job as well. Jeremy was already in Sydney. Lindsay had vanished. It was just the three of us. May and Charlie and me.

But Charlie kept the restaurants open. On restricted hours, admittedly, within the law, but he still needed to be out there. He needed to be seen in public, to show he was the same old Charlie, working the tables and laughing with the guests. He'd always fought his body in that sense, his looks, and he'd won. For a time he seemed to be holding it together. His smiling face still appeared in the social columns, and only May and I could see the strain behind the smile.

But as more evidence emerged and all of it pointed straight at Charlie, something started to crack. The restaurants emptied. The Inquiry was getting too big, too serious, there was nothing enticing about Charlie's criminal connections any more. People wouldn't speak to him. His face started appearing in the political pages, and they didn't even call him a restaurateur now, he was only a purveyor of prostitution and illegal gambling. And people didn't see his smile any more, they saw only a beefy, small-time thug with narrow, scheming eyes. Charlie stopped going to the restaurants. He managed them over the phone for a while, but then gave up on them altogether. Later still they'd be sold off, with everything else. But for the time being, Charlie withdrew into his house, with May at his side.

The Inquiry rolled on. I was called only once myself to testify. For a juggernaut that was transforming the entire state, it didn't look much. A single courtroom, a little overcrowded, with no power to try or convict, only to ask questions, and to compel answers. But through it passed an endless trail of penitents—government ministers, public servants, nightclub owners, police, madams, bookies, informers, petty criminals—and the sheer scale of the story we told was an avalanche. The newspapers could barely handle the weight of it, headlines could only scream so loud, outrage last only so long. And waiting behind was an echelon of criminal prosecutors . . . and *they* could try, *they* could convict.

So I stood in the dock. I was asked to admit that I had financial interests in Charlie's businesses, which I admitted. I was asked to explain what those businesses were, which I did, as far as I knew. I was asked to confirm that Marvin and Lindsay were also involved, which I confirmed. I was asked if I'd ever been directed about what to write in my columns, which I denied. Then I was let go. It hardly seemed like five minutes. Another witness was called. No one mentioned Jeremy. Let alone anyone called George Clarke.

The newspapers put me on page five, and they had surprisingly little to say. Maybe they were embarrassed about it being one of their own, maybe some of them had secrets not so different from mine. More likely I was just too small to be worth the bother. I was already unemployed and my old paper was folding and, besides, new scandals were breaking every few days. So my name was added to the long list of the exiled and condemned, and I was tossed aside for bigger fish. I had no idea what to do or where to go. I hid in my flat and drank, or wandered through bars where I would know nobody, see nobody. For a few months I sweated on the talk of criminal charges, but in the end all that I received were some angry demands from the tax department and a cursory visit from the police. Not the police I knew, of course, new police. Or at least, police who *acted* as if they were new. But even they didn't want me. I was already forgotten.

Charlie wasn't so lucky. His testimony at the Inquiry was front page stuff, and afterwards formal charges were laid and he was arrested. I went with May to his bail hearing, and when he was released I drove them home, the three of us silent. Charlie was losing weight, and drinking all the time now. He wasn't someone who knew how to spend time alone. His life was society. Without it he was crippled. I'd tried talking to him, but he was removed from me somehow, the connection was gone. Maybe it was because of May and me—in some way he must have known—and even the bond of alcohol couldn't break the distance. In the old days drinking had been a shared joy, a celebration together. There was no joy in it now. We were both drinking purely for oblivion, and that sort of drinking never required company. I dropped them off at their house but didn't stay, despite the entreating look from May. It wasn't for herself, it was for Charlie. But I couldn't see any way to save him.

I drove home and sat in my dark flat and opened bottle after bottle of wine. Later that night there was a knock on my door and it was May, the same old beaten tears in her eyes, and we started up again. Desperately this time, clinging to each other, cruelly aware of Charlie sitting alone in his house, abandoned by the both of us.

When the trial came I was called as a witness. I asked the defence lawyer if I would have any chance to speak on Charlie's behalf—to explain his character, the sort of person he was, how he'd probably known no more about the way things had really worked than I had.

The lawyer laughed in my face. 'A character reference from you?' he said. 'You want Charlie put away for life?'

So I stood in the dock again and blankly stated that I was an investor in Charlie's various establishments and that, yes, those included casinos and to some degree brothels, and that, yes, Charlie had spent time in these premises and knew what they were all about, and that, yes, bribes were paid to police and other officials, and on and on. Charlie sat quietly in the dock, looking pale and ill, and in the jury's eyes, I could tell, undoubtedly guilty.

It didn't help when he was called up himself to testify. Maybe the old Charlie could have charmed a jury, talked his way clear, but not the way he was now. His barrister at least got him to say that Lindsay had really run the darker side of things, that Marvin had masterminded it all, but the documents didn't bear his evidence out. Lindsay was gone. Marvin was on trial for other things, and everyone still loved him anyway. Charlie just sounded desperate and vindictive. From the gallery May watched with sad, drawn eyes. No one called on her to speak. One of the working girls had already mentioned May's habit of using the brothel rooms for sex with Charlie, and to the world at large she was little better than a prostitute herself.

The night before closing arguments we gathered, the three of us, at Charlie and May's house. We knew what the result would be and that this was our last dinner together. It was a surreal occasion. One of us was going to prison, but we were still the same people, the same three harmless people we'd always been. In all those long, drunken, wonderful nights, what had been so criminal? Who had been hurt? Everyone, according to the courts, and to the new spirit that was marshalling in the streets of Queensland. We'd hurt everyone, the fabric of society itself. Maybe it was true, but to the three of us that night, nothing made any sense. And Charlie wasn't saying anything. He was staring fixedly at the three or four years ahead of him. May and I faltered along with the conversation, but it was hard to find anything to talk about. All our memories, all our times together, led us straight back to the trial and to Charlie sitting voiceless, waiting for the sentence to fall. And if there was a wealth of things to say between May and me, it was impossible in front of Charlie. So we sat there, the three of us, the oldest and most familiar of friends and lovers, and chatted inanely about nothing. It was unbearable.

I escaped, finally, to their back deck, looked out over the Brisbane night. I drank steadily, feeling the welcome numbness grow, the world shrink in, the stars above fading to smudges in the sky. After half an hour or so May came out and said that Charlie had gone to bed and that I should leave. She looked exhausted. Like me, she was facing no criminal charges, but she was going to be a key witness at Marvin's trial, and she'd lost as much as I had. Meanwhile she'd been locked in a house with a husband growing ever more withdrawn, refusing her support, blaming her silently for something to which she couldn't even confess. We held each other there on the deck and May cried quietly and we kissed, the world shrunk finally to just the two of us. Charlie chose that moment to come out, his mouth open, as if finally he had found something he could say, some way to move forward, and he saw us there.

I watched the distinct expressions pass across his face. Shock. Pain. Anger. All in agonised slow motion. Then he was screaming at us.

'Not here! Not now! Wait until I'm gone!'

We all stood there. The anger drained out of Charlie as quickly as it had come, and he just shook his head, walked back inside. We followed him. Charlie sat on the couch and May sat with him, enfolded him in her arms, and I sat alone on a chair. And so we remained, not talking about it, not saying anything, just drinking, until one by one each of us fell asleep, and then it was morning, and time to go to court.

Charlie got his four years, and as we left the court May said, 'I can't see you any more.'

She went home to her empty house. It wasn't her house much longer. It all went, the house and the restaurants, to cover legal fees and tax debts and fines. May moved into a small rented flat of her own. Charlie went into the prison system and May visited him every time she was allowed. I went once to visit and was told that Charlie had no interest in seeing me.

I drank. I still had money and I was on unemployment benefits and nothing mattered.

I didn't expect to see May again, but one last time she arrived at my door, lost and alone and poised, quivering, as she would always be, on the horn between light and dark.

And as I always would, I took her in.

Later we lay on the couch in my big empty living room, the sky outside orange and night air flowing through the windows, and we talked about Charlie.

'It's terrible,' she whispered, the sadness splintering her voice. 'He won't talk to me, he thinks I'm with you. I've told him I'm not, I've told him I haven't seen you, that I won't see you . . . but he doesn't believe me. And it's killing him in there. It's like he's dead already.'

And in the depth of my being, to my lasting shame, I wished that he was.

'Never again,' she hissed, clutching my shoulders, her hair tangled about her face as she stared down at me, fierce and afraid. 'I had to tell you this, but never again.'

By dawn she was gone.

That was it, I thought, as church bells rang in the morning and the choir lifted their voices in song, praising a wise and merciful God. That's all there is.

But by then it was two years since the Inquiry had begun.

And the Queensland elections of December 1989 were drawing near.

THIRTY-EIGHT

Within minutes I was packed and we were in May's car, speeding away from the motel through the back streets of New Farm. From the passenger seat I craned around and watched out the rear window. There was no one following us.

'George?' May asked. 'Where are we going?'

For the first time I turned and really looked at her.

Maybellene, a decade older. Her hair was longer, and the curls were gone, leaving it straight and severe, and darker than I remembered, as if it had been dyed. Her face, though, had softened and grown more rounded. Her whole body had. It didn't suggest that tight, coiled energy that it had of old. She was a middle-aged woman. But it was May all the same. It was finally sinking through all the tension and panic of the last hour. She was really here.

'Just drive around for a while,' I said. 'Get us out of New Farm.'

She nodded. She didn't seemed surprised by anything I was doing. I'd barely noticed it in all the rush, but from me flinging open the motel door to bundling my stuff together and dashing back over to her car, she'd hardly said a word. As if she'd shown up almost for this very purpose. And now that there was time to talk, I didn't know where to begin.

'Jesus, May,' I said. 'I'm sorry about that . . .'

'It's okay, George.' She glanced from the road to the rear view mirror and then to me. 'I was coming to see you, but I saw that police car outside, and then that man, so . . . so I waited. When he left I thought you mustn't have been inside, but I had to check.'

I was staring at her, listening to the way her voice had deepened.

'I can't believe it's you,' I said. 'I'd given up. I thought you must be out of the state, or out of the country.'

She smiled, the old May smile, with its interior sadness. 'It's a long story, George.'

'And . . . you've heard about Charlie?'

The smile faded away. 'I've heard. About Marvin too.'

'Marvin?'

'It was on the midday news. That's why . . . that's why I thought it was time I came and saw you.'

'How did you know where I was?'

'Lindsay told me. Yesterday. I asked him not to say anything to you. I mean, I didn't know if there was any point in us meeting.'

And it all rushed up on me. 'But what have you been doing? Christ, May, have you been in Brisbane all this time?'

'More or less.'

'The police couldn't trace you. They said your name wasn't listed anywhere.'

Her eyes were cool, measuring me. 'Can you blame me for not wanting to be found, George?'

'They only wanted you because you were Charlie's next of kin.'

'We were divorced.'

Her tone was cold, but even after ten years, I knew her better than that.

'That was you, wasn't it. At the funeral.'

She looked away. 'I didn't realise anyone saw me.'

'I didn't. Not really.'

'I couldn't face it, George. I'm sorry.' And it seemed that was all she had to say.

I stared out at the streets gliding by. May was following the river as it curved around into New Farm's industrial fringe, only it wasn't industrial any more. All the old warehouses had been transformed into studio apartments, the factories into restaurants and shops.

She'd been here all along. And she hadn't known if she'd even wanted to see me.

She said, 'I've been reading the papers. About Charlie, about Highwood. They even mentioned you. Have you been up in that town ever since those days?'

I nodded, still staring out. It was easier than looking at her. 'I couldn't face Brisbane again. Until now.'

'What have you been doing?'

'Working on a little paper up there.'

'I wondered, but I could never call. I only had that old number anyway.'

'The boarding house. Did you call it a couple of days ago?'

She nodded. 'That was before I thought of Lindsay. I knew you would have seen him. And the old woman wouldn't tell me where you were. Neither would the other one. Emily.'

I looked at her and she was looking back, her eyes unreadable.

'Are you married or anything, George?'

'No, but Emily and me, well, you know . . . What about you?'

The smile again. 'No.'

'But what have you been doing, how have you lived?'

'I've been okay.' She laughed, unsteady. 'This is so strange, George.'

'And you really stayed in Brisbane? You never left?'

'Do you think I should have?'

'I don't know. I just assumed, after everything . . .'

'I came close. I really did. God knows, everyone else was gone.'

Including me.

'What about Charlie?' I said. 'Did you see him at all, before he died?'

'I didn't even know he was still in town.'

'What happened with you two . . . after the last time?'

The question didn't seem to bother her. 'After he got out of hospital I kept going out to the prison, but he wouldn't talk to me. Later he refused to even see me, and I stopped going. Then I got divorce papers in the mail.' She dabbed at an eye, but there were no tears. It was an older May. Harder, maybe. And it was all ten years ago.

'What about Marvin and Jeremy? Did you ever see them at all?'

'Why would I want to see Marvin? And Jeremy. I was thinking of Jeremy . . . I might have got round to it, I don't know. Have you seen him? Is he still in that house?'

'He's in hospital. He's dying of leukaemia.'

She sighed. 'I've left it all too late . . . but what's happening, George? When I heard about Charlie I thought that maybe it was just something that he'd been involved with since our time. From prison maybe. What else would it be? I was going to call you but . . .'

She stared at me, intent, forgetting about the road.

'George, for all I knew he could have died years ago. I'd given up on him. You didn't see what he was like in that prison, especially after the hospital. I buried him long ago. But now this thing with Marvin. What's going on?'

'What did the news say?'

'Just that he was found dead on a beach.'

'They think it was suicide.'

'Suicide? I didn't realise. I thought . . .'

'There's a note confessing that he killed Charlie.'

'*Marvin* killed Charlie?'

'That's what the police think.'

'You don't?' She was getting bewildered.

'Pull over for a minute.'

We stopped on a side street and May switched off the engine. We turned in our seats, facing each other a foot apart, and I told her the whole story. Aware, every minute, of her hands resting on her knee, only inches from mine. Of the smell of her. Of the new lines around her mouth. Of the body I'd known so well once, and how it was subtly different now, and of the desire to explore it further, to see what had really changed, and what hadn't, and whether it mattered. It was a helpless feeling, like the old days. May and I talking about Charlie, and me thinking only about her.

I told her everything. I don't know how I was expecting her to respond. Alarm or fear or anger. Instead a deep stillness came over her. Watching her hand, I saw it tighten and go white on her knee. A flush seemed to rise in her face, but she said nothing, didn't move. When I was finished she turned her head and stared through the windscreen. At the end of the street were the remains of a wooden wharf, and beyond that the slow flow of the river. But it wasn't the river she was seeing. I didn't know what she was seeing, what she was thinking.

'Poor Charlie,' she said finally, a brightness in her eyes that might have been moisture. 'He didn't deserve that.'

'You were Marvin's personal assistant. If this George Clarke and Marvin were partners, you must have met him. Christ, it was his property you tried to burn down.'

She nodded, still far away. 'I met him. Even before I started to work for Marvin. The first time was at Jeremy's place, not long after I moved in. They weren't friends but . . . Clarke . . . kept coming around. I was wishing he'd been inside that building we burnt. But of course I was on the other side by then. I was supposed to be grateful. He'd let me out of jail.'

'What was he like? Is he capable of all these things?'

'I don't know . . . maybe.'

'Do you know anything about him now? Where he lives? Where he works?'

'No. He kept to himself. That was the way he and Marvin wanted it.'

'I guess we should go to the police, then.'

She came back to the present, clutched my hand. 'I don't think that's enough, George.'

'What else is there?'

'You should get out of Brisbane. If everything you say is right, then he might have other friends in the police. Get away, George. Hide somewhere.'

And the feel of those fingers, long and slim, but so strong, digging into my palms . . .

'Hiding didn't help Marvin,' I said. 'I'm okay for the moment. They won't know where to go once they work out I'm not at the motel. My car's still there, but that's better. They knew my car anyway. They won't know yours.' I looked around the interior. 'It's a lot more luxurious, for a start.'

'It's hired.'

'You must have some money, then . . .' And it came to me again. I still had no idea where she'd been, how she'd survived. 'What have you been doing, May?'

'I've got money, but I don't want to go into that, George, not now. There's too much. What are *you* going to do? That's what's important.'

'Detective Kelly is okay, I think. I can talk to him.'

Her hands twisted in mine, worried. 'All right. But get out of Brisbane first. Call Detective Kelly from somewhere safe.' And her fingers were gone. She swung back behind the wheel, started the car. 'I can take you somewhere. Where do you want to go?'

'May, I can't just leave.'

'Why not?'

'There's . . . for one thing, I want to see Jeremy. He left me a message to come and see him. He said it was important.'

'All right. I'll take you to Jeremy. But then you leave. George, I've met this man. I . . . I saw what he was like, even back then. Promise you'll get away before you call anyone?'

'Okay, but . . .'

'Which hospital is Jeremy in?'

'The Royal Brisbane.'

She faltered a moment, her hands on the wheel, looked at me. 'The Royal?'

'I know. But it's only a hospital, May.'

She hesitated a second longer. 'Of course,' she said, and turned the key.

But of course it wasn't just a hospital. It was the hospital where one night, ten years before, everything had ended.

That night. The last night. Election night, December 1989.

THIRTY-NINE

It was a foregone conclusion anyway, the election.

I spent the day wandering though New Farm and the Valley, walking past polling stations and rallies, and I watched the revolution building. The Inquiry had gutted the old government, the premier had already resigned, Marvin and two other senior ministers were under criminal investigation, the police commissioner was in jail. On the streets people jeered at the posters of government incumbents. They tore up government how-to-vote cards and laughed at government volunteers. At one booth a dummy dressed up as the old premier was set on fire. Two years of inquisition and trial, of newspapers bulging with endless details of deceit and corruption, and before that three long decades of shame and anger and repression and lethargy . . . it was all reaching culmination.

I didn't bother to vote.

I stopped at bar after bar, jammed in amongst excited drinkers who talked of nothing but the ballot. No one recognised me, no one knew I was one of the old regime, one of the despised. I supposed I didn't look much like the George Verney of old. I was drinking all day, every day. I could see it in the mirror, if I could bring myself to look. The permanently bloodshot eyes. The swollen veins on my face, a raw transparency of the skin. When I shaved my hands trembled so badly that I constantly nicked myself, so I'd stopped shaving. My hair hadn't been cut in a year. And I could feel it in the way I walked. I was never quite *steady* any more. My legs ached endlessly. Everything ached and even with alcohol the nights were sleepless, my thoughts a bleary haze. I was sliding, step by step, into the deathly, empty-eyed shuffle of the chronic alcoholic. And worst of all, I stank. I still showered, and I was only fleetingly aware of the smell myself, but it was there. Embedded in my pores. Stale wine. Stale hopes. Defeat.

So I stood alone amongst the crowds. Election day wore on, and hour by hour a black depression settled over me. I didn't care that the government was going to fall, it deserved to fall, but still, it was the end. The official end. Once the voting was over and the government was gone, the whole thing would be only a memory. The purgatory I'd been floating in for two years would be over. I'd have no more connection to anything, no one left to blame, no more excuses. I would have to move on with life . . . and yet I couldn't see how or where. I could never work in the media again, and what else did I know? Where else could I start? The future had been a deep hole for so long, I'd simply let myself fall without thought, but now the bottom was rushing up and I was afraid.

I drank and drank, but there were too many people, too much noise. I couldn't handle it all in public. I loaded myself up with bottles of red wine and carted them home. From my flat I drank and watched the afternoon fade and listened to the growing rumour of vengeance from the footpaths. One bottle of wine, then another and another . . . by that time it was dark and the TV election coverage had started. Even from the first few booths it was obvious which way the landslide would go. No amount of bias in the electoral boundaries would save them now. But I thought that, with luck, I could drink myself unconscious by the time the result was final, by the time the new premier of Queensland raised his fist in the air. And maybe I would have made it. Maybe I wouldn't have woken up at all.

But the phone rang, and it was May, calling from the Royal Brisbane Hospital. Charlie had somehow got his hands on a prison guard's rifle, and used it to shoot himself in the head.

Later I would wonder if the same mood that had enveloped me throughout the day had also spread its wings around Charlie, sitting there in prison. Why else attempt suicide on election day, the very day that would mark the end of everything we'd ever been or shared? Had he even known what day it was? Had he cared? Or had the months of jail just built and built in him, and then there was a chance, a door left open, a gun case unlocked? Either way, he failed. The doctors would decide later that the length of the rifle made the angle awkward. He'd tried to shoot himself in the right temple, but instead the bullet had only made a furrow along the inside of his skull and exited just above his right eye. Charlie never even lost consciousness.

May was distraught. 'We did this to him,' she cried over the phone, 'we did this to him.'

I got in my car and weaved through the Valley streets to the hospital. My mind was fetid with alcohol and I felt sickened, with myself, with May, but mostly with Charlie, for being so weak, so stupid. At least if he'd shot straight it would be finished. It would be appalling, but it would be finished. This was even worse. Die, Charlie, I thought, die and let May and me be. And out on the streets the revellers were cheering as the government lost seat after seat after seat.

At the hospital I found May outside Charlie's room, slumped against the wall. A policeman had set up a chair by the door. He watched us vaguely. I knelt down before May and looked into her face, into her tear-reddened eyes, and she only stared back. It was months since we'd seen each other.

'He wouldn't believe me,' she said, broken. 'No matter what I said. But I haven't seen you, have I? I stayed away.'

'Yes,' I said. 'You stayed away.'

'It's been so hard. I've lost you both.'

'How is he, May?'

A wild sorrow shook her. 'His eye, George. They say he might lose his eye. And that's not the worst. His brain, the swelling, they don't know how bad, whether he'll ever . . .'

And tears took her again.

I knelt there and did nothing. The policeman watched us.

'I'm going in,' I said to May.

'He's sleeping. They've sedated him. They're waiting, before they operate.'

'I have to see him, May.'

'I know, I know.' She wiped her eyes. 'I'll come with you.'

We rose and the policeman lifted his gaze to me. 'You family?' he said. 'Only family inside.'

'I'm family,' I said.

'Are you drunk?' he asked.

'He's family!' May yelled.

And so we went in. There were two beds in the room, but only one was occupied. I wouldn't have known it was Charlie. The body under the sheets looked so thin, and the head was swathed in bandages. Only his left eye and lower face were visible, the lips dry and swollen. The eye was closed. There were still smears of what looked like blood on his jaw, and on his neck. A drip was attached to his arm, and a heart monitor blinked silently.

Oh, Charlie, I thought, you fool, you bloody fool.

Beside me May stood with her hand to her mouth, staring.

'How could he?' she asked. 'How could he?'

'He hates us, May. That's why.'

'There is no us.'

'He doesn't think so.'

We stood there, side by side at the foot of his bed, but a foot apart. Not touching. As if we had never touched. She shook her head, closed her eyes to blot out the sight of him. 'It's *killing* me,' she said quietly. 'I can't take it any more. I'd rather he'd just ended it.'

'You don't. You love him, May . . .'

'No, I love you.'

But her voice was dead. She had never said it before. And it was too late now.

Charlie groaned.

It was a hollow, despairing sound. A man arising to an awareness he'd done everything to destroy. His left eye fluttered and opened. He stared at the ceiling a moment, the eye glazed, but then he seemed to focus. His throat worked. His head shifted slightly, and with whatever vision the chaos of blood and swelling had left for him, he saw us standing there. His wife and his best friend, at his feet.

'. . . you . . .' he whispered.

May moved towards him. His hand lifted minimally from the sheets, stopping her.

'. . . get . . . away . . .'

The words were slow, thickened, as if his tongue wasn't working. Or maybe it was the damage he'd done to his brain. Maybe he'd speak like this forever. Was he already lobotomised, a crucial part of him lost beyond retrieval? And did he know? Did he know what he'd done to himself, in failing to die?

'Charlie,' May pleaded. 'Charlie, I want to help . . .'

'. . . can't . . . help . . . me . . .'

And a tear glittered in his eye, bright with a terrible, frightened confusion. He knew. He knew everything. His chest rose and fell in a sob, and his voice cracked as a red trickle emerged from under the bandages.

'. . . damn . . . you . . . damn . . . you . . . both . . .'

May choked. She turned to me for a second, speechless, then fled the room. I stared at Charlie a moment longer, at his single eye fixed on mine, shining with hatred for me or pity for himself, I didn't know. Then he was weeping, low and awful, and I stumbled backwards out the door, past the policeman who'd risen to his feet, his hand to his gun, wary. May was already gone, she was nowhere in the hall. I took a few aimless steps, I called her name once, and then the blackness swallowed me. The policeman was talking but I pushed him aside, reeling off down the passageway. I had to get out. Out of the hospital, out of this life, out of Brisbane, away from May, from Charlie, from everything. Enough, it was enough. More than one drunken coward could possibly bear.

So I ran out into the night where the government was crumbling and the crowds howled their victory and my car waited to take me away into the darkness and the rain of the mountains.

And Charlie cried, alone in his room.

FORTY

The Royal Brisbane. It was just a hospital. May and I walked through its front doors, and it was just a hospital, just a building . . . but with May at my side, and Charlie finally dead, as we'd both once prayed he would die, it was as if he was vindicated at last. The two of us together as he'd always known we would be, as he'd cursed us for being, that night. It didn't matter that he was wrong, that we were strangers now. The guilt felt the same.

Reception gave us the directions to Jeremy's floor, and we waited for an elevator, entered it alone. I pressed the button and watched the numbers slowly climb.

May spoke. 'I went back, you know.' She wasn't looking at me, was talking as if I wasn't there. 'That night. After I'd calmed down. I went back and held his hand and talked to him. I explained it all. I told him I loved him. That I forgave him . . . even for what he'd done to himself. I told him I wanted him to live. That I'd wait for him.' A laugh escaped her and was gone. 'It didn't make any difference. And I kept watching the door. I was hoping you might come back too.'

'I'm sorry,' I said.

'I'm not blaming you, George. You did the right thing. If you'd come back it just would have gone on. How would that have helped?'

'It didn't help you and Charlie that I stayed away.'

'No . . . we were beyond saving. But there was no chance for you and me either. Not after that.'

I could only nod. After so much time, and in a few words spoken between floors in an elevator, there was no way to rescue the past.

The doors opened, and at the nurses' station we were pointed to Jeremy's room. Outside his door May touched my arm, hesitating.

'I don't know about this,' she said. 'Should I go in?'

'It's only Jeremy. Things were always okay between you and him, weren't they? I thought you'd want to see him.'

'I do, but . . . my life has been so strange since then, George.'

'In what way?'

She stared at me, complex emotions moving in her.

'There are things you mightn't like . . . about what I've done.'

'I'm not gonna judge, May. As if I could.'

'It was so horrible after you left. I only saw Charlie a few more times. He wouldn't talk to me at first and then he refused to see me. It wasn't just the injuries . . . he was so bitter, so stubborn. So I thought, well, that's that. Time to get on with life. Everyone else was gone. You were gone. It was just me, and all I was doing was drinking, drinking far too much . . .'

I waited. I didn't know what she was trying to say.

'So I tried looking for work. I had plenty of experience. And there were jobs going, not in government any more, I wasn't that stupid, other jobs . . . but whenever I mentioned my history, that's when they'd realise who I was. After that, no one would touch me. I had to pretend I had no past at all, that I'd never worked anywhere.'

I said, 'You think any real paper in the country would have touched me either? We weren't in prison, May. We were the lucky ones.'

'I know that. I'm just saying I couldn't get a job. All I had was the dole. I was living in a disgusting flat, I wasn't doing anything, I wasn't going anywhere, there was just the drinking, and I couldn't see any way out. And then . . .'

And I thought that maybe I knew what she was going to say. And it meant nothing to me even if it was true. Not after we'd spent so much time in those sorts of places, and with those sorts of women, all those years ago.

But she didn't finish. She looked at the door.

'I'm sorry. This isn't the time to be talking about this.'

'May, you can tell me.'

She shook her head. 'Let's just see Jeremy.'

We went in. It was another twin room, and once again only one of the beds was occupied. Jeremy lay stretched out beneath a single sheet, sleeping. Tufts of bandages stuck out from under his back. A clear tube ran oxygen to his nose, and a drip fed into his arm. It was only a few days since I'd seen him, but this was a Jeremy visibly closer to death. I knew very little about leukaemia, how it worked or how it killed, but his naked arms were knobs of bones at the elbows and shoulder, and the skin was mottled with bruises. A reddish moisture stained his lips.

There was a chair pulled up by the bed, and I imagined it was where Louise sat, when she was with him. There was no one there now. I pulled up another chair and May and I sat either side of him, watching his face. The way he was laid out he might have been dead already, but his chest rose and fell, and a wheeze piped in his throat.

We waited for a moment. May's eyes didn't move from his face. At least I'd already seen him once and had known what to expect. For May it would be different. Would she be thinking of their first days together? It was Jeremy, after all, who had brought her into our whole world, luring her with wine and his distant, jaded charm. I wondered then, did May still drink? There was no smell of it about her, her eyes and skin seemed clear. But then it had always been that way.

She smiled at Jeremy, almost fondly, but there was something else there as well, a wariness.

'Should we wake him?' she asked.

'Jeremy,' I said, my voice low. 'Jeremy?'

His eyelids flickered, opened briefly, but he wasn't seeing us.

'Jeremy? It's George. And May is here as well. Maybellene.'

That seemed to reach him. He drew a deeper breath, opened his eyes again, rolling them from me over to May. Air whistled faintly from his chest, the hint of a laugh. 'Come for the funeral, May?'

She took his hand. 'You're not dead yet, Jeremy.'

'Close enough.'

'How are you feeling?'

'That's a stupid question . . .'

His eyes went wide for a moment and he shifted slightly, groaning. Then he looked at May again, puzzled. 'You're not Louise? Where's Louise?'

I said, 'This is May, Jeremy. Louise isn't here right now. You remember May.'

'I remember May,' he repeated, but his eyes were drifting.

'Jeremy, are you awake? It's George. You said you wanted to talk to me.'

May was watching me, worried. 'I don't think he really knows . . .'

'May?' Jeremy interrupted. 'May and George? The two of you? That can't be right.' He studied May suspiciously. 'What are you doing here?'

'I've come with George. I'm sorry, I should have come and seen you before.'

He smiled at her. 'I've got another one now, but she doesn't compare to you. Have you found a home yet, May? I heard that you had. I couldn't bring myself to tell George. Strange, May, very strange, but then you never could make up your mind . . .'

A nurse came through the door, a fresh drip bag in her hand. We waited while she switched them over.

'Don't talk with him too long,' she said. 'He's on very high doses for the pain.'

Jeremy was staring up at her like she was an angel. 'Can you send me a priest, please. I haven't had the last rites yet.'

The nurse felt his pulse. 'I didn't know you were a Catholic.'

'I'm the last one.' His eyelids were drooping, his voice fading away.

'He might slip off again with the new drip,' the nurse warned us, and left.

'Jeremy,' I said, 'we can't stay long. Louise said you wanted to see me.'

'I did,' he said sleepily, 'but I suppose you know by now.' A thought came to him and he roused himself a little. 'Did you ever find Marvin?'

'Eventually. But I've got some bad news. He's dead.'

He looked at me, perfectly coherent. 'No, it's Charlie that's dead. Marvin's writing a book, he's not dead.'

'Marvin died last night,' I said, aware of May's eyes on me, doubting.

'Oh . . .'

'But he told me what happened. To Charlie. They met someone else in that detox ward. Someone called George Clarke. You know who that is, don't you?'

He frowned. 'George Clarke?'

'You know. Back during the power dispute. You had to talk to him, to get May out of jail, remember?'

He shrank away from me, confused. He looked from me to May and back to me again. 'I know who he is. Of course I know.'

'That's who it was. With Charlie, in the substation.'

'I don't . . . understand.'

'It's all right. I'm gonna leave Brisbane for a while. But the police will handle it.'

Jeremy was still agitated. 'May? May, what's he talking about?'

May's head sank. 'It's all true, Jeremy.'

'But why?'

'I don't know.'

'But you must . . .'

I was missing something. 'Why should she know?' I asked.

Jeremy turned back to me. 'Hasn't she told you?'

'Told me what?'

I looked at May, but her head stayed down, her hands clutching Jeremy's.

'Oh dear,' Jeremy breathed. 'George, you have to remember how it was. I didn't want him in the house. But after I made that deal for May . . . he was always around. He knew I didn't like him, but he enjoyed that. I thought that's why he kept coming. But then later, when I heard, I realised it probably wasn't me at all. That's why I wanted to see you. I should have told you the other night. I knew how badly you wanted to know about May. But I didn't think you'd want to hear that, of all things.'

I was baffled. 'What?'

Jeremy shook his head, his eyes closing again.

'Jeremy?'

It was as if he'd fallen asleep.

May raised her head. 'Leave him be, George.' Her expression was calm. 'You don't need to pester him. I was trying to tell you, but I didn't know how.'

'May?'

'It's about where I've been for the last ten years. That's what Jeremy is talking about. He knows, he . . . he must have heard somehow.'

My world trembled on its last brink. 'What's this got to do with Clarke?'

She took a breath. 'That's where I've been. With him.'

She removed her hands from Jeremy's, composed them on the bed before her.

'I married him, George. He's my husband.'

And in his sleep, Jeremy nodded and sighed.

FORTY-ONE

We emerged from the hospital and this time there were no crowds on the streets, no fireworks in the sky, no government sinking into ruin. Only the afternoon peak-hour traffic and a sweltering sun descending into smog. Even the new government had come and gone since those days, governments came and went every few years in Queensland now, as fleeting as the seasons.

'I'll take you back to my place,' was all May said.

In her car we drove west, squinting into the sun. My mind was empty. The day had been too long, stretched too many nerves. All I felt was tired. I'd found May and it seemed she'd had the answers all along, but now I didn't want to hear them. Not from her.

'Will he be there too?' I said.

'I don't live with him any more. I haven't for months.'

'Why not?'

'Wait till we get there, George. Not now.'

So we drove in silence, out into the western suburbs, away from the Valley and New Farm and the centre of it all, out to where the hills rose and the television transmission towers blinked their warnings. We drove through The Gap and up along winding streets overhung by trees, then down a gravel driveway that didn't seem to have a mailbox or a number. There was a house there, surrounded by bush. Behind it the land dropped away to treetops and stone, and further below were the roofs of more houses, spreading down the lower slopes to join the city again.

May parked the car. The sun had already passed behind

the hills, casting shadows. The house was made of grey cement and glass, so dark it blended into the trees. I took my bag from the back seat and we went inside, where it was all white furniture and polished wood. A long wall of glass offered the eastward view, and May opened windows and sliding doors to let in air that smelled of eucalypts. I sat at the table and waited. There was nothing in the house that spoke of her. It was as anonymous inside as it was out. Rented, maybe, under whatever name she was using now. And secret from anyone who might want to find her. Police. Or old lovers.

She was at the refrigerator. 'Do you want anything to drink?'

'I gave it up.'

'Really,' she said, empty. She let the fridge door swing shut.

My bag was at my side. I dug into it and pulled out Charlie's urn, set it on the table.

'Do you want this?'

She looked at it, then came over and sat at the table, across from me. She reached out one hand and rested a finger against the lid for a moment, took it away.

'You keep it, George. He was your friend first.'

'I don't know what to do with it.'

'Neither do I.'

We considered the urn.

May said, 'I didn't have anything to do with Charlie dying, if that's what you think.'

I closed my eyes. Is that what I'd been thinking?

I opened them again, found May observing me. I said, 'Marvin told me Charlie blamed himself for the way it all went. He wanted to see you and me, to apologise, but he thought we'd hate him too much to listen.'

May's control faltered only for an instant. 'I . . . I knew he'd see it that way, sooner or later.'

'It's a pity your husband got to him first.'

She didn't respond.

'So why?' I asked. 'Why did it happen?' And it seemed I'd been asking that question forever, never getting an answer.

She studied the urn. 'Believe me when I tell you this, George. I don't know. I didn't know he had anything to do with Charlie or Marvin until you told me in the car this afternoon.' She thought. 'No. Until I saw that detective, outside your motel. That's when I knew.'

'Why then?'

'His name is Jeffreys. He's been taking money from George—my George—for years. From before the Inquiry even. They met years ago, when the police were breaking up the picket lines, during the power dispute. Jeffreys is a thug. He was then, he is now. And he does what he's told.'

But all I heard was *her George*. That's what she said. *Her George*.

I said, 'And I'm supposed to believe you knew nothing about Charlie until then?'

'Believe what you like, but it's true. I told you, I left George months ago. What happened in the detox ward, the way he behaved in front of Marvin and Charlie, that sounded bad, it would upset him. And God knows he wasn't well when I saw him last, but to do what he's done . . . don't ask me to explain it.'

'You haven't seen him in the past two weeks?'

'He doesn't know where I am. I'm not hiding or anything. I just . . . left that life.'

'Which was?'

Her hands moved restlessly on the table. She noticed them and caught one hand in the other, stared at them both.

'I gave up drinking too,' she said finally.

'You did?'

'Years ago. I still don't know what to do with my hands.'

She intertwined her fingers and held them there, on the table.

'How did you end up with him, May?'

'I was trying to tell you. I couldn't get a job, I didn't know what to do, I was on the verge of giving up altogether. And then he came to see me. I . . . I already knew him fairly well. All those visits he made to Jeremy's, and then of course, even more when I was working for Marvin.'

'How come I never met him?'

'It wasn't supposed to be public, him and Marvin. I wasn't

supposed to talk about it. And I didn't. But it was hardly ever that secret, George. If you'd ever really taken any notice of things . . .'

I stared at her hands. It was laughable. I'd never noticed anything, never understood anything, not until it was too late.

'Did Charlie know about him?' I asked.

'Charlie knew. Charlie was the only person I told. It worried him. He didn't like the sound of George. He knew all that stuff between Marvin and George was a whole lot more serious than anything we had going in the clubs. Even Charlie saw that.'

'So he would've known who Clarke was, when they met in that ward.'

'Maybe. I don't know how much Charlie remembered.'

I watched her for a moment, her eyes downcast.

'So,' I said, 'after the Inquiry, Clarke came to see you.'

She nodded. 'He said he'd heard I was still in town, and that I needed a job.'

'And you said yes?'

She looked at me, fierce. 'What was I supposed to say? I didn't have anything else. I was alone.'

'You burnt down his offices, May. You hated everything he stood for.'

'I hated everything Jeremy stood for, and Marvin. Even you. It didn't stop me then. Christ, George, the way my life had gone, it made a crazy sort of sense to end up with him. It was a full circle.'

Her tone was still defiant, but there was a pulse of such unhappiness in it that, despite myself, I felt the coldness in me starting to thaw. I knew how May's life had gone, how people had worked on her, and what it had done to her, inside. And I hadn't been there in Brisbane. I'd been safe up in Highwood, working out my conscience on a small-town paper and dating Emily. How was I any better? What would have happened to me if I'd stayed, if the rain and the night and the mountains hadn't intervened? And I was tired, too tired to hate May, who I'd never hated in my life.

I said, 'But you didn't just work for him.'

'At first that's all it was.'

'But?'

'I know it's hard to believe after everything that's happened, but I liked him. Even when I first met him, at Jeremy's place, when I wanted to hate him . . . I didn't. He wasn't like I thought he'd be, when we lit that fire. It's true, he couldn't care less about the union or what he was doing to them but, really, he'd barely noticed them at all. They were just people getting in his way. And he seemed so focused. So calm. He wasn't like the rest of us.'

'Jeremy sounded like he hated him.'

'They hated each other. George wasn't charming or stylish like Jeremy. He hadn't grown up with money. He thought Jeremy was . . . I don't know, spoiled. He didn't really like Marvin either. He thought Marvin was a fool. A con man. George was more serious. He didn't seem interested in flaunting things the way we did. He thought all that stuff we did with the clubs was just a distraction. And dangerous too.'

'He was right.'

She nodded. 'The Inquiry didn't bother him at all. All he had to do was dump Marvin. That was no problem. And of course what happened to Charlie, or to you or Jeremy, that was irrelevant. For George it was like the Inquiry never happened. Business as usual. A little . . . slow . . . for a while, maybe. But he still had all those contracts. No one seemed to care about that.'

'So you joined up with him.'

'You don't know what that was like. After those horrible two years, to be with someone who wasn't traumatised by the Inquiry, who wasn't looking backwards all the time, who wasn't just giving up. He was confident about the future. He could still see opportunity everywhere. It was like fresh air.'

'And what were you for him?'

'What was I for anyone? Even for you? I don't know. But do you know what he demanded I do before I could start working for him?'

'What?'

'Stop drinking. He was the one that made me give it up. No one I'd ever met wanted me to do that before. Not even Charlie.'

And pain ebbed through me because, no, I would never have wanted May to stop either.

I said, 'Marvin told me he was a big drinker.'

'He was. He is. But back then, it didn't seem to affect him. I've never seen anyone drink the way he could and not get drunk, not change.' She laughed. 'I was actually impressed by that. That wasn't like Charlie either. Or you. But he didn't think I should drink. He thought drinking was nothing but bad for me.'

'So you were sober and working for him.'

'And grateful, I was grateful. I had a life again. You did the same thing. Tell me it doesn't feel good.'

And I couldn't answer.

'Anyway, eventually we started up, him and me. It wasn't like anything I'd been through before. It felt like we were both sober all the time, really *there* all the time, even though he always drank. There were none of those nights like we used to have. It was quiet. But in lots of ways it was better. It was real. It wasn't always . . . blurred . . . the way it used to be. And for once I wasn't always trying to choose. Between one or the other. Between you and Charlie. There was just him, and that was enough.'

I was still disbelieving. 'And you got married?'

'We got married. It was a long time ago, George. It's hard to remember. It's true, there was always something removed about him, but it was good when we were together. He seemed so certain. So secure. After everything . . . it was what I needed.'

'Marvin said he was violent, May. That he'd hurt people.'

'I don't believe that.' She caught herself. 'I mean, not until now. I never saw him do anything like that, or talk about anything like that. He was strong, though, he could make people back down. Maybe he even did that to me a little, I don't know. All I know is that he seemed better for me than anyone else ever had been.'

'Even Charlie?'

'Charlie thought I was someone else. That's why it went so bad. I wasn't good enough for Charlie. Charlie was . . . Charlie was . . .'

She took her hands off the table, stared at them in frustration. I remembered what it was like, when you wondered if your hands were bent on betraying you, always reaching for a drink that would never be there. It was hard, May, it would always be hard. And suddenly I was remembering May on my couch in that big empty apartment, one hand reaching out for a glass, while the fingers of the other lightly touched my face . . .

She forced her hands down again.

'This time around, with George, I thought we at least saw each other for what we were.'

'So what went wrong?'

'It went fine for a while. The business was going well, the sub-contracting and the other things he and Marvin set up years ago. It wasn't strictly legitimate the way he worked, but God, whatever is? It was me, really. I was the problem.'

'How?'

She shook her head, wondering at herself. 'It was the nights. I missed those nights of ours. Those endless sessions. They weren't real, but real . . . real gets dull. The days were okay, I was always working in the day. But something was still wrong with me. I still wasn't happy.'

'What did you do?'

'What I always used to. I got drunk.'

'You got *drunk?*'

'Don't laugh at me. It wasn't funny.'

It was the old May, defiant and yet so unsure, and it washed over me again, how long it had been, how it had all gone so terribly wrong.

'I'm sorry,' I said.

'We were out one night, at a party. We didn't do that very often. He was a very private person. And sometimes I thought he was worried about being seen with me in public. In case someone remembered me, made the old connections, despite the fact my name was different now. He helped me with that. Got friends of his in the registry office to mix up the records, so there was no link. So I was someone new. But I wasn't someone new.'

'You were at a party . . .'

'Yes. It was with some of his business contacts. Overseas

suppliers. His lawyers. It was so dull and I was thinking, is this all it's come to, my life? So I just started drinking. I didn't even think. And oh . . . it was glorious. It all came alive again. The party, the night, everything. I wanted to go out, to see what was left out there in Brisbane, despite it all. I can't explain it. It's something that's in me. I could never just be one or the other, that was always the problem. I wanted George to come with me. I knew he wouldn't like me drinking, but I thought, for one night at least, we could be out there, together. Let it all go for once.'

'And?'

'He refused. Completely. He was furious, demanded I go straight home with him. At first I thought he was just disappointed, but it wasn't only that. I could see something else in the way he was looking at me. It wasn't that he didn't want to come out with me, he *couldn't*. He couldn't do it. It wasn't in him, the idea of cutting loose. He didn't know how.'

'Did you keep drinking?'

'No. It was just that once. He was so mad for so long.'

'So what happened next?'

'So I didn't drink again. But I watched him, watched everything he did. And I started to understand. It was all about control. I finally realised how hard he fought for control, all the time, every second of his life. Even when he was drunk he didn't let it slip. I think that's the real reason he wasn't involved with the syndicate. Not just because it was small time, but because he didn't understand it. The bright lights, the fast life, the indulgence of it all—all the fun we had. He couldn't do it. He was too cold. Too ordered. In the end I think he got so furious with me because I scared him. That side of me . . . just scared him.'

And I thought of May, a burning trail through the evening.

I said, 'Maybe that's what he liked about you as well.'

'Maybe. But whatever he saw in me, he wanted it kept quiet. He wanted *me* kept quiet. He was like that about everything. All those things from the old days, the clubs and the casinos. They were too visible, too chaotic. He thought his way of doing things, the quiet way, the steady way, was better.'

'He was right. He's the one that survived the Inquiry.'

She tilted her head. 'I don't know. He *thought* he had. But you could see it sometimes, eating away at him. Had he really? Could anyone just walk away from something like that?'

'And now questions are finally being asked about him. That's what Marvin said.'

She nodded. 'He's cut too many corners. Been too clever with the money. Not even clever really. Only half clever.' She pondered something. 'You know what used to infuriate me about Queensland the most? It wasn't just the corruption. Everywhere has corruption. But usually it's a little more discreet, a little more professional, it takes some brains. In Queensland, any fat idiot could do it. Queensland corruption was run by a pack of loud-mouthed amateurs. Like Marvin, like all of them. That's what made it the worst. And I thought that at least my George wasn't like that. I thought he was different.'

'He wasn't?'

'Not in the end. He didn't survive the Inquiry because he was smart. He survived because the Inquiry was never after him in the first place.'

'And now?'

'Now he's under pressure. They're talking about an official investigation. Another inquiry. And this time he's the target. That's when the drinking started getting bad. He's older, for one thing, and no one, no matter who they are, can stand the sort of drinking he's done all his life. Not without something giving. He'd get drunk—and I mean drunk like anyone else—and I could see how that terrified him. And that only made him drink more.'

'He couldn't stop? Like you did?'

'Don't you see? The drinking was his control, it was the thing that kept him together. Even when it started to turn on him, he couldn't let it go.'

And I thought of a different kind of alcoholism, where drinking wasn't an escape from reality, but an anchor that kept you *in* reality.

May was staring inwards. 'He'd start raving. About everything going wrong. About everyone being against him. He hated what he thought was going to happen to him. He was frightened he'd end up just like Marvin. Or even Charlie. And in his mind, they were about the most pathetic people there were.'

'What about you?'

'Me? I didn't know what he wanted from me any more. Most of the time it seemed he hated me too. I reminded him of too much, maybe. He'd catch me watching him and scream about how he wasn't like the other men in my past, how he was better than them. And okay . . . maybe then, maybe when he was like that, for the first time, I was even scared of him.'

'But he never hit you?'

'No. But it was still there. I didn't know what to do. It was like the old days again, with Charlie or Marvin, during the Inquiry. Worse even, because I'd been so sure he was different, and it turned out he wasn't any different. He was the same as the rest of us. As weak as the rest of us. I couldn't take it, George. Not all over again. I couldn't stay.'

Weakness. I thought of Marvin and Lindsay and Jeremy, Charlie, and even myself. And May was right; I could only see weakness. It was a simple fact about corruption, about Queensland corruption in particular. Would any of us have chosen the life we had if we'd possessed anything like strength?

May had turned away from me, was gazing out through the eastward windows.

'And I started thinking,' she said. 'This was the man who'd ruined my life. It was all because of him in a way. That power strike, the union, Marvin and Jeremy and Charlie and you . . . everything that happened. It all started and finished with him. My entire life, George, all the people and things I've deserted, one after the other, he was at the end of them all. And I *married* him.' She shuddered. 'It was like I was waking up for the first time since that damn fire we started, and I couldn't stand anything I saw.'

'So you left.'

'So I left. I walked out on him. Just like I have everyone else.'

Down below the lights of Brisbane were beginning to gleam, and overhead the sky was a hazy golden green. And

I was swirling. With everything. With the day, with ten years, it was all too much. And it was May, still May, her eyes as sad as they'd ever been.

'How did he take it?'

'I don't know. I didn't say goodbye. I just went. I haven't seen him since.'

'You haven't even spoken to him?'

She shook her head. 'Not him, not anyone.'

'You don't call that hiding?'

'I call it trying to work out what I want for myself, just this once. Not for Jeremy or for Marvin or for him. Not for Charlie or you. Just me. You know what I did when I got here? I bought a carton of wine. Twelve bottles. I put them in the cupboard. And ever since then I've been sitting here thinking, it's up to me now, no one else. Will I or won't I? Will I or won't I?'

'Don't, May. It wouldn't help.'

'And what would it hurt?'

We sat in silence.

'It doesn't matter,' she said finally. 'Charlie's still dead. And that's what I don't understand.'

'Marvin thinks something happened in that ward, that Clarke said something when it was just Charlie in the room, something he didn't want anyone to know. Maybe it was about this new inquiry. Can you think of anything like that?'

She shook her head. 'And anyway, what could Charlie have done? He was so far down that nothing he said would've meant anything to anyone. I heard the way George used to talk about Charlie. He was no threat. Not one worth killing.'

'He said that about Charlie?'

'About Charlie, about Marvin, Jeremy, everyone. He knew that none of them could touch him any more.'

'May,' I said, 'did he ever mention me?'

She turned away from the window and she saw me, sitting forlorn across the table from her. Something changed in her face, something that made her younger, that stripped away the years between us. 'No. In all those years, he never mentioned your name.'

'Does he even know about us?'

She touched my hand, shook her head. 'Oh, George . . .'

And I didn't understand whether that was an answer, or a refusal to answer.

She took her hand away. 'What's so strange,' she said, 'is that he was even in that ward. The whole mess only happened because he met Charlie and Marvin in that ward. He's never needed medical help before, no matter how bad he got. Even now, I can't believe he's come to that.'

But I understood one thing at least.

'May, can't you guess?'

She stared at me.

I said, 'The way Marvin described him, it sounds like he's almost drunk himself to death. You said it yourself, nobody can take it forever. Maybe it's just this investigation, the way everything's falling down around him. But May, if you just walked out on him . . .'

Her hand was over her mouth.

And I tried to make it gentle. 'Maybe that was the last thing. Maybe that's all he could bear.'

'But . . . but that means I'm the reason he was there. That means I killed them.'

'No, May, I didn't mean . . .'

But she was gone. She was up and away from the table. She moved back and forth around the room, her hand still to her mouth as if she might vomit.

'Oh God, oh God, not again. I've killed Charlie again.'

Then she was in the kitchen, throwing open a cupboard. I glimpsed bottles of wine. Red wine. More than one, a shelf full, a dozen. She pulled out a bottle.

'May . . .'

'No, George, no. Enough. I can't take this.'

She tugged open drawers, sent knives and forks cascading to the floor. She went down on her knees after it all. And then she had a corkscrew. She reached up and grabbed the bottle of wine, tore at the foil around the cork, positioned the corkscrew. She hunched over it, her entire body centred around that one place, that one moment, the opening of a bottle. And she froze there, kneeling on the kitchen floor. I could see the bottle shaking in her grip, her shoulders shaking.

May, my May, caught again, paralysed by choice, by the need and the refusal of the need. The corkscrew wavered in her hand. She looked up at me, pleading.

I didn't know what she really meant, what she wanted me to do, if she even knew herself. And with Charlie's ashes, unburied, unscattered, there on the table—what would he have wanted now, what would he have forgiven? I didn't know, I didn't care, I'd fought it too long.

I pushed back my chair and went to her. I knelt down on the kitchen floor and took the wine from her hands, took the corkscrew. In three quick twists I opened the bottle as if it had all been only yesterday. I took two glasses from the cupboard and filled them both. And all the while May watched me, her body shuddering, her eyes shining with the old fears and the old temptations, all the battles we'd already fought and lost together, and would lose time and time again.

I gave one glass to her, kept the other for myself.

I lifted the glass to my mouth. I smelt the dust and love of alcohol, the bloom of wine that, despite all I knew, promised everything, warm and dark and obliterating, a world with only the two of us again, me and her.

And there, on the kitchen floor, we drank.

FORTY-TWO

There was a figure somewhere out in the medical world. A percentage. It was ever-changing and disputed. Seventy per cent, eighty per cent, ninety per cent. It related to the number of alcoholics who, once dry, would relapse. There were those who said *everyone* would relapse at least once, sooner or later. And others again who argued that it was a meaningless question, that the fate of alcoholics couldn't be discussed in terms of sober or drunk, success or failure, that it was a matter of survival, of quality of life, of what was bearable and what wasn't. But all agreed that the enemy was not just the physical addiction, it was the spiritual one, the addiction of the soul. It wasn't merely the alcohol to which the drinker surrendered, it was all that alcohol represented, the joys it once held, the pleasures it heightened, the weaknesses it glossed over, the pain it numbed. All of it false, and proven to be false, and utterly destructive, but yet still perversely alluring, perversely insistent. And that was why the specialists were so keen with advice once you were sober—stay away from your old life, from your old drinking friends, your old bars and restaurants, your old patterns of behaviour, from everything that will remind you of what you've lost and given away. After all, you have gained far more than you have lost, they say. You are born again. You are shining and new.

But the siren song remains.

And I woke to the deadly kiss of her, my first hangover in ten years.

It was late afternoon, the sky outside the bedroom window hazy with a day already passing. And that was what felt the most familiar, not the hangover itself, not the dry mouth and the headache and the dull throb in the bones of my legs—it was the sense of time lost, of a day having escaped without notice. I'd forgotten it could be that way. One of the first things I'd noticed about sobriety was the way time flowed so smoothly from morning to night to sleep to morning again, without interruption. There was no blurring, no telescoping, no rush of the hours, no blackouts. You never lost track of time when you were sober. And that was also one of the most frightening things. What did you do with all that time, all that clear consciousness? If anything sent drinkers hurrying back to the bottle in the first few weeks it was that, the fear of eternal awareness, because in the end, for drinkers, awareness was the real danger. But now, having drunk again, I stared at the afternoon sky, disoriented, wondering where I was, and where the night and the day had gone.

And then, like the old friends in the bars who would always welcome you back, the memories came, and I lay my head on the pillow, blotting out the sunlight, knowing what I'd done.

I opened my eyes again. May lay sleeping next to me, the sheets thrown back, a light sweat on her skin. It was hot in the bedroom and my hair felt damp with it, the sheet below me muddy with sweat of my own. I was thirsty, but all I could see on the bedside table were fluted glasses stained with the remnants of red wine, and empty bottles.

We'd drunk until dawn, May and I, all of it in darkness, no lights switched on, no lamps or candles, only the glow of the city coming up from below, warm air creeping through the house as an evening breeze stirred the trees outside. Shadows the both of us, without voice for the most part, and then reaching for each other, moving across the rooms, losing our clothes but keeping our glasses and the wine, to the bed. There was sex in there somewhere, but as always the sex wasn't what mattered. It was the clinging, the force in May's arms wrapped around me, squeezing with something so violent it was almost hatred. And the drinking, her hand reaching out in the darkness, or mine, to find the bottle and bring it to her lips, to mine, offering ourselves up to it together. We were both so much older now, our bodies softer, but the fierceness in us was the same, and the knowledge that we'd always held about each other, about the crucial flaw that lay at the centre of each other's being . . . that was as intoxicating and damning as it had ever been. Only exhaustion and the growing light of sunrise had put a stop to it.

But there in the hot glare of afternoon it seemed like a dream. The dark house of shadows had become a dreary, neglected place in which no one really lived, and all I saw next to me was a tired woman who looked her age, sleep crusted in her eyes, and the stale smell of alcohol on her breath. And me—I was a husk, too old for this now, and in betrayal of everything I'd done to rescue my life.

And there was only one way to get the dream back. Only ever one way. The empty wine bottles still had brothers, waiting out in the kitchen.

I sat up, gazed bleakly out the window.

The other truth about alcohol was that whatever it was you drank to escape from, it was still there waiting for you when you woke up. The only change was that you felt worse, and more time had flown, leaving you and your problems with less.

May stirred, opening her eyes to stare at nothing, until it all came back to her as it had come back to me.

'Oh shit,' she groaned.

'I have to call Detective Kelly,' I said.

'And tell him what?'

'Whatever I can. I should have done it last night.'

May didn't answer. It was another line from the drinker's creed. Everything that should have been done never was.

I stood up, feeling hollow and dizzy. When had I eaten last? I couldn't even remember.

May said, 'I'm not going to back you up on this, George. I don't want you mentioning me to the police. You tell your detective friend about me and he tells Jeffreys, and Jeffreys tells . . . you know who he tells.'

'Maybe you should call him yourself. Clarke, I mean. It might help.'

'There's nothing I could say. Not after Charlie . . .' She

closed her eyes, as if it was all coming back again, overwhelming. 'Why don't you just leave it, George? Whatever he might have been once, he's dangerous now. Look at what he's done. Him and his detective. You push things, and that'll only give them a reason to come looking for you.'

'He'll come looking for me anyway.'

I left the bedroom and moved around the house until I found the shower. Then I stood under the spout with the water turned as hot as I could bear, as I had a thousand times in an earlier life, hoping against hope that water could wash the sin away.

It didn't. And when I emerged, May was slumped at the table, wrapped in a bathrobe, with a fresh bottle of wine unopened before her.

'May, what are you doing?'

She looked at me. 'There's six bottles left . . .'

Evening was descending on the house. Echoes of the previous night ran through my veins. But sometimes even an alcoholic can see the dream for what it is. I flicked a switch on the wall. Fluorescent lights blinked, throwing shadows under May's eyes and casting a grey pallor to her skin. The hangover flared in me, cold and nauseating. Welcome it, I told myself, and remember it. It's reality.

But May was opening the bottle. And there were two clean glasses there.

No . . . for pity's sake, no . . .

But they were just words in my head. There was nothing behind them.

I found my wallet, then picked up the phone and dialled, praying he would still be in his office.

'Detective Kelly here.'

'It's George.'

'George! Where the fuck have you got to? I told you to stay at the motel.'

'I had to leave.'

'So where are you now?'

My eyes were on May. 'I don't think I'll say, just yet.'

'What's going on, George? You know we need to talk to you. We can make that into a warrant if you force us.'

'Have you looked into those things I asked you about yet?'

'A few of them, but—'

'Tell me what you found and maybe I'll say where I am.'

'Jesus, George.' But I could hear him rifling through papers. 'Okay. Like I said, we got a few things, but they really don't mean much.'

'What are they?'

'The phone first. You're right, a call was made about two a.m. from Marvin's place to your motel. But like I said, what does that prove? It could have been Marvin himself.'

'It wasn't Marvin. And that proves someone else was there.'

'So *you* say.'

'What about the vodka bottle?'

'There were no prints on the bottle, not even Marvin's.'

'And that doesn't make you wonder?'

'Of course it does. But there could be explanations. Maybe Marvin knew the vodka would connect him with the sub-station vodka, so he wiped his prints off before he killed himself.'

'He'd supposedly just written a note confessing—why would he bother?'

'All right. But your theory doesn't help us either, George. It's been pretty much confirmed by forensics. Marvin killed himself. It was suicide.'

'Maybe it was—maybe he pulled the trigger himself, anyway. But someone else was there.'

'This George Clarke of yours.'

'Have you looked into him?'

'A little. You're right. There are a few noises just now about him and stuff to do with the old days. And it's true, some people seem to remember he had links to Marvin. But lots of people had links with Marvin.'

'So go and talk to him.'

'Why? Marvin killed himself. No one else did. And there's still nothing at all to connect Clarke to Charlie's death.'

'I've got another name for you. Detective Jeffreys.'

'Jeffreys—what about him?'

'I saw him outside Marvin's place two days ago. The day before Marvin died. I think he followed me there.'

'That can't be right.'

'It's right. So when he came looking for me yesterday, you can see why I didn't answer the door.'

'Was it you with that bogus call about Lindsay's place?'

'That was me.'

'I don't get it, George. What are you saying? Jeffreys knew where Marvin was all along and didn't tell anybody?'

'I'm saying a lot more than that. How much do you know about him anyway?'

'I'm not going to discuss another officer with you.'

'He works for Clarke.'

'Christ,' and he was angry now. 'Where are you getting this stuff from?'

'Why don't you ask Jeffreys yourself? Or ask some of your superiors about him. What's his record like?'

'His record is none of your business.'

But there was doubt there. Jeffreys was not one of his friends.

I said, 'He's the one who told you to close down the investigation into Charlie's death, isn't he?'

Kelly didn't answer.

'Just talk to him,' I said.

'I can't. He took some extended leave. Starting today.'

'Ah . . .'

'George . . .'

'C'mon, Detective, how much do you need?'

'A lot more.'

'Then I don't think I'll be telling you where I am.'

'You're making a mess of this, George. You can't hide out forever, and no one's gonna believe a word you say if you keep being so difficult.'

'Maybe I'll call you later. Go and find Jeffreys. See what he has to say.'

'Hang on, George, there's one thing you might like to know. You pissed Lindsay off yesterday. Jeffreys gave him a hell of a grilling and Lindsay hasn't had to put up with that sort of thing for years. He's pissed off at everyone. And he told us something about your old girlfriend.'

'What old girlfriend?' But I felt the pit again, yawning beneath me. Beneath both of us, this time.

'You aren't that dumb, George. Maybellene is in town after all. She called up Lindsay a few days ago, said she was looking for you. Lindsay says he told her exactly where you were. So have you seen May lately, George?'

'I haven't seen her in ten years.' At the table May's head shot up, eyes wide. 'Why would I want to? It was bad enough once.'

'You don't think it's odd she suddenly appears again, right now?'

'I wouldn't know.'

'Does she have anything to do with this, George?'

May was shaking her head at me, urgently.

I said, 'How much do you know about Clarke's private life?'

'What? Nothing. Why would I?'

'Find out who his wife is.'

I hung up.

May stared at me. The bottle of wine was open now, and the glasses filled.

I said, 'I had to say something. Once they work out you're his wife, then they'll have some sort of link to Charlie. At least they might start wondering then.'

'She shook her head again. And Jeffreys will tell George. He'll know I'm with you. Christ, think about what that will do to his state of mind.' She took up one of the glasses and drank. I watched as it passed down her throat, saw what it did as it hit, to her body, her eyes.

I said, 'Did you tell Lindsay where you're living?'

'No.'

I stared out across Brisbane. I thought about the city below and the bush around us and the gravel track that led back to the road. And I thought about the wine on the table.

'I think we should go.'

May sounded far off. 'No one knows I'm here. Not in this house. I didn't rent it under my name, the house or the car. And it's a big city.'

'It's tiny. We'd have to get food, leave the house sometime. We'd be seen sooner or later. They'll find out.'

'Go where, then? And why? For all we know he'll stop now. Marvin's confession wraps everything up for him, especially if one of the investigating detectives is onside.' Her voice faded away, hopeless. 'Maybe he'll leave us alone.'

I turned back to her. 'I don't think he's that rational any more. There was no reason behind what he's done so far, not that I can see. I think we should go. We can't just wait here to see if he finds us or not.'

Her hand was drawing sad circles around the rim of the glass.

'This isn't how I thought it would be. If we ever met again.' She drank. My mouth felt dry, but it wasn't the hangover now. 'Not the two of us, stuck in a house we can't leave. I thought we'd be able to do whatever we wanted. At last.'

'Tomorrow, May, we can leave tomorrow.'

'Where? Where is safer than here?'

I was struggling to think, trying to blot the thought of drinking from my head. This was important. It had to be somewhere we could disappear for a while—for how long I didn't know. I didn't even know how this could be ended, any more than Marvin had known. Time and silence, that seemed to be the only way. Until the police worked something out, at least. There were enough connections, they would have to see it eventually, at least track down Clarke for questioning.

In the meantime we needed to vanish. Another big city, then? Sydney or Melbourne, perhaps? Places where we knew no one and no one knew us.

But would *he* know people in places like that?

Somewhere else, then . . . if only the wine would get out of my mind, stop tugging at me, distracting me.

'Highwood,' I said.

May was disbelieving. 'Highwood? Your house in Highwood?'

'Not my house, of course not. Not even Highwood itself. But there's a place near there. A farm, someone I know owns it, right off up in the hills. It's miles from anywhere.'

'How would that be any better than here? It's your home town George. People would know you were there. Anyone could find out.'

'No, you don't know this place, or the man who owns it.'

She sighed. 'All right. I don't think it matters either way. But I'll come with you, for a while at least.'

She got up from the table, took her wine to the kitchen. 'There's food here, I'll make some dinner.'

And that was it. I'd made the decision. Now there was nothing to do but stay put until morning and . . . and the wine waited on the table.

There didn't even seem to be any battle inside me this time, no momentous decision. May was moving about in the kitchen. She flicked off the overhead light and turned on some lamps. The house felt warm and safe again, almost as if I had already drunk the glass, as if my mind had leapt ahead in anticipation. And it was just one night more, one night more, and after all, May and I might have so little time together, and I'd already fallen now, why fight, why suffer . . .

I lifted the glass, and all the lies and justifications faded away, leaving just one last clinging delusion.

'This friend of yours,' said May. 'He won't mind us dropping in?'

It was only for her.

'He's not a friend,' I answered, desolate. 'But I think he'll let us stay.'

FORTY-THREE

Not everyone had welcomed me to Highwood.

It was bad enough that I had blown in, raving drunk, from Brisbane. And while my notoriety in the media had been brief, there were still plenty of people in town who knew I had *something* to do with the Inquiry, and so viewed me askance. At least at first. Over time some of their fears were calmed by my quiet lifestyle and the fact that a man like Gerry saw fit to hire me, and that a woman like Emily saw fit to sleep with me. No doubt, too, my sobriety would have been duly noted. Still, there remained a few incorrigibly sceptical folk in the town who never accepted me—our own secretary, Mrs Hammond, in particular—and occasionally I heard of their dark mutterings, and their certainty that, sooner or later, I would turn out to be trouble.

One other man shared that certainty, but his reasoning was entirely different. Stanley Smith. He wasn't even a local. He was from Brisbane, just like me, and just like me he'd fled to Highwood, seeking refuge. But that was as far as the similarities went. Stanley had arrived in town years before me, and he wasn't running from the fall of a government, or from any such consequence of the Inquiry. He was running from the government itself, and his only opinion about the Inquiry was that it should have happened far sooner, and that the government and all its ilk couldn't have fallen quick enough. I was one of that ilk, and he detested me on sight.

In the late '70s and early '80s Stanley had been a university lecturer in philosophy and ethics, and his life, understandably, was one long cry of outrage at the way things worked in

Queensland. He organised street marches when the government made street marches illegal. He attended communist party meetings when the government had made it known that the Special Branch monitored and listed every single person at such meetings. He demanded freedom of information when the government hadn't even heard of the concept. He chained himself to bulldozers when the government sanctioned the bulldozing of mangrove swamps to build tourist resorts. He reported on the Aboriginal gulags that the government denied existed. He organised sit-ins of gay men and women in public bars after the government had forbidden publicans from serving them. And year by year he refused to vote, claiming that until the electoral boundaries were properly redrawn, there was no point in the process anyway.

He was fined for not voting and, refusing to pay the fine, went to jail for it. He was arrested for marching and chaining himself to bulldozers and, refusing to pay the fines, went to jail for that too. For being a suspected communist he underwent years of phone tapping. For being a suspected homosexual he underwent the indignity of police peeking through his bedroom windows at night. He was forbidden entry onto Aboriginal reserves and into most government buildings, by restraining order. Special Branch agents attended his every lecture at university. Traffic police routinely pulled him over for alleged speeding offences, or seatbelt offences, or roadworthy offences, or to breathalyse him . . . almost as if they tailed him wherever he drove. And when none of those things shut him up, half a dozen heavily armed riot police stormed his house early one morning, trashed the place, and arrested him for the possession of ten pounds of marijuana which had magically appeared under his bed. Stanley spent two years in prison for dealing in a forbidden substance, lost his tenure at university, and finally got the message. *That* was the way things worked in Queensland.

So he gave up and retreated to Highwood. He bought himself a few hundred acres of mountain scrub about ten miles out of town, at the end of a disused logging track, then went on the dole and set about building a house, a haven from a world that had become unspeakable. After a few friendly raids by the drug squad, who combed his land up and down for plantations and who always chose to arrive at three in the morning, he bought himself a pack of dogs and began collecting guns. They left him alone in the end, partly because they were convinced that having spent so much time and money on his property, it was unlikely he'd ever darken the doors of Brisbane again, and partly because the Inquiry came along, and suddenly the authorities had their own problems to worry about. It was too late for Stanley, however. Terminally embittered, he applauded the fall of his political nemesis, but he had no great hopes for the incoming government either. He stayed in his hills, and his only obvious acknowledgement of the new age was that, for the first time in his life, he really did start to smoke marijuana, and set up a small plantation to boot. Justice at last, of a sort.

Most of this I learned from Gerry during slow days at the newspaper. Gerry was probably Stanley's only close friend in Highwood—an independent editor's natural affection for a defeated radical, perhaps. Indeed, occasionally Stanley would recover enough of the old flame to fire a letter off to the *Highwood Herald*, railing against some local injustice in a dense welter of academic references and political dictums. Gerry would glance through them and think of his readers, then tear the letters up and drive out to Stanley's farm with a carton of beer, to offer solace for the old days.

Stanley, in his turn, was dumbfounded that Gerry could then befriend someone like me—an ally of the very forces that had turned Queensland so rotten for so long. He refused to be in the same room with me, but Gerry didn't seem to mind. Defeated radical, defeated establishment, Gerry apparently couldn't see much of a difference.

Which was why, possibly, that when it came to Stanley's biggest protest of his Highwood days, Gerry sent me to cover the story. This time Stanley's cause was the last thing his friends from the old era would have imagined. It was gun control. He was fighting *against* gun control. The federal government, faced with a massacre of terrible scale by a lone man with a semi-automatic rifle in Tasmania, had decided enough was enough and was setting out to reform the gun laws. And

Stanley, his house racked with lethal weapons of all types, and no longer capable of trusting any sort of government, no matter what its intentions, saw one last battle that couldn't be lost. He sent in a cheque to take out a full-page ad in the *Herald*, declaring revolution and rallying all gun-bearing townsfolk to the barricades.

Gerry read it over with a sigh. 'Go out there and see him, George. Calm the poor old bastard down. I can't print this.'

'Me?!' I said, horrified. 'He'd shoot me on sight.'

'Oh, I don't think so. It would hardly help his argument, would it?'

'Gerry, he hates me. From his point of view I'm part of the whole problem.'

'That's what I mean. Talk about old times with him. Get his mind off it, make him see this gun thing isn't so bad, that it was far worse in the old days, the police state and all that. Hell, you two have lots to talk about. I've always thought so. Tell him you'll do a story on him if he wants. He can make his point, but I'm not gonna print this. It'd start a bloody riot.'

And so I drove out there.

Stanley's property was to the west of town. The road was gravel all the way, climbing up towards the high edge of the escarpment. Near town farms lined the road, dairy cattle grazed in cleared fields, but the further I went the more tangled the hills became, and the bush closed in. Most of it had been logged at least once before, and here and there were stark quarries of naked rock. There were fewer houses, fewer signs of farming. I crossed creeks that in heavy rain would block the way, climbed up the sides of gullies where moisture gleamed on stony walls. And finally the road dwindled to two ruts of dirt that picked their way around the hillsides, bisected by clumps of rock that knocked against the bottom of my car. It was a track that only one vehicle ever used, and that vehicle was Stanley's old Toyota four wheel drive, because his property was the end of the line. Only ten miles, but it took me something close to an hour to cover the distance.

I came to a gate strung between two tree stumps. The gate was laden with signs, jagged black letters painted on sheets of old fibro. No Trespassing. Beware of Dogs. Shut This Gate Behind You. And one that was presumably fresher than the others. Owner Armed and Will Protect Property.

Not exactly welcoming.

I got out and opened the gate, then drove through and was careful to stop again, close the gate behind me. From there it was one last steep, rattling climb before the track levelled out onto a small shelf on the hillside. To the right the land dropped away into a deep gully, its floor an impenetrable mass of trees and vines. Ahead the hills climbed into a high ridge, densely forested, that rose to the southern rim of the escarpment. And to the left was a parcel of level land, partially cleared, upon which Stanley had built his homestead. It was a world enclosed by sky and mountains and trees, into which the sun would shine for only a few hours a day, and there was no other sign of habitation in the valley. Only Stanley and his dogs.

The house itself was built of grey cement bricks roofed with corrugated iron, and for all the years that Stanley had been there, it did not quite look finished. Piles of bricks and a cement mixer waited at one end, and for a verandah a few sheets of tarpaulin had been stretched from the eaves to some nearby trees. Still, it was sizeable and looked neatly built, and under the tarpaulins were arranged comfortable armchairs, a large wooden table and a brick barbecue. Up behind the house was a water tank, several small sheds, and finally a low structure that I took to be the kennels. Even before I turned the car off, I could hear the dogs barking. I waited in the car until Stanley emerged from the house. It seemed safer to assume that if any of the dogs were roaming, they would at least not attack without his command. Nor, I was relieved to notice, was he carrying a gun.

But he wasn't pleased to see me.

'What the hell are *you* doing here?' he said.

He looked as angry at the world as I'd been told he felt. Fifty years old, perhaps, but short and wiry, dressed only in ragged pants, the hair on his chest tufting white. His head was nearly bald and his square black-rimmed glasses were spattered with paint. His face seemed to be all bone—a passionate face, hard and intelligent, and perhaps a little crazed. No wonder he'd scared the life out of the authorities in the old days. They knew, as politicians had always known through the ages, that a man who looked like that, so lean and hungry, could never be trusted to keep his mouth shut or play the game right.

I leaned out the car window. 'Gerry sent me,' I said. 'To get your side of the story.'

'He's got my side of the story.'

'He's not sure it's legal to print something that incites citizens to actual violence against the state.'

'That's the one right we *do* have! A government living in fear of its people is the only government that might actually listen to them. History proves it time and time again.'

Beyond the house, the dogs were barking ceaselessly.

'I don't disagree, but surely there are other ways to say it. If we could run it as a story, as an observation, rather than as a declaration of war . . . I mean, there are some people around who get a kick out of shooting things just for the sake of it, politics or no politics, and if you get them all fired up, well, people could get hurt.'

'Can't help taking the official side, can you?'

I got very serious. 'Trust me, Stanley, I have no more love or faith in governments than you do. And I should know, I've seen them from the inside.'

He stared at me a moment, then turned and faced the kennels. 'Be silent!' And all the dogs stopped in mid-bark. He turned back to me, smiling coldly. 'You can get out of your car now if you want. I only let them loose at night, when I'm asleep.'

And so I interviewed him. We went inside and he showed me around his house. It was surprisingly well appointed. The floor was only polished concrete and the walls of brick, but there were rugs everywhere, wall hangings and paintings and four or five large bookshelves, all crammed. The furniture was sturdy and warm, there was a large open fireplace and a wood stove and lots of candles and kerosene lamps. He had a generator out in a shed which he ran for several hours a day to keep the freezer and the hot water going, but there was no electric lighting, no television, and no phone. He would have preferred a solar panel to the generator, but his little valley didn't get enough sunlight to make it feasible. Otherwise there were a couple of bedrooms, an office that was overflowing with magazines and journals and one manual typewriter, and finally, taking up one wall of the living room, his gun collection.

I knew nothing about guns, had never even touched one in my life, but I took photos as he posed before them and pointed out various makes and models of rifle. There were twenty at least, some of them apparently quite rare and expensive.

'They bring these new laws in,' he said, pointing, 'and I'll have to surrender this one, and this one, and all of these. All they'll leave me with is a twenty-two or something. If I'm lucky. Even then I'd have to join a gun club, and build some sort of safe to store it in. What would be the bloody point?'

'Do you actually use all these guns?'

'I shoot a bit. You get feral cats up here, wild dogs that come around and fight with my pack—so, yeah, you need a gun for the vermin. And I got some targets set up about the place. It's a skill, you don't just stand there and blaze away.'

'And that sign on your gate?'

He considered the guns. 'When I first got here I had the drug squad busting down the door at all hours and they could have done any damn thing they liked. They already had, back in Brisbane. For all I knew, one of those nights they might have just popped me and been done with it. Who would have stopped them? So I got the dogs, and I started getting guns. I'd had enough.'

'And now?'

'You think those times won't come round again? Queensland is permanently fucked, believe me. We got more Nazis in this state than Hitler did.'

'A few lunatics . . .'

'For now.'

'But it's precisely those people who are most dead set against gun control, just like you.'

'Exactly. You want them to be the only ones with guns? Because law or no law, they're gonna keep theirs. So I'm gonna keep mine.'

I jotted notes in my pad. I didn't understand him at all.

'What will you do if the laws get passed? Will you give the guns up?'

'Fat chance. I'll bury them somewhere off in the bush. And good luck if they wanna search up in those hills.'

'And what would you say to all the victims of shooting deaths in the country? What would you say to their families?'

'Welcome to the fucking real world. I didn't hear any of them offering to help when I was being crucified.'

We would never be friends.

But Gerry printed the article and not long afterwards the new gun laws were passed anyway, and Stanley refused to surrender a single cartridge. Graham took a couple of police out to his place, but the guns had disappeared from the wall, and Graham knew there was no point combing the scrub for them. Stanley blithely stated that he'd destroyed them all and was happily abiding by the law. Of course, his distant neighbours still heard him firing rounds at various times of the day or night, hundreds at a time it seemed, till it sounded like combat, so it was safely assumed that somewhere up in the hills, Stanley was still fighting his war.

Where better, then, for May and I to retreat?

On the run, as we were, from one of the very enemies who had sent Stanley into exile in the first place.

FORTY-FOUR

The plan had been to reach Highwood by early afternoon.

That was the plan, but I'd forgotten about life with alcohol. It was already beyond noon when I woke suddenly, aching and ill, and from there we never really caught up with the day.

I squinted at the daylight, confused. Then I lurched out of bed and got to the phone. There was no way to call Stanley direct, so instead I called Gerry at the newspaper office.

'George,' he said, 'I heard about Marvin. It's been in the city papers. Who'd have thought he could do something like that to Charlie? I mean, I know he was rotten and all, but . . .'

I was rubbing my eyes. It was hard to think straight. Empty wine bottles were everywhere. 'He didn't do anything, Gerry, but it's a long story. The thing is I need to get out of sight for a while. I was thinking of Stanley's place.'

'Why? What have you got to do with any of it?'

'I *know* Marvin didn't do anything, and no one is supposed to know that, that's the problem. And right now I don't want to be seeing the police either.'

'As bad as that?'

'As bad as that.'

'So what do you want me to do?'

'Go out and see if Stanley is home. Tell him I need to stay there for a while. He won't like the idea, but his place is perfect.'

Gerry sounded doubtful. 'Why would Stanley want to get involved with your problems?'

'Just make sure he's home and that he knows we're coming.

I can explain the rest when I see him. He'll help. Not because he likes me, but because he hates other people even more.'

'We? Who's we?'

'It's me and a friend. And, Gerry, don't tell a soul about this. I don't want anyone in Highwood to know we're there.'

There was a pause. 'George, I've had a few calls from Emily. She's been trying to reach you for the last couple of days. She's worried, especially since this Marvin thing.'

But when I thought of Emily, something in me quailed. I had no idea how I could explain things to her, not without going through all the ancient history I'd never wanted her to know. And then there was May. How could I ever explain May?

'No. Not even Emily. I'm sorry, Gerry, I'll get to her eventually, but not yet.'

'Okay, if that's the way you want it.'

We got off the phone. May was standing in the bedroom doorway, her hair tangled and some of the old curls emerging defiantly . . . a memory of the younger May that jarred with her face, so much older, and tired.

'Get packed,' I said.

But then we had to wait for almost three hours, until Gerry called back. We sat at the kitchen table, not speaking, watching the clock on the wall tick around. There was no more alcohol in the house, nothing to dull the hangover or to alleviate the deepening depression that I'd learned years before was actually a chemical thing, the symptoms of withdrawal. I needed another drink. I listened constantly for the sound of a car in the drive, for footsteps in the gravel outside, but there was nothing. Maybe they'd never find us here, no matter how hard they looked, but I could never be sure. May felt it too. She'd withdrawn into herself a little. We both had. She was right. In the old days we'd always been in hiding of a sort, from Charlie, but this was different. There was no excitement in this, no spice of betrayal. This was a trapped, suffocating sensation, with no conclusion in sight.

Finally the phone rang and it was Gerry.

He said, 'Stanley will meet you here at the office.'

'The office? I wanted to go straight out to his property.'

'He's not convinced, George. And besides, he's gotta come into town today for supplies.'

'Someone will see us if we just roll up the main street.'

'You don't have to. Just park round the back. No one will notice. By the time you arrive I'll be the only one here. And it's not as if the whole town is on the lookout for you, George. Why would they be?'

I considered it. We'd have to pass through Highwood either way, and a quick detour to the lane behind the newspaper office would hardly make it worse. We wouldn't be in my car, we'd be in May's, with its tinted windows. And it was getting too late to argue. I didn't want to spend another night in Brisbane.

'Okay.'

We were in the car and on our way, with May behind the wheel. We stole through the western suburbs, and on the city outskirts we stopped at a suburban mall and stocked up on food. It was already a big enough favour that I was expecting of Stanley. I could hardly demand he feed us as well. In the supermarket I found myself watching the aisles, studying the other shoppers warily. It was paranoia, another reason to get away. We visited a bottle shop as well, bought cartons of beer, bottles of wine. We didn't speak about why. But if May and I were going to bury ourselves in the safety of Stanley's place, then there would inevitably come a long dark night sometime, with no one there but each other and nothing to do but wait . . . and after what we'd already done, what was there to discuss, what defences were left? All the rules were in abeyance.

We stacked the food in the car and got back on the freeway, passed Ipswich, out onto the Cunningham Highway. Away south and west the mountains rose in sharp blue lines. There were no clouds today, no haze. It wasn't as hot either, and anyway, the heat was different out here. It wasn't caught sweltering between street frontage and footpaths and a river that barely flowed. Instead it baked off the ground and rose to an open sky. And as Brisbane fell behind I felt the tension in me uncoil minimally and the hangover fade, with the speed of the car, the breadth of the countryside, the presence of May beside me. We came to the turn-off and the road sign, just as

I had that night ten years earlier. Highwood, it said. From a newly formed habit I looked back at the highway as we turned. No one followed, and the bitumen rolled away behind us, empty and clean.

'You know,' said May, 'maybe this is right. This feels better. We're out in the open, we can breathe.' She smiled at me. 'All my life I've been stuck in the city. I can't even remember when I last saw the stars properly.'

I agreed. The sprawl of Brisbane, all its problems and memories, could only be a quagmire for the two of us. This was better. Much better. I pointed at a notch in the line of the mountains.

'That's where we're heading,' I said.

But the light was already fading by the time we hit the foothills. May steered the car up the winding road as I tilted my head out the window. Dusk was falling beneath the trees, and it was much cooler here after the warm day below. I smelled earth and rotting leaves. Birds called in long mournful notes. And when we broached the last rise the forest closed in darkly, as it always did, and in moments I saw the rutted track that led off to the substation. I caught a glimpse of grey steel, the top of an electricity tower, the wires marching away towards the mountains' rim, and abruptly I was remembering everything. The cold concrete floor and the pale frigidity of Charlie's skin. I knew who was responsible for it all now. Somewhere down in Brisbane they were still searching, and sooner or later they would find out we were gone, and then . . .

We cleared the trees and Highwood approached. The western ridges flung deep shadows over the valley. A tractor hurried homewards across a paddock, and in another field cattle huddled outside a milking shed. I wound up my window against the air, and to hide my face behind the tinted glass. This was no casual homecoming. Then we were on the outskirts of town. There were cars moving on the streets, people in their yards, lights switching on in houses . . . but no one lifted a head to so much as watch us go by. We turned into a small lane that ran behind the main street. Halfway along was a large fenced yard that formed the back of the *Highwood Herald* building. There was a shed beyond the fence, for parking cars. Gerry's was already there, alongside a muddy Toyota four wheel drive. We pulled in and parked beside the others, and May switched off the engine.

I studied the yard. It was an empty space of sand and weeds. A chill breeze tugged at a loose flyscreen. And though it was not yet fully dark, a naked light bulb burned above the back door to the office. We'd arrived, this was my home, but there was no sense of welcome. Highwood felt like a town I'd never seen before.

'Let's get inside,' I said, and we slipped across to the door.

It was open. Gerry and Stanley were waiting for us in the main office. And the first one who spoke, to my amazement, was Stanley. His feet were on Gerry's desk, he had a can of beer in his hand, and he lifted a finger in greeting.

'Hello, May,' he said.

May considered him for a moment. 'Hello, Stanley,' she replied.

I stared at them both. Stanley propped his hands behind his head and smiled at me.

'You *know* him?' I said finally, to May.

'He was one of my lecturers at uni. Why didn't you tell me it was Stanley?'

'Jesus Christ.'

'Relax, George,' Gerry said. 'We've been sitting here wondering who your friend could be. It wasn't that hard.'

'You haven't told anybody?'

'Not a soul.'

I sagged. In the corner of the office was a small refrigerator. It served only the one purpose. I went over, took out a can of beer and opened it.

Gerry raised an eyebrow.

'Don't ask,' I said.

'All right. But what's the story, George?' He indicated the computer screen behind him. 'I'm getting the next issue ready. Are you telling me what I'm printing is wrong?'

I looked at the headline. 'Disgraced Minister Confesses to Highwood Slaying.'

I sat down, hardly knowing where to start.

It was only seven days since I'd left town. A simple week. Too much had happened. My head still wasn't clear. I swigged on the beer, tasted the cold bitter flow, was hardly even aware of it. A simple week ago, I had finished with drinking forever . . .

I did my best to explain. About Marvin and Charlie and the detox wards, about Lindsay and his house on the beach at Redcliffe, about the fisherman and his turning out to be a senior police detective, about bottles of vodka and a man with whom Marvin had once been in partnership, a man who had installed a substation for Highwood years before, a man losing his grip on the world. And at my side May waited and nodded, and Gerry and Stanley listened without saying a word.

'Clarke,' Gerry pondered, when it was all finished. 'I remember the name. There were stories . . . especially during the Inquiry . . . but nothing ever happened to him, did it?'

Stanley was opening a fresh beer. 'I remember the bastard. The prosecutors didn't even look that hard for evidence. They never did, with people like him. Still, it was fucking obvious he and Marvin were in each other's pockets. Believe me, if I hadn't been in jail, I would've been down on the picket lines during that power strike.'

'I was,' said May. 'It didn't do any good.'

Stanley studied her. 'What happened to you, May? How'd you get mixed up with people like this? You were smarter than that.'

'Who was smart, Stanley? You ended up in prison on drug charges. I ended up working for one of the most powerful ministers in the government.'

'He was corrupt.'

'Everyone was. The whole state was a joke. What was I supposed to do? Join you in the street marches and get my head kicked in?'

'Might have turned out better. Look at you now, looking for somewhere to take cover.'

'What d'you think *you're* doing up here? Wherever we started out, Stanley, we've both ended up in the same place.'

He sipped on his beer, thoughtful. 'We hardly got here by the same paths, May.'

'Can we stay out at your place?' I said.

He frowned. 'You've got a nerve, you've really got a

fucking nerve. It was people like you who screwed me, and now that you're screwed yourselves, you want me to help.'

'They didn't screw you,' said Gerry. 'Maybe they went along with it all, but it was people like Marvin and Clarke, they're the ones who really made Queensland the way it was. They were the sort of people who were annoyed by you, it was their little deals you were interfering with, that's why they set things up to send you to jail. Who were these two?'

I said, 'I was drunk most of the time. I don't even remember half of it. And I never knew you existed.'

But Stanley's eyes were on May. 'She did.'

May didn't answer.

'Either way,' Gerry insisted, 'surely you don't want someone like Clarke to get his hands on them? He walked away from the Inquiry without a care. If he makes George and May disappear, then he walks away from all this too.'

'Everyone walked away from the Inquiry,' Stanley muttered. 'Everyone that mattered.'

'He didn't,' said May. 'Not really. And it's caught up with him now. All we need is some time, Stanley. To let the police work it out.'

'The police?' He shook his head, disgusted. 'It's none of my business.'

Gerry was gentle. 'How can you say that after all these years? Wasn't that always what was wrong? No one wanted to make anything their business. Except you.'

Stanley stared angrily at Gerry while May and I waited, silent supplicants.

'All right, then. Stay if you think it'll help.'

I glanced out the window. It was almost night.

'Do we need anything?' I said. 'We bought food.'

He looked me up and down. 'Have you got warm clothes? It's still pretty cold up in the hills.'

I blinked. All I had were the clothes from Brisbane. I turned to May. She shook her head. 'I didn't even think,' she said.

'Haven't you got anything out there?' I asked Stanley.

'Not in your size. I live alone, you know. I don't usually cater for guests.'

'Get some stuff from your house,' Gerry suggested.

'I wanted to avoid going there.'

Stanley thought. 'Your house is on the way. We can see if anyone is hanging about the place and, if not, you can duck in for a moment.'

We ventured out into the back yard. The sky was still glowing orange in the west, but down in Highwood the evening was deepening. Stars gleamed above and the streetlights were on. And it was getting colder, the breeze picking up, touched with a distant frost.

'Is that your car?' Stanley asked.

May nodded.

'Then I think we'll all go in mine,' he said, 'Some of the creeks are still up and the track's a mess. Gerry nearly tore his sump off, coming out this morning.'

Gerry nodded. 'Leave yours here,' he told May. 'No one will even see it in the shed.'

So we transferred our gear across to the Toyota and climbed aboard. Gerry leaned in to say goodbye. 'I'll come out in a day or two. But you know you won't be able to hide out there forever, George. You could talk to Graham. I don't think you'd have any worries with him.'

'Eventually maybe, Gerry, but not yet.'

'Graham is still a cop,' Stanley added, starting the engine, 'and that's never good.'

We backed out into the lane, and then onto the street. There was no one about. It was only dinner time but already Highwood looked shut down for the night. Smoke curled up from chimneys. Summer might have been months away.

We crossed the creek and climbed up the western slopes. A car passed us and then another, but they were only headlights sliding by. Then we were up above the town and on the gravel track that went by my house. It was the same track that ran on out of town, all the way through the bush to Stanley's place, and it was deserted. We drove slowly by the cottage. It was dark and closed up, and there was no sign of anyone nearby, not a car or a person. Stanley continued a hundred yards or so further on, then switched off his lights. He u-turned and cut the engine, rolled silently back to my driveway.

'Make it quick, then,' he said.

I turned to May. 'Come in and see what clothes of mine you want.'

We stole across the front yard. The wind rattled in the trees, and down below the lights of the town glowed, little havens of warmth. The front door was locked as I'd left it. I dug out my keys and we were inside. We waited there for a moment in the front hall, but the house was silent. In the darkness I led May through to the bedroom, then I pulled down the blinds before switching on the bedside lamp. The room seemed like someone else's, small and cheerless, but it was untouched. No one had been here, no one was waiting. I opened the wardrobe and the cupboards and, whispering to each other, we searched for clothes. Jumpers. Jackets. Boots. All too big for May, but warm at least, and at the bottom of one drawer we found a smaller woollen pullover that belonged not to me but to Emily. We folded them all over our arms and I switched off the light.

Heading back out we paused for a second in the darkened kitchen. It was at the back of the house and there was a large window over the sink that gave a view of the mountains climbing away into the night. From here the town wasn't visible, no sign of civilisation was, it might have been an unexplored world. Westward there lingered a greenish hue of sunset, and the rocky outcrops and the forests that crowded them were etched in a perfect line against the sky. And above, the multitude of stars were blazing.

May stared at it all. 'It's beautiful,' she said, looking up at me. 'If I'd come here ten years ago, none of this would have happened.'

'It was impossible then.'

Her eyes were lost, her face only a pale blur. It was the May of my memories. A shadow, a voice in the dark.

'I'm glad I found you again,' she said. She leaned up and kissed me, her lips startling and warm in the cold air. I kissed her back.

It was only a moment—it seemed that all of our times together had only been brief, just touches—and then we were at the front door again. But maybe it was true, maybe there was a curse over May and me, and it wasn't done yet. For even as we opened the door the sound of an engine welled up, tyres crunched in the drive, and for the second time, the last time, we were caught in the untimely glare of headlights. We froze there hand in hand, staring at a car we couldn't see. It might have been anyone behind those headlights and for an instant I knew it had all been for nothing, that they had found us anyway, and then another set of headlights clicked on. They were from Stanley's Toyota and they shone across the first car, pinning the driver clearly. It was Emily, staring at us, open mouthed.

I dropped the clothes, stepped away from Maybellene. Emily's hands were working at her seatbelt, and then she was out of the car.

'George,' she said, coming towards me, then stopping. Her eyes went to May, to Stanley in his four wheel drive, back to me. 'George, what's going on?'

And there were no words. 'Emily . . . it's a bad time . . .'

'I've been trying to call you. I thought you were in Brisbane, but the motel said you'd gone, said you hadn't even paid your bill. And I was at the school and I was driving home and I just thought I'd come up and check.'

She was staring at May again.

And I was thinking that this was how it must have felt that other time, for May, when it was Charlie who'd caught us and May was the one torn between her two loves. I'd only ever thought of it before from my point of view, from the third party's view. But I was in the middle now, and this was worse, far worse.

'This is May,' I said. 'She's . . . she's from back then. I can't explain it all now, Emily.'

And her face looked as fragile as ice. 'I'm sorry, George. I should have left you to it. It's nothing to do with me.' She was backing away towards the car.

'Emily, wait.'

'No, George,' and the anger was there now. 'Don't worry about it. I'll go.'

'I can explain,' I said, not believing the words were coming out of me. But she was already back in her car.

'You don't have to,' she said, fumbling with the keys. I'd never seen her so frantic, wouldn't have thought it could happen, not to someone like her, someone who'd already lost her husband and been burned and stayed forever in this town and survived. 'I've always known. It was always going to happen. You don't have to explain a thing.'

Then the engine was revving. I could see she was still speaking but couldn't hear what she was saying. The tyres sprayed gravel as she reversed away, and she was gone.

Only moments had passed. I was still just five yards from May. She stood waiting on the steps, watching me, her whole body one sad, painful question.

The lights of Stanley's Toyota flicked off.

The three of us hung in darkness.

Then Stanley's voice came. 'Christ, George,' he said. 'Is there anything in your life you haven't fucked up?'

FORTY-FIVE

I should have gone after her.

There were plenty of excuses as to why I didn't. I was numb, couldn't think where to even begin an explanation. And May was there. Stanley. I couldn't just abandon them to follow Emily home. We weren't even supposed to be in town, there was no time . . .

But I still should have gone.

Instead May and I climbed back into Stanley's vehicle and we headed out west into the hills. I was hardly aware of the journey. I pulled cans of beer out of the back and drank. A sickness had possessed me, and all I noticed were trees and rocks in the headlights, the black glint of water as we splashed through creeks, and the lurching of the vehicle as Stanley ground gears and swore at the road. We seemed to wind into darkness forever. May sat wordless in the back seat. All I could think of was the expression on Emily's face, staring at us through the windscreen.

What had I been thinking? Where had the ten years between Emily and me gone? Was that all I thought she deserved?

But of course I wasn't thinking, hadn't been thinking since the phone had rung that morning weeks ago and I'd first learned Charlie was dead. All I'd been doing since was responding, reacting, running. Nothing had changed. Maybe I had given up the drinking once, but I was still a fool, still a disaster to my partners and my friends and my lovers.

And if that was so, then what was the point in not drinking anyway?

The beer seemed too thin. I thought of the bottles of wine in the back, dark and full of their liquid balm. What had I been staying sober for? *Who* had I been staying sober for? For myself? For Emily? For May? No, not for May. For May I didn't need to do anything, didn't need to fight anything. With May I could simply surrender and descend . . .

We were at the gate to Stanley's property.

'Well,' he said, looking at me, 'make yourself useful.'

I got out. The night was full now. There were no lights, no other houses for miles. On all sides the hills reared as black shadows crowned with stone. Water trickled somewhere below, and from far up on the ridges there came a muted roar like distant surf—it was the wind, grown stronger up here in the hills, surging and ebbing though the forest. It was a night wind in a jagged sky, hemmed in by the mountains, bright with stars. I opened the gate, Stanley drove through, and I closed it behind him. Then we climbed on up the last rise.

I heard the dogs barking, and they loped into the headlights, five or six of them, black shapes with shining eyes and red mouths.

'It's all right,' Stanley said, opening his door. 'They won't do a thing if I'm here.'

Then he was amongst them, stroking and murmuring. May and I got out as well, and for a moment the dogs milled about us before Stanley moved off, calling them behind him.

'I'll lock them up,' he told us. 'Get your gear unloaded.'

May was gazing around, studying the place. Stanley had left the headlights on, but it was still too dark to see much. Only a stretch of ground and the outline of the house. Everything else was night and cold and the hollow thrum of the wind. She wrapped her arms around herself.

'It's like we've fallen off the earth,' she said.

'That's the idea. And don't wander too far. The land drops away over there.'

'God, what a place.'

'Wait till morning. It looks better by daylight.'

She nodded, but she seemed haunted and small.

'It'll be okay,' I said.

She looked up at me. 'About before . . . I'm sorry she had to see that.'

'So am I.'

I wanted May to ask me what it all meant with Emily, to make me say something at least about what I felt for her, or about what I felt for May herself, and about what I hoped might happen if this was ever finished.

But all she did was stare around the darkness again. 'I don't like this place, George. I don't know if we should have come.'

We unloaded our gear. By that time Stanley had the dogs locked away and had lit a kerosene lamp. He took us inside. The living room was dim in the lamplight, but otherwise much as I remembered it. In fact it was exactly as I remembered it. The gun rack was still there on the wall, laden with weapons.

'I thought you buried them,' I said.

Stanley was lighting some candles.

'I dug them up. Graham won't be coming out here again. And don't tell me you aren't glad they're here.'

'No . . . I just hope we don't need them.'

'That's the thing with you, George. You hope for the best, but you never prepare for the worst.'

We tried to settle in. The spare bedroom held two narrow single beds squeezed in amongst piles of boxes and books. May and I unpacked and donned jumpers and thick socks. When we came out again Stanley was using a cleaver to chop up meat and bone for his dogs. A kettle was hissing on the hotplate of a wood-burning stove, but the house was still cold.

May inspected the living room. 'It's a nice fireplace,' she said.

'You won't need that,' Stanley answered. 'The stove's enough. I'm not gonna spend all day chopping wood.'

'Would you like me to cook?'

'You ever cooked on a wood-burner before?'

'No.'

'Think you better just stay out of my way then.'

He took the food out to his dogs. May looked at me mutely. I picked up one of the wine bottles and went to work with the corkscrew. There was nothing I could do about Emily now anyway. I wanted to stop even thinking about her, and beer wasn't going to be enough. May found some glasses and held them out for me to fill. When Stanley came back from his dogs we were deep into the first bottle. He eyed us both for a moment, me in particular. Then he got to work on dinner.

May and I huddled in the armchairs. Despite the stove and the extra clothes, we couldn't get warm. Stanley didn't help. He banged about angrily in the kitchen and wouldn't talk to us. We said little ourselves. There was no television, no radio, nothing to do. Outside, the wind began to dip down from the upper slopes and whoop around the house. Candle flames quivered as errant drafts slid under the doors, and shadows jumped on the walls. Despite the cold May and I went out into the night to inspect the wind, and to escape Stanley's silence. We cradled glasses of wine in our hands and stared skywards. There was a deeper iciness to the air now. A front must have been moving up from the south, some last vestige of a winter already gone, straying north. The sky was still clear, but there was no moon, and the land was shapeless.

'This won't work,' May said. 'Stanley isn't going to forgive us. No matter how long we stay.'

I drained my glass. 'We'll go somewhere else if we have to.'

'Or maybe it should just be me that goes.'

I shook my head in the darkness, not even certain if she saw. Back inside we poured more wine and Stanley served dinner. We ate and retreated again to the armchairs. Air rushed around the house. The minutes ticked by and occasionally from outside a dog would yelp or whine. Stanley would cock his head and listen for a moment, then relax again. 'They don't like the wind.'

Finally he took out a worn leather pouch and rolled himself a joint. He offered it to us wordlessly, but we both refused. I stayed with alcohol, even though the wine didn't seem to be working. There was no comforting cloud seeping into my mind, only a creeping unease, and thoughts about Emily. I opened another bottle of wine. Stanley watched, wreathed in marijuana smoke, a grim presence in the room.

'Would you like a glass?' I asked him.

'No.'

May was right. Stanley wasn't going to accept us. Maybe I'd been wrong all along, thinking we could survive here. But if we went somewhere else, left the state altogether perhaps, May and me together, what did that mean? And what about Emily, waiting alone in Highwood? Was I going to make a choice that final? I didn't know. It was too big a question, and the wine felt like a weight on my tongue.

May broke the silence, pointing to the joint in Stanley's hand. 'Is that how you make money now? Growing that?'

'It helps.'

'You're not worried about breaking the law?'

'Not that law.'

I said to him, 'You should visit Brisbane now. It's changed. Everything that we got in trouble for is legal. The bars never shut, there're casinos, lap-dancing . . .'

He looked at me. 'You call that better?'

'Isn't it?'

'You can drink all night, lose your money and watch naked women? Who ever cared about any of that?'

May sounded sad. 'Everyone did. In the old days.'

Stanley shook his head impatiently. 'If I'd thought any of those things mattered back then I would have been out there protesting against them. But why bother? Of course the licensing laws were ridiculous, of course they were there to be broken, of course there'd be an underworld. I didn't have any problem with that. It was the bigger things.'

I said, 'You don't think the Inquiry improved anything then?'

'The small things, maybe. The obvious things. Maybe not even them. In another generation the Inquiry will be a memory and it'll all be like it used to be. Nothing else ever changed. It's entrenched in this state. It's the people themselves.'

May nodded. 'And it's worse here. Always worse than the rest of the country. It's like there's something in the air.'

Stanley blew out smoke. 'It's always been that way. Queensland was appallingly governed, right from the start. Go back a century—the big pastoralists owned the government then, and sheep were all they cared about. Meanwhile we were falling behind the southern states in everything else—industry, infrastructure, education. People were starting to wonder why. So the parliament said to the voters, it doesn't matter if you're poor. You're tougher than those southern states, you don't need good roads or good schools, you're harder than that, you're different. Ignore anyone from the south who laughs at us, ignore anyone who suggests things could be better. In fact, be *suspicious* of anyone who says things could be better. They don't understand the Queensland way.'

The wind rose and fell, and sheet iron moaned on the roof. Stanley studied the ceiling until if fell quiet.

'That's where it started,' he went on, 'this thing about Queensland being different. You're rough and ready, they said. You don't need sophistication. You'll get by because you're simple, decent, hard-working folk. Be satisfied with less, be satisfied with backwardness. No, be proud of it. Because you're unique here in Queensland.'

He flicked the stub of his joint into the empty fireplace.

'The worship of ignorance. It's an excuse, that's all it is. It's the excuse of rednecks and backwaters and corrupt governments the world over. The saddest thing is that people believe it. They get used to it. They accept whatever leftovers they're given. And meanwhile the bastards at the top keep scooping the heart out of the place.'

He stared at the cold grating.

'What insufferable shit we were all taught.'

May was silent, gazing into her glass, and I thought of Marvin and his campaign slogans and the way the old premier had beat the Queensland drum whenever his popularity sagged.

'It was years ago,' I said. 'It's not that way any more.'

The marijuana burned in Stanley's eyes. 'You're a fucking idiot, George. Who are you hiding from here? You think people like Clarke would have survived this long anywhere else?'

May was staring deep into her wine. 'He used to laugh about it. Poor old Queensland, and all its idiot voters.'

'Everyone laughs at Queensland,' Stanley brooded. 'That's why it'll never change. The rest of the country loves having us to laugh at. It's the only attention we ever get. So of course we oblige. We perform on cue.'

May wasn't listening. 'He's not laughing any more.'

Stanley glared at her. 'Don't expect any sympathy from me. For him, or for you two either. This is my home, you know. You two have come smashing in here just like the police used to, and you expect me to . . . Christ, I don't know. I don't even know who's worse, you or him.'

I said, 'We haven't killed anyone.'

'I don't think you could, George, even if you needed to.'

'You think that's a bad thing?'

'It's a weak thing. I don't get you, George. Gerry said you had something, but I could never see it. And then I thought—well, he gave up drinking. That must show some sort of character. And I thought, well, he's with Emily. She's got some strength to her so he must be worthwhile somehow, if she's with him. But here you are, back where you started. Back on the drink and back with your old drinking partner and back fucking things up for everyone else.'

He was furious, the skin of his face taut with a lifetime of injustice.

'You're the worst of them all. You don't think, you don't question, you just drift along with any sort of viciousness like the old days, and then you act surprised when it turns on you, never mind all the people it crushed in the meantime. At least the real pricks like Marvin and your friend out there—they're arrogant and greedy and dead wrong, but at least they run their own lives, at least they take some responsibility, as least they *act*. You, George, I don't know what you do.'

I stared at him, my face burning, and I could think of nothing to say.

'Leave him alone,' May said softly.

For a moment Stanley turned on her, then he slumped, and the anger in him died.

'Fine,' he said. 'You two are welcome to each other.'

Outside the wind rose like an ocean rolling over the hills, and sank away again. I looked at my wine glass and drained it.

'We'll leave if you want,' I said.

'Forget it,' he answered. 'You're here now.'

No one said anything. I refilled my glass. My skin was still prickling. It was suddenly too hot in the room. I rose and went to the door, stepped out into the night. The wind cut against me and in the darkness my face cooled, but the wine remained, a fog over my thoughts. I didn't want it there any more. It didn't matter what I wanted. Alcohol would always move at its own pace, a matter of flowing blood and the liver. Will had nothing to do with it. I took another mouthful.

Above me material billowed. There were still only the tarpaulins stretched to the tree trunks in place of a verandah. Filled with air, they strained towards the sky. The door opened, and I sensed May behind me.

'He's got plenty of reasons to be bitter,' she said.

'He's right, though. Look at us, May. All those years.'

'We didn't mean it to turn out the way it did.'

'We never even wondered how it might turn out.'

'No . . .'

'And you and me . . . and Charlie. Look how we treated Charlie.'

'Look how everyone treated Charlie.'

'But us—he didn't deserve that from us.'

She didn't answer for a time. 'This is about Emily, isn't it?'

It was. I could see her face again. I thought of her away back in town, sitting in her empty house. What sort of future had been there for us, what was I abandoning? What sort of future was there now, for me and for May? And what were the consequences? Think for once, I told myself. Think! But only the fog remained.

I said, 'What are we going to do?'

'You and me, George? I don't know. When it's the two of us, I've never known.'

We stared into the night.

I said, 'I have to at least go and see her.'

She nodded. 'I understand. I remember what it was like.'

'I mean, the thought of her alone, wondering what's happened, not knowing . . . I can't leave it like that.'

'No. You have to talk to her. I never could with Charlie, but I should have.'

'It's not even that late yet. She'd probably still be awake.'

She stiffened. 'You're going now?'

'It's better now. This late no one will notice me driving

around town. It's better than going during the day. And I don't want her to . . . to have to try and sleep, without knowing.'

'But you've been drinking. Won't that bother her?'

I drank again, the wine tasting tart and dry, without any pleasure in it at all. 'She may as well see me for what I am.'

May pulled away. Her arms wrapped around her chest, and she sounded a thousand miles distant. 'All right, George. If you have to do it, then do it now. But I still don't like it here.'

'There's Stanley. He mightn't want us, but you won't be alone.'

'It isn't Stanley. It's this place. It's so dark. It's so deserted.'

And I heard a sadness in her voice, deeper and more final than ever before.

'It'll be better tomorrow,' I said. I couldn't think of anything else.

We went back inside and I told Stanley I wanted to borrow his vehicle.

He shook his head in disbelief. 'What on earth for?'

'I'm taking your advice,' I said. 'I won't be long.'

They came out to see me off, Stanley carrying a kerosene lamp, the flame flaring in the wind. He handed over the keys. 'Just take it nice and slow, okay? And don't forget to close the gate behind you. But don't worry, I won't let the dogs out until you get back.'

May leaned in through the window and kissed me. 'I hope you can work something out with her,' she said. She was smiling, but I saw the effort in it, the loneliness.

'Wait for me,' I said. Then I was rolling down the hill, and in the rear view mirror they were just flickering figures in a tiny pool of light. Then they were gone altogether.

FORTY-SIX

The town was deserted.

I drove down the main street, the footpaths empty, the stores and the cafes all shut down, their display windows gone black. Wind whipped along the gutters. I came to the park where the memorial to Emily's dead husband stood motionless amidst trees that bowed and shook. On past the courthouse, its clock showing close to midnight, and then beyond to the police station. A light glowed above the door, but there was no one there, not tonight. No crime stirred in Highwood. There was only me, and I wasn't so certain now. The wine was leaching from my body and my head ached dimly, and I was afraid of what I had to say.

I drove on. Beyond the school and up towards the national park, past dark houses and sleeping families. And there was Emily's place. Her car was parked outside, and behind the blinds of her bedroom window, a lamp still burned. She was awake.

I climbed out, looked up and down the street. There was no one to see me, no lights suddenly switched on, no faces peering from behind curtains. I walked up the footpath and knocked on the door.

Even though I had a key.

I waited. Noise came from inside and Emily opened the door. She must have come from bed. She was in pyjama pants and a T-shirt, her hair was tousled, and her eyes were red.

'George,' she said, and she tottered slightly, leaning against the doorpost. A small note of hopelessness sounded inside me. She was drunk.

'Emily? Can I come in?'

'Sure,' she said, and walked back inside. I followed her. There were no lights on in the living room, but a small oil heater was set up in front of the couch, a blanket pooled on the cushions. She hadn't been in bed, she'd been sitting there in the dark. There was an empty bottle of wine on the coffee table, and another three-quarters gone. And a single glass.

'Do you want some wine?' she said. She had never asked me that question before. And her voice was frightening, colder than the air outside.

'No,' I said.

'So you haven't taken up *all* your old habits?'

She was curling herself in the blanket again, lifting the glass and drinking.

I didn't answer. She would never notice the alcohol on my breath now. And to accept a glass, actually drink in front of her . . . I couldn't do it, for all that I had intended to hide nothing. The balance between us seemed so precarious as it was.

Emily considered the wine.

'I like drinking, George,' she said. 'All those years of staying sober, just for your sake. Tiptoeing around it every time someone so much as mentioned alcohol. You know what? It was boring.'

'I never wanted to stop you.'

'But you did, all the same. It's no fun drinking alone, George. And I should know.'

'Emily . . . May needed my help. You don't know what's been happening.'

She was gazing at the little flames in the heater. 'You wouldn't ever tell me.'

'I thought it was over, I thought it would never come back. I didn't want you to know about those times.'

'And now it's come back anyway.'

'Some of it has. I don't know why, not really. But Charlie is gone. And Marvin. Jeremy is dying. There's only May and me left.'

'I don't even know those people. You barely talked about

them. You talked about May, though. In your sleep. I heard it. I always knew.'

'You don't know it all . . . but the thing is, May and I have to stay out of sight for a while. There's someone . . . it's a long story. But I couldn't tell you I was coming up here, or that I was with May. I'm sorry you had to find out the way you did.'

'And how long is it going to be this way?'

'I don't know.'

'And when it's all over? What then? What about you and her?'

I forced myself to tell her the truth. 'There's so much that was never finished between her and me . . . I don't know.' And I didn't know, but from Emily's point of view, that was as good as making my choice.

She shook her head. 'Why here? Why did you have to come back here?'

'It's the safest place.'

'Only for you.'

I tried to reach her. 'Emily, nothing has been decided. Nothing can be, until this is over. But I'm not just going to disappear. I'm not forgetting everything. The last ten years, I wouldn't have got through them without you.'

'Not now, George, not that.'

'No, listen. I had nothing when I came here. I would have just gone back to the old ways if it wasn't for you. You were so good to me.'

She look at me, sickened. 'Good? I don't want to be *good*. I'm not a fucking saint. It's all I get from this town, ever since that damned fire, but Christ, George, do you think that's what I wanted from you?'

And it occurred to me that both May and Emily could look back to a fire that forever changed their lives. One lighting the flame, and the other fighting it.

'I know it isn't,' I said, 'but compared to the way I used to live . . . '

'The way you used to live? You missed that life, George. You shut it all away, but you missed it. And I only got what was left over. You didn't think I could even understand what you were like back then, let alone that maybe I could be that way myself. Only your precious May could be like that, no one else.'

She drank again, grimacing.

'And now you've got her back. *She's* not good. You and her, you drank and you cheated on your best friend and you ran brothels, and you *liked* it. You decided she's the only one who can give that sort of thing to you. So of course you could quit drinking, if she wasn't around. But you never even gave me a chance. All I was allowed to be was good. Jesus, it's such a fucking pointless word.'

'Emily . . .'

'Get out of here, George. I don't want to talk about this now. I'm drunk.' She gave a sour laugh. 'Now, finally, I'm drunk.'

I stared at her. 'It's not as simple as you think.'

She emptied her glass, not looking at me. 'I know. I'm not as simple as you think either.'

I bowed my head. There was no answer, and the sight of Emily drunk disturbed me. Maybe she was right, that it was a side of her I didn't want to see, and that wasn't fair. But fair or not, it wasn't like it was when May and I drank. There was no invitation there, no link, no kindred pull towards alcohol, no core of darkness in Emily that echoed my own. Maybe it was there, if I'd ever let myself look, but I hadn't, and it was too late now.

I stood up. 'All right. But we still have to talk about this.'

She was pouring the dregs of the bottle into her glass. 'Goodbye, George. And tell your police friends not to bother me any more. It's your business, not mine.'

I paused. 'Police? What police?'

'They came round tonight. They'd got it all wrong. They thought you were here.'

I sat down again. I put my hand on her glass before she could lift it. 'Emily, what police are you talking about? Are you talking about Graham?'

She blinked at me vaguely. 'No . . . no, the Brisbane police.'

'No one is supposed to know we're here. Not even the

Brisbane police. Who was it? Was it Detective Kelly and his partner, the ones who came up when Charlie died?'

My alarm was getting through to her now. 'No. It was another detective. I don't remember his name, but he showed me his badge.'

The world seemed to be slowing to a single moment.

'What did he look like?'

'I don't know . . .'

'Was he a big man, fairly old, white hair?'

'That was him.'

I was scarcely breathing.

'What did he want?'

'He said he was looking for you and May. He said that you'd told them you were coming to Highwood and that you'd said you'd be staying here with me. He expected you to be here.'

'And what did you say?'

'I said as far as I knew you were at home.'

'And did he believe that?'

She shook her head. 'He said he knew you weren't home, that you were supposed to be staying somewhere else. So I said that maybe you were at Stanley's place. I'd seen you three together. He said, oh, the plans must have been changed. It didn't seem to be any big thing.'

'May, when was this?'

'A couple of hours ago. Why, what's wrong? I saw the badge, George. He was a detective.'

I was on my feet. I stepped towards the door, came back.

'Police,' I said. 'You said there were *police*.'

'That's right. There were two of them.'

'And the other man?'

She thought. 'I didn't see him, really. He stayed in the car. They were parked right out front. I could tell there was someone else in the car, but I didn't really see him.'

I grabbed her hand, hoping against hope. 'Emily, did you tell them where Stanley's place is?'

She was staring back, not understanding, but knowing that something was wrong. 'Yes, I did.'

And I was running out the door.

'George,' she yelled after me. 'What is it? What have I done?'

But I was in the street and the wind had me and I didn't stop to answer.

They were here.

I started up the four wheel drive, revving the engine madly as I searched for the gears. Then I was in motion, u-turning, racing back down through the sleeping town, past the staring windows of the houses and the pale light over the police station. There was nowhere else to turn, no one to help. Highwood may as well have been a graveyard. I was utterly alone, a single speeding vehicle, tyres shrieking on a corner, a wail in the night.

They were here.

How had it happened? So easily, so quickly. I'd been so sure they would still be combing the streets of Brisbane for us. Eventually, I'd assumed, they would try Highwood again, but even then they would only have found my empty house. There would have been nothing to suggest they drive an hour up into the hills to find us. No one else would know, no one else could tell them. And where could they have gone from there? It should have worked, we should have been safe.

Unless they were already here. Waiting.

My mind worked, a blur of terrible thoughts. Maybe they'd left Brisbane even before we had, Clarke and his fisherman. Detective Kelly had told me that Jeffreys had taken leave the previous morning. Maybe they'd abandoned the search in Brisbane even then and come to lie in wait in Highwood. In that case I'd run right into their arms. And I'd led May into the trap with me. They could have spent yesterday and today watching the town and then, finding nothing, turned to Emily. Why would Emily hide anything if a policeman came knocking at her door? Especially if he pretended to be a friend, to be expecting to see me.

But Emily shouldn't have *known* anything. If she hadn't caught May and me on the steps of my house, she would've thought we were still in Brisbane. Or if Stanley hadn't been there then at least she wouldn't have known it was his place we were using. There would have been nothing for her to tell.

Or if I'd gone after her straightaway, if I'd explained the need for secrecy, that no one was to be told where May and I were, not even the police, especially not the police.

It was the curse again, the doom that plagued May and me wherever we went. There'd been only those few hours of opportunity. If they'd called on Emily earlier this afternoon, if they'd waited until tomorrow, they would have missed us. If I'd gone straight to Emily and told her the truth, told her everything. If things had happened any other way . . .

But they hadn't.

And now they knew. And May and Stanley were sitting out there, shut away in the house with the marijuana and the wine, and no idea what was coming their way.

I was on the track, the Toyota bouncing and lurching as I pushed it too hard and too fast. Two hours . . . what had they done in those two hours? I hadn't seen any other cars on my drive into town, but what did that mean? Once they knew where we were, would they wait till morning, or would they go straight out to the property? And in that case, why hadn't they arrived even before I'd left?

Or had they been waiting again? For the night to get deeper, for the hour to get late, like they had with Marvin. So that when they arrived we wouldn't be eating dinner or sitting around the fire, we wouldn't be listening for a noise at the door. We would be asleep. Defenceless.

They wouldn't know that Stanley would have loosed the dogs by then.

They wouldn't know about his guns.

But if they were on their way there now, or if they were there already . . . Stanley was going to keep the dogs locked up until I got home. He and May would be waiting for a car in the drive. For a knock on the door. The guns would still be on the wall.

I was hunched forward in the seat, staring out through the windscreen. The Toyota whined and roared with every ditch, but it was too slow. Trees and rocks stood out as the headlights slewed crazily, and beyond them the darkness waited. But something was different. I could see the shadows and folds of the hills, where before all had been black. I glanced behind me and saw, barely creeping into the sky, the moon. It was riding the wind over the high eastern ridges, waning and yellow, and framed against it a far rocky point angled upwards like a fang. The sight chilled me. I was too slow. I would not get there in time.

Water splashed around the wheels. The eyes of some animal glowed red on the track and I caught a glimpse of grey fur as it bounded aside. On a switchback curve I felt the back tyres slide out and the side of the vehicle lightly kissed a wall of stone. Leaves and branches smacked against the windscreen. All of it lurid, a cinema screen unrolling before me. They were ahead of me somewhere, always ahead, as they had been from the beginning.

Then finally through the trees there came the reflective flash of white paint. Stanley's gate. I slowed down, ready to leap out and unchain it. Then I saw that the gate was already hanging ajar, and in my memory came the clear certainty that I'd closed it when I left.

I rolled to a stop, staring stupidly. And as the engine fell away to idle, I heard it. The barking of dogs. And gunfire.

I would never be able to explain what I did next. Later it would come to me that I should have revved the Toyota again and charged through the gate and up the hill, headlights blazing. It might have made a difference if I'd done that, right then. I didn't know what was happening up at Stanley's house at that moment, and I would never really know . . . but it might have made a difference.

Instead I turned off the engine and lights, and I sat there, half out of the door, listening. I didn't know what it was that made it impossible to reason or decide or act . . . but all I did was sit there, paralysed. Frozen by the sound. Fascinated, in a disbelieving, shrinking sense. Not even thinking about cowardice or fear, although that's all I would think about later. Right then I wasn't thinking at all. Just listening, as if this was something distant, unconnected to me.

There was nothing to see. The shots were coming from up on the hillside, over the last rise. As the wind rose and fell the sounds rose and fell in unison. Dogs barked ceaselessly. And the shots, like the wind, came in gusts. A flurry, a rattle of loud cracks fading away to individual reports, then bursting out again. Different tones, some high, some low. And yelling. Male voices, indistinct and hoarse. In my mind I could see Stanley's vast array of guns, but I could go no further. How much time had he had, what warning?

I looked behind me, back down the track towards town. I could go . . . I could go for help. Back to the nearest house, the nearest phone. Call Graham and the police. Call someone. And anyway, couldn't anyone hear? There were neighbours in the distance. The shots were loud and the wind would carry the sound. Someone would hear.

But even if someone did hear, what would they do? It was Stanley's place. He was always firing his weapons, day or night. No one would care.

I could still go myself then . . . now . . . I could get away.

I realised I was shaking.

And above me, the gunshots had stopped.

I cocked my head, but there were only the dogs now, yelping and howling. And the wind. It streamed down the hill and sighed in the trees, unperturbed. And that was worse.

Something up there was finished.

I waited, tense and straining to hear. The stars swung in their slow arcs, paled by the moon. Nothing happened. No one came down. And I didn't go up. Time was an agony. All I wanted to do was drive away. Whatever had happened up there, whoever was still waiting—what use would I be now?

I had to command my legs to move. They felt weak, drugged. I got out of the Toyota, took a step towards the gate, then another. I eased past the signs and the posts. Then, just visible in the faintest of moonlight, I could see the track climbing up. I crouched low and followed it.

It was only a hundred yards, but it stretched out like eternity.

As I approached the top I was almost crawling. The first thing I saw was the dark shape of a vehicle. It was just over the crest—another four wheel drive. Both its front doors were open, and though within it was all darkness, I could sense it was empty. I crept on. Then I was over the rise. I could see across the patch of level ground, a network of restless shadows, to the bulk of the house. The windows were lightless, but halfway back towards me a small flame burned on the ground, flaring in the wind. I couldn't tell what it was. There was nothing else, and all the while the dogs barked in their kennels. I longed for electricity, for a spotlight to ignite and throw everything into stark relief so I could see. But there was no electricity here. This had all started with a power failure, with groping in darkness, and now it was ending that way as well.

I stared and waited. The wind sang and trees swung back and forth and shadows fled across the earth. But one of the shadows didn't move. It was a few yards in front of the four wheel drive, and as I stared I knew what it was. I inched forward. I made out arms and legs, spreadeagled. There was a hint of a white shirt beneath a suit, white hair crowning a face that was invisible, buried in the dirt. A fisherman cast up from the sea. Motionless.

I was very close to him now, crawling, and my hand touched moisture in the soil. His own hand was barely a foot away, streaked with what looked like ink, seeming to reach out towards mine. Between our fingers something densely black and small lay on the ground. I stared at it, not daring to touch.

Someone coughed.

And across from the little fire, in the jumble of darkness under the tarpaulins, someone moved. Glass glinted. And then shapes resolved themselves into a man, sitting against the trunk of one of the trees. For a moment I caught a profile—a hard face, unrecognisable from the photo I'd seen of it decades before—then it was gone again. But the man remained. And the glint of glass was from a bottle. I watched as he lifted it to his lips and drank. He was barely fifteen yards away.

My hand jerked forward of its own accord and touched steel. For the first time in my life, I picked up a gun.

His head turned.

'Hello, George,' he said.

FORTY-SEVEN

The flame on the ground flared again, and finally I recognised what it was—a broken kerosene lamp. The glass was smashed, but kerosene was pooled in the base and it was dripping to the ground, burning. The wind plucked at it and blue fire danced in a tiny circle of grass, illuminating nothing.

Clarke spoke again.

'That is you, isn't it?'

I stared, but he was still only a voice and a shape. The moon was no help. He could see me, perhaps, by its light, but in amongst the shadows of the tarpaulins, he was a phantom.

I lifted my arm, the gun feeling giant and obscene in my hand.

'Don't move,' I said.

He seemed to peer my way, then he gave a low laugh, rested his head back against the tree. 'I'm a ghost, George. Bullets have been passing right through me all night.'

His voice had a weary air to it, faint over the wind.

I was too far away. I edged around the fire, avoiding its small circle of light, keeping my arm as straight as I could, the gun wavering in his direction. Closer, until I was under the tarpaulins myself, hidden in the darkness again, my back to the door of the house. There was no way to be sure, but I knew he was watching me, silent.

'May?' I called out. 'Stanley?'

The dogs set up a new round of howling, but there was no other response.

'They're not in there' he said, close by now. 'I've already looked.'

His voice was low, and not young. Hoarseness frayed at the edges. I recognised what it meant. He was exhausted, and drunk. Very drunk.

'If they're gone,' I said carefully, 'then what are you doing here?'

The bottle was in his left hand. He raised it and took a mouthful.

'Waiting,' he said.

It wasn't a vodka bottle, it was a wine bottle. Perhaps it was even one of my own. It didn't matter what he was drinking. It was all the same in the end. A poison. I thought of everything May had told me about him, everything Marvin had told me. What had the last few weeks done to him? If he was a sick man when Marvin and Charlie had seen him in detox, what was he now? What was happening inside his head? And what did he see, in all the wind and darkness?

'Your friend is dead,' I said.

There was no reply, only a watchful shadow.

I searched for a sign of May or Stanley, but the world was all shifting shades of grey. Where had they gone? What had happened up here? The wind rose again. Leaves spattered like rain on the tarpaulin above us, and out in the yard the kerosene sputtered fire. The lamp . . . had Stanley heard a vehicle driving up the hill and come out to meet me, lamp in hand? And instead of me it was someone else . . .

'Just don't move,' I said again, not knowing what else to do.

He gave no sign he'd even heard, or cared.

I yelled names into the night and only the dogs answered. I thought of the house behind me, the hills all around, and no ideas came. I wished for light, for day, for anything. But it was just me and him and the gun in my hand.

'We gave your name to the police,' I said. 'The *other* police. They'll work it all out eventually. You should get away from here while you can.'

Then, in the endless shifting of shadows, I saw his eyes for a moment. They were wide open. Fixed on me.

'I'll tell you something about names, George,' he said, and he was more than just exhausted, the words seemed empty of any emotion at all. 'Until recently, I'd completely forgotten yours.'

'So what do you want with me now?'

'You? I don't want anything with you.'

'Who then?'

But he only laughed, and tilted the bottle.

'May doesn't want to talk to you,' I said.

'Really, George? We'll see . . .'

There was something about the way he said it. His right arm swung up slowly, languid almost. I caught a glimpse of his mouth, smiling, and I saw it in his hand, a short black gun barrel, pointed directly at my head . . .

And I pulled the trigger.

I didn't even mean to. My finger was squeezing back before I understood what I was doing. Nothing happened anyway. Something in the gun clicked, but there was no explosion, no flare or recoil. And he was laughing softly, leaning back against the tree, his own gun still pointed at me.

'There's a safety on that thing somewhere,' he said. 'Or maybe the magazine is empty, with all that shooting. It was pretty crazy up here for a while.' His head lolled back and he called out to the night. 'May! Get down here or I'll shoot George!'

And we waited, both of us, staring up into the hills. The wind pulled at the tarpaulins and the trees danced and the dogs barked as if they would never stop, but no one answered. My fingers were running vainly over the gun for a catch or a switch, but it was all steel and sharp edges, and I knew nothing about weapons.

'Poor George,' and the mockery was as elusive as his voice. 'Always chasing after other men's wives. At least Emily's husband is dead. Nice monument, though.' He proffered the bottle. 'You want some of this?'

'Don't come near me.'

'Not a drinker?' He sounded surprised. 'I heard different . . .'

'May won't come down,' I said.

'She will. You know her, George. It's hardly the first time she's run away. From Charlie, from you, from me. But she always comes back, sooner or later.'

'Why come after her, then? Go home and wait for her there.'

And his tone was disapproving. 'I think we all know it's a bit late for that.'

There seemed nothing else to say, nothing else to do. All the evasion and fleeing and pursuit, it had come to this. And I didn't know what was supposed to happen now, or who was supposed to decide. My thoughts pursued each other through the darkness, going nowhere. Minutes went by. No one spoke, there was only the wind in my ears. Clarke drank and I sat and the mountains stared down upon us and far above, unconcerned, the moon continued its infinite orbit of the earth.

Until I couldn't bear the waiting.

'Why her?' I said.

He had been watching the sky, it seemed, but now the shape of his head turned my way.

'What?'

'Why May? Why did you track her down after the Inquiry? Of all people.'

'She needed a job.'

'She burnt down your property, for Christ's sake. Why her?'

His head sagged again and he straightened it. 'You know, of all those people who lit that fire, she was the only one who really meant it. The others were shit scared when they got caught. Not her. She was just angry.'

'She hated you.'

He shook his head. 'May didn't know who she hated. She was a black hole, George. People could fill her up with anything they liked. Jeremy did it. Marvin did it. Maybe even you did it. But it was never what she wanted . . .'

I didn't answer. I wished I'd never asked the question. There was nothing I wanted to hear from him. Not about May.

'You people wasted her,' he added. 'You pissed her away on those clubs and casinos like she was something cheap off the street.'

I let the scorn into my voice. 'But you were different?'

'I gave her a way out. I got her away from that goddamn Inquiry, I got her off alcohol. It's more than any of you ever did.'

'And what did she have to do for you?'

'Nothing. Nothing she didn't want to do.'

'That's not the way she tells it.'

He only waved the bottle, dismissive.

'Maybe you're right,' I said. 'Maybe we wasted her. But you didn't get it right either. The way we were back then, the way *she* was . . . it's a part of her.'

'That was just the drinking. She could never control it.'

'Like you can?'

'Yes, like I can.'

'She didn't want to control it. None of us did. That's why we drank. That was the whole point of those days. If you don't understand that, you don't understand anything about her.'

He was amused. 'You think you do? There's more to her than just a fucking drinking partner, George. Even May worked that much out.'

'Then why is she back with me? You know what we've been doing the last few nights? You know how many bottles of wine we've drunk, me and her?'

The gun lifted again, and his voice went low. 'Be careful what you say here, George.'

And the threat was there . . . but this wasn't the substation, and I wasn't Charlie. He was alone now, just as I was, and we were in a forgotten corner of the world, beyond the reach of any power grid or electrical line. Out of anyone's territory, his or mine.

'This isn't just about May,' I said.

'It isn't?'

'What about Charlie?'

'What about him?'

'Why did do you what you did to him?'

'Ask May. She brought me here.'

'What does May have to do with Charlie?'

The arm holding the gun slipped down again, as if it was too heavy to hold. He drank another mouthful. 'We didn't mean to kill him, you know. We only wanted a few answers. If the poor fool had just told us . . . but he just stood there with that beaten up-face of his and snot running everywhere.

And then he went and pissed himself. What could we do then? He's the one, George. He's the one to blame for this whole sorry mess.'

'What answers? What wouldn't he tell you?'

'Where May was hiding, of course.'

The wind swirled up and the world seemed to go darker, but it was only in my mind, a dawning of comprehension that was a darkness, not a light.

'May?' I said. 'He wouldn't tell you where *May* was? Is that what you mean?'

He seemed to shrug. 'What else? Why do you think I ended up in that detox ward? It got bad, George. I'd been looking for her for weeks. When I woke up I didn't even know where I was. But there was Charlie. It was like a sign. I should've known she'd run back to her old friends. I begged him to tell me where she was, George. I begged him. That's all I wanted.'

'But Charlie didn't know . . .'

'He knew. I saw his face as soon as I mentioned her name.'

And finally I understood. That's what had happened while Marvin was sleeping, while it was just Clarke and Charlie in that room. It wasn't something about Clarke and his crimes that had sent Charlie off into the hills, looking for me, it was something about May . . .

I felt weak. 'Charlie didn't know where May was. He hadn't seen her in years.'

'Oh, he knew. He wouldn't tell me a thing, not then, but as soon as he left, Marvin came in and told me about Highwood . . . and now look where May turns up. Charlie knew all right.'

'No. No. She wasn't here. That wasn't what he meant.'

I didn't want this to be possible. Charlie had wanted to fix everything up for May and me, Marvin had said, to apologise. And in that ward he'd heard that May was still in Brisbane, alone and in hiding, with Clarke searching for her, a man Charlie had never liked, a man desperate and capable of violence . . . that's when he'd come looking for me. For her sake.

Clarke was gazing at the sky, his voice like mourning. 'I only wanted to talk to him. So I got Jeffreys to pick me up and we went round to that little ward in Bardon. Charlie wasn't there, but they were glad to see a policeman, they wanted to report that a car was missing. They gave us the description of it. After that, well . . . Highwood is only a little town. I remembered it from years ago. It wasn't hard to find him.'

'He was coming to see *me*. May wasn't up here.'

Clarke wasn't listening. 'But when we got up here all we found was Charlie, all alone in the street. There was no May. So we took him off for a talk. Somewhere private. Just for a few quiet words, and maybe a drink . . .'

'He didn't know . . .' and it was a refrain I seemed to be repeating to no one but the night and the wind and the dogs. 'There was nothing he could tell you. You did it all for nothing.'

'It was an accident. And we didn't know about you then. Charlie never mentioned your name. We only found out the next day that you even lived up here. I could barely remember who you were. He should have said something. We might've let him go if he'd said something. We might have gone straight to your place.'

And more weight piled on my soul. Charlie had been coming because he wanted to help May, maybe even to help me, to heal all the old wounds. And then he'd died for not saying something as simple as my name. Had he known that? Had he realised what he was doing, and chosen the pain, the vodka bottle at his lips?

I looked up at the stars, as numerous as the mistakes we'd all made.

I said, 'So then you had to find Marvin.'

He swigged from the bottle, almost conversational. 'That was thanks to you, George. We couldn't find him anywhere. But then Jeffreys heard you were in town, you were looking for Marvin too. That was interesting. So he started tailing you, and the very next morning you drive out to Redcliffe.'

Mistake upon mistake.

I said, 'And Marvin wouldn't tell you where May was either.'

'No.'

'He didn't *know*. Neither of them knew.'

He didn't speak for a long time, his head tilted, questioning.

'Are you serious?' he said.

I nodded. 'You had everything wrong.'

'I'll be damned.'

We fell silent. It was like talking with a spirit. Fading in, fading off, with news of an afterlife where nothing was as it was supposed to be. The sound of the dogs had dwindled to mutters and growls, the kerosene shrunk to a single thread of fire. Even the wind had rolled away.

Clarke stirred. 'Still, Marvin knew other things, George. Too much. We couldn't just leave him. And besides, *someone* had to take the blame for Charlie.'

I didn't need to ask about the rest. How they'd got in, the suicide note. I remembered what Marvin was like, the terror he was in. There was nothing he wouldn't have done, once they had him. Anything for a few minutes more . . .

I said, 'Why on the beach?'

'That was his idea. He wanted it to be there. So we went down with him and let him have a last bit of scotch, and then we gave him the rifle. There was no harm in it. We took his glasses, he was always blind without them . . . and there was only the one bullet.'

I looked down at the dark shape of the gun in my hand.

'And that left me.'

'That left you. I still didn't think you had anything to do with it. Who was this George person, anyway? I didn't know, you see, that you and May ever had anything going. It was Marvin who told me. He said you two were in love once. He said if anyone would know where May was, it'd be George. He said that maybe you'd even mentioned something about seeing her. He was spilling his guts about you, George. He was pointing the finger. If we'd left him alone and gone straight off to blow your head away, he couldn't have been happier. No, don't feel too bad about Marvin.'

But I thought of Marvin's blind eyes, trapped and squinting on the beach, looking for any way out, his last moments ticking away . . . and my hand was still on the trigger of the gun.

I would have squeezed and squeezed and squeezed if I thought it would have made any difference.

Clarke's voice went on, running endlessly. 'So I finally saw where I'd been going wrong. May wasn't with Charlie or with Marvin, she was with you all along. And then when we found out you'd skipped from your motel room, I smelt May all over the place. I was in your motel room, George, and I could *smell* her. She'd been there. So back to Highwood we came. We never should have left. You had May up here all the time.'

'No. I only met her in Brisbane. And it wasn't until after I'd seen Marvin. He was lying—I didn't know where she was either.'

He laughed, shook his head so much he slid sideways, had to force himself upright. 'Isn't that fucking typical? Fucking Marvin.'

But I felt beaten. Cheated by everything I'd believed.

'So all this . . . all this was just to find May?'

He was tilting the bottle higher now, to drink. It was getting empty. He swayed, straightened himself again, and I could tell he was peering at me, intent.

'It was a terrible thing she did to me. She just disappeared, George. Why do you think I ended up in that ward?'

And I'd had enough of all this.

'You didn't end up in that ward because May left you. You were there because you're sick.'

'I'm not sick. It was just that one night it got to me. I can handle the drinking, don't worry about that.'

'No, you can't. No one can.'

'Maybe *you* couldn't . . . '

'And I know it's falling apart for you. I know there's gonna be another inquiry. A serious one this time, just for you. That's why you can't take it any more.'

'Don't worry, I can handle that too.'

'All over again? After the last time? May didn't think so. That's why she left.'

He was tapping at the bottle glumly. 'May knows me . . . she knows I'll survive.'

'She doesn't. She said you were just like Charlie and Marvin were, years ago. She said you were worse.'

'Bullshit. I'm nothing like any of you. I mean, look at you, George . . .'

'I gave up drinking at least. That's more than you could do.'

'My drinking isn't a problem!'

'You can't even admit it!'

He reared up, threw the bottle away.

'May! Goddamn it! Come back!'

As if in answer the wind soared in one vast tumbling rush. The tarpaulins cracked like sails and the kerosene flared one last time, a tattered flame, then snuffed out. The darkness seemed total, no shadows, no moon, no stars. Then the wind receded. The night fell back into place, and I realised something else. The dogs had gone silent.

Someone said, 'Are you two finished fighting over her?'

Where the flame had been a figure now stood, outlined against a patch of sky, a rifle at its shoulder, aimed directly at us.

'Stanley?' I breathed.

'You okay?'

'I'm okay, but . . .'

I glanced sideways and Clarke was upright, his arm extended, the gun pointed straight back at Stanley.

'Where is she?' he said.

'Up on the hill.'

'Then you get her down here, right now.'

Stanley's voice was calm. 'She won't be coming down. She can't.'

The gun seemed to waver. 'What are you talking about?'

'Is she all right?' I asked.

'No, George,' and I wasn't even sure which one of us he meant. 'She's dead.'

FORTY-EIGHT

He refused to believe it.

He screamed things and stumbled between Stanley and me, waving his gun and threatening to shoot us both, but Stanley just stood there with his rifle pointed patiently.

'Come up and see then,' he said after some time.

And at that Clarke fell silent.

We passed around the back of the house, each of us with our weapons still in our hands, none of us speaking. The dogs watched from their kennels, and before us a hill rose, dark and waiting. We began to climb.

Later Stanley would tell me a little of what had happened. In the end, I'd only been a few minutes behind Clarke and his detective, nor had they been expecting Stanley to be armed. They'd simply driven through the gate and straight up to the house.

Inside, Stanley and May had heard the vehicle coming. Thinking it was me, Stanley had gone out with a lamp. Or perhaps some sense had warned him, because first he'd taken down a rifle from the rack. He'd seen a four wheel drive that wasn't his, he'd seen two men he didn't know, climbing out the doors. They'd all stared at each other for a frozen moment, then the men had pulled out guns of their own, and the shooting had started before even a word was spoken.

And eternally I'd be left to wonder—was there anything I could have done? If I'd arrived five minutes earlier. Or even if, when I finally had arrived, I hadn't simply waited at the gate. Listening. Afraid. My hands cold on the steering wheel . . .

Meanwhile, Stanley had run back inside the house, even as Clarke and Jeffreys sprayed the walls and windows with bullets. He'd yelled at May to get down, then dashed about the room, extinguishing the candles. He'd seen May on the floor. He'd thought she was doing what he'd told her to do. Then he'd got back to the windows, started returning fire. He'd kept firing until someone in the night had cried out, and then everything had gone quiet. Stanley hadn't waited. He'd grabbed May and they fled out the back door. By the time they were in amongst the trees, May was flagging. He'd dragged her behind him. And by the time they were higher up he'd realised that her shortness of breath, her gasps, weren't just from the running. And that there was something wet and warm on his hands.

We climbed.

It wasn't far, through trees and undergrowth that were pitch black and strangely still. The canopy above swayed and hummed with the wind, but down on the ground nothing moved. I smelled the resin of the trees and felt the crunch of fallen branches under my feet. Every sense was aware, every sound and touch acute. And yet none of it meant anything, my mind was empty. I was walking in a dream with two silent sentinels, Stanley before me, a faceless man behind.

The trees thinned, and there was the sky again. The moon had lifted clear of the hills, and it shone a cold and pure white. We emerged on the hilltop, amidst grass and stone, and all around the night fell away, a jumble of grey and noise and the great tide of air. And there was May.

It was probably one of the first shots that came through the windows, according to Stanley. As if she'd been standing there at the glass, waiting to see who it was coming up the road.

Which of her men. Me. Or him.

She was on her back, her face to the stars, her skin pale against the ground. He eyes were open, darker than they'd ever been, and one hand lay over a black stain that spread across her chest.

Oh May, I thought.

Then I was shoved aside, and Clarke was sinking to his knees next to her.

'May.' And he was clutching her arms, urgent. 'May. It's me. I'm here.'

Her lifted her shoulders and her head sagged back and I knew it was true, she was gone. Like a vision I was remembering the feel of her hands on my shoulders, her fingers and all their desperate strength, gripping me, angry and afraid and wanting . . . wanting something. I'd never known what. Would never know, now.

'Wake up,' the man was saying. 'C'mon, May. Wake up.'

'I told you,' said Stanley. 'She's dead.'

And later I would ask Stanley if she'd said anything at all, given any message, any last clue. But there was nothing. She'd drifted away, while Stanley had heard me down at the house calling her name. And while we'd argued about who loved her most, Clarke and I, she'd died.

Clarke was on his feet again, wheeling, the gun pointing madly from Stanley to me.

'*You* did this. Get back to the house. Call an ambulance.'

'There's no phone out here,' said Stanley. 'There's nothing.'

He stared at us, not understanding. He staggered in circles about her body, his hands to his head. I could see him now in the moonlight—an aging, confused, inebriated man. Like a thousand I'd seen before. In pubs, in gutters, in boardrooms. Alcohol didn't discriminate, and out here, with the night to strip him of identity and wealth and influence, he moved in the same drunken dance we all did, and towards the same end.

He fired his gun.

He wasn't even aiming at us. It was just one shot, flying off somewhere into the night, and then Stanley and I watched as he pulled the trigger again and again and the gun clicked emptily. He stared at it, threw it away.

'I'm taking her home,' he said.

And still we only watched, as if that was our sole purpose there, to witness. He bent to May, got his arms beneath her and tried to lift. Whether it was her weight or his drunkenness, he toppled sideways with her body. May's head cracked against rock, the sound of it hideous, and then she rolled face down into the earth.

'May, oh Jesus, May, I'm sorry.'

He bent over her again, weeping, rolling her back and brushing the dirt from her face, from her hair, from her eyes.

I realised Stanley was looking at me. I stared back, not understanding. He reached over and took the gun from my hand. His fingers moved over it and something clicked, then he put it back in my hand and threaded my finger onto the trigger. His hand still on mine, he pointed the gun at the back of Clarke's head. Then Stanley took his hand away. And waited.

I stared down my arm. The gun felt different now. It was alive, potent with power, as if blood pulsed within it. Loathsome . . . and yet, all it needed was the squeezing of my finger. It would leap at the faintest touch, and all that power and potency would blaze and pass and a man would be dead. This man. The one who had killed Charlie and Marvin and May, and who ruined our lives even before he ended them. He would be dead and it would be over. After ten years and more than ten years. All the past, the drunken lost years, the hurt and the sadness, the Inquiry and the whole wretched business that was my life, that was Queensland itself . . . no, Queensland wouldn't change, Queensland would go on, but my part in it would be done.

He had May in his arms again, had struggled to his feet. He was talking to her, but I couldn't understand the words, only what was behind them, the despair. Tears blurred my eyes. I couldn't kill him. What point was there now? I'd known it all along, I was no avenging angel. Nothing could be brought back. Not even May. Let him live. There was nothing left for him now anyway, without her. Only the descent into alcohol, and inquisition, and arrest. What purpose would it serve, what was there to take from him? All three of us, May, him and me, alone in the end.

I lowered the gun.

Stanley stared at me a moment longer, then in one motion he lifted his rifle, only inches from Clarke's skull, and fired. I didn't flinch at the explosion, or at the brief bloody flash, and I stood motionless as his knees buckled and his body slumped and settled, almost gently, over May.

The wind seemed to have died, the whole world gone quiet.

Stanley lowered his gun. I could sense the fury in him.

'That's the problem with people like you,' he said to me. 'It's always someone else who has to finish it.'

And he turned and walked away.

FORTY-NINE

We buried May on the hill.
    It wasn't what she would have wanted. The hill, the mountains themselves, they meant nothing to her, she'd never even seen them until the night she died, and then they had only frightened her. I didn't know where her heart would have wanted to rest, Brisbane or somewhere else again. That was the problem with burials. There was no way to ask, no way to be sure. And either way, there was nothing else we could do.
    We buried the two men deep under Stanley's marijuana plantation, and tipped their vehicle into the gully. It left a path of broken, tangled trees, but the gully itself was impenetrable, and Stanley said that within a few weeks there would be no sign that anything had ever been there. As for the men, Stanley was certain that even if the police raided his place one day and actually found the crop, the last thing they would ever do was dig beneath it. And as for May . . . we left it to fate. Surely the curse that had haunted her all her life would finally let her be. There was no reason anyone would want to look up there anyway. The world was full of hills.
    The following night Stanley drove me back into town, to the offices of the *Highwood Herald*, and dropped me off next to May's car.
    'That's it for you and me, George,' he said.
    I didn't bother answering. I drove May's car down to Brisbane and to the house she'd rented. I wiped the steering wheel and the doors and the dash—every place I could think—for fingerprints. Nothing was in her name, she'd said, but someone would track it down eventually, and it was

important that I left no trace of myself. I opened the house and did the same in there. Then I left the keys inside, closed the door and walked away, down through the streets, until enough distance and time had passed, and the dawn was coming. Then I hailed a cab over to New Farm, to the motel.

I hammered on the door until the manager woke. I apologised for disappearing without warning, I paid the outstanding bill on the room, and retrieved my car from the garage. Then I drove back to Highwood, unlocked my own house, and finally slept.

Gerry came by later that day, surprised at seeing my car in my driveway.

'What's happened?' he wanted to know.

I said, 'May decided she'd rather go back to Brisbane. So she went.'

'Just like that?'

'Just like that.'

'What about Clarke, and this detective of his, what about them?'

I was tired. I couldn't even muster a lie. 'I don't know, Gerry. It's out of my hands.'

'I don't understand. Are you going to talk to the police?'

'They already know all they need to know. And, Gerry, it would be better if you never mentioned to anyone that May was up here. Not even to Graham. Just let it be, for my sake.'

'What about Stanley?'

'He'll tell you the same thing.'

Gerry studied me, his eyes going cold. 'What happened out there, George?'

'It's over. It sorted itself out. That's all that matters.'

But there was something new in the way he looked at me, as if after all that he'd tolerated in me, my past and my weaknesses, he had at last seen something too distasteful to live with.

'Okay,' he said, 'I never saw her.' He started to go, paused. 'But I don't think I want you working for me any more, George. I think we'll just . . . call it quits.'

And I could understand that.

A day later, Detective Kelly called.

'Is she with you, George?' he wanted to know.

'Who?'

'May.'

'I told you, Detective. I haven't seen her.'

'That won't do, George. We worked out she's married to Clarke. And now it turns out he's missing too. So what's going on here?'

'Have you talked to Detective Jeffreys yet?'

'No . . .'

'Why not?'

'No one knows where he is either.'

'Ask *him*, when you find him. Ask him about the rest of it too. I've already told you everything I know.'

He was silent for a time. 'You said you were going to disappear for a while, George. What happened to that?'

'All I really needed was to get out of Brisbane.'

'And do you still think Clarke was with Marvin when he died?'

'I can't prove anyone was there. Can you?'

'You know we can't.'

'Then I might as well forget about it.'

'I think we'd better come up there and talk to you in person, George.'

'So come on up'

But no one came.

I would never know what they decided themselves, the police, but officially they and the papers stuck with the wrong story and Marvin went to his grave a suicide and a murderer. The public tone was one of bafflement—how could their old hero end up so disgraced? Corruption was one thing, but this . . . people felt disappointed and cheated, which perhaps was how they should have felt all along when it came to Marvin. Clarke and his wife made the papers as well. They were listed as missing, presumed to have fled the country to escape the investigation into his business affairs. No one mentioned his old connections with Marvin and the rest of us, nor anything about May's history. Perhaps the police were happy just to bury it all, to farewell the long decline that was the Inquiry.

It was the end of it, that was for certain, and there weren't really any survivors.

Which only left Emily.

And I couldn't face Emily.

It wasn't her fault that May was dead. How was Emily to know what would happen, just by answering her door to a detective? It was my fault, if anyone's. My fault that May was even *in* Highwood, and that Emily was left there alone, not knowing. My fault, too, that Marvin was dead, I'd led them straight to him. Even Charlie had only suffered and died because he was unlucky enough to be looking for me. The blame stretched back through the years, back to all of us, Marvin and Lindsay and Jeremy as well, and the disaster we'd all created . . . all the alcohol and long nights and the money . . . in the end, all the way back to that first drink Charlie and I had shared over dinner in his parents' little restaurant, when Brisbane was a different place and the only thing we wanted was somewhere to drink after closing time.

But Emily . . . she had nothing to do with it.

Even so, I couldn't go around to her house. Every time I thought of her I saw May's face staring up into the night. I couldn't conceive of what I would say to her, what I could explain, how I could tell her that whatever had been there for me and her, there was nowhere it could go now. Not with May's body between us, not with May's eyes as dark and empty as if the sorrow of her whole life was welling up into them. I couldn't even tell her May was dead. It was another secret, on top of too many others. I knew it was even worse to just leave things so unspoken, so incomplete, but I still couldn't bring myself to do it. Go and see her, I told myself. I screamed it inside my head. At least do that one thing, for her sake, finish it properly!

But Stanley was right.

I didn't go and see her. Instead I rang my landlord and told him I was leaving the house, and I started packing up my belongings. There wasn't much and I didn't know where I would go, but there was no need for Highwood now. There was nothing left from which to hide, no exile, no wanderers waiting to return. On the day before I was due to move out

I read in the paper that Sir Jeremy Phelan, distinguished public servant, had died in hospital after a long illness. So it was only me left. Lindsay was still out there admittedly, but really, it was only me.

I called Jeremy's number and Louise answered.

'He left me the house,' she told me. 'Everything.'

'I don't think he had anyone else.'

She laughed sadly. 'Even his wine cellar. You wouldn't believe his wine cellar. He kept collecting, even when he couldn't drink any more.'

'He had you to do that.'

'George . . . come round. I don't know what to do with myself. Come round and I'll open some wine and we'll drink to Jeremy.' Her voice fell. 'I'm sorry. I forgot you don't drink.'

'I'm not so sure that's true any more.'

'Really? Well why not then?'

And it was there, the siren call, faint and tinged in my memory with immense sadness, but still there. Maybe it was only an echo of May . . . even from the first meeting I'd seen something of her in Louise. Something not so shining and fierce as May, something quieter and less bent on its own destruction, but even so, there was that familiar shadow within her, and in her eyes. Maybe something lesser was all I was capable of anyway. The call would never be so strong with someone like Louise, and the addiction never so deep, but nor would it be fatal.

'I might,' I said. 'I'm leaving here tomorrow, and really, I might.'

And then it was my last day and there was only one thing left to do.

I climbed into my laden car and drove down through the town. The morning was clear and warm. I'd been expecting that somehow, despite the progression of summer, it wouldn't be that way. When I'd first arrived all those years before, Highwood had seen what I needed and had granted me two blessed weeks of mist and rain and cold. I'd been hoping, maybe, for a similar farewell . . . but whatever had kept the town and me so attuned in those days was gone now. It would be a hot day.

It was just on eight a.m. I drove up past Emily's school and two early children were running through the gates, but I didn't look for her. I drove on to the edge of the town, where the hills rose again to the border of the national park. I parked the car. When I returned to it I would have to decide which way to go. One direction would lead me over the mountains and down into New South Wales, as I'd intended once, long ago. The other would lead me back down into Queensland. Neither choice made any sense or held any promise, but I would choose one or the other. I was a physical body, I was a presence in the world, and I had to exist somewhere.

But not yet.

I took a backpack from the car and walked across to the sign which heralded the beginning of the walking trails. The map hadn't changed. There, at the upper extremity, eleven kilometres away, were Redemption Falls, where they'd always been. I took no note of the name. This time I wasn't walking to heal myself, or running from anything, and I no longer sought salvation.

I was going to bury a friend.

I plunged into the forest. It was cool and green in there, and for all that I remembered of wet rock and rain and aching legs, the walking was pleasant. There was a wind in the tree tops, but it was only the faintest of whispers, and birds sang clearly through the air. I met no one else. The miles rolled by, and the hours. I recognised nothing. It had been too long ago. My legs started to stiffen, but I had water in my bag, and food. And even if I arrived back at my car tired and sore, then wherever it was I stopped that night, I would find a bar and I would order a tall cold beer to soothe the muscles, like any man did. Like any man had the right.

Then I was walking alongside a small stream. Through the trees ahead the sky appeared blue and cloudless, and I came to the cliff top. The stream tumbled over the last few rocks and disappeared and beyond that . . . beyond that was a gulf of air and the distant peaks and hills of a different country. It was noon and the sun blazed down from above and hawks circled in the sky.

I sat on a rock and opened my pack and took out the urn.

I thought about Charlie, but I was still no closer to an answer. Where would he like to be—Queensland or New South Wales? We stood there on the very border and it was only a matter of choice. The same choice that was before me. To leave or stay. Was it Queensland, after all, that had destroyed Charlie and me? Was there really an essence to the state, a crucial flaw that warped its inhabitants and closed down their minds, made us small and fearful? And even if there was, what was there for either of us in New South Wales? A state so much bigger and stronger, and yet so cold, so superior, so full of scorn for places that were small. Wanting them to be small. What had Stanley said that night? The rest of the country needed Queensland to be the way it was . . .

And I thought of May, tugged and pulled all her life by men who wanted her to be what they needed. Until between us all, we'd torn her apart.

Which way would Charlie want to go?

I watched the sky. I remembered what the psychologist had told me. Burial was for the living, not for the dead. So don't think about what the dead would want, I told myself, answer the questions of the living.

I was a physical body, I had to exist somewhere, but that didn't apply to Charlie.

I stood up and uncapped the urn. I stood on the very lip of the falls and poured the ashes into the stream, just at the point where the water tumbled over the edge. Up here at the top it was Queensland. A hundred metres down, at the bottom, it was New South Wales. In between I could see that the little funnel of water fanned out into a spray and eventually to a mist, and then to thin air. I watched the ashes go over, watched them diffuse into a grey cloud, drifting.

I walked away.

The choice was still mine to make.

But Charlie—I was hoping he'd never touch the ground.